W9-BWI-330

Zone of the Interior

Books by the author:

WEEKEND IN DINLOCK
GOING AWAY
ZONE OF THE INTERIOR

Zone of the Interior

by
Clancy
Sigal

Thomas Y. Crowell Company
ESTABLISHED 1834 NEW YORK

 Published simultaneously in Canada by Fitzhenry & Whiteside Limited, Toronto.

Designed by Ingrid Beckman

Manufactured in the United States of America

Library of Congress Cataloging in Publication Data

Sigal, Claney.
Zone of the interior.

I. Title.
PZ4.S5715Zo [PS3569.I4116] 813'.5'4 76-4831
ISBN 0-690-01091-5

1 2 3 4 5 6 7 8 9 10

To Margaret Walters

Author's Note:

THIS IS FICTION, a work of imagination. Although set in Greater London of the 1960s, all characters and incidents, except for obviously public figures and places, are invented. To the best of my knowledge Clare Community Council, Conolly House, King Edward VIII Hospital, Meditation Manor and their personnel do not exist except in my mind. Any similarity to persons living or dead is purely accidental.

I am living very badly now and just to stay alive is an ordeal, but I see something better. It is vague, and is a possibility at best, but I know a place, a refuge where people love and live.

—George Jackson to his mother.
From *Soledad Brother: The Prison Letters of George Jackson*

England exploded, didn't it? I don't know when. . . .

—Paul McCartney

I AM BACK. After several years coming down—maneuvering like a weightless astronaut in space—I'm on earth again. Most of us are still alive.

Once a year I get a Christmas card from Les O'Brien. He quit mental nursing after Conolly House folded, but soon got bored with 'healthy' people and reenlisted at another hospital, this time near his native Newcastle-on-Tyne. Conolly House alumni occasionally visit or phone me. Herb Greaves and Gareth de Walden are still somewhere inside King Edward Hospital. Clem, who married and emigrated, teaches high school in Salt Lake City. Yorkshire Roy works off his money hangups as assistant head cashier in a Leeds bank. A. C. Corrigan runs a Merseyside Free School. Jeff H. almost got shot as a TV cameraman in the last Arab-Israeli war. And Robin Ripley, the unit's honorary boy, has become a housewife and mother in Wokingham. Barney, Jack, Hurricane Hodge, Derek, Wally, Percy-the-radio and the others I've lost touch with.

The Medical Research Council recently published a study confirming that fewer Con House patients are rehospitalized than schizophrenics who are treated conventionally. So it was worth it.

Being an adopted Londoner, I can't help running into Clare Council Mafiosi. Once I shared a Vietnam protest platform in Trafalgar Square with Con House's founder, Dr. Dick Drummond. The grapevine tells me that Major Straw has opened a spiritualist bookshop in Hampstead. Once in a blue moon Davina sends a letter from Australia, where she qualified as a social worker and has set up a home for unmarried mothers in Melbourne; she's much happier working with women instead of mad men. And Alf, with his keen nose for a growth industry, has launched several more therapeutic communities which have become so respectable they get government grants-in-aid.

Jerry Jackson's dead, of course. And Lena. I sometimes lay flowers on her grave in Golders Green (like Jack the Ripper revisiting the scene of his crime). I've had plenty of time to figure out my responsibility for killing both of them; it's something I live with. The doctors' wives—Sybil, Nancy and Vivienne—sank without trace, like movie extras no longer needed. In the blaze of charismatic publicity surrounding Dr. Last nobody remembers them, the real victims.

Willie Last himself is back from a spell of Buddhist meditation in Bangkok. While he was there Thailand was used as a U.S. Air Force base for massacring Indochinese, which he didn't seem to mind, or even know. But then his current lecture audiences (at five bucks a head) aren't bothered either. Dr. Last's exodus from radical politics suits their mood. Into a happy second marriage, he also seems to have forgotten his views about the oppressive nature of the nuclear family. The important thing is not to use your mind at all, he now preaches.

For months after I quit Clare Council he tried hard wooing me back. He'd 'accidentally' bump into me in the street or find excuses to phone me to "clear up some ootstandin' matters." Once or twice he waited in his black Bentley outside my apartment, but drove off when I brandished the composition rubber sap I always carried with me then. His accosting me in public to pinch my cheek and call me "Brither Sid" got so bad I had an argy-bargy with him on a streetcorner that almost got us arrested.

For a while remorse—even terror—almost killed me. That too has ebbed, leaving behind only the cramps, headaches and night sweats I took with me from America years ago. Coral, who got me into all this in the first place, now advises me not to "stop on" bitterness. "It was just a damned silly way to cure a bellyache," she says in that maddeningly brisk, absolute way of hers.

Since leaving Last's group I've gone back to basics. During the Vietnam war I stuffed envelopes and picketed the American Embassy with our USA-Out-Of-Indochina Committee, and now in the local tenants' association I petition neighbors for a safer road crossing—learning all over again how to work with a minimum of manipulative bullshit. Most times I don't think I'll make it.

But there *is* something new and better. What I want to understand is how I, from the radical working class, missed it so wildly. Why did we follow Last into the desert? Why, after all my experience in unions and the Communist party, did I fall for the dialectical soft soap *again?* And why, with so much to politically rethink in the Sixties—the rise of multinational corporations, the alleged disappearance of the boom-and-bust cycle, the growth of women's consciousness and the international left's approval and use of terrorism—did I seek refuge in near-Fascist irrationalism?

And was it all so crazy?

It's hard to run away from the old days in Con House and Meditation Manor, even harder from the problems they raise. Somehow it's in the air around us. Nowadays even school kids read Last, family therapy is clinically fashionable. Once the media b.s. died away, Last's disciples and others working along similar lines went on to do something with the idea. Informal therapeutic communities such as Alf's have probably saved the sanity of countless people, and even the big State hospitals are taking this approach seriously.

Slowly the idea of not strangling the mad, indeed of honoring them with kindness, seeps through. The politics of madness takes its place as one of many reform movements. It will not, of itself, revolutionize English society (what can?). But we—Conolly House graduates, Manor escapees, friends and survivors of Clare Council—are in circulation. And so is the need to humanize an increasingly irrational and mechanistic system. Wherever we are we spread the word.

Now for the ordinary thing.

1

I THOUGHT the world had exploded or been blown apart by something. A gigantic spasm had occurred that shriveled and exposed people, made ideas obsolete, tore the mask from institutions. It was a new era in which the desire for change/rebellion clashed with a tired, frightened conservatism—both currents being deeply poisoned by the 'German disease,' as I called it. The 1930s had unstoppered a genie of self-destructiveness that we could not put back in the bottle after V-J Day '45. I knew, perhaps too well, that I overidentified a social cosmos with my personal problems: the sexual-political frustrations following on the breakup of the U.S. Communist Party, the 1956 Hungarian repression and the premature fading of the English New Left's star.

I'd always regarded myself as 'normal.' On the streets of Chicago, Detroit and Chattanooga, growing up in the 1940s and in my Hollywood jobs I'd always avoided the far out for the everyday and unsurprising. I wasn't snobbish about square. Greenwich Village (class of '50) confirmed my straightness: dope made me sneeze and I fell asleep during orgies.

Up to age thirty-three in 1961 I was optimistic about life. After years of failure and frustration I'd hit a streak of good writing. My first novel had sold well in England and been paperbacked in the USA, and I was driving down the homestretch of my second with plenty of gas to spare. I was securely based in English left politics and had resumed my old American habit of holding fast to one woman, Coral, while fucking a lot of others. The life I'd left the USA to find was in my hip pocket.

Then 'it' began to happen again.

Head- and stomachaches, vertigo, cold sweats, unexplained fevers, a rising anxiety: all the discomforts I'd suffered prior to my first book. "Oh, those are just writing pains," Coral had pronounced before shipping me off to the first of many psychiatrists she hoped would take a little pressure off me. (And because I woke her at 3:00 A.M. to talk, which she said wrecked her for the next day's writing.)

On the day my second novel won a literary prize in America I was due to see yet another trick cyclist. Dr. Willie Last.

I'd gotten his name from Coral—my 'connection'—who'd heard it from Fred Bradshaw, an ex-coal miner novelist. I checked with Fred. "Willie's okay," he said over the phone. "A working-class Scot, about our age, Marxist of sorts. I don't go to him but a couple of my friends do. He's supposed to be great with artistic layabouts like us." Since I was very high on Bradshaw's latest book, *North Country Blues,* I rang for an immediate appointment.

Last was the umpteenth doctor I'd seen in the past few months. Freudians, Jungians, Freudo-Jungians, neuropsychiatrists, a faith healer (Coral's idea), a herbalist, two won't tells and an LSD therapist. Most of them confirmed my worst fears about psychiatry. I hated their smug superiority, the middle-class philistinism behind a pose of scientific detachment. In Eisenhower's America I'd learned to steer clear of psychotherapists when I saw how they influenced comrades to 'adjust'—that is, drop out of radical politics. Some Hollywood doctors actively helped patients turn stool-pigeon during the blacklist purges, and in one or two cases I knew they'd even acted as unofficial FBI spies. So the blinkered Toryism of English shrinks came as no surprise. Almost unanimously they urged me to drop writing if it caused me so much pain.

I'd stayed longest with the LSD man. A Harley Street hustler with a deathbed manner, he mainlined me on a mixture of lysergic acid and pethedrin in a gloomily antiseptic room with oxygen tanks and a female nurse who looked horribly like Judith Anderson as the mad housekeeper in Hitchcock's *Rebecca.* Every hour he popped his bald head in to see if I was still alive: "*Out* go the bad thoughts, *in* come the good thoughts—right-ee-o, Mr. Bell?" Afterward he summarily bundled me into a taxi in a semidelirious state to dry out at various friends' houses. Once, when I collapsed with shakes, he bad-temperedly let me sleep over—paying extra, of course. He fired me when I started doing handstands on his desk and composing eighty-thousand-word poems under the influence. Also LSD wasn't helping my theater reviews for the *New Statesman* and *Vogue.* I wept and sobbed in all the wrong places and laughed uproariously in the middle of Ralph Richardson's big speeches.

It was spring, Friday the thirteenth, when I rang Dr. Willie Last's bell.

He came to the front door himself. All my previous shrinks had had snooty housekeepers. "Och, Sidney Bell, is it? Come in, mon. It's a pleasure tae meet ye. I've read yir wurk." He sounded like a younger version of Dr. Angus Cameron, Tannochbrae's kindly old country doctor in the BBC-TV series, "Dr. Finlay's Casebook."

He warmly shook my hand and took me up a dark musty-smelling staircase to his office. This was on the top floor of a shabby building on North Gower Street, beside Euston Station at the unfashionable end of Bloomsbury. I preferred its flaked, peeling paint and broken pillars to the elegantly sterile facades of Harley, Wimpole and Cavendish streets where my other doctors had practiced. There was a bookie ('turf accountant') on the ground floor, a barbershop above it. Camden Town hereabouts was full of dingy little hotels, trade union headquarters and in Tolmer Square the cheapest, friendliest cinema in town. (You can't find it now. Like so much of London's lovely muddle the movie has been bulldozed and the square hardly exists anymore.)

Last's office was different, too. The carpet was threadbare. Everything looked as beat-up and secondhand as Henry Fonda's first law office in *Young Mr. Lincoln.* The only furniture was a rolltop desk and swivel chair where Last sat; patients had a choice either of a moth-eaten easy chair or a leather couch so decrepit it looked ready for the junk heap (and that's just where he found it, he said). The high-ceilinged room was badly lit by a single overhead bulb, its one soot-blackened window faced the brick wall of an adjoining warehouse. Dr. Last apologized for the poor view. "Th' landlord tried tae unload a street-facin' window on me fer an extra fiver a week but I tol' th' thievin' bastid where tae shove it."

What a pleasure to hear plain working-class talk after all these months of oily uppercrust medical accents.

When I defiantly settled in the overstuffed easy chair, Dr. Last didn't blink an eye. Most shrinks spent whole sessions arguing over my refusal to lie on their couch. Instead he pulled out a long black cigar from a silver case, nonchalantly lit it, drew and puffed with almost fierce concentration. As the blue smoke curled around his softly aquiline features, I studied him.

Last was the youngest doctor I'd seen so far. Two years my junior—I'd looked him up in the Medical Register—he looked like the kid brother I'd always wanted and never had. With his long Teddy Boy sideburns and rather artistic-looking 'wings' of thick, disheveled, curly brown hair swept back from his broad forehead, he was more like a Bill Haley rocker than a stiff-necked doctor. This impression was curiously reinforced by his simple single-breasted black suit, slim-jim tie and old-fashioned ankle-high boots, an outfit he wore all rumpled and scuffed as if he'd just slept off a hangover on Brighton Beach. He had a doctor's delicate hands, which constantly played with his cigar or kept inserting a phallic-looking Vicks inhaler up his nose to clear up a breathing difficulty he seemed to have. Watching me watch him he arched his eyebrows and grinned conspiratorially. He fingered the lapel of his jacket. "It's er, um, ah my mai-dical disguise. But at hahrt I'm really a civilian." Like Billy Budd he had a slight, charming stutter that, at moments, rose like a cry of pain.

The most compelling thing about Last was his eyes. Gelid, gray and hooded, they habitually stared into infinity, batting up and down every few seconds with an almost hypnotic, stroboscopic effect. There was so much sorrow in them. At times his young-old severely sensual face clouded over, as if he'd seen the Dark Angel, or as if the person he confronted was obscurely injuring him. Later it became all too easy to translate this into: "I've done something bad to him" and want to set him free of all my terrible, boring secrets. It only made it worse when he flashed a radiantly forgiving 'us humans are sech shitpots' grin and said, "Mon, tha' wis a *stuipid* thing tu'h've done!"

For openers I did my usual stunt of outsilencing the shrink. But Dr. Last seemed to enjoy the absence of words. We sat together without speaking in the semidarkness for what seemed like ages, then he leaned forward in his anciently creaking chair. "How's Freddie Bradshaw, then? Haven't seen him since Arnold Wesker's pahrty."

Ah. He'd read my books and knew my friends.

Seeing how gun-shy I was, Dr. Last gently broke the silence. "That Chicago of yirs was nae such a picnic fer ye, was it?" (He pronounced it "Chick'-aw-go.) He said that parts of my novel, *Running*, reminded him of his own childhood in Dundee, and in his faint stutter he told me about growing up poor in prewar Scotland. The Tayside tenements, Saturday night punch ups, stand-up sex in hallways and gas oven suicides could have come out of Jake Arvey's 24th Ward in the 1930s. "Of course," he boasted, "we'd've regahrded yir Yankee depression as fan*tas*tic prosperity."

Unlike my other shrinks, Dr. Last wasn't afraid to talk about himself. Though he wasn't too specific about his parents, I got a strong feeling he'd had an overprotective mother and an absent cipher father. That, too, sounded familiar. A fantasy-ridden, sickly stammerer (like me), he'd literally read his way up from squalor (ditto). A spinster teacher had been so impressed with his precocious appetite for Darwin, Marx and Schopenhauer that she wangled him a prized Grammar School scholarship, which smoothed his way to Aberdeen University. There he stumbled across A. J. Cronin's novel *The Citadel*, about a poor Scottish lad who becomes a rich society doctor. "I thought, 'Tha's th' ticket, Willie.' " He enrolled in medicine as an insurance policy against poverty, he admitted. But the higher reaches of philosophy—"birth, death, who guards th' Portals, does Gaw'd exist an' all that metaphysical jive"—continued to obsess him. "Books on th' great 'Why?' of life turned me on like a James Bond." To prolong his adolescent speculations he specialized in psychiatry. "It seemed as guid a way as any tae combine haid an' hahrt, airthly an' spiritual—an' still make a decent wage."

Internship for Last-the-young-philosopher proved traumatic. Qualified psychiatrists were so scarce that he was appointed as head of several mental wards in Ayreshire immediately after graduating. "They gave me this hunk of parchment tae stick up on my wall, an' th' next thing I was in th' madhoose shit up tae my neck. They haven't let me come up fer air yet." With controlled fury he described his early days in Scottish asylums, where the standard treatment was insulin injection. By comparison, 'shock boxes'—electro-convulsive therapy, ECT—had been almost merciful. His gruesome tales of how patients' bodies bloated and nearly exploded turned my stomach. "We butchered them in droves, in th' firm Calvinist conviction we wair savin' their minds."

In the greatest detail Last told me how he'd gone south to work in a Dorset hospital while undergoing training analysis. "Tryin' tae do eggistainshul psychiatry in a National Health loony bin was purty spooky. Th' staff thought I was crazier'n th' patients."

For the first time in almost fifty minutes I spoke up. What, I asked, was existential psychiatry?

He took a long thoughtful puff on his cigar. "Talkin' tae a bloke an' listenin' tae what he says."

At two pounds ten shillings (about $7 then) per hour, Dr. Last was the cheapest shrink I'd found. "I do Freddie's friends at a trade discount," he cracked in his soft Scottish burr. (England was great for breakdowns. The Stelazine, Librium, Parstelin, Valium, Nardil, Tofranil and Equanil I lived on cost next to nothing on the National Health.)

First we tried "th' formal route," as Last called it. Three afternoons a week, face to face, talking. I was unhappy, I said. I'd come from America a left-wing Marxist. England had almost ruined my socialism, my sex life and my self-image. I slept with comrades' wives, hated my two books and, most ominously, didn't enjoy flea pit movies anymore. Almost overnight a whole generation of my father- and mother-figures—Hemingway, Gary Cooper, Hoot Gibson, Mrs. Roosevelt, William Faulkner, the CP-USA leaders Dennis and Foster—had died. And at Ascot races last month a man standing at the rail next to me had had a heart attack and died in my arms. A growing fear of travel crippled my work, and I was sick of X-rays, barium meals and conflicting diagnoses. Only lysergic acid diethylamide took me out of myself, but it was illegal in England except under strict medical control.

For a few sessions we desultorily talked about the Freudian roots of my aches and pains. "Ye've done this neat li'l trick on yirself," Dr. Last said. "Internalized yir maw's fear an' hatred of ye, treatin' yirself as yir maw treated ye. Ye're nae bein' so guid tae yir own li'l bairn, th' yew within yew. Take more pity on yirself, mon." My guilt at no longer doing a nine-to-five job he lightly jeered away. "Aw hail, Sid. Wha's so all-fired noble aboot addin' surplus value tae th' capitalist system. An' yew a Communist, too!"

With the aid of diagrams in his book, *The Unhealed Heart*—I'd started carrying it with me—Last explained my tortured relationship with Coral. "Obvious. Ye're engulfed by her depersonalized fantasy of yir perception of her collusion wi' yir imploded false self system." He dismissed the affair as "bad faith," closing the subject.

At last. A shrink who played it straight from the shoulder. Who didn't sandbag me with value judgments behind a wall of therapeutic 'objectivity.' And who didn't try to impose his ideas on me.

My silences deepened; not being allowed to discuss Coral throttled me. To 'demystify' our sessions and get me moving, Dr. Last filled in the gaps with more data about himself. I learned he was married to an Edinburgh property developer's daughter, had a five-year-old daughter named Rabbie (after Scottish poet Robert Burns), owned a 1955 Bentley, shared a house in north London with another psychiatrist and smoked an endless supply of rare imported Havanas—a grateful patient's gift, he said. With little else to talk about we soon discovered a common passion for Bessie Smith records and old war movies. Several times we played hookey from sessions by sneaking off to John Wayne revivals (*Sands of Iwo Jima*, *Flying Tigers*) at the Tolmer cinema around the corner from his office. ("It's as guid a catharsis as ye're gointa get on th' couch, Sid.") We cried at a British Film Institute showing of John Huston's documentary about combat fatigue, *Let There Be Light*, and afterward agreed that madness was merely a type of civilian shell shock. Dr. Last, who'd never been in military service, doted on my army stories. He could sit for a whole fifty minutes absorbed in my tales of mock assaults and simulated river crossings. Though I'd never fired a shot in anger he envied my "sojer's reflexes."

Come again?

For radicals, he explained, the army could be as much of a university as prison traditionally had been. Military discipline broke down those twin curses of Western civilization: sanctity of the individual ego and petty bourgeois concepts of privacy. As examples, he cited the Algerian and Vietnamese n.c.o.'s who learned their anti-imperialist trade in the French army and then had gone home to lead the liberation struggle.

This appealed to my unslaked guilt about having been just too young for combat in World War II. "Don't worreh," Dr. Last said, "there's *another* war fer ye tae go tae." Behind the puny shadowboxing of parliaments and parties shaped up a rather different sort of conflict, truly global in dimension if not yet visible to the untutored eye. Sooner rather than later a new "ravelushnry caydree"—bereft of guns, power or even self-consciousness—would take over responsibility for changing society from Trotskyism, Stalinism, social democracy and other manifestations of the left's moral decay.

Like an old warhorse hearing political alarm bells, I pricked up my ears. Who . . . what was he talking about?

His eyes took on that faraway, flittering cast. "I hope ye never find oot."

Even as a kid I never could resist a dare. What secret was he challenging me to find? Whatever it was, it must be more important than my petty personal problems that made him look so bored. So I stopped even trying to talk about myself. (Anyway, certain childhood incidents had been too hard for me to recall, and he lacked enthusiasm for digging into painful areas.) By unspoken agreement we padlocked the formal route. And just sat there, staring at each other.

I apologized for the long silences. "Tain't yir fault, Sid," Dr. Last said. " 'Tis th' way th' mai-dical cookie crumbles." The doctor-patient relationship, essentially pecuniary and exploitative, was a parody of the larger system of false human relationships under capitalism, he said. It forced us to treat each other as Things. In bourgeois psychoanalysis the I-thou encounter—he'd started me on Martin Buber—degenerated into a deadly game of mutual seduction in which his professional advantage over me enslaved him as well. He was bored out of his mind by the 99 percent of his patients "who root aroun' like pigs in their own emotional shit tae buy my attention." He leaned forward intently. "I'm invitin' ye tae set us both free."

How? I asked.

Dr. Last slyly grinned. Then leaped from his chair, grunting and gesticulating. I ducked. His hands chopped the air in front of my face. Then, arms swinging loose and low like an ape, he made as if to grab me. I got up and backed away. "Have you gone nuts?" I asked.

"Now ye're catchin' on!" he chortled.

Dr. Last called it "dancing," or Zen applied to psychotherapy. (And handed me Alan Watts to read.) Making faces and no-touch karate replaced talking between us. "Anything tae shake th' shackled mind loose fr' its moorings an' let th' soul rediscover It-Self," said Last.

Things pepped up; or rather, our I-thou encounter revived. It was like being a kid again, relearning how to play by improvising around Last's wild leaps and snarls. "Tha's th' ticket, laddie," Last encouraged, "*ye're gittin' thar!*" By shifting seats we reversed roles. I, smoking a cigar, mimicked his accent, "So ye're havin' trouble passin' water in th' mornin', Mr. Last. Ah, um, er, oh. Nae doot an eggistainshul disorder—an' so on an' so forth. Try pissin'. Haw haw hee hee!" Last pretended to be me, including the nail-biting. "Gee, Sid—what's the meaning of it all? Is there any point to life? I think, I mean, I guess. Gee whiz." Then Last kicked off his boots and jacket and told me to lunge at him. When I did he thumped me. He hit me again when I retreated. By rules he alone invented (and changed in mid-game), I got smacked no matter what I did. Only by contorting myself till Last was satisfied could I escape his blows. He had to help extricate me from a ludicrous, humiliating pretzel bend—one leg over my shoulder, my tongue hanging out, arms immobilized, fetal. "An' *tha'*," Last said gleefully, "is th' double bind."

An added bonus was that 'nonverbal communication'—grunts, belches, squeaks, whistles, coughs and spits—cleared up my old catarrh condition.

When, unaccountably, my anxiety got worse, Dr. Last bucked me over to his personal guru, a pioneer existential analyst named Dr. Phineas Maud, in Southwark. "Finny's an' ol' charlatan, but he's got a knack wi' noorotically sane types like yew." Dr. Maud, a large, grandmotherly man in his late sixties, charged me three times as much as Last, and told me I was a monkey chasing its tail. "You think therefore you're ill, sir. Constipated on ego. Take the laxative of self-LESS-ness and *lose your mind.*" There was no 'I' only an unfound 'me,' he briskly explained, ponging me back across the river to Last, who welcomed me with a warm brotherly hug. I'd passed some sort of test by going in against Dr. Maud, and Last meant to reward me.

"Right, then. Are ye disposed tae take a wee dram—an' I don' mean Johnny Walker?"

On a late Saturday afternoon, when the Gower Street house was empty of its bookie and barber, Last locked his office door and dug under the sagging couch for his black medical bag. It contained wood racks of Sandoz glass vials and unlabeled bottles of distilled water. He used a razor blade to saw off the cap of one of the vials, pour its colorless fluid into a tumbler of the water and mix it carefully. Then he switched off the overhead bulb. I thanked Last, drank and waited. At this exact moment, I knew, many of my friends were hiking from Aldermaston to London on the fifth Easter Campaign for Nuclear Disarmament—the only one I'd ever missed. Where was Coral—marching or sleeping with someone else? Her son was in Wormwood Scrubs for chaining himself to railings outside Number 10 Downing Street. Fleetingly I wished I was chanting and singing with them, then pushed all that aside.

Last, silent and sober, sat with me in the dark office till after midnight. For eight hours I fought wild beasts, flew around the world, drowned in my father's jism and commanded an Assyrian legion. Aldermaston, Coral, snatches of ban-the-bomb ballads kept breaking in, but I shrugged them off. Toward the end when I was strangling on my infantile pule, Last wiped me off and soothed me. Then he drove me back to my apartment, gave me a supply of sleeping pills and a tranquilizer called Largactil, wrote down his home phone number and told me to ring him anytime, even Sundays.

I couldn't wait to do it again.

Mutual trust, like LSD doses, grew. In fortnightly bursts I went from 75 milligrams to 150, and when I leveled out at

200 mg Dr. Last asked mildly, "Care fer a li'l company?" And for the first time he mixed acid cocktails for both of us. Raising his tumbler he saluted me:

"So stand by, yir glasses staidy
Th' wurld is a wurld o' lies
Here's tae th' daid awraidy
Hurrah fer th' next mon who dies!"

Robert Burns? I asked.

"Nae," he replied. "Errol Flynn in *The Dawn Patrol.*"

Though I quickly learned to quote Kierkegaard, Jaspers and Sartre—Last's favorite thinkers—back at him, our deeper values and images came from a common lore of old Hollywood films. On acid I often 'saw' him as Clark Gable (*Command Decision*), or Tyrone Power (*A Yank in the RAF*), or Robert Taylor (*Bataan*), or Spencer Tracy (*Test Pilot*)—all the leading men of my movie-haunted youth crashing through the silver screen to supply a drama my life sadly lacked. I was too bashful to mention such fantasies until, one Saturday afternoon while we were Indian wrestling on 200 mg each, he casually grunted, "Y'know, this reminds me of Burt Lancaster an' Kirk Douglas in *Gunfight at OK Corral.*" "Not Burt Lancaster, it was Rock Hudson," I pedantically corrected him. Even swacked I knew my movie stars.

But Last had turned a forgotten key in my chest. I almost fainted with emotion.

Comradeship.

Like secret lovers we met after hours in his office, my flat, Hampstead Heath, hotel rooms. By now we both carried "emergency rations": small chamois bags of come-down pills and bottles of pure water. But only Last kept the LSD. It was perfectly legal for him to give it to me but he wanted to control my supply as a way of protecting himself. To this end, we also devised a secret code.

"bacon 'n eggs"	was	LSD
"tomatoes"	was	distilled water
"cats' litter"	was	Largactil

On the phone we sounded like Russian spies. A deliciously furtive feeling of an enemy out there spying on us drew us together, and like kids we slipped into a make-believe world of military fantasy. In battle after battle—Thermopylae to Alamein, Agincourt to Stalingrad—we perfected a 'buddy system,' fighting and dying together as spearmen, tank drivers, crossbow archers and paratroopers. We used each other's LSD-blown minds like an H. G. Wells time machine, to travel together into the future and back into the past. Sometimes we chastely danced about Last's office, feeling unearthly musical zephyrs through our barely touching fingertips—to an unsympathetic eye a grotesque satire of a bad Dante Gabriel Rossetti painting. Or, as sparring partners in ancient Greece, boozily, warily circled each other, stark naked. Then, body to body, we tackled, pushed, clutched until The Other surrendered. Once, when our sweat-glistening bodies lay atop one another, we discovered our penises were erect. This didn't bother Last at all. "Buddha's bisexual," he breathed, grabbing my cock with a comradely lunge.

Bucked up by LSD and Last, I flexed my phobic travel muscles by flying to Sweden. (It was the day Marilyn Monroe died.) My "battle assignment"—I was getting used to Last's metaphors—was to enjoy a short holiday and return safely. By Copenhagen I was drenched in sweat, trembling. Forcing myself to reboard the plane, I got to Stockholm blind with terror, my tongue parched, my chest filling and cracking with the ice water of fear. A note ("PLEASE RETURN TO DR. W. LAST, GOWER ST. LONDON WC 1") taped to my stomach, I shivered in a Stockholm hotel for a couple of hours, then checked out, defeated. On the SAS flight back I sat with a towheaded Swedish businessman; he looked exactly like me. Was me. At Heathrow I barely managed to ring Last and beg him to come get me.

Back in his office he consoled me by saying that I mustn't take too hard my tactical retreat from Sweden. "It's jes' yir first taste of th' heroic journey, yir reentry intae th' proto-original situation."

My what?

Last said that for months it had been apparent to him that my neurosis was caused by my having "forgotten" that I was a hero in the ancient mold. Heroes were twice born. First through their natural mothers, then through a symbolical sequence usually involving a trip—a sea voyage, descent into Hades, even return to the original country of exile. Many embarked, few came back.

After being swallowed by the metaphoric mother (the sea, a whale, the mother country), the hero usually had to fight his way out of her belly to a state of rebirth. Oedipal conflict with my human mother had been a groping, imperfect expression of this yearning for the dangerous journey to a new, second life. Psychoanalysis and LSD—even my abortive Swedish holiday—were vivid evidence that I was now ready to begin my real, truly Heroic Voyage.

I was fascinated. What he said dignified all those bloodcurdling quarrels with my mother and gave ritual value to experiences, such as the Coral fiasco, I was so ashamed of. (And hadn't Coral herself often told me that society's malaise was caused not by capitalism but because "we're all so starved of ritual"?) More, please.

Last duly loaded me up with more books from his personal library. Evens-Wentz's *Tibetan Book of the Dead*, Huxley's *The Doors of Perception*, mystical volumes by Alan Watts, Arthur Waley and Gerald Heard ("th' baist type of Ainglishmon"). He even let me glance at the as-yet-unpublished manuscript of his second book, *The Sanity of Insanity*, written while on acid holiday at Millbrook, Timothy Leary's farm in New York. And on Last's say-so I plunged into the work of Mircea Eliade, an expert on primitive religions.

A whole new world opened up. Shamanism, initiation rites, possession cults, rebirth symbolism: all the things I'd slept through that semester of Comparative Religion 113B at UCLA. What a fool I'd been!

"Gawd's holey fy-ool," Last gently amended. My thirty-odd years of ignorance and spiritual flabbiness, he said, had been the Tao's way of preparing me for the final, self-healing Voyage.

Where to? I asked.

"Schizophrenia," he replied.

Like a ticking time bomb the word had lain under the skin of our talks from the start. Now it exploded.

Vaguely I knew Last had come to public notice through his work on schizophrenics. His book, *The Unhealed Heart*, a study of the family strategies adopted by mad youngsters, I'd found beautifully written and seemingly well researched. (Although later he told me that all the cases were from one particular area in Scotland.) In our LSD sessions he'd often hinted that acid was merely a crude chemical substitute for "th' real thing"—the sacred ecstasy of his more psychotic patients. Now he got down to cases.

Half the hospital beds in Britain, Last said, were occupied by mental patients, 50 percent of whom were so-called "schizophrenics." But these people were neither insane nor ill. Their madness was a relatively sane response to a society that denied the holiness ("whole-y-ness") of human experience; in fact, they were relatively less mad than most normal people, who by definition were divorced from their psychic roots. "After all, 'twasn't th' mad who butchered fifty million of their fellowmen in wars this century."

Medically speaking, the problem was that British therapists had forgotten ("if they ever knew") that schizophrenia was a condition of broken-heartedness, not split-mindedness. "It's nae a disease but a state of awareness," Last argued. Schizophrenia never existed *in* a person, only between people. It described relationships, not a sickness. Yet doctors insisted on treating schizophrenia as a medical entity, with complicated tortures disguised as remedy. "In effeck, they smash ye over th' haid wi' ECT or drugs or 'supportive therapy' tae blot oot what's possibly th' best thing tha's ever happened tae ye—th' visions an' inner voices which may be yir only hope of recovery." In this sense, modern medicine was less progressive than in the Middle Ages, which by regarding the mad as possessed by demons, at least had respected their possibilities for sacredness, Last said.

Anti-shrink as I was, even I was startled by the venom of his dislike for his colleagues—"a careerist cabal of public-school sadists, time-servin' quacks an' knife-crazy leucotomists." Mental hospitals were "Auschwitzes of th' soul"; most psychiatrists were "mind butchers" who induced the 'disease' of schizophrenia which existed only in their own disordered brains. At best, therapists were "mai-dical mechanics retreadin' overexposed minds till they pairminently blew oot'; at their too-frequent worst "*feld-polizei* huntin' doon sassiety's natural deserters—th' shock truips of th' comin' psychic ravelushun."

I sat and listened to Dr. Last describe young schizophrenics as existential guerrillas—"th' lead scouts of a Children's Crusade fightin' tae retake th' Holeh Land of oor Primal Unspoilt Selves."

Their 'illness' had taught them how to crash through the arbitrary barriers between mind and body, space and time, "inner an' ooter"—how to live naturally in a landscape usually occupied only by saints and geniuses. "Th' mad are Columbus, Lenin an' Colonel Glenn all tangled up in one unhappy knot, heroes wi'oot th' ticker tape, travelers wi'oot a passport who minesweep a booby-trapped road all of us must travel one day." But normal people victimized those who "re-minded" them. Families *colluded* among themselves to *mystify* their most sensitive kids, a form of *disconfirmation* and *social violence*, which placed the victims in an *untenable position*. Official medicine further *invalidated* these psychic Absolute Beginners by turning them into unpersons; i.e., patients. For daring to question, in however distorted and fragmentary a way, the constipated rigidities of capitalism, "th' best young minds of oor generation" got locked up in hospitals or were laid out cold on couches like so many guppies. That was how the bourgeois state neutralized its potentially fiercest rebels. But the armies of mind-expansion were too strong to stop now. Already, in forms too numerous and slippery to effectively police, the Word was out. Pop music, hallucinogenic drugs, miniskirts and New Wave satire—these signs of a general youth dissatisfaction with the status quo—were in reality harbingers of a psychic earthquake that would shake humankind to its foundations.

Even without undue family or psychiatric interference, Last concluded, the voyage of the madman—he used "mad" interchangeably with schizophrenic—was perilous. Most inner-space travelers lost their way. They needed Guides, "someone who's bin up th' Magic Mountain an' doon again, who knows th' safest routes." Older societies had honored this guide-priest-voluntary madman; ours scorned him. The task was to 'resacralize'—"re-member"—this Forgotten Healer.

Was Dr. Last such a one? I asked.

His eyes flittered in despair. "I'm nae so sure any more. I may be too far gone by now." Several years of medical practice had dimmed his lights. "It requires a person of fresh ootluik an' "—he looked steadily, meaningfully at me—"a real talent fer it."

My flesh crawled. It was like going to a chiropodist for bunions and being told your gangrenous leg had to come off.

Dr. Last hastened to assure me I was mad "only in th' eggistainshul sense." Unlike most schizophrenics—his lumping me with them I now felt more as a compliment than insult—I had options. I could (a) keep running away from my forgotten, transcendental Self; or (b) "go double or quits," risk all on spiritual rebirth. It was entirely up to me; he didn't want to influence me one way or the other. Yet he strongly implied that (b) was more "authentic" and the only long-term solution to my problems. "Ye've seen so many shrinks ye may've taken Western orthodoxy as far as it'll go. Why nae gi' th' East a chance?"

The 'East' was Lastian shorthand for the "innair wurld" where Zen Buddhism, mental illness and psychogenic drugs merged. The end product was a mind stripped of its barnacles, of its sick-making tendency to think itself into tight corners. This No-Mind, a blissful emptiness of the soul, induced *atman* where ego totally vanished. One was still, at peace (and presumably without stomachaches).

To illustrate, Dr. Last sat perfectly silent and motionless for the next thirty minutes or so. When I tried doing likewise I fell into dozing daydreams . . . about where Last had his attractive sideburns trimmed, how many mpg his Bentley did, what his wife looked like. At session's end Last looked immensely pleased with me. "Nae doot aboot it, Sid. Ye've a real vocation fer No-Theng."

Shy and awkward, I began talking to Last in language absorbed from him and his books. Life was "ontological insecurity." People "perceived" or "were perceived," never saw or were seen. I bandied words like "modality," "experiential," "pathogenic nexus," "false self-dissociation" and "collusion." *Maya*, *prana*, *chakra* and *atman* came as easily to me as reading the baseball results in the International *Herald-Tribune*. Soon it became second nature to think of Last and myself as Very Special, a separate breed. "Amnesiac, strangers tae oorselves an' tae others, fallen sons of Prophecy experiencin' th' insignificance of oor significance rather'n th' significance of oor insignificance, sane tae th' point of extreme alienation." We were "eggistainshul heroes despite oorselves"—psychic parachutists dropping behind enemy lines to rescue that scattered band of Israelites (schizophrenics) upon whom the Light had broken through. Together, "brithers of th' Light," we'd achieve "th' Kingdom, th' Pahr an' th' Glory"—"rediscover freedom in its Absence, die in th' flesh an' be reborn in th' Spirit."

Feeling like an 82d Airborne trooper I relaxed into the warm slipstream of Last's rhetoric. "Nae a famine o' bread oor a thirst fer water. But o' hearin' th' words o' th' Lord . . . absolute an' unconditional risk . . . th' body o' Christ Crucified . . . ravelushun . . . raissurection . . . Black Nativity . . . Th' Man o' Sorrows . . . Mission . . . Task . . . sorties . . . frontal assaults. . . ."

The words mattered less than the speaker's willingness to put his body on the line with mine.

Gratitude (and LSD) flowed through me. For Last and his Children's Crusade I felt ready to fight tigers bare-handed. He cautioned me not to underestimate the risks. My present angst was a tea party compared to the suffering of a real schizophrenic. " 'Twon't be as easy as spendin' a coupla weekends with th' coal miners," he said. Couple of weekends indeed!

To limber me up for the Great Voyage, Last laid out a strict program of diet and meditation. I must destroy my ego and "die" in an egoless wilderness. Detach myself from emotions and things, eat no meat. My psychic bones must be crushed to a pulp, my soul burned to a symbolic crisp. Only then would I feel "th' Alpha an' Omega, th' Non-grace of Nae-Gaw'd." This might or might not make me into a better writer, Last said. Bad luck might becalm me, as it did so many psychotics, in a Sargasso Sea of incoherence. But it was a gamble worth taking if I wanted to break the 'code' of wisdom buried in the schizophrenic depths. Examples of mad double dutch Last quoted to me sounded so much livelier than the earthbound prose I was sick of writing that I couldn't wait to try to do it for myself.

> *Craziness, Last said, was purely a subjective judgment, mainly a function of 'congruity' between doctor and patient. But what if, I asked, a doctor who thought his patient sane was himself mad? Last replied, "Waal, le's jes' say their collusion is nae worse'n a lot of others. I've seen in this wurk."*

All that late summer I "killed time"—which in Eliade was no joke but indispensable to ecstatic flight. As an exercise in nonbeing, I skipped meals, refused to answer the phone and doorbell. I choked off human contacts, and spent more time alone in my apartment. My step grew springier, my waist trimmer on a 95 percent vegetarian diet. I felt lean, mentally alert—and bored. The time I was meant to kill merely dragged. Fewer friends came by (mainly American women passing through London, the English hardly ever drop in), and free-lance jobs tailed off. With nothing to do but take LSD and wait for my-Self to dwindle to No-Theng, I got itchy. Halfheartedly I scouted publishers' parties for women or sat around Soho pubs waiting for literary lightning to strike again. As a kid I'd dreamed of being Captain Marvel or the Lone Ranger. Instead I'd become a coffeehouse dandy out of a Frank Yerby novel.

Where was my socialism?

For the first time in my adult life I was free of political assignment. (It started at age seven with a clemency petition for Bruno Hauptmann, the Lindbergh baby snatcher, which I'd dreamed up because I thought he was getting a raw deal.) Until last spring, when I squatted behind Bertrand Russell and Arnold Wesker at the Committee of 100's sit-down in front of the Defense Ministry, I'd been active in England. The Campaign for Nuclear Disarmament and circuit riding the northern New Left clubs had kept me honest. But my base, the *New Marxist Quarterly*, had collapsed after auctioning itself into the sternly revolutionary hands of its present Old Etonian proprietors. The out-of-London left clubs, my sport and joy, quietly folded one by one, and I had less reason to leave the metropolis. Coral, having gotten me out of her system by writing a play about us, was busy with fresh raw material—her leading man—and with furnishing her new house. Even Mosley's fascists, usually good for an idle afternoon's punch up, were disappointingly quiet. All I had 'left' was writing. By last autumn's huge Trafalgar Square demo I'd been hospitalized with vertigo and had to watch Coral, Danny Fior and several other pals get arrested on the ward TV.

Our mass movement had fallen apart. Suddenly even the illusion of power was smashed.

> Men and women stand together
> Do not heed the men of war

we'd sung, holding aloft our unsleeping antinuclear sword for Chiswick, Ealing and the rest of the green and pleasant land to follow. But CND got stuck in the single-issue rut; the New Left failed to touch rank-and-file workers and trade unionists. Revolutions had broken out everywhere—the Congo, Cuba, even in the USA with freedom riders—except in England, where the heady days of anti-Suez riots and 250,000-strong CND marches were nothing but a memory. London was no place for a bored, unmarried man full of aimless political juices.

I felt swindled by the English ability to shrug off their recent idealistic jag. (Anger and all that.) For all our shouting about The Bomb and smashing the class system, we'd hardly laid a glove on the British upper crust. Eleven straight years in power may have slightly frazzled the Tory party, but I'd been in England long enough to know that a 'Socialist' Labour government would ride to the rescue of the system in time to hand it back in good working order to its natural owners. This collusion between Britain's major parties made the Republican versus Democratic battles back home look positively genuine by comparison. The only real result, I sometimes thought, of the great 'post-Suez renaissance'—all the marches and meetings—had been the thawing of a hitherto frozen cultural establishment to absorb new talent like Fred Bradshaw, John Osborne, Doris Lessing, Danny, Coral, me, etc. Partly revived by our fresh blood, the Draculas of the old order emerged stronger than ever. I'd escaped cooption in capitalist America only to get waylaid in socialist Britain.

Where was I? Still on the New Left. But where were they?

Although a few Committee of 100 (ex-CND) diehards hadn't got the message, most of us New Marxists did. Myself included, we scattered to the academies and professions. With some resentment I woke up one morning (or so it seemed) to find my comrades were no longer free socialist spirits but job holders.

For this I left Hollywood?

My choice seemed clear: either throw in with the Direct Actionists, whose tactics—such as disrupting U.S. Air Force bases—might get me deported from Britain. Or take cover behind the hedgerows of middle-class respectability. I futzed about, wanting it both ways. After the highs of packed New Marxist meetings and CND's mass singsong, I didn't fancy the hard graft of 'community work' (where was my community?). Was there, I thought, a hope of politicizing psychoanalysis?

It hadn't been possible with previous doctors, including the old

Bolshevik Coral first sent me to (an ex-lover of hers). "Ah zo, very interesting!" he exclaimed like the Nazi in "Laugh In," shining a dazzling spotlight in my eyes from his dark corner of the hospital office. He pressed a desk button. "For manic deprezzives mit paranoid ten*den*cies like yourzelf, perhapz von teeny touch ECT, electric therapy." The velocity with which I shot out of his office propelled me to a posh South Kensington lady shrink who didn't know Karl from Groucho, had two black maids and an investment banker husband, and an amused curiosity about why I puked at meetings and fainted at demos. "So much for the political pleasure principle," she observed. Every time I tried to connect my 'cotton wool' feelings, my angst, with the capitalist system, she shook her head disapprovingly: "My eye." Later shrinks sacked me to avoid endless political bickering.

Dr. Last eased my anxiety by 'placing' me politically. "Ye're a soul-sojer strayed fr' his duity on th' Long Roman Wall." Oh *yes.*

Exactly where Last stood politically puzzled me. Was he CP or ex-CP, Fourth International Trot or what? He affably ducked a straight reply. "Don't worreh, Sid. I'm one of *yew.*"

Swell. Still, his habit of weaving poetic generalizations rather than baldly stating the facts of his early life made me curious. Were any of the schizophrenic families he wrote about his? I couldn't be quite sure if the father who tied a lead weight to his adolescent son's penis to prevent erections or the mother whose idea of toilet training was to hold her baby out of a fourth-story tenement window weren't in fact Last's. By looking stricken and changing the subject whenever I asked a direct question, he somehow implied an unimaginably horrifying childhood. My only clue to his real past was his addiction to tough-guy lingo. To argue was "puttin' in th' buit." Disagreement was "I knocked him four ways intae Wednesday." His metaphors invariably involved punching, slugging, bashing, kicking and stomping. What a helluva bruiser he must have been! Or had he devoured the same Jimmy Cagney and George Raft movies I had? Was he, like me, slightly reinventing his childhood?

If so, we were even closer than I thought.

Sheer habit kept me in touch with a few old friends, but they were fairly cool to my latest interests. Coral, who was developing a 'rational' mysticism in sessions with her Jungian shrink, smiled indulgently. "Ah, darling, you're sweet. That corny old occult stuff went out in the 1920s with Elinor Glyn and cloche hats." Pete Rich, my downstairs neighbor, grumped: "Don't tell me about hoodoo, kid. A gypsy fortune-teller once conned me out of fifty quid on a Grand National sure thing." My drinking gang in The George, the pub around the corner—Larry the Australian scuba diver, Flo the bus clippie and Arnie the taxi driver—assumed it was a passing phase.

Dr. Last was not surprised by their indifference. "What'd ye expeck, mon? Ye're askin' people wi'oot wings tae fly."

I rejoined my copilot and strapped myself in for takeoff.

Under LSD, Last and I coupled our Quests. His (he said) was to retrace his blood to its primal fountainhead, its ultimate cosmic source; mine was to fly as high as possible on my broken wing (my literary 'wound'). These were our Flight Missions. Not for the first time Last said he envied me. More than anything he yearned "tae junk th' whole charade an' go fer broke—tae fly straight tae th' burnin' hahrt of th' Secret Gaw'd." But he was held down by family and professional chains. He turned his somber, direct gaze on me. "I wisht I had yir freedom of action."

I felt so sorry for Last, slumped tiredly in his shabby chair as if he hadn't slept for centuries, that suddenly I wanted to give him the only gift in my possession: my life. As befitted a cosmic spaceman, I sloughed off airthly drags, such as jobs, friends, parties. Anything that slowed me down got dumped overboard. So no more all-night pub crawls around Covent Garden, and no more voyeuristically hanging about with teenage rockers, Bayswater whores, GIs and other fringe people. Wha', in Gaw'd's name, c'd *they* teach me?

Even when the editor of a glossy magazine fired me for writing "over our readers' tiny heads," I kept riding mushroom lightning with Last, including side trips on mescaline and psilocybin. After all, hadn't the *Daily Express* once complained I used three-syllable words? Who were these media muttonheads to criticize me?

Soon no flat or office seemed safe or big enough. I needed elbow room. After I warmed up with jaunts to Dublin and Paris—ringing Last every few hours to make sure someone was at the other end of my lifeline—he pronounced me fit to take on the Great Mother Beast herself: the USofA. I hadn't been home in seven years. Now, a few weeks after the Cuba missile crisis killed antinuclear politics in Britain (and which I spent rolling on his office floor with Last, both of us naked), I took a writer-in-residence job at Huron College in Detroit. Last and I embraced as brothers at Victoria Station. "Re-member," he said. "Th' life ye're tryin' tae grab is th' yew tha's tryin' tae grab it."

I spent exactly nine months in America, a full 270-day gestation period coast to coast. Everywhere I had been inside the monster's belly—teaching angry Detroit dropouts, riding Georgia back roads with field workers of the Student Nonviolent Coordinating Committee, manhandling a compressed-air sandblaster alongside Puerto Ricans and blacks in a New Jersey plastics factory—had confirmed the truth of Last's favorite axiom: "Th' Draidful has awraidy happened." On the 271st day I flew back to England, burned out with travel exhaustion, but having survived my Descent into Hades. I hurried back to London to organize a new life for myself.

In my absence unemployment in Britain had risen to a million, and Alec Douglas-Home, a relic of Munich appeasement who hadn't slept with Christine Keeler, had become Prime Minister. Valerie Hobson was playing the greatest role of her life as Profumo's loyal wife, Labour's Hugh Gaitskell had died and a mad cop named Sergeant Challenor successfully framed some of my Committee of 100 chums for booing the Greek queen. 'Arold Wilson and the Beatles swam out of the Mersey toward fame and fortune, and my taxi driver assured me that a Rt. Hon. Peer had masterminded the £2 million Great Train Robbery. Coral was dating the Bronx method actor hired to impersonate me in her new play, *Scorpions in a Bottle.*

None of that mattered now. America, living proof of imminent world crack-up, had taught me I'd never 'make it'—climb Last's mountain in time to lead survivors down to safety—unless I cut out the crap and frivolity. Such as watching TV, eating in good restaurants and drinking at The George with Larry, Flo and Arnie. Or, for that matter, writing for money and crass ego gratification. And the fewer lady friends the better. (I was reading the two Thomases, Aquinas and Merton.)

I packed away most of my books, canceled the TV rental and newspapers, and wrote a personal note to *I. F. Stone's Weekly* suggesting that the proprietor see a good psychoanalyst. Firing the charwoman, I scrubbed, washed and vacuumed the apartment myself to remove all trace of Arnie, to whom I'd lent it. To reduce casual contact I told the greengrocer what to deliver and leave outside my door twice a week. After renewing the lease, I got my solicitor to draw up a will and had a private doctor give me a full physical checkup (National Health doctors hate doing this), went around to Coral for a goodbye fuck and installed a new lock and steel grille on my front door. Now.

Last met me in his office with an embrace.

He looked haggard, I thought. Listening to my American saga, my nine-month Trial and Quest, he seemed worried and abstracted. Even when we playfully reversed chairs—me leaning forward (like him) with a leering, half-cocked nudge and matey wink, him rolling around in feigned, tongue-tied agony (me)—or shot nonsense koan at each other, his handsome face fell into a dim-eyed frown. I coaxed it out of him.

"Oor li'l gruip is havin' a bad time. We need money, support, allies. I cannae carry on wi'oot help. It will fail."

What group? I asked.

Last explained that in my absence he and a few trusted friends had got together for the purpose of buying a house for themselves "an' others in trouble." Two of the group were psychiatrists who, like him, had a large backlog of patients they didn't know what to do with—talented, fractured people who'd exhausted their alternatives and now faced either suicide or "mind butchery" (mental hospitals). Last dreamed of a Place, a "community of brithers," preferably in the country, where patients and doctors could go mad—and ultimately sane—in maximum love and safety. Where the insane distinction between staff and patients would no longer exist. And where, away from the pressures of a berserk society, "we c'n breathe back tae life th' still-smolderin' sparks of oor fergawtten selves—re-create th' Lost Time when we were better. . . ." Last's soft gray eyes melted away to a distant Atlantis, as though, momentarily, he'd lost sight of me.

My questions brought him back to earth. There were problems, he admitted. A potential angel had just died and other promises of help had fallen through. These disappointments "an' vayreous crawss-personal tensions" threatened to sink the project. My offer to increase his fee elicited a wan grin. "Ah mon," he murmured, "as if 'twere as easy as tha'. 'Tisn't jus' th' cash. We need *innair* strength."

My first Saturday back we locked his office door and mixed each other's LSD with the distilled water he kept stashed under the sagging cracked-leather couch. Having teetotaled in America to assist natural rebirth, I had a double dose, 400 mg. That evening we dined out, high. It tickled Last to stroll into Quaglino's on Piccadilly, order and consume an expensive meal with wine, smoke a stogie and chat up the maître d'—on 1000 mg pure acid. What a constitution! At less than half that dose I commanded a Manchu palace guard under Whitechapel's sewer system: blotto.

Toward Sunday night, after an hour of hard arm wrestling in his office, we began easing down. Suddenly I cried out, "The light! The light!" Sprawled with my eyes shut, I thought I'd gone blind.

I felt a head in my lap. Last, sobbing. I stroked his thick brown hair, slowly, contentedly. "Sid," he whispered, "i's beginnin' fer ye. Th' road ahaid is rough an' bluidy bu' now there's nae turnin' back. Ye've seen th' Great Illumination." Smiling, I kissed him and fell asleep.

It was a whole new ball game after that. I stopped being Last's patient and became, in his words, a co-worker. Like a flower his life opened to me.

One by one I came face to face with the group, starting with the other two doctors.

The first time Last invited me home to dinner I met his collaborator, Boris Petkin. A hulking, lantern-jawed, former Communist organizer in his native East End, Dr. Petkin had a soft, faintly menacing snarl that reminded me of Mike Mazurki, the lovelorn thug in *Farewell, My Lovely.* In his assertively 'prole' clothes—drip-dry shirt, baggy Marks & Spencer cord trousers and rubber-cleated Tuff shoes—he moved slowly and clumsily like a *shtetl* wraith. Petkin had interned with Last in Dorset. "It was turrible, turrible," he'd grimly boast in his flat, grinding Stepney accent.

"Willie and me pulled the shock box on hundreds of the poor sods. Christ knows how many we actually killed." The Petkins—wife Vivienne, an ex-mental nurse, and three kids—shared Last's house in Islington.

The group's other doctor was Richard Drummond, a Canadian psychiatrist who ran Conolly House, an experimental unit for adolescent schizophrenics at a hospital outside London. He had little of Boris Petkin's plainspokenness. When I asked Dr. Drummond to explain about Conolly House he stared blankly at me, then said: "Within a micro-social nexus the holistic hungers of the community members dialectically reinforce my narcissistic violence, but produce a negation of a negation in which we abduct one another from our arbitrary roles. Thus, a wholly new politics emerges: an anti-imperialism of the mind." Babily plump 'Dr. Dick' (as Last told me Drummond's patients called him) was a sharp dresser and drove a custom-built yellow Morgan. He lived with his black American wife Nancy and their four children at the hospital.

An invisible line divided the doctors from the group's nonmedicals who Dr. Last called his "noncommissioned officers."

Despite his lack of medical status Alfred Waddilove, a ruddy-cheeked bachelor, was even closer to Last than Dr. Petkin. He looked after Last's business affairs and made himself useful in a thousand little ways. ("My adjutant," Last joked.) All I knew about Alf was that he'd once been a patient of Last's down in Dorset and had followed him to London where he now owned a small travel agency in Shaftesbury Avenue. Intensely, doggedly loyal, he gazed admiringly at his ex-analyst during meetings. "Willie's like a national monument," he said wistfully. "He needs protecting—especially from himself."

I did a double take with Major Anthony Straw, M.C. What was an ex-battalion commander (Royal Corps of Military Police) doing in Last's group? "Bugger me if I know, coz," said the small, bristling, moustached officer-turned-City businessman. "Willie says I've joined up again for the duration—of what I'm still not quite sure." After resigning his commission in 1956 as a protest against the British withdrawal from Suez, Major Straw had drifted from one semimanagerial job to another trying to find a use for himself. "Frankly Sid, civvy street almost clobbered me before I met Willie." Last, enamored of all things military, had fastened onto Major Straw when they accidentally met in a pub. "Almost a pickup, really. As soon as I told him my background he practically saluted and called me 'sir' ". Separated from his wife, Major Straw had found virtually another home with Last's family in Islington. "Good show!" he'd bellow in his parade ground voice if anybody in the group made an especially telling spiritual point.

It was easy to think of the group's only woman, Davina Mannix-Simpson, as just another of Last's boys. She deliberately defeminized herself by wearing tweeds, shapeless sweaters, flat-heeled brogans and a timid, self-deprecating grin. In a way I found this sexy. Hadn't Joan Fontaine looked this dowdy before Laurence Olivier or Tyrone Power brought her back to life with a kiss? Davina, a BBC Religious Programmes producer in her mid-thirties, had met Last while taping him for "Thought for Today." "It was something he said in the interview that shook me up so. 'The existence one is attempting to make viable is the person who is endeavoring to appropriate it.' Or words to that effect." Encouraged by Last, she'd quit her job to plunge into nudism, Flamenco guitar lessons and learning to arc-weld cast iron sculpture. "More and more I see what Willie is on about, this madness thing. It just means conquering your inhibitions, doesn't it?"

I was, in Last's phrase, the "sacred seventh."

I couldn't help noticing how, for a group dedicated to schizophrenia, we were all firmly anchored in middle-class sanity. Dr. Last called this "purrchase in th' wurld," essential if we were serious about helping others. "At this sensitive stage in oor development as a britherhuid—nae tae speak of oor failures as sheer hyoomin bein's" (with a bitter laugh)—"we cannae risk takin' in th' truly mad. 'Twould be unfair tae them an' tae oorselves." No chronics or uncontrollables, he decreed, nor anybody "not viable." In other words, none of Them; i.e., patients currently labeled actively schizophrenic. (Ex-patients were okay.)

I was disappointed. I wanted to share Last's life concern and felt "inauthentic" palavering about mental cases I hadn't even seen yet. (Also, I didn't want to be left behind in the dodo's class with Alf Waddilove, Major Straw and Davina, who were medically unqualified to deal with crazies.) I badgered Dr. Last about schizophrenics, but he was too busy and merely recommended more books. And when I approached big Boris Petkin he glowered, "Do you expect me to give you in five minutes what it's taken me twenty years to learn? You must be joking!"

Frustrated, I turned to 'Dr. Dick' Drummond. Though his work load was at least as heavy as Last or Petkin's—he looked after two hospital wards in addition to Conolly House, an out-patient clinic and had a private practice as well—Drummond let me hang around him and ask questions. His style—he was as fond of dialectical contradictions as of rich food—I found infuriating at first. He never used a simple word if a dozen double-barreled ones would do, and it was easy to get lost in his fog of Marxist-cum-Sartrean circumlocutions. But under all that vague Germanic rhetoric was a deeply serious purpose, which he explained this way: "I want to help build a community where, for the first time in history, people can actually love and hate *each other* and not another (oneself) in the other, thus experiencing toward oneself one's own disowned hatred of the self-disowning other and pass the point of perfecting ourselves beyond the further imperfectibility of our perfect imperfection." Only when drunk did he talk straight. "Conolly House is the last chance for some of those kids. Maybe I can help a few make it."

I begged him to let me visit his institution.

"You understand, of course, that existentially speaking, you'd be scaling a mountain peak of phenomenological indeterminacy there," Dick replied after a little hesitation.

When he refused to forbid me to come—his way of agreeing—I packed my bag and hopped a Green Line bus from Marble Arch, heading west. Along Bayswater Road, past Notting Hill through Shepherds Bush (then still intact), past Lime Grove BBC-TV studios and Acton, onto the M-4 and the semi-industrial suburbs of Ealing, Southall and Hayes. Past Heathrow airport, tiny streams and beacons in the scrub fields, past Slough's soulless streets to golf courses, cows and stockbroker villas just beyond Eton College, spitting distance from Ascot and the ruritanian towers of Windsor Castle. Small meadows, citified villages, the outer spokes to London's huge wheel. In a short stretch of country, between the Chilterns and North Downs, a rural caesura, Low Wick, gateway to King Edward VIII hospital.

Hefting the bottom part of my old infantry pack, I swung down from the busload of cloth-coated, stony-faced shoppers and nervously walked toward the yellow brick chimneys poking up above a thick stand of trees between Low Wick village and the main road. Past the war monument, with fresh flowers, around a small brackish pond frozen over, to an untended gate house. Drawing a big breath I stepped onto hospital grounds, into another zone.

Days and Nights in Conolly House: Winter

LATE SATURDAY A.M.

A tall, high cheekboned boy in bare feet and a dirty terry-cloth robe blocks my way into Conolly House, a two-story, yellow brick building at the far end of a paved crescent of similar wards. As soon as I start up the cement steps of the wire-meshed front porch—all the other porches are enclosed by glass—the youth snaps to attention, an invisible object in his hand.

"Pree-sent ARMS!" he shouts in a make-believe American accent. Whistling "Sweet Georgia Brown" he goes through a dazzling display of Harlem Globetrottery, syncopatedly slapping and shouldering his 'rifle,' finally flips it up into the air and catches it like a rescued infant (both arms moving in and out like a fireman holding a net), strokes it once or twice, then arches way back legs apart to tootle "High Society" as if it was a clarinet. Finished (note perfect), he comes to attention again, smiles broadly and steps aside to let me in. As I pass him his smile wavers. "Carry on," I say, mock military. "Fuck ya!" he retorts and raises the 'clarinet' threateningly.

Opening the unlocked front door I'm attacked, not by Clarinet-stick but by an aggressive smell of Dettol, body sweat, cigarette smoke and rancid milk. It's like a stone wall you have to walk through. Clarinet-stick follows me down the freezing, acrid corridor. "Carry yo' bag, suh?" he whines and shuffles like Stepin Fetchit. I gingerly sidestep another bathrobed boy, hands wrapped lovingly about his body, rocking rhythmically in place, a small puddle at his combat-booted feet. From the kitchen on my left a wild-eyed blond-goateed character leaps out balancing a foot-high stack of white bread and sloshing cup of tea. He stops short, holds himself rigidly and spits:

"I am the Life
I am the Man
If you don't like it
Kiss my can."

"Ah, fuck off Greaves," amiably says my tall bespectacled escort, " 'e jus' arrived." He points to a door and in an Uncle Remus accent with echoes of Fats Waller says, "Dat's de Big Bwana's wigwam o li'l white brother." He jitterbugs away 1940s style. "See ya latuh, alligatuh." I knock and walk into a small office cluttered with wooden file cabinets, a desk and more folding metal chairs than I think can possibly be fitted in. One wall is covered from floor to ceiling with a mural depicting (to me) hairless schmoos paddling a coffin across a sea of blood. The title scrawled at the bottom is *Christ Redeems Us from the Shrinks.*

Three men stare balefully at me. One, a tubby 200-pounder with grease-slicked hair and scared, overbright eyes, wears a nurse's uniform—a white knee-length coat with green shoulder boards—that looks like an 1890 cowboy's duster. He hands me a paper form. "Name, address and religion." A moment's panic: they think I'm a patient.

"It's okay, Bert," gently smiles a man in civilian clothes behind the desk. "Mr. Bell, is it? Welcome to our happy home. I'm Les O'Brien."

As soon as my bona fides are established the staff men relax a little. Dave Foster, in his early thirties with a broken nose and cauliflower ear, looks at my bag and says neutrally to the younger nurse, "Bert, show Mr. Bell the way to Doctors Quarters." Foster has on a compromise uniform, a short, white, red-epauletted coat over a business suit and tie.

But I'm staying in Conolly House, I say. Les O'Brien spells it out, "Mr. Bell is a w-r-i-t-e-r. He's come to do us for the Sunday papers, I expect."

Quick, careful glances among the nurses.

Oh, I say, I'm not at Conolly House as a reporter. "I'm here as myself."

"Ballocks," snorts O'Brien. "You're here as Dick's protégé, a late Christmas present to us from the old boy network." Nurses Bert Karp and Foster sit up a little straighter. I can almost hear them thinking: if Bell is the boss' friend, go easy on him.

Loftily I refuse to be labeled. Dick Drummond assured me that Conolly House was an 'anti hospital' opposed to rigid roles. So I'm neither patient nor doctor nor nurse. Not even a writer. I'm who I 'elect' to be. "I'm here because I'm here because I'm here."

"Ah ha," Les O'Brien chortles, "a new recruit to the cause. I know what Dick tells you innocents about this joint. But we're the slobs who have to pick up the pieces after you go. I suppose you'll write a book—*Down and Out in Conolly House* or *Now Let Us Praise Famous Nut Cases.* Or are you here, Mis-ter Bell, to help out? We sure could use some."

Bert Karp bows out in a gust of diplomatic coughing.

I'm in Conolly House, I wearily repeat, as myself. To write, go mad, help or not help, what difference did it make? Without rancor O'Brien grins. "Good god, another effin' tourist."

Nurse Foster too finds he has urgent duties elsewhere. O'Brien and I are left alone.

For several months he's been just an anonymous voice at the other end of the telephone line to Conolly House. Whenever I call Dick I usually get Les, his chief nurse. At first I can't spot the accent: north country, musical, strong. The voice, slow and cautious, always seems to be laughing at itself. "Good evening, *Mister* Bell. Dr. Dick's not around tonight, will any of us plebs do?"

Slumped in a swivel chair at his scarred, tea-spattered desk, his legs stretched out before a one-bar electric fire, O'Brien looks almost frail. His fingers are blackened, his teeth are half-rotted by nicotine; his large rocklike face looks tired. Only the small black eyes glitter fiercely. In his old shabby suit he seems undersized, fatigued. When he gets up I see he is, in fact, about my height, athletically built. It's as if he has two heights: fully erect and also set in an automatic, watchful crouch which somehow diminishes him. He's either an ex-boxer, I think, or an on-the-run whorehouse gambler.

Before we can grapple at closer quarters, Clarinet-stick soars in. "Where th' fuckin' fuck are my fuckin' clothes, ya fuckin' fuck?" he asks. Then bursts into helpless laughter and hugs O'Brien. Seeing me he straightens up and plays "It Ain't Necessarily So" on his nonexistent instrument. O'Brien says, "You're high as a kite, Jerry. No civvies till you come down." He unlocks the wall medicine cabinet and mixes something in a glass of water from the basin tap. "Here's your calm juice, boy-o." Noting my surprise O'Brien laughs shortly. "Sure we dope 'em if we have to. What'd you expect—the millennium?"

Jerry drinks his drug and lets out a mighty Tarzan yell. Satisfied, he shuffles out fingering "How High the Moon" (Stan Getz version). O'Brien says that Jerry Jackson has been in and out of mental hospitals since fifteen. "He's twenty-four now. Escapes now and then, but always hides somewhere he can be spotted easy. Last month th' rozzers found him sleeping inside a sentry box at Windsor Castle up the road. He's got it down to a fine art, including playing mad to get his Largactil."

O'Brien shakes his head. "Oh, he's pretty crazy is old Jerry Jackson, no mistake. Right up th' bloody spout." He falls into his Charge Nurse's chair and points a long, burned-looking finger at me.

"The true definition of madness, dear sir, is that you get caught. Found out. Arrested, admitted, diagnosed. The clever ones around here play possum, kiss a little arse and get out. Jerry isn't so clever. He's honest. Just a nice English working-class lad who's made one mistake too many. And keeps making the some small mistake on and on and on." O'Brien throws back his head and gives a terrifying laugh.

A Geography Lesson

On our way upstairs to a room reserved for me Les O'Brien gives me the one dollar tour. I wave to Jerry Jackson-the-clarinet slumped sleepily on his cot in a six-bed dormitory opposite the staff office at the ground floor back. "Observation Dorm," says O'Brien, "for nervous nellies and first admissions." Most of its windows have been kicked out.

We sidestep a dainty pile of shit under the swaying, self-embracing dummy in the corridor. The smell of urine from him is dizzy-making. Is that hum coming from him? Boys in pajamas or street clothes mooch around guzzling tea or glued to transistor radios or talking to each other—or to themselves. For the first time I become really aware of how noisy Conolly House is. It's like the wild track from a circus movie, and grows louder and more snarling as we move along, as if something was on our scent. An elephant-sized teenager has two small plastic radios clamped to both ears. To block out the noise? In the rather cheerful, brightly curtained dining room next to Obs Dorm there's a carnage of broken tea mugs, unwashed dishes, tipped over chairs and chunks of leftover food on filthy tables and floors. Greaves, the goateed rhymster I bumped into earlier, idly noodles the keys of a half-gutted old upright piano in the corner,

"Hegel, Marx, Hume and Russell
Put my mind in a Sixth Form bustle
Lawrence, Leavis, James and Joyce
Gives me very little choice."

Conolly House's nerve center is a large, messy room nearest the front entrance. There, half a dozen or so boys, at lazy alert, sip tea, smoke, watch "Saturday Sportsdesk" on an old 19-inch TV. A boy exhorts the soccer match on screen, "Th' kingdom of God is within you. . . . Aw fer fuck sake, you're offside, ya stupid git!" Another boy talks to himself. "I . . . I saw something when I flew. The plane in front of ours crashed. It's very easy that. Yes. Crashing without a plane." Comic books and soccer magazines lie scattered among defiantly unused ashtrays. It all reminds me of World War II documentary films about life aboard a combat aircraft carrier. Except no pilots' ready room ever had this weird an assortment of furniture: a velvet chaise longue, beach li-lo, doubled-over mattress, poof cushion, a hammock slung between massive armchairs, odd lots of metal seats and a plush red-leather executive's chair with a headrest monogrammed in gold, DIANA DORS. Surprisingly, no graffiti except one neatly scratched above the door lintel:

SHANGHAI EXPRESS

Two large corner windows, looking out on the front lawn and driveway, are smashed and stuffed with rags against the January chill. A lovely fire in the grate. I feel sucked in by the welcome warmth, a card party smell of ash, old beer, poker tactics.

Across the freezing hall from TV lounge there's a kitchen equipped with a shiny tea urn and, farther back, a main toilet. Why's it all so cold? O'Brien says, "Dr. Winstanley, the Medical Superintendent, won't turn on the furnace till the boys stop bustin' windows. And the boys keep knocking the windows out as a protest against the cold." His tone suggests that around here this is perfectly reasonable logic.

The second floor is like rush hour in a pop record factory. A turntable somewhere blasts Chubby Checkers' "Let's Twist Again," behind that a *katyusha* mixing "Light Cavalry Overture" with Lonnie Donegan's "Don't You Rock Me Daddy-o," plus assorted screeches, scrowls, woofs and weeps. O'Brien gingerly knocks on a door nearest the upper staircase then steps aside like a homicide detective expecting a hail of bullets. The door opens a fraction and we're almost bowled over by a thundering niagara of sound. A hot-eyed, tousle-haired kid wearing earmuffs (or enormous headphones) peeps out, slams the door in O'Brien's face. For just a flash I saw inside, a roaring catacomb of wires and electronic gadgetry. O'Brien raises his voice above the din. "Percy is our resident deejay. Plays anything but requests."

On this landing are another large toilet and dormitory and some private rooms. ("For them as desires solitude if not exactly peace and quiet.") Also what O'Brien calls the "Anything Goes Room," which is the cleanest I've seen, the only one with intact windowpanes. An unmarked punching bag and an unused set of watercolors stand in the corner. "Sad case really," says O'Brien. "Our first O.T.—occupational therapist—had this great idea. Set aside a place for the blokes to do whatever they felt like—kick, punch, break, smear, shout. Naturally nobody ever uses it." He laughs. "She eventually went crackers, I hear."

In the latrine there's a dirt-encrusted bathtub with attached leather straps and piles of old canvas, a relic of forced hydrotherapy that Dick Drummond junked along with ECT and habitual drugs. A neatly dressed black boy bends over in one of the doorless toilet cubicles hacking out loud, mechanical coughs. He hardly notices O'Brien slipping some cellophane-wrapped pastilles into his jacket pocket. "Glycerine," says O'Brien, "so Abe don't tear his larynx all to shreds."

Upstairs here, most of the doors and walls have words like 'Paris,' 'Berlin' and 'Moscow' chalked on them. When I query O'Brien he just shrugs. "Stopovers on the way to China, I imagine," and explains no further. He opens the door to my room, which has clean towels, running water and a pleasant view of the Berkshire countryside. Someone has neatly swept up and left fresh crocuses in a tea mug on the table. O'Brien says, "Robin Ripley's doin' her earth mother bit again." With friendly, skeptical eyes he watches me unpack, then says he goes off duty for the weekend in a couple of hours. "So if we don't see you again," he sticks out his hand, "it was real nice meetin' you." I know that tone from the West Riding coal fields: stay if you dare.

Watching O'Brien disappear amid a catherine wheel of Percy-the-radio's sound explosions, a small fear uncoils inside me. Jesus I'm cold.

Alone. On the bed, listening to a rising tide of angry static through my walls. Does Percy ever sleep? Will the smells from downstairs come up to strangle me? Is Jerry Jackson violent? As I put my things away I think: well, Magic Mountain it's not.

A Recon

Shielded behind my chair-barricaded door and a copy of Buber's *I and Thou*, I decide to die facing the noisy enemy rather than be pounded to bits in my rathole.

Peek out, cautiously. Corridor empty, freezing. Edge along a hall, past upstairs dorm. No one there except a few sleeping forms curved under blanket mountains. In the adjacent latrine black Abe, popping O'Brien's pastilles into his mouth, adds to the clamor with dry Morse code coughs. Hack-hack . . . uck-uck-uck.

Tippytoe, holding my breath, past Percy's musical howitzers

firing like *Custer's Last Stand* plus the Goons at full tilt. Easy, easy. Don't scare them. I'm terrified.

On the stairs an Asian boy in black pajamas buttoned to the neck soundlessly flits past me. Jesus, he could've garroted me before I heard him.

Downstairs, I approach a knot of boys around the stainless steel water boiler in the kitchen. In thin robes or shirt-sleeves—don't schizophrenics feel the cold?—they drink mugs of tea and watch me pour hot water into a plastic cup of Nescafé and spoon in honey I brought with me. "That's right," says a giant with a lobster-red face and large arms and legs that stick out of absurdly ill-fitting pajamas. "Assert your indivi-*duality* right at the start. Saves trouble later." I offer coffee and honey around, no takers. "In the war," says a pencil-moustached boy in a three-piece business suit with his wallet prominently exposed from his jacket side pocket, "thy Yanks dropped food packages on our heads and we haven't recovered yet." He's got a Yorkshire lilt and nervously checks the time on his wristwatch.

A. C. Corrigan, a stocky, muscular freckleface with a mane of bright red hair and dressed in civvies, introduces himself and the others in a broad Liverpool accent. He says, "You're gointa study uz nuts, right ol' whack?"

I'm here, I repeat, as myself.

"Bu' tha're not on a Section 25 or 29—a Detention Order?" demands the Yorkshireman, Roy Battersby, who vigorously shakes his wristwatch to see if it's working. No, I say. "Well then," he winds his Rolex with the superior air of someone who has established what's what and who's who. "Don't let it go to thy head then lad," he adds smugly.

For almost as long as I battled O'Brien I defend myself against the boys pressing me on why I've come, who I am. When they boast about their records in previous hospitals, I rather guiltily admit that I always managed to dodge the bin before this. A languid-looking boy in a high-neck sweater festooned with CND buttons says matter-of-factly: "Your mother and father must be dead then. Some people have all the luck." He constantly combs and recombs his shoulder-length dark blond hair, checking his work in a hand-held mirror. He is called Jeff H. (After the movie actor Jeffrey Hunter, I'm told later).

I tell them about Dr. Last's project, our hope of making a place like Conolly House, only freer.

"Oh-ho!" shouts the awkward red giant Barney Beaton, cinching up the strings of his pajamas as if strangling someone. "While your pals are tax-deducting amateur schizophrenics you're here talent scouting among us professionals." Yorkshire Roy adds, "After us they'll be dead easy, raght?"

"Well," warns Beaton, "make sure you do a craft-y job of it. Nothing I dislike more than shoddy work." His piping voice—oddly childish in such a bulky body—takes on a nagging, adult gruffness. "Don't know what's wrong with today's help. Satisfied to swill their tea, draw a hundred knickers a week and watch naked ladies in *The Mirror*. When I do a thing I do it proper."

Beaton launches into an excruciatingly detailed account of a day in his father's Holborn printing firm where he was learning the business. "I dead-bored the Number Sex-tie double-pecker bust to the fallopian, got my *Times* to follow the leader, sardined to Take-A-Chancery Lane, banged the time clock, checked the chaps, goggled the gauges, pricked the pros, tampered with the temps, screwed the stackers, inserted the inkers . . ." Losing him for several minutes, I pick him up again. ". . . and, broad-ly speaking, give or take an extra eight inches, made a cunt-plete ballsup of it." Back to his own adolescent voice. "It isn't fair, you know. In the good old days the youngest son was entailed to the Colonies to feed the starving hoojie-woojies. Now he stays home and lets his parents eat him." He roars, "Isn't that so, Kurse Narp?"

Which nails the beefy, brylcreemed young nurse I met in O'Brien's office. Caught flat-footed eavesdropping outside the doorway, Bert Karp blusters in, his face almost as red as Barney's, and pretends to refill his tea mug at the urn. Dipping me a sly wink he bellows: "GOOD LADS REALLY, MR. BELL! WOULDN'T BELIEVE ALL THEY TELL YOU THOUGH! HA HA!" The boys look at Karp with a mixture of pity and derision, and before they scatter Barney Beaton makes a twirling motion with finger pointed at his head and loudly whispers, "Careful—he's psycho-pathetic."

Nurse Karp corners me against the kitchen sink. "Now then, Mr. Bell, you're a man of the world. Frankly, what do *you* make of the pH factor?" The what? I ask. Karp smiles confidently at me and strides off with an immensely knowing air. As bewildered as the boys, I gape after him blankly.

Nurse O'Brien is what I need for my nerves but he's busy in the office conferring with a palely handsome young man in shirt-sleeves who has his feet lazily up on O'Brien's desk. I assume from the snatch of talk I barge into that he's a staff colleague of O'Brien's. ". . . Roy's identity crisis stems from his mother's imploded false-self system and—" is all I hear before bowing out hastily. I'll get some fresh air instead.

A little later, on the front lawn I almost sprawl headlong into the flailing fists of an angry young bull encased in a visored helmet and a motorbiker's black leather outfit with HEAVEN'S DEVIL studded on the back of the zip jacket. He explodes in all directions like the American boxer Hurricane Jackson, hitting out blindly. Several boys easily dance in and out of his reach. Immersed in R. D. Laing's *The Divided Self*, Herb Greaves gracefully ducks and weaves through the wild swings without once taking his eyes from the page. Everybody but me in this incredibly precise ballet knows how to move. Dodging a looping left I stumble into the arms of the young staffer I saw with O'Brien minutes ago. He steadies me. "Relax. There's a trick to it," he advises calmly. He walks up to the furiously milling boy and says: "Time for your ECT, Hodge." The visored boy freezes, then gallops off in terror.

"Never fails," says the staffer. "They gave it to him once."

In the cold darkening air my rescuer and I feel each other out by tapping a partly deflated soccer ball back and forth on the scrub grass. His name is Clem Woodford. "Don't worry," he says, "I won't cross-examine you. We've got used to sightseers like you. Con House ought to charge admission." He says he's lost count of the Americans and/or reporters (he uses the words interchangeably) traipsing through the ward. "They ask questions, take notes, then vanish like the dust. Christ knows what they make of us. Probably swallow Dr. Dick's story hook, line and sinker." He savagely kicks the ball over my head. "You'll lie," he says without enmity. "They all do."

Six P. M.

Supper of dehydrated eggs, shrapnel-hard peas, soggy chips, watery carrots and spine-straightening tea. Dining room empty except for two girls at an oilclothed table with a couple of patients. The boys' dates or staff? A Saturday night bonus for all-male Conolly House? Feeling like a wallflower I slouch to a far table and moodily munch alone. One of the girls comes over. "Terrible grub, isn't it? The Management Committee's trying to poison the lot of us." Coal-black hair braided in a halo around a lovely moon-pale Renaissance face, she leans across to shake my hand. "I'm Bronwen Jones, soon sing. After the wedding bells we're seeing sail-on." Mmm. Green split-to-the-thigh skirt, form-hugging red sweater, long white stockings: with her low melodious voice a Welsh nationalist vision, I think madly. Sexy. Crazy too, probably.

"Bronwen, bring Dr. Bell over," shouts the other girl, elbowing her table-mates to make room for me. "Move over, ya bums." She's slightly older, mid-twenties, thinner, with long brown hair, crew-neck sweater, butt-tight pedal pushers and sandals: a Los Angeles hipster with a south London accent. When I learn the thin girl is Robin Ripley I thank her for the flowers and cleaning my room. "That's okay," her grainy husky voice reminds me agreeably of Anita O'Day. "Dr. Dick says you're trying to learn how to go crazy. Anything we can do to help. . . ."

Saturday evening, the unit is a bellowing half-empty chassis. (Some boys have weekend leave.) On top of the other noises—Greaves' piano, a low but piercing hum from Gareth the rocking-and-pissing boy, black Abe's metronomic cough, crashing plates, the occasional tinkle of a breaking window, various transistors—Percy-the-radio shoots Ray Charles' "Hit the Road Man" at us at 100 rpm. Blasted from all sides, I try to sort out first impressions. To my untrained eye Conolly House has at least three levels. An articulate core—Jerry 'clarinet' Jackson, Yorkshire Roy, A. C. Corrigan and Barney (including some like Hurricane Hodge who use only body language). Next, visible and unseen sound raisers: Percy, and the fat boy with two radios permanently clamped to his head, and whoever mans the portable pickup, which is moved around so much it sounds like a drunken ghost. (Sometimes, I swear, the dining-room piano is played by poltergeists or Peter Lorre's hands amputated from an old horror movie.) And an underground of withdrawn, silent boys whose Presence, in Dr. Last's phrase, is in their Absence. Altogether about two dozen youths, early teens to mid-twenties, in their first or second breakdown, from a West London catchment area plus a bit of imported talent from the provinces. All diagnosed by one or more doctors as "acute schizoid," "paranoid schizophrenic," "severe personality disorder," "florid acting out," etc., etc. One or two have committed petty crimes but most are from solidly respectable English families. They've come, as I learn, by a variety of roads from 'voluntary' (informal) admission to outright kidnapping—Orders under Sections 25, 29 or 136 of the 1959 Mental Health Act.

It's like the army: hurry up and wait. Except that the chaplain, Dr. Dick Drummond, isn't due to punch t.s. tickets till Monday morning. A long, long weekend.

After Robin and Bronwen disappear somewhere, night takes over Conolly House. Its temperature drops, corridors seem longer, walls higher. Outside more alien. As if angry at the two girls' departure, Percy-the-radio explodes Billie Holiday's "Love for Sale" nightmarishly loud, driving us into stunned sadness or up the pole. Soon the unit responds to Percy's call, and the schizophrenics' field song of slamming doors, switched on transistor radios and obscurely ambiguous sounds rises like thick vapor. The adolescents' symphony is unanswered. The hospital remains dead, silent and dark.

A familiar depression descends. Or is it my old American reflex? I'm always blue Saturday night without a girl.

Sunday

"LEGGO MR. BELL'S TAPS!" bellows a voice in my Seconal-drugged ear. Groggily I turn over, glimpse two hazy figures wrestling over my washbasin. Door slams. Silence. I drift off into a dream that I'm Fred Astaire dancing up a staircase of pajama'd cockneys singing,

> "We din't meanya
> Tuh catch schizophrenia. . . ."

Instead of Ginger Rogers, an outraged male voice yodels, "NO-O-O-o-o-o!"

Wrapped in a hospital-issue gown I stumble downstairs in time to see burly nurse Bert grapple with Gareth, who is rumpled, uncombed but not smelling too badly yet. Bert, at least fifty pounds heavier, tugs and strains at the robot youth who simply leans into him without budging: perfect zenmanship.

What's up? I ask.

"Little basket," sweats Bert, "won't wash." Does he always wash at 7:00 A.M. Sundays? "He does when *I'm* on duty." With a triumphant cry of "Gee up, lad!" Bert uproots Gareth and drags him kicking and squalling into the latrine. Shivery with cold, I carry my honey jar and instant coffee into the dining room where Herb Greaves sits alone before a breakfast of two pots of tea, four bowls of milk-sloshed Weetabix heaped with sugar, an everest of Wonder Bread and a two-pound can of lemon curd. (A normal meal, I'm told, for thin-as-a-rail Greaves. Yesterday I heard Bert theorize that schizophrenics manage to keep slim by burning up abnormal amounts of energy. What about vast Wally Walters, the boy hiding between his two radios? Bert: "No tellin' *how* big he'd be sane.")

Greaves slams shut his copy of Goffman's *Asylums* and, taking three trips to transfer all his breakfast paraphernalia, moves to another table when he spots me. Hunched over his cereal he snarls: "They rubbed out Baby Face Gaitskell to win the next General Election. Who did the Transport House mob think they were kidding? At the funeral in dark glasses Two Finger George Brown, Frank (Lucky) Cousins, Scarface Harold Wilson. . . ." Though his tone is threatening it feels as if Greaves is presenting something to me.

"What about Double Crossman?" I suggest.

Surprised, Greaves looks up. He didn't expect an answer in kind. He laughs uneasily and lowers his scraggly head to his arm, trying to keep up his end of the dialogue. What comes out is a confused torrent of census statistics and Guinness Book of Records minutiae. Looking me straight in the eye he winds up with the United Kingdom 1963 health budget ". . . for growing green meddlers in mental hothouses."

"REALLY SAD CASE THAT!" interrupts Bert Karp. Water-drenched from his battle with Gareth, he plunks himself down at my table and points with a steaming tea mug at Greaves. "Lad there failed his exams! Lost his student grant! One morning—w'd you credit it?—goes up to the university clock tower and starts chucking down Walls meat pies!" Nurse Karp giggles. "Must be thankful, though. In America eh? he'd of sprayed 'em with a tommy gun. Ha ha!" To make a joke of it he mock-machine-guns Greaves. A light dies in Greaves' eyes, and he relapses into a dull monotone like Barney Beaton's yesterday. (Is he parodying Beaton? Or consciously faking out Bert?) "So I lazurezed at seven and put on my marks and sparks and went down to kelloggs and typhoo and raleighed to the lecture hall and morpheused to professor thompson model cabbages in economics and oxoed in the wimpey and matissed while doctor freedman embalmed marx and raleighed lumpward to wrestle with my allen & unwin and watch pie-in-the-sky with my stalins and beautyrested until morning and put on my lillywhites and bannistered to the stanley matthews . . ."

"Hold on!" Bert shouts. "Why aren't you in class today?"

Greaves peers contemptuously at him. "Today is Sunday, you stupid nit."

His voice rises rapidly, shrilly. ". . . and sat my exams and waited for the results and listened to my parents say how they'd slaved all their lives for this moment and. . . ." He stops. Me: "Then what happened?"

"Then it happened," he says dully. His eyes are cold, glazed.

"What happened?" I persist.

"I can't remember." Greaves shuffles off.

Alone with Karp I ask if the fight I dreamed earlier in my room was real or not. Real enough, he says. Around sunup he caught Vince, a fourteen-year-old deaf kleptomaniac, tampering with my washbasin. The room I now occupy used to be his, and he keeps returning to adjust the slightly leaky faucet, Bert says. How can a 'deaf' kid hear a trickle even I can't?

Bert gives me a I-know-you're-asking-out-of-politeness-because-you-really-know-what-I-mean look. "It's an established fact, isn't it, Mr. Bell, that paranoid schizophrenics hear better than us normal people. Y'know, higher frequencies, like dogs. It's called the pH factor."

Eight A.M. Signs of life. Like some great perfect engine Conolly House sparks, moves. Doors open and shut, someone's built a cozy coal fire in the TV lounge grate. From upstairs Abraham cracks open the day with his first cough: it's as if an unseen conductor has raised his baton. Like a Dmitri Tiomkin chord when the Sioux appear on the horizon, Percy's amplifiers—asleep since three this morning—suddenly boom Mitch Miller's "And The Caissons Go Rollin' Along." We're off!

Staff shortage means that on Sundays from 7:00 A.M. to 2:00 P.M. Bert Karp—a constable's son who failed the police cadet height minimum by one inch—rules the roost alone. Like a mechanical gnome in a Swiss clock he whirls through Conolly House furiously crackling paper, coughing, banging doors, inspecting rooms, rattling tea mugs. Whenever we pass in the corridors he winks and shouts, "NEVER LETS UP, DOES IT MR. BELL?" Later, the young staffer Clem Woodford, a copy of Camus under his arm, joins me for elevenses in the kitchen. He bemusedly watches Bert scurry around in an endless, self-defeating effort to discipline the unit, and observes, "That bloke Sisyphus must've been a weekend duty nurse in a mental hospital."

Sunday is Con House's longest day. The nearest cinema is in Farningstoke, five miles away, and the village pub is shut all day. Nothing to do but stew, and wait for

Visi-Tears

In the thin cold sunless air figures toting laundry bags and napkin-covered wicker food hampers slowly, funereally invade the hospital landscape's frozen silence. Heads down, legs moving stiffly like luckless infantrymen going into trenches they know are booby-trapped, mothers, fathers, aunts and uncles head for their loved ones in the hospital's thirty-odd wards. Inside Conolly House anxiety (and Bert Karp) rouse some boys, parents a few more. Several boys won't get up, their relatives huddle fretfully over sullen blanket lumps. The parents look at least as bewildered as their sons—and much more frightened. In the TV lounge florid Barney Beaton towers menacingly over his mother and father and pretends to film them through his eyeglasses. "Hold still dammit, while I shoot you," he commands. Mrs. Beaton, almost as tall as her six-foot son, turns sweetly to her husband, a little flabbergasted man in a trilby who stares at them both during the visit: "There George, I told you. He *is* better."

I slip into a rocking chair beside the Liverpool redhead A. C. Corrigan, and from behind *News of the Worlds* we eavesdrop on the patients and their families:

Derek Chatto is an apple-cheeked boy in immaculately white sneakers, white linen trousers and white tennis sweater. Playing chess with his father he slaps his head in chagrin: "Sorry, dad. I'm making all the wrong moves again, aren't I?"

Beefy Wally Walters, with the two radios still at his ears, "Aw, don' cry, Mum. I don' blame nobody but meself."

Eric Raw, a gaunt, beak-nosed character: "It's all my fault, isn't it?"

From the small quiet family knots around us spout geysers of apology—"sorry . . . sorry . . . my fault. . . ."

Beside me A. C. shakes his red-maned head crossly. " 'Twould make th' fuckin' angels weep. Beggin' forgiveness of th' very jokers what slung 'em in here. Except good old Barney."

Barney, by this time shouting insults and threats, lunges at his parents. Even when he is hammerlocked and boisterously wrestled out of the room by nurse Bert, hardly a single visitor looks their way. A. C. says, "If we took no notice like that, th' shrinks'd call it 'shallowness of affect.' " The ability of some families to totally ignore what they don't want to see is one of the contributory factors in the breakdowns of their sons, he says.

Afterward, postparental blues. From Conolly House's shattered windows the families can be seen streaming out the front gate, heads slightly higher, stride jauntier, a refreshed army of survivors. Boys who've had them tend to weep in corners or drift around lost in morose brooding. Jerry Jackson loudly sighs, "Wisht someone'd visit me. Somehow it don't seem fair for th' brunt tuh fall on a few unlucky bastids."

Dark, late afternoon. There have been five nurses changes since I arrived yesterday. Conolly House (I'm told) goes up or down according to who's on duty. Weekends, without Dr. Drummond and O'Brien, can be dicey.

It's down now. Boys gather around the unit's cracker barrel, the kitchen tea urn, to mend one another's troubles out of pure orneriness. For openers, the sharply dressed Yorkshire dude Roy Battersby announces: "Mah mam's mah best pal." No mother can be a boy's best friend, the others jeer. Jeff H. (né Bernie Mendelson) scoffs, "If she knows you want to fuck her she can't be too friendly."

Roy irritably winds his Rolex. "Not everybody wants to do tha' with his mam," he mutters uncomfortably. One or two boys, drilled in Drummond doctrine, say it's the other way around, mothers impose their sexual hangups on kids.

Little beads of sweat pop out on Roy's forehead. Without ever taking his eyes from his watch, he slowly pulls a multibladed Scout knife from an inside jacket pocket—his wallet is still blatantly exposed from his outer pocket—selects a blade and starts carving his initials on a steam pipe. "Ah'd never let my mother visit me here. She'd be contaminated by thy dirty minds—or one of tha'd take a punch at her." The idea of his young, divorced mother in Halifax being beaten up by Con Housers obviously pleases Roy, and he suppresses an involuntary belch of laughter. "Mind," he adds piously, "it's only wha' she deserves for fiddlin' wi' mah brass." His mother burgles from his post office savings account, he insists.

Other boys chime in with similar tales of how their parents rob them.

Staffer Clem Woodford says crisply that they're "reifying a metaphor," misidentifying stolen money with their sexual double bind.

Roy glares suspiciously at him. "Don't confuse me, Clem. That's Dr. Dick's job. Tha bluddy Socialists want to take over everything." Though I've often seen them together, horsing around affectionately and even strolling arm-in-arm, Roy can't stand Clem asserting his staff authority. Wally Walters also objects. "You'n Dr. Dick wanta educate us outta bein' sick, Clem. You can't. We're born that way."

Roy's temper rises. "Ah know when Ah started to get sick and when Ah started to get well. Nobody's born with it."

"And nobody is sick and nobody is well," lectures Clem.

In a swift, deadly movement Roy whirls on Clem, the Scout knife upraised. Clem stands his ground and merely gazes coldly at him with folded arms. No one interferes. Brandishing the knife while checking his wristwatch—no mean feat—Roy slips into that dreamlike narrative I've noticed some boys substitute for physical violence. "Ah remember goin' down into th' cellar and saw this knife. A safety not a flick. As soon as Ah opened it Ah wanted to stick it in somebody. Ah went upstairs and tried to stick it in mah mother. Then mah aunt. Ah wanted to shove it in them. For a long time whenever Ah saw a knife Ah put it away, hid it, threw it down drains. Now Ah don't have to do tha' anymore."

"Why?" demands Clem.

Roy looks agonized.

"C'mon," pursues Clem, "say why."

Roy, shaking with anger, shouts, "Ah don't have to say why." Desperate to keep control he holds his watch right up to his eyes. I can't resist: "*Quelle heure est-il*, Roy?"

He turns the knife toward me. "Did tha call mah mam a whore?" Maybe this is no game for *novilleros*, I think. Jeff H., a veteran picador, quickly diverts Roy from me by sidling up and running a languorous, braceleted hand through Roy's neatly parted hair. "That's just French for suck his cock," Jeff H. bats his eyes flirtatiously. Roy practically has a spasm patting his hair back into place; he'd rather die than not look 'proper.' (Even the scruffiest Con Houser, I've noticed, will spend hours on his coiffure.) "Tha leave me mam out of this," Roy shouts on the verge of tears. "Money's money an' th' other thing's just tha. She's never even seen mah foldin' stuff. Ah mean my hard lolly." He looks ready to kill someone.

"Come off it," says Clem. "You're interiorizing an ontological—"

That's too much for A. C. Corrigan. Till now an amused spectator, he slumps to the cold cement floor clutching his heart like Victor McLaglen at the end of *The Informer*. "Ur-r-gh-gh. Plugged troo de ol' ticker wid anudder Drummondism!" A. C.'s act breaks the tension, and the boys' laughter washes away Roy's murderous rage. When Jeff H. bitchily observes that Clem can't resist playing doctor while Dr. Dick's away, Clem flushes and retorts that if more patients played doctor there'd be less need of loony bins.

A. C. suspiciously: "None of dat New Left shit around here.

After all, I'm Catholic, almost made it as a priest." Suddenly he slaps his head comically. "Wad am I sayin'? Here I am in Con House. Up th' bluddy Revolution!"

Clem grins disgustedly. "That's right, you scouse opportunist. Join the winning side." A. C. says that's how he survived all these centuries. "When I wuz a Roman centurion I did a deal wid th' Gauls in case our regiment got defeated."

Someone asks, "How come you made it in here then?"

A. C. wraps his husky arms around Clem, swings him off his feet and whoops with laughter. "Th' fucken English just won't listen to Irish reason."

A Twilight Jog

I like Clem Woodford. Though too prone to Drummond jargon, he mixes easily and unpatronizingly with the patients. I gratefully accept his offer—perhaps made to regain his professional composure—to show me around the hospital. We put on thick sweaters and set out trotting to keep warm in the afternoon's dying light. A number of trees and young saplings have the Latin names of their species neatly printed on cards at eye level. "The gardener probably picked up the habit from the doctors," says Clem unsmilingly.

A two-lane driveway leads us to the Main Administration Department (MAD), a huge penitentiary-style building whose cornerstone was laid in 1845 by Queen Victoria. Extending from either side of Reception—a slightly smaller replica of Wren's St. Paul's (including a miniature dome)—are quarter-mile-long wings in pseudo-Palladian that house the kitchen, various workshops and wards. The wooden window frames, painted in bright white, resemble iron bars. Inside the mazelike corridors of Main Block—so like an even madder Pentagon, right down to the little electric trolleys soundlessly driven by porters and trusted patients—Clem points out the back (geriatric) wards, MSW (mentally subnormal wing), tiny library and O.T. Hardly a soul in sight. Then it's outside again for a rapid sweep around the trendy, spireless chapel, prefab Patients Canteen and a crematorium discreetly tucked behind some tall trees.

What strikes me is the heavy silence. It strangles the cold dusk air. Grass, bushes and privets are micrometer-cut, paths neatly sterile. It's scary. "You're catching on," says Clem. "What they teach you here is where you went wrong—*you made a fuss.*" He calls England a "mortuary state" in which resigned silence is the greatest civic virtue. "We ran the world for a couple of hundred years. Now the Olde Curiosity Shoppe has gone bust—but it's a crime against the Mental Health Act to tell the owner."

Clem concedes that 'King Eddie' is a liberal hospital compared to others he's seen. Most wards, though segregated by sex, are unbarred, unlocked, open plan. "Except Winnie Wing over there." He gestures at an imposing mock Tudor mansion partly concealed in a grove of hedges; its double-barred windows remind me of Count Dracula's castle. Winston S. Churchill Wing, the violent unit "for the stroppy ones," is one of the swords the all-powerful Management Committee holds over Dick Drummond's head. "If the lads sail too near China they're shipped up there for a bit of the Twisted Towel Treatment—wrapping a wet towel around a patient's neck till he blacks out."

"What's China?" I ask. Clem shrugs enigmatically. "Go ask a Chinaman."

A Socialist Baedecker, Clem gives me a (sometimes literally) running commentary on King Eddie. Most of the smaller units in the large fifteen hundred–patient National Health institution are immediately prewar, which by British standards makes them modern, and much effort has gone into brightening the surrounding landscape. There are new flowerbeds, fresh paint everywhere, dulcet ward names (Sunny Side, River View, Honeysuckle). Main Block, the hospital's nucleus, began life as a nineteenth-century workhouse—for the poor, debtors and mad—named Addleford, and was reincarnated as King Edward VIII Hospital only during the Prince of Wales' abortive reign in the 1930s. For over a hundred years, due mainly to a lucky succession of enlightened superintendents, Addleford functioned as a remarkably progressive institution "for its time." King Eddie has tried to live up to its reputation by treating patients if not humanely at least less barbarically than most other asylums. In the great surge of post-VJ optimism Aneuran Bevan, the Socialist Health Minister, opened an assembly hall and several new villas whose intentions shone from their names: Keir Hardie, Sylvia Pankhurst, George Lansbury—the saints of British radicalism. A ward specifically devoted to research and experiment was named in honor of John Conolly, the great nineteenth-century humanitarian doctor often called "the English Pinel" after the liberator of France's lunatics.

"Typical of Atlee's crowd to throw a few medical minnows into a sea of capitalist sharks and expect them to survive," says Clem as we turn homeward and retrace our steps. Labour's first postwar government modernized the buildings, but left basically untouched the old upper-class bias of English medicine. Thus, the shadow of a punitive, almost forgotten Poor Law still hangs over the hospital and prevents it from coming to terms with Conolly House. "Talk about double binds. Admin sends us their most disturbed patients—then blames us for being disturbed. We can't win."

Con House looms out of the darkness. Clem says, "Man, we're a bloody microcosm of British social democracy. Potentially the most creative experience of our time—and mostly a big fat drag."

A gigantic explosion cuts him short.

A classic Hammer horror scene greets us. Several boys slosh about in Golden Syrup seeping in from the smoky, gas-smelling kitchen into Con House's main corridor. Herb Greaves bangs out "Lord, Let Me in the Lifeboat" on the piano while Mr. Wu, the Asian Flash, runs soundlessly screaming up and down milk-splashed stairs. A human skeleton in pajamas hanging in tatters from his emaciated frame moans, "Aye, blame it on poor Eric." Upstairs, Percy's loudspeakers blare the Beatles' "Help."

It looks like a bomb has hit the TV room. Chairs, ashtrays and Sunday papers are violently scattered, the windows have been punched out rag stuffing and all. In front of the exploded TV set Robin Ripley, the girl who cleaned my room yesterday, calmly bandages the bleeding hands of a small muscular Irishman angelically crooning "Ave Maria" (pop version).

We find A. C. Corrigan sheltered under the upturned chaise longue and reading a newspaper. "What happened?" I ask.

"Not sure," he replies. "I think we just found a way to lick the English Sunday."

Monday

"NO-O-O-o-o-o!"

Gareth's outraged cock crow awakens me to my first working day in Conolly House. Without looking I know that Bert Karp is hassling him. And I don't bat an eye when little Vincent, the 'deaf' klepto, dashes into my room and swings a hammer at my surrogate skull, the (allegedly) leaking faucet. Here only thirty-six hours and already I'm an old con.

After 7:00 A.M. I shadow Les O'Brien on his early morning rounds. Before most boys are up he's consulted the offgoing nurse, wheeled in a trolley of two dozen precooked breakfasts from the hot meals lorry, studied the roster for overnight admissions, written several reports, turned over some blanket lumps to see if they're still breathing, liaised with police in Windsor about a drunk and disorderly furloughee, soothed a worried parent by phone, filled in countless forms and found time to sort out stray insomniacs, including me.

Con House Game (1)

When I tell O'Brien that someone should blow the whistle on Bert Karp's habit of bullying Gareth, he smiles innocently: "Who's stopping you?"

"I'm not staff. You're paid to do things like that."

O'Brien lights a cigarette. "Sez you and Mr. Tasker, the Chief Nursing Officer. But Dick Drummond, my *other* guvnor, says I'm paid not to exercise 'inauthentic authority.' Which twin has the Toni?"

Ten A.M.

Group therapy in the TV lounge made positively arctic by yesterday's fracas of busted windows. This 'therapeutic hour' is all that's left of the structured day Dr. Dick promised the authorities in order to get a unit of his own. Attendance optional. About nine or ten patients, exuding a why-not-humor-th'-guvnors aura, sprawl half asleep or read the morning papers. Staff—O'Brien, Dave Foster, student nurse Karp and a leggy, plump girl in a low-cut peasant blouse—look more fraught. Bronwen Jones, the pale Welsh beauty I last saw on Saturday with Robin, is also here. I plop down on a mattress between A. C. Corrigan and Clem Woodford and say, "What's Bronwen doing here? I thought female patients had their own meetings."

A.C. says, "Yeh, well I guess she's mad to marry that twit Singh." When I look blank Clem says that Bronwen is engaged to a staff psychiatrist Dr. Lewis Singh who the boys call "Screwy Lewie." She happens to be Con House's full-time social worker, and the short, *zaftik* girl is Sally Peel, the occupational therapist. Clem adds, "They're the establishment, we're the bloody masses."

I do a slow doubletake. If Bronwen is 'staff' . . . then Clem is a patient. Before I can digest this, Dr. Dick Drummond appears.

Places, everybody.

No Biz Like Show Biz

Morning 'community meeting' (group therapy) reminds me of my old job as an office boy with a New York theatrical agency. I soon got used to tap dancers, tumbling acrobats, singing Siamese twins and ventriloquists double somersaulting over the wood barrier, pulling lighted cigars from my ear, sneaking up behind me to imitate Mae West or Humphrey Bogart. What performers!

First on (natch!) is Jerry Jackson who bounces in tootling "It Don't Mean a Thing if It Ain't Got That Swing" on his invisible clarinet. He skids to a stop in front of Dr. Dick. "H'lo Devil!" he says. Dick, bolt upright in the Diana Dors red leather chair as if it were a Sing Sing hot seat, gazes at Jerry unresponsively. Jerry bitterly complains: "What a fuckin' wasted life. I wanta preach. Do God's work. Brownwen, give us a kiss, luv." ("He'd faint if she did," A.C. whispers to me.) Jerry isn't sure what to do—except not lose his audience. He flings his long arms into the air and shouts, "Yowsuh yowsuh yowsuh, Jesus is my Savior Cugat. But where's Abbie Lane? Dublin, ya say? Doublin' is where I am, too." He sings, "How I-rish up-on a star. . . ." His weak puns move no one. Dr. Dick remains silent as a stone. Jerry's eyes dart from side to side with real pain. "Ha ha, fuck me, silly cunt, ain't I? Got tuh stop swearin'. Why? Been bottled up all my life." Nobody helps him. They've seen his act too often.

Slowly, despairingly, Jerry capers around the room riffing Ellington's "Take The A Train," beautifully syncopating it in a low flatted key. He breaks off helplessly. "Th' other thing. I forget. Feelin' an' . . . Feelin' an' . . . *Fuck me, I can't remember.*" On impulse I help him out by picking up the Johnny Hodges' alto-sax part. Nodding happily Jerry segues in, and we play it back and forth, riding it to the end with a final skippy eight-bar "Everybody's Doin' It."

No applause. Jerry puts on his Satchmo growl. "Le's blow dis dump, Misteh Bell. Ah sho does hate charity gigs." He blows spit out of his invisible trumpet and flops in a chair, his back to us.

Herb Greaves, Jerry's rival for top banana, has already taken over. Slapping his pajama'd knees and snapping his thin bony fingers like castanets, he busks around the TV room:

"Mac the Knife
Eden unheedin'
Phallick Fuckless Home
Boom boom boom."

His voice rises shrilly.

"Fatso Hogg's
In a fog
Christine Keeler
Won't let him feel 'er."

When Sally the O.T. giggles, Greaves, shaking with schizophrenic ague, shrieks at her:

"Mods 'n rockers
Suck their cockers
Misses and prisses
Lack such blisses."

Jerry and Herb are hard acts to follow. A few try but just get in each other's way.

"She's going, she's dead, she's my mother. . . ."

"I am Christopher Marlowe, Françoise Sagan's lover for sixteen years. Cunt. K-A-N-T. . . ."

"I was the husband and father. I chose the three-piece suite. It's not fair. . . ."

"Oh God, progress, where is it?

"Is this a house of God? One two three my father is a flea. . . ."

"Here I am and there is no hope. I am God and I will destroy the Luddites. . . ."

"Through my wishing and through my horn, through my mother and through my spawn. And that is love. . . ."

"Belt up!" "Stuff it!"

The acts succeed one another at a dizzying pace. Everybody has a point to make, a case to present. To a newcomer, it's like listening in on a dozen private lines at once. I can't help noticing that this scheduled community meeting seems less productive than the more spontaneous kitchen session yesterday.

Con House seems to have only one firm rule: no meddling by staff. Even when the boys boil over with rage—"YA FLIPPIN' 'ORRIBLE MOTHER-BUGGERIN' SOD YA!"—or take lethal-looking punches at one another, no one in authority lifts a finger. And they suffer for it. With nothing to do but look on passively, the five Drummond-trained staff stare at the tips of their shoes or morosely yawn in an ecstasy of repressed irritation. The male nurses especially squirm with the effort not to clout one or two of the loudest mouths.

The threats and insults build up to a nerve-shattering climax. Something's gotta give.

"Right then," Dr. Dick rasps. "What's it all about anyway?"

For the rest of the therapeutic hour what it's about is the unceasing shellfire of adolescent anxiety raining down like shrapnel. From a bottomless pit of boredom the boys issue raucous complaints about the food, the filthiness of the ward, the madness of other patients, etc. Including "Who th' 'ell is Dr. Bell anyways?" (I am, depending on who you talk to, [a] a Scotland Yard detective, [b] geriatric patient, [c] atomic scientist working on a nuclear cure for schizophrenia, or [d] Harold Robbins researching a sexy book on Con House. Check one.)

Over all this, resplendent in an off-mauve Hardy Amies suit, royal blue Asser & Turnbull shirt, Liberty tie and Bally winkle-picker shoes, Dr. Richard Drummond presides like a haute couture baby Buddha. He uses his patients' formless fury—much of it slung at him—like clay, to sculpt tiny nodules of self-awareness for them. With cold, precise passion he limits his therapeutic role to a few clipped, factual comments. When Wally Walters in his usual rhyming slang confesses to having murdered his father ("Pushed 'im down th' apples an' pears wi' me own German bands"), Drummond downgrades it to a prosaic pub scuffle. Robbery-obsessed Yorkshire Roy is reminded that he chose to move his cot next to Vince, the unit's semipro thief, and that he is in for hurling a bayonet not at his mother, as he likes to boast, but at her favorite china set. Big Barney, who periodically phones the national newspapers to report the nurses' attempts to do him in, is told the 'poison' is nothing more fatal than Largactil.

I'm put off by how hungry some boys are for punishment. Longing to be 'corrected' with drugs and other forms of restraint, they scorn, even despise, Drummond's leniency. "So weak, so babyish, hasn't the guts to handle us like a man," croaks Eric Raw whose hunger strike Drummond refuses to terminate with forced feeding. Dr. Dick's battle to preserve their 'right to suffer' in the face of bitter hospital opposition only makes them sicker, several boys tell me. Threats to report him to the Medical Superintendent are fairly common.

All grist to Drummond's mill. Having read the case histories and met the culprits (parents), he knows what he wants. "If possible, to have the community mutually reproduce triadic aggression and thus reinvent an interpersonal technology of demystifying the ontological basis of alienation." Translated, that adolescents in their first breakdown may relate to one another's problems by reenacting within the group patterns of family manipulation. (For example, two boys will join together as a parental team to elect a third as a victim-child, practicing techniques of confusion upon him which the therapist tries to make explicit.) I'm too new to see how Dick's theory works in 'praxis.' It's still ish kabbible to me.

On the fifty-ninth minute exactly Dick sneaks a look at the clock above the wall mirror and scootles out of his chair like a reprieved Death Row inmate. I try to head him off, but he brushes past me wordlessly. "Don't take it personal," says Wally Walters. "Dr. Dick don't believe in individual therapy."

Session's over. Bodies slump; staff look wiped out. Everybody's suspended, quiet. Through a jagged windowpane we see Godot drive off in his yellow Morgan toward two other wards he's responsible for (part of his deal with the hospital).

A. C. Corrigan stretches and yawns. "Okay, kiddies. No more auditions for now. Backstage again tomorrow for 'Okla-coma!' "

Midafternoon. Those who are going to get out of bed, have; sleeping blankets sleep on unmolested. Les O'Brien knocks off for a cuppa tea with me before bicycling home to Slough. Like most nurses he cannot afford a car.

Les Talks

As Senior Charge Nurse, O'Brien has chalked up almost twenty years in English mental hospitals. "Long enough to know that the gift of mental nursing is knowing when *not* to act at times of crisis or mass anxiety."

Jabbing that finger in my chest, he bares his teeth at me. "Listen, Mr. Bell. This unit exists on a knife edge. Everybody from ward orderly to Regional Board chairman has heard, or think they've heard, about us here. For every Yank pseudoshrink who drops out of the sky to temporarily feel us up, there are ten hospital brass hats itching to bury us. We make them nervous. At least half my job is to keep them from getting *too* nervous." And he suddenly drops his head, roaring again with that sad laughter.

The real victims in a mental hospital are not patients but staff, O'Brien says. "We're like the man on th' flying trapeze. Frantically swingin' between Dick's revolution and the orthodoxy of the other doctors. And nobody's down below waiting to catch us either—just patients dying to see us lose our grip. Eventually we become as mystified as the most deluded back ward zombie."

The chronic problem at Conolly House is that staff has almost nothing to do, O'Brien says. Drummond saw to that by encouraging the abolition of 'role bound' rituals—compulsory reveille, basket weaving O.T., floor polishing, etc. But he left staff high and dry when it came to finding adequate substitutes for their diminished prestige. "The suspicion you can run a large mental ward with only one staff member—or none at all—has grown into a demoralizing certainty.

"This place undermines us now, our idea of ourselves, our job, even our families. Dave Foster's wife is a King Eddie nurse, too. She hears all the internal gossip, fills up on the fears we provoke. What d'you expect she tells Dave when they're home together? Even my old lady, who's never seen the inside of a bin, sometimes gives me hell because of what the neighbors and their kids whisper. 'So you work in that 'orrible Conolly House,' they say, and it goes on from there.

"All it needs to bring the house of cards down around our ears is just a little fresh air from the outside. Very nerve-racking. So—patient and staff alike—all our energy goes into sustaining the organization of a mental hospital, bolstering it. Nobody around here wants to do themselves out of a job. So the whole sordid nonsense of 'patient' confirming 'doctor' in the doctor's disconfirmation of the patient endeavoring to keep staff 'sane' who must keep patients 'mad'—everybody conning everybody else—never ends. The boat never docks, the plane never lands, who we are and what we are is lost in a limbo of total, civilized madness. Agghh."

Supper. Semiraw potatoes, greasy greens, charred chops, tasteless blancmange. (For every £1 spent on the physically sick, the Government pays out only seven shillings, or one-third, on mental patients, says Les.) Outside workers trail in, those with wage jobs at nearby factories got them by Dr. Dick who pressured local firms into hiring a few stabilized cases. (At Con House's inception he experimented with make-work programs which the boys contemptuously rejected.) One of them, Bob Featherstone, a husky extrovert who day-labors in a brewery, digs into his dinner across from Robin and me and gabbles on about his case. "Sure do miss my kids," he says with Billy Graham sincerity. "The missus too, of course. I shouldn't be here, you know. It's just society's way of invalidating dissenters. Forcing us to go to pieces for them, right Robin? All the same, wish I could play with my little kiddies is all." After Featherstone goes, Robin—a patient at all-female Pankhurst ward but who takes her evening meals with us—spits venomously on the floor. "Disgustin', ain't he? A child molester. Been in the nick for it. Ain't got no kids of his own. I could kill him." Her eyes say, I mean it.

It's amazing how many boys 'Drum-talk,' i.e., couch their problems in left-existential terms they've picked up from Dr. Dick. Clem says that even Con House patients soon learn how to suck up to staff. 'Soft bird'—easy time leading to a fast discharge—is what it's about, he suggests. "You play at what the doctor says you are. Don't argue; talk, shit, eat and throw fits when it's convenient for staff—and hope your ward consultant had a good breakfast before he sees you." 'Drum-talk' also stems from wanting to cash in on Con House's notoriety. "There are fashions even in madness," Clem says. "And we're 'in' this season."

Jeff H., the star-struck CNDer, is a skilled model patient along these lines. Wild Aztec-eye paintings adorn his dormitory wall space, and he loves impressing credulous visitors with bon mots like "I take the line of least existence." The boys call it "singing for your supper."

Eleven P.M.

Night ghosts. More activity, fear. The overnight nurse, 'Mad' Monahan, a pug ugly in a nurse's jacket, stalks about radiating disapproval. His spirit intimidates even the noise. Door slams, transistors, even Percy's gargoyle amplifiers seem perfunctory, cowed. Damn. I don't *like* being in a nuthouse at night without a staff friend.

As if in reply to my unvoiced prayer, a knock at my door. Dave Foster, O'Brien's sidekick: "Care for a quick pint, Mr. Bell?" Passing darkened Patients Canteen, Foster says, "Gettin' on all right? Th' chaps treatin' you fine? Sometimes I wonder who's mad and who's sane." Even in the cool blackness I can feel his eyes testing me. I agree, we quote Last and Drummond dutifully to each other, enter Staff Club. Spanking new, gleaming bar, spacious dance floor. Foster takes our drinks to a small group of men in dark suits at a table. "This is Mr. Bell, Dr. Drummond's assistant." They look just like detectives at Chicago's Fillmore District police station. I don't argue. Careful talk, weather, soccer, whose relations live in what American city. At last one asks, "D'you find *that* place a little . . . queer?" All, including Foster, laugh softly.

"How do you mean?" I ask. "Well, all that. You *know.*" One or two shake their heads sympathetically at me. A little scared, I say it's all right, everything is okay. Sure, sure, they nod. I'm stood another Scotch. We drink in silence. One nurse leaves, puts his hand on my shoulder. "If you need any help let us know." The others nod in emphasis. When Foster and I are left alone he says, "Good boys, those."

Returning by myself, crossing the dark, great hospital. All wards blacked out except Con House blazing like a bonfire. Inside cold, quiet. Fearing Monahan, I tiptoe past the office up to my landing where Percy suddenly opens up with *1812 Overture.* The cannonading music releases a storm of window breaking, door slamming. Angry footsteps as nurse Monahan bounds up the back stairs and heads straight for me. *It's not my fault*, I want to shout. Jangled, I say nothing, slip into my room and lie down. Pray to Hine-nui-te-po, Great Lady of the Night. A chest spasm knocks me to the floor. Oh no, I think, not while Monahan's on. Slowly I climb back into bed while my *chakra* squeezes me to an inch before death. No no no. I sleep.

Tuesday

All day in a pale cold nausea. Sweating, feverish. The stench and disorder—*Con House's lack of direction*—gag me.

Why doesn't anyone volunteer his case history? My readers will want to know. Robin Ripley obliges, alas. By the time she finishes telling me how her parents shaved her head for messing about with boys, blamed her for a younger brother's suicide and forced her into an abortion at sixteen and then threw her out of the house, I collapse with stomach spasms. "Gee Mr. Writer," she helps me to my room, "you oughta meet my ward shrink Dr. Goldstein. He says I pack the meanest punch in the business."

Choked with rage I march into O'Brien's office and reel off Robin's chronicle of parental torture. "Take it easy," he advises, "she only told you the good part."

America, America

In general, the boys look upon my nationality in a friendly light. One calls me 'Ginger' after Ginger Fiske, the first U.S. pilot to die in the wartime RAF. Another sings "Yankee Noodle Randy" whenever he catches me flirting with Bronwen. That both Dick Drummond and I are North Americans confirms a long-held suspicion that the Yanks have already taken over the country. The image they have of my native land I suppose we have only ourselves to blame for. Herb Greaves says, "The social mess-up in America was caused by the religious inaccuracy of the immigrants. They thought they were leaving England for theological reasons. That was a lie. They were going to get jobs with Boeing Aircraft." Jerry believes Benedict Arnold played sax for Glenn Miller, and some boys think that the late Senator Joseph McCarthy is the American president. One patient summarizes American history for me like this: "John Wayne landed at Plymouth Rock and killed the Indians on Thanksgiving because they stole his sister, Poke-a-mon-in-the-ass. In the war General Ike Eyes-on-Power conquered England, which has been living on surrender terms ever since. Jackie Kennedy shot her husband so she could marry Peter Lawford. Anyway, that's what Alistair Cooke said on the wireless."

Barney Beaton stands up for me. "One thing I've got to hand to the Americans."

What's that?

"Coin-operated laundries."

Patients

Today I witness a hallowed Conolly House rite. Every morning, come rain or shine, Mr. Tasker, the Chief Nursing Officer, makes his regular inspection round. Tasker, a ramrod-stiff ex-Colonial police inspector, is noted for his view that mental illness will disappear if military conscription is reintroduced. His disciplinarian soul is horrified by Drummond's blurring the roles of doctor, staff and patient. (He was genuinely puzzled, I'm told, on his first day when nobody stood to attention as he entered the Main Staff Room.)

As a spectator sport Mr. Tasker is unbeatable. At 10:44 precisely he pokes his head out of Honeysuckle Ward next door, sniffs the air suspiciously and reconnoiters Con House as if expecting a bomb to go off. Slowly he walks around the building, dourly shaking his head at the state of the lawn or broken glass panes, then ceremoniously inserts a key from a bunch at his waist into the back door—though he knows it is always kept open. He then calls out for O'Brien or Foster to accompany him. Drummond's is the only ward Mr. Tasker will not enter unescorted. Once inside he hardly breathes lest the (admittedly exotic) smells asphyxiate him, and he always backs out like Clyde Barker after a bank job. Apparently this routine hasn't varied in Con House's two-year history.

The boys love Mr. Tasker's visits. Minutes before he is due those who are awake crowd the windows impertinently cheering him on. Why do they play up to the Chief Nurse's paranoia this way? I ask.

Wally says, "Aw, 'ave a 'eart, Sid. 'ow else is th' silly ol' gaffer gonna know 'e's sane?"

Eleven A.M. The office. Staff 'group' a faded copy of community meeting immediately preceding it. No vaudeville, just foot shuffling and strained silences.

Ticktock, ticktock goes the wall clock. Who's to nurse the nurses? Who else—Jerry Jackson.

High, he sails in with his usual act, to the tune of Fats Domino's "Blueberry Hill."

"I found my thrill
On Calvary Hill
On Calvary Hill
Where I met Je-hee-zus! . . ."

Les groans, and Jerry pats his knee. "Know jus' how ya feel, ol' china. I coon't put up with me another minute neither." He vaults over the desk and knocks the files in the air. When no one stops him he panics and soft-shoe shuffles around the office to get a reaction. Staff stare at Jerry with repressed fury, but make no move to stop him. Only when he shimmies out of his pajama bottoms does someone crack—with a bull-like roar Bert Karp is on him with a half nelson, causing Bronwen, the social worker I'd mistaken for a patient, to hiss: "Let him alone, you nasty little sadist!" Red-faced and confused, Bert tightens his grip. And for nearly half an hour, with Bert sweating to keep his hold on a groaning, delighted Jerry, staff argues among themselves over what to do about him. It's an old Con House dilemma, I'm told. When does a patient's legitimate need to act out violate the rights of others? And who draws the line?

Like most theoretical problems around here it gets resolved pragmatically when O'Brien loses patience. "Damn it, Jerry, if you don't belt up I'll knock you through that door." Looking pleased as a pistol at having got a reaction, Jerry scampers out yodeling Cab Calloway's "Hi-dee-hi hi-dee-ho!"

It's back to ticktock ticktock.

Con House Game (2)

To break the tension I ask O'Brien for a tranquilizer.

"Why?" he asks.

For an acute anxiety attack, I say.

O'Brien points to a printed notice on the medicine cabinet: FOR PATIENTS' USE ONLY. "Sorry," he says, "but you're not a patient—or so you say."

What's the difference? I protest.

"I didn't make the rules." O'Brien grins from ear to ear.

I try the cabinet. Locked. When O'Brien tantalizingly jingles the keys in his jacket pocket, Sally giggles. Bitch.

My temper rises, O'Brien flatly refuses. "If you can play God, so can I."

Furious and embarrassed, I slam out.

Clem, who was present, finds me miserably pacing up and down the driveway, and takes my arm. "You'll need a lot more practice before you can play the Con House game with a master like Les."

"What's the Con House game?" I ask.

Clem scratches his head. "Dunno. Been playing it over a year and still haven't found out."

Lantern Slide: *Clement Attlee Woodford*

To cool me off Clem walks me out the unattended front gate to the main road and tells me some of his story.

A true son of the upwardly striving, working-class dormitory suburbs, Clem is neatly split between wanting to be a militant Socialist and a conventional bourgeois success. He blames this on his ambitious, frustrated mum who from his earliest days spurred him to excel his ungogetting Tory carpenter father. (Being staunch Labour herself, she hopefully named him for Britain's wily postwar prime minister.) "Sod her." Mainly to defy his mother Clem more or less deliberately failed his crucial eleven-plus exam, and left school at fourteen—"to be a pop star or a famous revolutionary—or both if I could swing it." He wiped tables in a Soho coffee bar featuring Tommy Steele, then traveled with a left-leaning skiffle group for whom he became road manager. By the time he was nineteen, just when English pop was taking off, Clem had become impressario of several folk and prerock groups. "So there I was, helping to start a real revolution, and my name in the newspapers, too. I drove a red Mercedes and read the *Guardian* for my conscience. It was a great party for a while except I forgot to invite my real self." At twenty, suffering from "premature businessman's menopause" (his own term), Clem hallucinated he was invisible and overdosed on purple hearts. The casualty intern advised him to enter King Eddie where he was diagnosed "schizoid identity crisis" and landed up in Con House.

"Trying to kill myself was the best thing that ever happened to me." In Dr. Dick Drummond he finally found a father to look up to. "My old man lets everyone walk all over him. Dick makes a science of that kind of masochism to stomp his enemies," Clem grins. Drummond has taught him that working within the system to beat it is no sin, and on Dick's advice Clem is studying for his university entrances to qualify as a psychiatric social worker. "Or rather, an anti-psychiatric one." His mother couldn't be more delighted; she always wanted him to have a respectable white-collar job. Clem is aware of the irony that is easing him back into the career rat race, which almost destroyed him. "Dick says it's a negation of a negation—the dirty joke at the end of the dialectical rainbow."

Clem feels profoundly grateful to Drummond. "He showed me what revolutionary socialism today is all about. Trouble is, you have to be crazy to know it."

The Village

In the still cold January air Low Wick looks deserted. Occasional prim, bundled-up shoppers hurry along the narrow pavement, avoiding us. Cars zip by nonstop.

Low Wick is a small Home Counties village, with a charming medieval church, a tiny subpost office-cum-newsagent, a few shops. In front of the church there's a yellowing placard on an otherwise empty bulletin board:

KEEP BRITAIN TIDY

Another zone.

We enter a grocery. Inside a bell sounds like a burglar alarm. Before coming forward the baldheaded proprietor gives us the 'King Eddie stare'—a fixed, glassy look that makes one feel transparent. (Low Wickers have picked this up from hospital staff, I assume.) "Keep it simple," Clem says out of the side of his mouth. "Last week he almost phoned the police when I asked for mortadella instead of ham." A couple of middle-aged women shoppers strenuously ignore us.

Careful, I warn myself. Clearing my throat I nervously ask for a "nag of buts, chiss sweese and a har of joney." The two shoppers roll their eyes up at the shelves. "Why *of course*, sir." The proprietor frozenly smiles and stacks the counter with boxes of Kleenex. What? Harpooned by his stare I drop a ten shilling note and flee, sweating. My unease mounts at the other shops. To avoid the previous confusion I bark "Granny Smith!" at the fruit-and-veg man who goes white as a sheet. The lady in the ABC bakeshop gives me a queer glance when I ask for cherry pie instead of the English equivalent, tart. At the newsagent, to recoup my losses, I put on my lordliest accent when asking for the evening papers. (Suppressing an urge to add, My name is Sidney Bell, no doubt you've seen me on the BBC, I have a luxury apartment near Buckingham Palace and regularly dine with Iris Murdoch, Ken Tynan and the Duke of—) The girl behind the barley sugar jar hands me the paper and remarks: "Fancy, a mad elephant in your kitchen." I back out in confusion and run for my life back toward the hospital. "Slow down, Sid," Clem laughs, chasing me. "It's in tonight's edition." He shows me an item about a circus pachyderm which escaped and broke into a woman's house in Bedford. I don't feel safe until we're back inside Con House.

Some safety.

What I've feared most happens. In the depressed, post-Dr. Dick afternoon Hurricane Hodge leaps up from his chair in the TV lounge and lashes out blindly with his fists. Hits nobody (yet), just viciously spars—huh! huh! he breathes heavily, muttering "Cunt Sonny Liston, I could smash him up. Bang whump!" In his black leather motorbike outfit ("HEAVENS DEVIL") and visored helmet which almost swallow him up, he knees an imaginary opponent in the testicles. Hodge, a judge's son, usually assaults only himself or, when hallucinating badly, "IRA scum" (anyone with an Irish name). He aims a kick at the chess board Derek Chatto is silently studying, and sends it flying into the air.

"Who you staring at, cunt?" he swings a punch that grazes my ear. From their gin-rummy game in the corner the nurses, Les O'Brien and Dave Foster, studiously don't look up. So far, Hodge's violence is as ritualized as Jerry Jackson's number. No sweat. But gradually I detect something else, and so do some other boys who edge away from Hodge a little more nervously than usual. But not A. C. Corrigan, who laughs scornfully from behind his copy of *Encounter*. Hodge rushes over and whooshes tremendous punches mere inches from A. C.'s head. A. C. frowns, but doesn't flinch or stop reading. As Hodge dances around shooting out near misses at him, it goes wrong. Suddenly A. C. uncoils and dives at him, and they crash to the floor, rolling over and over, arms and bodies locked. A. C.'s genial, freckled face is contorted by rage. A few boys leave in alarm when they realize it's out of control. (Con Housers are more scared than the sane of losing their tempers, and often go rigid with fear at the slightest sign of physical violence, I've noticed.) One or two work off their disturbance by trying to separate the fighters. Eric Raw weakly pulls at their legs and chirps, "Mama, Daddy, it's all my fault." A. C. easily shakes him off. I've not seen the Liverpool redhead so angry before; the change in him frightens me more than Hodge's frenzy. His smile vanished, his face tight, A. C. pins his opponent to the floor and raises a fist to annihilate him. Hodge stops clawing and scratching to lie absolutely still, compliant. A. C.'s fist hovers irresolutely, he glares down at Hodge and almost seems to come apart in the struggle to control himself. Then, as if waking from a bad dream, he looks around dazedly, and forces his fist to open. Still astride Hodge, A. C. dusts himself off and, slightly shamefaced but with immense dignity, gets up and walks back to his *Encounter*.

Hodge creeps along the floor to A. C. Sadly, "I'm a sissy. Are you a sissy? I'm a sissy. That's my situation." He leans thoughtfully against A. C.'s leg, stroking it.

My heart thumping, I look at O'Brien and Foster, who are so immersed in their card game they haven't noticed a thing, it seems.

Class Notes

Why do middle-class Con Housers seem crazier than those from the working class? Clem says it's because if you're poor you don't have to be too mad to get locked up as a schizo. Affluence bestows softer options—private therapy and scaled-down diagnoses ('anxiety tension' for psychosis). "So posh kids have to be really up the spout before we receive them."

When I grill others about the sociology of madness the responses are more equivocal. "Class doesn't matter here," says Barney Beaton, "it's what's insane in a man that counts." Or as Jack Sweeney says, "In the country of the blind the one-eyed boy is kink."

Drummond once told me that young schizophrenics knock themselves off at double the national average for suicides. Today word came in that Harvey Keegan, an ex-Con House patient, committed suicide at home. Harvey (1) swallowed lye as he (2) strangled from a bathroom shower fitment after (3) eating 100 sleeping pills. Why the overkill? I ask. Jeff H., once Harvey's best friend, says "His parents were always after him to try harder."

Toward midnight, in the darkened TV room, shapes corral around the dying fire to watch tonight's BBC Epilogue: a Cabinet Minister's appeal to save African wildlife. The TV screen has shots of game wardens in open Land Rovers pursuing water buffalo and other dumb beasts to stun them with tranquilizer darts. "Some," the Minister says, "have contagious diseases which must be caught in time to spare the herd. The most beautiful and sturdy specimens will be transported to zoos for citizens to enjoy. Practically no shooting is done nowadays, it's all the modern painless way with high velocity fast-acting drugs. This is both humanitarian and efficient."

Robin Ripley, Barney, Yorkshire Roy, Bob Featherstone, Gareth, Jerry and I watch without comment.

WILD TRACK:

"Peace be with you, Mr. Bell."
"Peace be with you too, Jeff H."
"That'll be the day."

After midnight, Con House's anxiety turbine turns over faster. Montovani's "Strangers in the Night" rides over Barney's mournful ocarina and the strange flittering noise Mr. Wu makes racing up and down the stairs. In darkened Obs Dorm Jerry, masturbating, groans "Don't look, Jesus. Don't look . . . oh, Jesus, th' Mother of God is suckin' me orf. Tell 'er tuh stop . . . oh, Jesus." Upstairs, tired after constant patrols, I open the wrong door. In the dark broom closet a pair of yellow eyes peers out. Backing away I spy deaf Vincent lurking around my door with a hammer. I duck past him, lie sweating on the bed. Then, from Aeon 149, a Shaft of Light pierces my chest. For the next hour sweat and struggle to expel the yowl inside me. Another Seconal, and amid a symphony of crashing doors and tinkling windows I drop asleep.

Wednesday

"NO-O-O-o-o-o!" Gareth, 7:00 A.M.

"HEL-L-L-o-o-o there!" Dr. Dick's way of greeting patients, containing as it does a permanent note of surprise and despair, sounds exactly like Gareth's protest cry.

At the breakfast scrum this morning a small, slight boy with an engaging smile whispers to me, "You may be working for the FBI. I heard it on the Jimmy Young show. If I tell you something my yesses and noes, my stresses and foes, may make matters worse for me." I laugh. Sally Peel, the O.T., snaps, "So Nigel got it a bit wrong. Yesterday a nurse told me you were from Interpol."

The smiling boy, Nigel Atkinson, is back after a month's hibernation under blankets. Refreshed and clear-eyed, he goes around shaking hands at the community meeting as if everyone else had been away on a long trip. "H'lo Clem, haven't seen you lately. . . . Where have you been keeping yourself, Roy?" Dr. Dick, who fought the hospital bureaucracy to let Nigel sleep it off without drugs, is powerfully pleased at his voyager's safe return. He asks if Nigel has any tips he picked up while 'away.' Nigel busily scribbles on strips of paper which he distributes around the room. Mine reads: "THE ACHILLES HEEL OF PRESENT-DAY MORALS IS PREMARITAL SEXUAL INTERCOURSE—Lord Longford."

Most schizophrenics, O'Brien insists, are strictly homemade, as earthbound as the families that drove them dotty. But he does concede the existence of the rare 'one off job,' a patient with genuine paranormal sensitivity. Fifteen-year-old Nigel may be one: he claims to get signals from spaceships circling the earth and to have visited Venus. To most doctors, his talk, sprinkled with references to Master Jesus, Mars Sector Six, Jupiter 92 and Saint Goo-Ling, is a symptom of mental unbalance. However, O'Brien took the trouble to find out that Nigel is actually a paid-up subscriber of the Aetherian Society of Fulham, a large, respectable organization devoted to psychic research whose members hold beliefs similar to Nigel's—a fact that no doctor ever bothered to learn. Why then is Nigel still on a Detention Order?

O'Brien says, "Oh, little items like setting fire to his school and cutting down his mother's rosebushes. But that's not what really upset his folks. They decided he was mad when he stopped talking to the family and passed written notes instead."

Sheep May Safely Craze

The boys say I can't properly do my job—whatever it is—by hanging around Con House all day. "Come see how the other half-wits live," A. C. urges.

A visiting U.S. Third Air Force band concert in the large raftered Assembly Hall. King Eddie runs a good 'rec' program—films, dances, day trips, patient-produced newsletter, etc. Dutifully the 'sheep'—as the boys call them—are herded in. It's my first look at the mass of patients.

Almost instantly my previous fears wash away. Were these the monsters I feared? But they're so docile. The largest proportion are what Barney Beaton calls "my old friend, Jerry Atrick." Neat, shabby people, many in their sixties and seventies (and older), with caved-in dentureless faces. Most in civvies, long ago having lost the impulse to escape. Though the hall is well heated, a number of patients ritualistically rub their hands together as if to dispel a permanent chill. Hard to tell the difference, in the mad elderly, between men and women. Above lean anonymous bodies are unisex masks of total powerlessness. Quite a few whiskered women, which A. C. says is due to excessive ECT and dope. Even the younger sheep, sitting apart timidly, have got that infinitely grieving hangdog look.

An overwhelming air of mutual cooperation fills the hall. A twitch here, a tremble there, one or two brave souls hopping from seat to seat but otherwise total compliance. The slightest sign of unprogrammed life, even scratching one's palsied leg, is immediately seen to, quelled by a small army of starched nurses from Jamaica, Belfast and Galway who automatically reach over to stop aged limbs quivering, fingers tapping. Rebellion is reckoned any spontaneous movement, except those specifically licensed. Look at that old man who periodically bounces up to walk to the other end of the hall, bow and mechanically kiss an elderly woman whose only acknowledgment is to scratch her nearly bald head after every kiss. The fact that the nurses don't bother to stop the old man is like telling him he's already dead.

On stage there's an annual prize-giving for flower arrangements and home-baked cakes in Occupational Therapy. A member of the Hospital Management Committee, a matronly woman dripping costume jewelery and goodwill, hands out Gift Shop tokens—and says, utterly without irony, that she hopes to see everyone again next year. Then Mr. Tasker, the Chief Nurse, effusively introduces the GI bandmaster, a fat Warrant Officer in blue dress uniform who bows, beams and raises his baton. "Stars and Stripes Forever" cascades down on the patients, all those disciplined ranks of mothers, fathers, sons, daughters, orphans, the workers-clerks-lower civil servants of Home Counties England. Almost all served militarily or as civilians in at least one war: were bombed out, shot at, industrially dragooned, semistarved during Austerity. Companions of the 1926 General Strike, the long Depression and Dunkirk-to-V-E Day, they sit in attitudes of stiff, regimented gratitude as Britain's nuclear guests serenade them.

"Bunny Hug or Lambeth Walk, Mr. Bell?" Robin Ripley coyly flutters her long beautiful lashes at me.

We've trailed the sheep to Patients Canteen, a long low hutlike building surrounded by implacably kept hedges. Much less money has been spent on its plastic seediness than the new, glossy Staff Club. To a stream of incongruous rock 'n' roll records patients (mainly white, a few black) queue up for tea at a portable urn or, serenely immobile, rest in folding chairs spaced at mathematically regular intervals against the insulated-wood walls. Except for Robin and me—she's an excellent dancer—the floor is occupied by middle-aged women locked in each other's arms, sweeping past in long graceful glides from a thousand Women's Institute dos and Joe Loss weekends. A pair of elderly ladies in identical Clara Bow haircuts and scotch plaid skirts walk carefully about in time to Bill Haley's "Rock Around the Clock." In a dim echo of previous courting patterns old men segregate themselves in the adjacent snooker room, while a few teenage boys and girls hardly dare look at, let alone dance with, each other. Robin says, "You can always tell the new fish. They're the ones itchin' to have a go at the opposite sex. Soon get that knocked outta them."

Herself a patient for the past five years, Robin explains that some old-timers have been locked up since King Eddie was known as Addleford in the 1920s. Post-Edwardian spinsters banished from their families for an unmarried pregnancy; the deaf and dumb; undetected autistics and mild subnormals; alcoholics and homosexuals—or simply homeless men and women who lost their kin and had nowhere else to go. "Poor old things," Robin laments with real sympathy, "were just born a little early. Wonder what's wrong with us that'll be respectable one day?"

Hemmed in by nurses, policed by sternly jolly Social Directors, the Canteen's habitués wear invisible straitjackets—until A. C. Corrigan, a chocolate cigar stuck into his wide mouth, swaggers in like Edward G. Robinson's *Little Caesar* cradling a toy tommy gun. "Stick 'em up, screws! Somebody phone th' warden—we're takin' over!" Behind A. C. bursts in a gang of obscenely healthy-looking Con Housers screaming like wild Indians. They sound—but are not—violent.

Pandemonium. Like angry chickens staff and patients scurry this way and that, reacting as if the Devil himself had just walked in. Herb Greaves grabs a burly Social Director—one I'd seen forcing patients to dance—and whirls her away in a no-nonsense foxtrot. Other boys invade the floor with an impromptu war dance that empties out the Canteen in nothing flat. Then, led by Jerry fingering "St. James Infirmary Blues," a bunch of us return in triumph to Con House for tea. By the time we arrive the staff grapevine, racing ahead of us, has reported that a mob of schizophrenics tried to rape a Social Director and set fire to Admin Block. Robin smiles philosophically. "If wishes were pennies th' nurses around here'd all be millionaires."

Trimly pugnacious Robin is part of what I'm coming to think of as real staff: experienced patients with know-how. It's confusing. Would Clem or A. C. be unofficial staff if Jerry and Herb weren't superofficial patients? Is nonstaff 'staff' staff to staff-staff (paid)? If Dr. Dick doesn't believe in patients, who then are the boys? And Les, Dave, Sally, etc.? Who's caring for whom?

In the sweet pregnant pause between supper and Krakatoa's nightly eruption, an argument in the kitchen: Is Religion Really Necessary? To my surprise, the boys and Robin agree that it is. "How come this is th' greatest country in th' world?" demands Jerry Jackson. "I'll tell ya. We licked th' Huns *'cuz everyone done 'is part.* King George conquered 'is stammer, right? An' ol' Winnie 'e swore off imported cigars so ships'd've more room for guns. Well now it's our turn. Some people got to make th' Christian sacrifice so's others c'n survive. It's like a law of nature, i'nt it?" Arch-Tory Barney Beaton has the last word. "Without the Queen, police, banks and headmasters we couldn't have the Archbishop of Canterbury."

Dr. Last failed to prepare me for how conservative most schizophrenics are. The ones in Conolly House seem very suspicious of Dick Drummond's mild attempts to radicalize them by relating their personal problems to larger social issues. Royalism is so rampant that some boys see the present occupants of Buckingham Palace as a court of last resort for them. Written appeals to the "Virgin Queen, Mark II" are routine, even the occasional phone call to nearby Windsor Castle (almost always diverted to the local police station). Nigel has an electronic bug planted in the Queen's cleavage, he says, and Percy's radio antennae are permanently tuned toward the family home, Sandringham. Hurricane Hodge, the judge's son, has a scheme to kidnap "that Greek sod—I mean god" (Prince Phillip) and use the million pound ransom to rescue the Queen Mother from Churchill Wing where she's being held a prisoner.

"Why this royal mania?" I ask Jeff H. Combing and recombing his hair in a mirror, he says, "Well, they're the perfect British family, aren't they? And we adore them exploiting us."

After rocking with Gareth, coughing with black Abe, arm-wrestling with Barney, jamming with Jerry, arguing Socialist politics with Clem, analyzing Nigel's visions and regaling Jeff H. with my Hollywood tales, I retire to my room, wondering who's on tonight. Dreading Monahan, I masturbate, don't wake till morning.

Thursday

Rain. Two more days to go. Still no word or sign from my host Dr. Dick. What did I expect—a medal?

A problem. I'm here representing Last's group, on a kind of training course. To learn, toughen myself in the roaring fires of all-out schizophrenia. What's the form of my Presence in Conolly House? Since I'm not a patient, doctor, nurse or social worker—not even a journalist—who am I? How often I've met this predicament in the outside world. Well, I'll do what comes naturally. Dr. Last calls it "inventing" myself. I call it "gathering material for a new novel." My anxiety assuaged, I relax into incessant note taking.

I'm beginning to see how a sense of family realities is the best qualification for mental nursing. Dave Foster says, "Y' know th' difference between these lads and myself, Mr. Bell? At the right age I laid one on th' old man and when he hit me back I had him up before the Salford magistrates on a charge of assaultin' a child. Got to th' old bastard before he got to me."

> *Though nurses still warily 'mister' me, I feel myself slipping irresistibly into a subculture of patients. The boys become 'us' not them. With each passing day I'm terrified at the small difference I see between articulates and withdrawns, between both and myself, between Conolly House and the outer world. Once I accept—as I must to live here—Gareth's rocking, Abe's coughing and Herb's rhymes as 'language,' then all bets are off. Urgent for handholds, I try to apply the boys' standards, which aren't the most reliable. Just as—or so O'Brien tells me—mental patients carry staff's inadequacies and repressed violence, so some boys bear the cross of others.*

A news flash starts it.

Herb (the poet) Greaves strolls through Con House town crying:

"Clash us
Mash us
Sonny
Bunny."

What happened? I ask.

Someone says, "Clay beat Liston last night."

All day Liston's compromised shadow lingers over the unit. Because most newspapers championed Clay as the clean-living Olympic ideal versus the black hoodlum beast, the boys naturally identify with Sonny. They haven't had a real folk hero since the Great Train Robbers.

Clay's suspect victory and a cold drizzle sharpen Con House tempers. Copying Hurricane Hodge's act, the boys, aching for a legitimate target, torment one another—and find one when community meeting's roulette wheel, bouncing all week from Jerry to Herb to Barney, finally comes to rest at the unsteady feet of Gareth. His furious farting and puling, which consistently evacuates the dining room, has finally triggered a demand that something "be done" about him—preferably far away from Con House.

"And what part of yourselves are you trying to exile—to get rid of?" asks Dr. Dick.

A mild cheer at this, Drummond's standard riposte.

A short sharp argument follows, between Drummond and those patients whose grip on reality (and middle-class attitudes to tidiness) is threatened by Gareth. Con Housers take mental hospital logic to absurd extremes. Yorkshire Roy, who'd shit sixpences if he could, insists that the British taxpayer put him under care to be cured of a neurosis "and not to play nursemaid to incurables Ah c'd name but won't." With sweet reasonableness he trots out premises I'm to hear over and over again with regard to Gareth, Abe, Mr. Wu and other solitaries: they require special care unavailable in Con House, the more serious psychotics may 'infect' respectable breakdowns (such as Roy), the withdrawns are too far gone to help, etc. ('Withdrawn' is to Drummond's patients what 'schizophrenia' is to most civilians, a convenient wastebasket.) Anyway, Gareth is an unfair burden on staff, piously adds Jeff H. "Look how Kurse Narp has deteriorated since he took an interest in the little zombie." Barney, our law 'n' order champion, suggests castrating Gareth or dumping him on the Isle of Dogs—for his own good, of course. "He'll never get better around us bifurcated spectaculars."

I'm disillusioned to find an illiberal lynch spirit even here. "It's a democracy," O'Brien tells me. "Why shouldn't they enjoy the great English blood sport of invalidation like everybody else?"

Lantern Slide: *Gareth de Walden*

Who is he, this seventeen-year-old Con House baby?

An adolescent *golem*, permanently wrapped in an unspeakably filthy robe, his surprisingly handsome but slightly out-of-focus head lolling brokenly on his square almost athletic shoulders, whiskers just starting to sprout around his meaningless grin, eyes clamped down to slits or staring unseeingly upward, snot like Old Faithful issuing regularly from his nostrils, dirty socks crumpled around his devoutly unwashed ankles encased in combat boots, he's content to grapple with himself eighteen to twenty hours a day. What energy he spends securing his space!

What . . . who . . . smashed Gareth? I can't, of course, ask him. His speech is mainly body movement, hops, wiggles, rocking, trotting, bending, skipping, shuffling and smiling. What you get out of Gareth depends on how you relate to teenage infants who opt for premature senility as the safest alternative to 'growing up.' Most Con Housers are divided in themselves between love and hate for him, and almost all have had a 'Gareth crisis' when he brings out the parent in us. The day he told Clem—Gareth speaks when he wants to—I was a "phony," I spent in bed, utterly crushed.

Normally he is taken for granted like a familiar old piece of furniture—ignored, pushed aside, bumped into, even sat on. Boys with middle-class pretensions (e.g., Roy and Barney) can't stand him, while cockneys like Jerry and Wally love teasing him, rumpling his hair and boxing with him like a tame bear cub. Gareth, son of a Bloomsbury publisher—his younger brother is at Eton a few miles down the road—laps it up. He adores being spoon fed, babied. How we envy him! Every now and then, sucking on Jerry's fingers or mooning in

Bronwen's arms, he'll open his eyes quite wide and intelligently straighten up for a fraction and . . . not quite . . . wink.

Meeting ends on a whining note. Why, asks Jerry, is Gareth never sedated when he, Jerry, seven years older, is doped and has his civvies taken away at the slightest infraction? "All I had was a vision, an exaltation—th' trees, th' sky, God makes me new. Hallelujah!"

Sprawled on the chaise longue, O'Brien growls, "It ain't your rapture, you nit, but the way you handle it. Yesterday you wheeled a male geriatric into Female Nurses Quarters askin' if they'd like to do two old codgers a big favor. *And* serenaded an ECT session with "It Ain't What You Do It's the Way That You Do It." *And* rang up your vicar pretending to be a vice squad detective who'd just arrested his daughter in a Soho brothel."

No kiddin', Jerry's expression proudly says, *did I do all that?*

All day Eric Raw scowls at Bronwen Jones, muttering "You are there to play on my mind. I am your victim." Suddenly he slugs Wally Walters, an innocent bystander. When Wally kicks him out of TV room, Bronwen smugly does her Drummond bit: "What part of yourself are you trying to get rid of, Wally?" Wally dusts himself off. "My inflamed paranoids, ya silly cow."

A Shell of Himself

The mind/body dissociation that Last told me to look for in schizophrenics often assumes sadly comic forms in Con House. Take Keith Whitworth, a twenty-year-old plasterer's apprentice from Putney. Ever since his admission he has held one hand to his right ear while keeping his head rigid and making soft ticking sounds. Born in a '44 doodlebug raid, he believes his brain is a left-over V-bomb which will go off if he dislodges the 'pin' by moving his head or if he drops his hand from his ear. The ticking sounds he makes all day are maddeningly irritating. Finally Jack Sweeney, the angelic-looking little Irishman, can't stand it. Today in TV lounge he reaches over and slaps Keith's hand away, which causes Keith to go rigid and say "pop!", thus releasing the firing pin. He waits in horror for his brain to explode. When it doesn't he starts to tremble and shake. Big tears of disappointment roll down his face.

But isn't he relieved to still be alive? I ask.

Keith sobs, "I'm a dud."

Little nervous fights break out all afternoon, and I retreat to the kitchen and bang pots and pans together to settle my nerves.

Trapped.

Hurricane Hodge, burning with the fevers of the Clay-Liston match, windmills in and corners me against the sink.

Whoosh! whoosh! his fists whistle past me.

My guts freeze. Oh no, I can't hit a *patient.*

I duck a murderous right.

It's him or me.

I yell: "You insane creep—you need a good lobotomy!"

Hodge falls back as though I've struck him, then hares out the kitchen door as fast as he can.

From the doorway Jerry Jackson grins jubilantly. "Oi—ya jus' lost yer cherry!"

Les Talks

Jittery and ashamed of my clever-dick tactic, I seek O'Brien's counsel. What should I do if a patient actually hits me?

"Make a decision," he says, "based on your old Chicago street savvy. Or do they always use machine guns in the Windy City?" A relaxed attitude to violence is basic to getting along in Con House, he says. He and Dave Foster were drafted in by Drummond because they're northern working class. "And up in Geordie-land they may be anxious about a lot of things, but nobody thinks you're mad for thumpin' th' other guy. In fact, it's a way of life."

Les says the first ten years of his nursing career were spent straitjacketing, massively drugging or physically restraining patients. "Or kicking the living daylights out of them." On his very first day as a student nurse a patient armed with a jagged bedspring made for him. "No Tynesider hesitates in such a situation. I hammered him. And kept hammering them whenever they stepped out of line.

"I was in rough shape myself most of the time. But what could I do? The longer I stayed a mental nurse the less qualified I became for anything else. The more time toward promotion, the deeper in I got stuck. I was pretty hard then."

Originally Les came from the northeast, Newcastle-on-Tyne. Joined the army in '44, demobbed two years later. Joined the merchant navy. "But Peggy my girl said she wouldn't marry a salt-water sailor. So I packed it in and looked around for a shore job. Pensions, all that. Just after the war they were hard up for mental nurses so I says why not it's all the same. I was nineteen." He laughs softly. "The mental hospital scene in 1947 was—not too gentle." Later, the 1959 Mental Health Act, giving patients the right of appeal and voluntary admission, improved the scene in some ways, made it worse in others. "In the bad old days you had to be legally certifiable, right round th' bend, to get into a bin. We got some real lulus then. But at least staff and patients knew where they stood with each other—at the opposite ends of the sanity spectrum. Reassuring in its way.

"But today only one in sixteen patients is detained compulsorily. That forbidding old iron gate is a bloody revolving door into a psycho supermarket. Short stays in hospitals are prescribed like Enos salts, and we ain't such an exclusive club anymore.

"But what th' hell does that do to us nurses and doctors? In the end your average underpaid nurse knows all he's got to defend himself with is his statutory authority. Take that away and he's got nothing. Patients ain't that stupid. Out of panic and insecurity—you'd be surprised how many *have no idea* why they're here—they try to dissipate their mental fog by manipulating their legitimate rights to unbalance us, the already unbalanced staff. I wish I had a shilling for every patient who quotes Laing at me when I tell him to wash a dish or two.

"Since '59 we don't even have the instinctive physical response of a right ol' clip 'round th' ear-'ole. So we're forced to keep patients down with newer, more subtly mystifying techniques—which is what got most of them in here in the first place.

"We don't bash 'em nearly so often. Sometimes, God help me, I wish we could."

A peaceful, wet afternoon. Con House rests between explosions.

A sudden sweet crashing chord, the most beautiful blues, sets me up. On the dining room upright Herb Greaves idles his bony fingers. Pure prowling Kansas City, the best I've heard since the States. Greaves' lean sharp face, usually so taut and hysterical, is relaxed, softened by the heavy bass runs of "Sweet Lorraine" and "Piney Brown's Blues." James P. Johnson lives again in Berkshire, England.

Interludes don't last long in Con House.

As soon as Greaves spots me in the doorway he reverts to his 'mad' mask, a bluesy Lon Chaney with brylcreemed locks. Jerry Jackson skates in to blast a Beiderbecke "Indiana" while Barney Beaton huffs and puffs "Beer Barrel Polka" on his toy ocarina. "Eee eye addie o!" A. C. joins in with the Mersey football chant, and Jack Sweeney adds "Nature Boy" to Gareth's jiggling hum. It's a ghastly mixture, so to bring order out of chaos I kazoo "Lay Me a Pallet on the Floor" through cupped hands and tissue paper. In different tunes and tempos we pound down to the finish line, exploding on the last bar exactly together. M'Gaw'd, I haven't felt this good since I played washboard in the *New Marxist Quarterly* skiffle band.

Jerry removes his spectacles to wipe his eyes. "Fuck me," he cries, "wasn't that sinful though?"

High on jazz-induced euphoria I fall in beside Gareth's shuffle. Up down up down, winter wonderlanding the corridor. After half a mile indoors I drop out, exhausted. Bronwen, watching, says: "You'll burn yourself out, Sid. I only do the rocking in place with him, never the running.

WILD TRACK:

Jerry Jackson: "You devil, you cunt, you bastard."
Me: "You sonofabitch, you double cunt, you turd."
Jerry: "Okay, cunt. God bless. Take care."

Each night after supper I chair-blockade myself in my room to type up "Battle Report," the day's notes, on the borrowed office portable, and in the morning I faithfully put a carbon copy into Dr. Dick's box. (He never mentions it to me.) Not wanting to be a stoolpigeon, I give the boys pseudonyms. In effect, I'm dealing with three versions of each patient: his 'real' self, his schizophrenic 'shadow' and the name I invent for him. Talk about juggling acts!

The mad can be truly nasty to one another, but they also have a tact, an instinctive grasp of how to handle crises. Sometimes, when a numbing, nameless panic immobilizes me, Robin or one of the boys will help me walk it off or shoot snooker with me till my mental storm abates. Tonight, restless, I switch TV channels incessantly, jumped on and off the latrine scale, make mountains of toast which I don't eat, rush up and down the stairs on patrol, even talk to myself. Wally Walters watches me with the calm, shrewd gaze of a scout for a first division team. "You're comin' along jus' fine, Mr. Bell. Soon try you out for th' Seniors."

Two A.M.

Because I'm the only nonstaff adult available in the small hours, my room has become a nest for night ramblers. Tonight, we dream aloud of what it would be like to break down in a gentler, freer place. When I tell them my idea of Last's community—the monastic layout, hierarchy of Adepts, strict female exclusion, etc.——the boys listen respectfully. Then little Nigel says, "Why don't you be honest and come right out with it? You'd like to go to Eton."

Bloody Imperfects.

At 5:00 A.M. we break up. Och, i's bin a lawng bluidy deh.

Friday

My last day.

An intense quiet pervades the unit, as if it takes all the boys' energy to face another long weekend. Jerry stares into the lounge fire, Wally's two radios distantly squeak "Land of Hope and Glory," which seems to radiate from his head. Slowly the room fills up with patients wanting a last contact with Those Who Go Home. At 10:00 sharp Drummond materializes. Scanning us with perpetually surprised eyes, he moves in warily, like a counter-puncher not knowing from what angle the first blow will land. What possible variation of the common ore can be dug up today?

"HEL-L-L-o-o-o there!" My heart leaps, sinks. Drummond is greeting someone else.

Carefully, he settles into the Diana Dors chair (his by tradition) and swivels his fleshy, well-barbered head from side to side: *who are all these people,* his baby-blue eyes seem to say, *and what are they waiting for?* Sitting (unacknowledged) near Dr. Dick most mornings, I hurt for him. It would drive me mad, too. Knowing what's wrong, having isolated (insofar as humanly possible) schizophrenia's nonbiological virus—the social violence of love's old sweet song—he must now stand by impotently while his young lions lunge against bars which he, Drummond, feels he helped create. He can do little more than suffer with them. Well goddamn it—I can almost hear him thinking—at least I'll not rob them of their dignity with my self-indulgent pity. Deliberately stripping himself of the tricks of compassion, he almost vengefully play-acts at being a doctor pretending to be a doctor who refuses on principle to 'be' a doctor but wants his patients to know he isn't a doctor pretending to be a 'doctor.' To hell with bourgeois psychotherapy.

Herb Greaves strolls in wearing boxing gloves.

And so it goes, my last meeting, with its usual conundrums, hungers. Eric Raw, his gown open to reveal a body now wasted to less than 100 pounds, hurls himself at Drummond's feet. "It's not my fault, is it Dr. Dick?" Drummond stares down at him with infinite terror and sorrow. "I don't know, Eric. Maybe it is." At 10:59 Dr. Dick levitates like M. Hulot out the door, followed dumbly by his staff. Greaves, inexpressibly angry, removes one of his boxing gloves, aims and hurls it, whap, hitting Sally's plump ass in the doorway. She jumps, but smiles patronizingly on seeing who did it. Desperately Greaves keens:

"In olden days
With golden lays
And Tories had no mores
You swung 'em high
You made 'em sigh
Debbies weren't bebbies."

In staff office:

Me: "I'm going tomorrow. Can I come back some time?"

O'Brien: "Sure. It's been a mutual education. (Laughs.) Just disguise the names."

Nobody believes I'll be back.

Jerry Jackson, who worships at the altar of American jazz, says goodbye in his own way, by sliding into my room on imaginary roller skates triple-tonguing Jack Teagarden's "Hold That Tiger." He asks me to help him symbolically masturbate. I know the routine. Faster and faster I accompany him with hands krupaing on knees. "No!" he shouts helplessly. "Yes!" I reply. Shaking, quivering with joyous rage, he lays down his 'trombone' to lock his hands. "No . . . no," he whimpers, tearing at his locked hands. "Yes yes!" I roar. His body shakes violently, and with all his might, his weeping eyes almost popping out of their sockets, he pulls against himself. He's getting there. "Ah . . . no!" His hands spring apart and flop limply, and half-collapsed with the effort he turns to me. "Madness is th' confusion of reality with . . . fuck it, I forget." Sadly, the wild light gone from his eyes, he pats my shoulder and shuffles to the door. "Sorry ol' mate, ya did yer best."

The Good Citizen

On a last walk Clem and I are joined by one of his pals from another ward, Max Heath, editor of the hospital newsletter *Far Out* and a patient for about ten years. In that time Max hasn't traveled more than half a mile from the hospital; beyond a certain 'safety line' he panics. He has the settled, dapper manner of an old lag, and moves and speaks in a nasal monotone born of presenting himself in a stereotyped way to hundreds of medical case conferences. Yet he's deeply proud of the hospital and its liberal Superintendent, Dr. Winstanley. Why doesn't Max come and live at Conolly House? I ask. It might be more congenial than his present ward of aging chronics.

Max goes evasive. "Er, all that dirt and mess at Con House. The noise. No; it would undo all the progress I've made."

Con House is charged with impending weekend. Staff happier, us moodier. Tomorrow I 'R & R' back to my apartment, my Buber and Eliade, my near-vegetarianism and Yoga, games of existential solitaire and Zen coins-in-the-can, and Dr. Last. Only one more night to go. . . .

At supper Herb Greaves, shivering with anger, comes at me. His knuckles are chalk-white around an upraised, gleaming butcher's knife. *Oh shit,* I think, *he's going to kill me.* Where's O'Brien, Clem? No one interferes.

Feebly, like Lew Ayres reaching for the flower seconds before the Armistice in *All Quiet on the Western Front,* I croak: "What do you have against me, Herb?"

Greaves grabs my overdone lamb chop and rams it into his mouth, singing:

"Sunday painters
Part-time feinters
Weekend blighters
JUDAS WRITERS!"

He finishes tearing at my chop, puts the bone on his head and walks out.

Weak with anxiety and relief I beg a pill off Mad Monahan, then sleep through a night of Percy's highest-fi, one of Gareth's wailing nightmares and Jack Sweeney fracturing his hand (again) on anti-IRA Hurricane Hodge's indestructible jaw. In the morning Jerry Jackson shakes me awake. "Oi Mr. Bell, there's some bird downstairs wants tuh take ya home."

From here on my life had twin poles: Conolly House and 'Clare Community Council,' a name we in Last's group chose after much soul searching. "Gaw'd damn it!" he blew up as we agonized over 'Yin-Yang Center,' 'Liberation Hall' and 'Albert Schweitzer Clinic' (the latter for fund-raising purposes). "Why nae nail oor colors tae th' mast an' call oorselves after th' mad Ainglish poet, John Clare?"

So moved, seconded and ordered. Alf Waddilove, Last's ex-patient and business advisor, was instructed to draw up tax exemption papers for:

CLARE COMMUNITY COUNCIL
for the
Study and Treatment of Mental Illness

Last assigned each of us a 'task,' according to a military-style Table of Organization (T/O):

Dr. Boris Petkin	House hunter
Dr. Richard Drummond	Ministry of Health liaison
Alfred Waddilove	Fund raiser, accountant, Charities Commission and local government contact
Anthony Straw (ex-Royal Corps of Military Police)	Legal officer

Sidney Bell (me)	Public relations
Davina Mannix-Simpson	Recording Sec'y

Last's assignment was to "rove responsibly."

Our targets were:

a) to find a rural house and grounds for a healing center.

b) to raise cash for this.

Over a magnum of champagne we Clare Councillors pledged 10 percent or more of our annual incomes, and as the clock in Last and Petkin's house struck out 1963, we hugged, kissed and promised ourselves a Place by next New Year's Eve.

At 7:00 the following morning, rather to his wife Sybil's annoyance, I woke up Last to tell him my latest LSD vision. On his doorstep he sleepily scanned my four-page memo with accompanying sketch (see overleaf), which described an all-male community "on the edge of London." Laid out like a medieval town, it was governed by a nuclear core of Perfectii, or Brothers, who studied and prayed in a shedlike temple far apart from the un-Elect (women, children, cats and dogs). Girdling this Inner Sanctum was a ring of mobile prefab huts inhabited by the mad and broken down—i.e., patients who might also be any of us. Unlike the wives and families of the Perfectii, who were segregated in an Outer Zone where they contentedly raised chickens and bees to make the community self-sufficient, the mad always had free access to the Nuclear Brothers. Decisions were by democratic majority of the Sacred 7, ties to be broken by the F.O.C. (Father of the Chapel, a term I borrowed from my National Union of Journalists). Circulating my memo at the next Clare meeting, Last coughed indulgently. "Er, um, I'm sure ye'd agree naebuddy bu' Sid c'd've written this."

Reactions varied. Dr. Petkin, the East End Bolshevik, asked if medical Brothers could charge fees. Major Straw inquired about security—"Sentries or Alsatians?" Alf Waddilove, the travel agent, insisted on seeing a cost-effective analysis, and the Canadian blueblood, Dr. Dick Drummond, wondered if we could move somewhere warm and sunny like Provence. Davina hesitated. "Is there room in your scheme for a Brother Sister?"

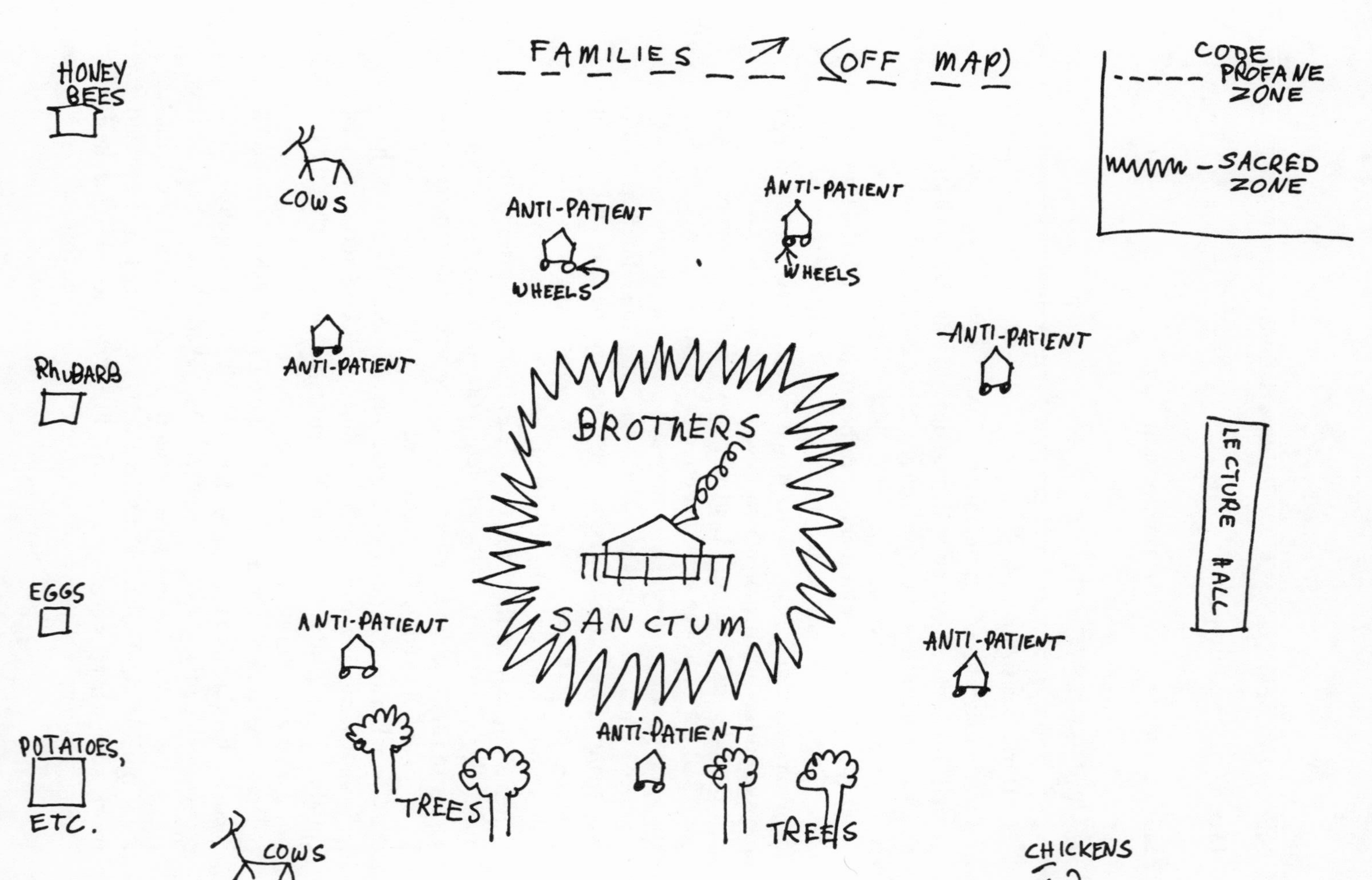

FAMILIES (OFF MAP)
CODE
PROFANE ZONE
SACRED ZONE
HONEY BEES
COWS
ANTI-PATIENT
WHEELS
ANTI-PATIENT
WHEELS
ANTI-PATIENT
ANTI-PATIENT
RHUBARB
BROTHERS
SANCTUM
LECTURE HALL
EGGS
ANTI-PATIENT
ANTI-PATIENT
ANTI-PATIENT
POTATOES,
ETC.
TREES
TREES
COWS
CHICKENS

From the start Dr. Last fostered a 'two track' approach to Clare Council. To outside laymen it was advertised as a "new direction in family therapy," But for us Sacred 7, the group was a vehicle for working out our individual transcendental destinies, "oor way tae th' innair light."

Didn't this mean that family therapy was only a front for our own personal salvation? I asked.

Last smiled tolerantly. "Surely ye ken th' distinction between a shallow pretense manipulated tae preserve th' privileges of a blindly selfish elite an' a genuine dialectic embodyin' th' reciprocal interplay fr' innair tae ooter, Light an' Dark, I an' Thou?"

Um, sure.

In long evening talks, with acid, dining together or driving around the Home Counties looking for a house with the right 'baraka' (vibes) and price, I finished hammering out my battle assignment with Last. My nine months in America had convinced me that life had no Center, no real point; existence was a sham, a veil of *maya.* Like good prose it had to be ruthlessly boiled down to No-Theng until it disappeared into the Cosmic Vacuum, the origin of all creation. Only this way could I climb the Mountain, die and be karma-released.

Last nodded approvingly as I replayed what he had taught me. "Ye've set yirself a real mon's task there. Sid. Only a fyool—Gaw'd's Fyool—w'd try it." He punched me affectionately in the chest. "Ye stuipid bluidy Jew."

Despite my lifelong atheism Last insisted I couldn't escape my Jewishness. "It's stamped inside ye, like DNA–RNA. Ye'll have tae learn tae be a Jew tae stop bein' one."

So to Zen Buddhism, Siberian shamanism, Tibetan reincarnation, Buber-Sartre existentialism and lysergic-acid pantheism, I added 'astral Judaism.'

A vast, almost physical joy seized me. I was still unhappy in the old personal sense. My journal is filled with references to worthlessness, frustration, guilt. But in a little-used corner of myself a soft light had appeared. It was to this tiny glow-spot that I directed my Self.

At this moment Lena reentered my life.

"*Gruss gott*, stranger," she grinned from behind the steering wheel of a shiny new red MGB GT coupe parked outside Con House. It was she who'd come to take me home. How had she located me? Lena winked. "A friend of Willie Last's told me where you were. It's a small world, *liebchen*." In the backseat she had a picnic hamper of Liebfraumilch, pâté de foie gras, Parma ham, roast chicken and cucumber salad, which I fell on like a starving man. A week of English mental hospital food had temporarily deranged me. As she amusedly watched me rip into the chicken, we drove back to London and brought each other up to date.

I hadn't seen Lena since two or three Aldermaston marches ago, not since (or so the rumor went) she'd gone off and become a Greek shipowner's mistress. When I asked what she'd been up to recently all she said was, "Spending my winters in Capri with a friend." She had, she said, a large flat-cum-workshop in Notting Hill Gate and was learning to make jewelry in it.

My relief at talking to someone so unpsychiatric was short-lived. Up at my place Lena revealed that (a) her current boyfriend was in analysis with Willie Last and (b) she was seeing a shrink too, her fourth in a year. Lena noted my surprise. "Well, why not?" she said defensively. "I'm not paying—Irv is." Irving Goldman, her rich American fiancé, was a hot-shot theatrical producer who subsidized her car, apartment and psychiatrist—"a Harley Street *mishugenah* with a Schickelgruber moustache and the manner to go with it. *Oi gewalt*, quel bore."

Given Lena's long, complicated history of relationships with men, I wondered if a woman doctor mightn't make more sense.

"What's the difference? Confidentially I think they're all nuts." Lena thought psychoanalysis was a big joke, but she didn't want to cross Irving, the latest in a long line of authority figures starting with a soldier father killed at Stalingrad and which included even me. "Jewish father figures, *naturellech*."

Lena was a Hitler war baby from Bavaria whose friends and lovers—except the Greek shipowner, I assumed—were almost all Jewish. "Why not? We Krauts have a lot to atone for," she cracked. I saw that she hadn't lost her old habit of making compulsive jokes about her personal guilt for the Holocaust, which was hard to take seriously. After all, she was born in 1940 and had been only five at war's end. Our great bond was that I'd once passed through her farm village en route to Occupation duty in 1945. She idolized GIs, of whom I seemed a living reminder. "You were all so tall and good-looking in your uniforms," she said. "Bloody great gum-chewing gods."

Of course I didn't remember Lena from all the other German urchins I passed out chocolate to, but I'd never forget our first meeting as adults. During the first Aldermaston march I'd gone to sleep in Reading Town Hall, along with a hundred other ban-the-bombers, when this suede-coated girl with the sweetly swinging hips who I'd marched behind all day slipped into my sleeping bag. "They ran out of beds upstairs," was all she said in a thick German accent. We didn't screw, mainly because I was afraid to risk spoiling my already tattered reputation with the Socialist-puritan comrades by making love to a girl who looked well below consent age. (Not to mention Coral's jealous rages.) In fact, Lena had been nineteen or twenty then but acted much younger. She giggled a lot and was starry-eyed over Elvis and The Pretty Things. Also she dressed in a casually expensive style that emphasized her slightly boyish youthfulness. Upper-class Englishmen educated at all-male schools and Hampstead intellectuals with a thing about Germans usually went gaga over her.

Without real skills but with plenty of bobby-sox charm, Lena was a kind of mascot-au pair to the N.W. 3 literary and Central European exile crowds. She used these jobs to learn the language and accumulate time to qualify for residence in Britain, which didn't stop her resenting her benefactors. "I cook their meals, scrub their floors and wash their babies' nappies—and they expect gratitude too," she sneered. Her menial position in liberal, affluent households had given her a cynical insight into London's middle-class trendies who boycotted South African sherry but were not above working her eighteen hours a day. "Some of your radical friends paid conscience money to bring the little Nazi girl over to reeducate her. Some education!"

Rubbing shoulders with well-off intellectuals had given Lena a taste for the good life, not only sports cars and St. Laurent clothes but literature as well—especially the poet Sylvia Plath, a friend of some of Lena's patrons, who'd killed herself in London last year. "She really knew what it was like to hate a German father she'd hardly known." Almost offhandedly Lena admitted to several suicide attempts lately. "Just experiments—like some of Sylvia's poetry," she said. Then she brightened. "I almost forgot—I finally passed my O-levels!"

Could she, Lena asked, see more of me? "That is, if you're not currently occupied elsewhere."

I smelled a rat. Who really had told her my whereabouts?

Lena puckered her pretty, freckled face. "I told you. Irving found out from his shrink, Willie Last. Irv thinks you and he may have a lot in common and wants to meet you."

Why didn't Irving come himself?

Lena laughed. "For Irv that's much too direct. He's a pretty devious type. Anyway, Last advised against it. Said it was 'therapeutically unwise'—or some such rot. Irv won't make a move these days without Willie Last's say-so. He's mad keen on the bloke, really."

Was Lena merely Irving's go-between?

"Hell no," she giggled. "I've been waiting years for you and Coral to break up." Lena also frankly wanted to take a mild revenge on Irving. "If he thinks he can manipulate this stupid Kraut, maybe I'll show him a thing or two about manipulation."

Lena's candor melted some of my suspicions. Had she been Sent to help me? (Her car would come in useful; I'd stopped driving after a smashup in Indiana last year.) Or was she tempting me back to my corrupt, lazy old ways? I decided to test her.

I was already 100 percent committed, I said firmly. To my Task. I'd renounced meat, partying and (hammering home the point) "desacralized" sex.

Lena's first response was a spontaneous yelp of laughter. "*Du?* Of all people! *Du machst einen Witz!* What a waste!" My frown instantly sobered her, and she grew serious, like a suddenly chastened child.

This was my last chance, I said, and if I failed I'd never get another. Only total, committed mind-body discipline would get me There, to the peak of Mount Analogue. To further impress Lena I outlined my normal day. Come rain or shine, up to eighteen hours daily, I applied myself to deep meditation, headstands, Hatha Yoga and Tai Chi, and Eliade's translations of shamanic texts, and held my tantra breath up to three minutes. ("Gosh," Lena said, "I'm a good swimmer and can't do that.") My diet consisted almost entirely of honey, herbal tea and nuts, and I used only distilled water so as not to weaken the LSD. Evenings were spent at Clare Council or casting my I Ching. Since editors had got tired of getting no answer at my telephone, fewer free-lance jobs came my way. I almost never went out to films or plays anymore.

"And who supports you—the State Department?" Lena asked.

A little savings and royalties, I said. Anyway, I wanted—like Simone Weil and the worker-priests—to mortify my flesh by sharing the condition of the poorest wage slave.

Lena looked around at my four-room semimaisonette commanding a private key-only garden, my Heals deep-pile rug, Bang & Olufsson stereo in custom-built sideboard, inlaid teak typewriter desk, and white leather chairs, and said dryly: "Those worker-priests must live pretty good."

I brushed aside her childish sarcasm to list my terms. Any woman who helped me had to bind herself to certain rules:

1. No visits without prior permission.
2. No gossip about me with third parties (i.e., Irving).
3. No sex unless preceded by religious meditation and prayers.

Lena stared at me incredulously. "In other words, just to see you I have to enlist in your private army?"

Aptly put.

Sitting on my $1,200 Indian laurel and beige leather T-form couch, she poured herself another stiff Glenfiddich, then slowly nodded. "Well, why not? Now that he's got Willie Last, Irv finds me a little boring. Maybe helping a wandering Jew like you will get rid of my concentration camp nightmares."

Ah. That was it. *I* had been Sent to help Lena.

We sealed our soldiers' pact in bed—after meditating, of course.

Afterwards, she happily wandered into my kitchen to cook me a meal but couldn't find anything in the cupboard except nuts and distilled water. "My God," she exclaimed, "not even a piece of cheese for the mice. That's crazy!"

Mad, I sternly amended, not crazy. But I couldn't tell if she'd heard me.

As Lena chauffeured me to the first of many Clare meetings, I uneasily asked about Irving. She said, "Oh him, he'd give a million of his dollars to be in your shoes, Sid. Not because you're sleeping with me—he's so involved with Last he wouldn't care if I fucked the whole regiment of Coldstream Guards. No, he's dying to be invited to one of your Clare Council meetings."

Several nights a week Lena dropped me at The Angel, Islington. It was (then) mainly a working-class area but with lovely Georgian houses tucked away in the side streets and squares. I waited till she drove out of sight then hurried along Upper Street beyond The Green, turned left and—to throw off Lena or other would-be pursuers—backtracked along Liverpool Road past the Royal Free Maternity Hospital to Dudesley Square, nipping round the corner to Number 4 Crimea Street. You could spot Last's house a mile away. Though one of an identical terrace of three-story detacheds, his was the only front garden so littered with kids' toys and domestic junk. The peeling paint and uncared-for exterior stood out from the other, tidier homes like a huge WELCOME sign.

Always first to arrive, I banged the Buddha-shaped knocker on the door.

Normally, we Clare Councillors met behind locked sliding doors in the study-office Last shared with Dr. Petkin at the back of the house. Once, in an excess of feminist zeal, we invited the wives but that had proved abortive. Sybil Last, an attractive, haunted-looking woman, had sulked in a corner resentfully flipping the pages of *Woman's Own* while loudly exchanging domestic complaints with Boris' wife, long-suffering Viv, who kept applying cold compresses to her chronically migrained head. Now shooed upstairs, the ladies always left behind a truculent backwash of dirty dishes and diapers.

Whipped on by Last, who kept us lubricated on Scotch and coffee, we Clare members crashed through a seemingly impenetrable jungle of business agenda—the writing of by-laws, sponsor hunting, finance reports, etc.—until, long past midnight, when we were looped on booze and exhaustion, Last would mercifully signal a break. Off flew his tie, jacket and ankle-high boots as he rolled his neck around his shoulders like an Olympic shotputter warming up. He blew through one nostril then the other and fixed us with a hooded, impish glare. "Ye're dyin' on yir feet, Brithers. Shall we dance?"

Sometimes till dawn we 'danced'; that is, wrestled with Last's consciousness-raising Zen riddles, striving to 'break through'—to where Con House's Jerry Jackson and Herb Greaves already lived.

> Q. Why did the peacock scream?
> A. " 'Cuz naebuddy luiked at him."
>
> Q. How do you fuck yourself?
> A. "All too easily."

And so on and so forth.

From word games we advanced to making faces at one another, then animal sounds. Braying, honking, baaing and mooing helped break down our middle-class defenses—and often produced a sleepy, terrified child or irate neighbor's phone call. BBC's Davina was especially good at flapping her arms and screeching like a great angry bird.

"Tha's th' idee," Last shouted. "Bein' ridiculous is oor secret weapon against schizophrenia!"

Returning to our human forms we'd sit in silent hand-holding meditation, until Last closed the meeting with a short prayer. To clear my head of cigar and Sufi smoke I often walked down Pentonville Road to the St. Pancras Station taxi rank. But I never quite got rid of an optical illusion: two pairs of eyes, glowing with hostility, at the upstairs windows of Number 4 Crimea Street.

That was silly. Sybil Last and Vivienne Petkin had been asleep for hours.

It was marvelous to be involved again. Not since CND and the *New Marxist Quarterly* had I felt that old go-to-meetin' jolt, the long-absent joys of political communion. (Perhaps, like heroin addiction, passed through the mother's umbilical cord?) I slipped back, hooked again.

To get to know my Brithers better I did my Con House thing and rushed around taking their case histories. But when I approached Dick Drummond he just groaned and turned away, as he did whenever he saw me at King Eddie; Boris looked down at me and said: "Piss off." The nonmedics were easier to talk to.

Alf strenuously avoided the group's metaphysical side to concentrate on bookkeeping and holding down his ex-analyst's wilder business fantasies. His ten years as Last's patient had taught him how to make himself virtually indispensable. "The thing is, Willie needs me now at least as much as I used to need him. Without someone like me to kick around what would he do to himself?" Alf, who had struggled up from being a semiliterate farm laborer to managing his own company, said he owed it all to Willie Last. "The least I can do is pay him back," he said without any trace of irony.

Major Straw's twenty years as a professional soldier I gleaned mainly from his dyspeptic, right-wing outbursts. "Turns your stomach, doesn't it, old man. All those ban-the-bloody bombers and lying Whitehall politicians with their Russki-lovin' trollops. I didn't enlist after the Munich betrayal in order to see Yid bankers like Rothschild—pardon me, Sid—sell this country to the Americans—no offense, Brother. Or force our empire kith and kin to kiss the black arses of mission niggers like Banda and Kenyatta. Was it all for nothing at Arnheim and Cassino, then?" After distinguished service in World War II, followed by Far East antiterrorist operations and with the Gloucesters in Korea, Tony Straw had been a staff officer at the Suez invasion. "Dammit, we almost grasped the nettle there," he said bitterly. "Pity your John Foster Dulles had to stab us in the back for a few New York Jew votes." He sighed. "I suppose you're a bolshie too, like Boris. Hunted you fellers with the Seventh Gurkhas in Malaya. Oh well, as Willie says, it's all the same at the center of life's great mandala."

I was beginning to find Davina the most likable and candid member of the group. "If you had met me B.W.—before Willie—I would have given you the cold shoulder for asking such personal questions, Sid. It's simply not done in my circle." If not quite top drawer, the Mannix-Simpsons of Tunbridge Wells were still posh enough to be received at the Palace. "Daddy went there to collect his Order of the British Empire for services to banking and the Conservative party. Mummy lives for Crufts when she can show off her corgis once a year. I'm the family tearaway." Educated to do nothing but marry well, Davina had fought tooth and nail for the simple right to work—which she won only by compromising with her parents and agreeing to "come out" as a deb. After six years at Benedene, an exclusive girls' boarding school where she played field hockey well enough to get into the Wembley Girls Finals, and a few more years at the BBC, which kept her in the ghetto of "women's programmes," Davina was overjoyed to be in Last's male-dominated group. "It's rather like being in a harem with the ratios reversed, isn't it?"

Because Boris' background was so much like mine, I had another go at him. But he just stared coldly at my notebook and snarled, "Are you making a copy for the FBI?"

Davina eyed me suspiciously. "You're awfully keen to pump us, Sid. What's your, er, angle?"

Hoping to build bridges, I told them all about my aches and pains, the bustup with Coral, and my search for a fresh subject that would get me over the hump to my next book. Boris, the ex-CPer, affected dismay. "So it's not the schizophrenics you want to help—only yourself?"

My hackles rose. How well I knew this type of Party oneupmanship: shaft your comrade in the name of the People. What did Boris have against me? Before I could defend myself Last jumped in. "Come off it, Boris. Brither Sid's lit'ry narcissism an' eggistainshul rootlessness are th' best possible bona fides fer th' long struggle ahaid. Scattiness may be his particular form of Gaw'd-haid." I wasn't sure I liked being 'helped' with veiled insults, but Last mollified me by taking me aside in a friendly way. "Don't let Boris git yir goat, Sid. He's prawbly a wee bit jailus of oor bacon an' eggs." That was our code word for LSD, about which the group had mixed feelings. Half scandalized, they also envied my acid relationship with Last, our playful little winks and nudges and in-group jokes. ("I had a heroic breakfast yestidday—double rations o' bacon an' eggs an' hardly any tomatoes.") Only Boris strongly objected.

"Com—Brothers!" he glowered. "How can we demystify capitalist irrationality if we ourselves are always pissed out of our minds?"

Boris' thunder fell on increasingly deaf ears, because once the Clare Councillors saw how LSD gave me a privileged position with Last, they fell over themselves to try it. (Only Davina loyally abstained, the better to serve us as 'sitter.') Poor Alf upchucked on his, but Dick Drummond and Major Straw were soon buzzing the acid heights like true barnstormers.

Last's amusement at their first clumsy trips was tempered by a nagging worry. Despite all his precautions—the Orphan Annie code, secret rendezvous and his insistence that only he carry the LSD vials—what if a scandal-mongering newspaper exposed him? (BEATNIK DOCTOR IN DRUG ORGIES WITH PATIENTS.) "Th' bureaucratic ol' turds"—he meant his disciplinary body, the General Medical Council—"'d love nuthin' better than tae nail me up on th' cross of 'profeshunal misconduct'—jes' like yir Yankee fuzz crucified that *uther* Willie." The martyrdom of Wilhelm Reich, the orgone therapist railroaded into a federal prison by U.S. postal police, haunted him. Last constantly reminded me that my slightest false move could ruin him—and then he'd pointedly add: "Bu' don't fergit, kid. If my life's in yir hands, *vice versa.*" Each of us had the power to destroy the other: I by going berserk and denouncing him as the author of my madness, he by certifying me into a lunatic asylum. This "balance of terror" kept us honest, he claimed. "Y'know, like Billy th' Kid an' Doc Holliday holdin' cocked Colt .45s at each other's haids."

His brutal frankness charmed away my old pol's reflexes, which in previous groups always had operated to spot who among my comrades had "disaster insurance" denied to me. (For example, almost to a man the *New Marxist Quarterly* editors were buffered by family money or social influence.) The really nice thing about Clare Council appeared to be the equal sharing of risk between medics and nonmedics alike. Nothing that Alf, Tony, Davina or I might suffer seemed anything like the awesome power of the General Medical Council to banish our three doctors into professional outer darkness. "Boris, Dick an' me're like hyoomin mine detectors in th' nae-mon's-land of schizophrenia. One misstep—an' BLAMMO!"

Gradually I realized that Clare Community Council was the antiworld to a large medical Establishment, which I'd barely glimpsed at King Eddie hospital. Last's views fell on ground well fertilized by my talks with Les O'Brien.

The "ainemy" was a shadowy, all-powerful elite which—through the British Medical Association, G.M.C. and other professional groups of doctors—controlled the minds and bodies of fifty million Britons. The difference between State and private medicine was less than it seemed; in fact, the National Health, which I'd always regarded as the pearl of England's welfare society, was a greater medical tyranny. Superficially progressive innovations, such as open-door wards and group therapy, were mere fig leaves to disguise the system's totalitarian brutality. Even clinical liberals like Maxwell Jones, R. D. Laing and David Cooper were mere "window dressin'."

If all that was true, why did Last stay in such a rotten setup? I asked.

He, of course, sneered at his participation in "th' maidical game." "But by th' time I woke up I was in too deep. Ye've got tae wurk *somewhere.*"

Shouldn't Socialist doctors work in the National Health rather than private practice, which catered to a rich minority of patients?

"As Lainin told us, Brither Sid, th' real ravelushnry exploits *all* th' ainemy's contradictions." Though Last agreed that the State had spent a lot of money and time training him, fairly early in his career he had had to "go private" for the tactical flexibility it gave him. "And the lolly," Boris bluntly added. (Last and Petkin funded their family research with fees from private patients like Lena's Irving. On his own, Boris held a free psychiatric clinic in his old Stepney neighborhood once a week. Dick's gilt-edged income left him freer to remain a State employee.)

Last chuckled bleakly. "Anyway, private wurk minimizes th' harm we do. We see fewer patients."

Last's refusal to give up his despised medical identity he justified in terms of *realpolitik.* A doctor carried more weight than a layman in the battle to penetrate official medical lethargy. In his lexicon this was a 'combined ops' in which the three doctors, or 'officers,' were 'point men,' while us noncoms were 'coverin' fire,' guerrillas striking at the very heart of the system. (He often compared us to Fidel's *compañeros* and Chu Teh's Eighth Route Army during the Long March.) But until ready to mount a 'craidible major offensive,' we would cloak our deeper, more mystical aims in a 'tactical smokescreen.' Hence, no wild and woolly frontal assaults, no militant oratory that might scare off potential angels.

Shades of the CP-USA. Such pussyfooting (we used to call it

'Aesopianism') had confused our old movement far more than it had given us useful allies, I reminded Last. I hadn't come to Europe to lie for yet another cause.

As one man the Councillors went all silent and cold while, narrowing his eyes, Dr. Last puffed hard on his cigar. Then, softly but with spine-chilling finality: "I ken how oor prevaricatin' must stick in yir craw, Sid. Ye probably had tae do more'n yir share of belly-crawlin' an' arse-lickin'—objectively necessary, of course—in Joe McCarthy's Amahrica, eh? I woon't blame ye fer droppin' oota th' Britherhuid."

Stunned, I said I didn't *want* to resign. (And bitter tears welled up in my eyes as I vividly flashed back to that awful Saturday afternoon when the Roosevelt Road Rockets, hankering after a new right fielder, had asked me to turn in my priceless red and blue team sweater just before the season's biggest game with the Pulaski Pythons.)

Then they went after me in full cry. Dick Drummond got in first by sternly suggesting that I'd benefit from a close study of the anti-Nazi resistance in Germany for whom lies and subterfuge had been essential to survival. And did I think I was more authentic than Jean-Paul Sartre who had demonstrated the ultimate in existential good faith by defending Soviet labor camps even after the facts were known?

I pointed out that the comparison between ourselves and the German underground was wrongheaded. British social democracy, as flabby as it was, wasn't fascism. And as far as good and bad faith went, the American CP had degenerated more from its own self-delusions than from FBI persecution.

Before a good argument could develop Last suddenly offered to resign. "Th' implication seems clear fr' what ye're sayin', Sid, that I'm leadin' ye all intae moral quicksand. P'raps I'm th' one who should go."

This really put me up a tree, with accusations of disloyalty (and worse) whistling about my ears. Boris rumbled with rage and old anti-American resentments. "Easy enough for you to be the simon-pure Socialist in another man's country—why not go back and try it in your own?" His radical veneer fell away to reveal a bilious patriot. "And anyway, where th' hell were you Yanks when the bombs were falling on London—poofing around in your

Caddylacks and waxing rich on munitions contracts, no doubt?" ("Hear! hear!" echoed Major Straw who, in the welter of existential argot, had been quietly starving for an issue he clearly understood.)

Nobody came to my defense. I didn't like the odds.

Last magisterially raised his hand to quiet the angry voices. "Aw, th' puir laddie meant nae real harm," he smiled supportively at me. "Brither Sid is gittin' so close tae th' Light he occasionally loses his airthly bearin's. Right, kid?" (Though I was two years older he always addressed me as his junior.) I grasped the lifeline he held out by nodding dumbly, gratefully, and slowly the group relaxed to let Last bind us up together again. Our tempers, he said, had been rubbed raw by "th' wounds o' waitin'." Like Mao and Fidel in similarly fallow periods we had to learn to cultivate revolutionary patience, to use the present unproductiveness ("oor Yenan an' Sierra Maestra") to rethink tactics and gird for battles ahead. "Freud, Jung an' Harry Stack Sullivan might've bin okay fer delayin' actions. But fer th' close-in knife wurk necessary fer *oor* Great Leap For'ard, there's nuthin' tae beat mind-commandos."

Us.

In this battle for the mind our heavy ammo was Last and Petkin's tape-recorded interviews with schizophrenics and their parents. Though I never was permitted to meet 'Judy S.,' 'Ronald P.' and 'the Harrisons,' I knew they were living proof that schizophrenia didn't exist, except as a disorder of the whole family, a pathology of domestic murder that made living corpses out of guileless children. The key to the dominant bourgeoisie's death grip on our vitals was . . . the Joneses next door. Since the ainemy's secret weapon was a socially conditioned lie, liberation could be won only by confronting capitalism's joker-in-the-pack, the 'normal family.' "What holds the system together isn't so much fear or even intimidation," declared Dick. "It's love. So our main task, Brothers, is to demystify, in ourselves first and foremost, this degrading and enslaving myth. Love, Brothers, is the horrible beast that awaits us all at the end of the dark tunnel we're entering."

Of course. Why hadn't I seen it before? That's where we American reds and English new lefties had gone wrong. How often on my way to Catford New Marxist Club or Potters Bar Labour Society I'd wondered what *really* went on behind the tightly drawn curtains of the semidetacheds my train zipped past. Last and Petkin's family studies tore the curtains aside, satisfying both my journalistic zeal and political hungers—and not for England only. Change the names and the case studies might have come from Chicago, Leningrad or Timbuktu, Last said.

Zowie. I'd struck oil again. Once *again* I'd 'accidentally' found myself inside a small, mobile cadre (like the early CIO organizers) so strategically placed that a few clever men pressing on a weak point could overturn the system, move it. Here was a power base beyond my wildest political fantasies. And this time we wouldn't be held back by "laggardly elements," sympathizers with minds of their own. Clare Council was so deeply rooted in the fertile soil of schizophrenia, people whose psyches we were so tuned into (and anyway were so deranged), that we never needed to consult them.

How could we lose?

It all fitted superbly with post-Stalinist Socialist humanism, Christian Marxism, existentialism, Freudian revisionism and even the later developments in Malcolm X's thought—all the recent trends.

It was a strange yet oddly familiar politics. Though the "maidical kawn-text" was new, the tone rang sharply true to some earlier Party-type hustles. Including that old Movement axiom: trust your enemies but spit on your friends.

Clive Flynn, for example.

A middle-class dropout with a Cambridge First in economics, he had been sent to us by his analyst (and Last's guru), Dr. Phineas Maud. Flynn was an angular, quiet man in his late forties who had left a cushy job with the Foreign Office to teach himself carpentry, and his expertise was invaluable on house-hunting expeditions. But at Clare meetings he refused to croak like a frog or waddle like a duck, just grinned skeptically and said little. ("Sheepish sort, wouldn't you say?" Boris whispered loud enough for Clive to hear.) Admittedly, it was pretty unnerving to flap your arms and goose-honk while Clive gazed calmly, quizzically over his pipe at you. This, together with his volunteering to work for Clare Council full time without pay, froze us. What was he up to?

At the meeting after Clive made his offer, he was "interrogated," a mixture of court-martial and PhD viva voce Last had made each of us undergo. My own initiation into Clare Council had hinged on his single question: "If ye were a Partisan on th' run how w'd ye dispose of a captured ainemy sojer?" Thoughtlessly I had answered that I'd probably leave the German behind, alive. "An' endanger th' entire mission?" demanded Last, almost failing me on the spot.

Now, faintly amused, Clive sat before us in the study of Number 4 Crimea Street.

Boris Petkin peremptorily cleared his throat. "Clive, what's your commitment to the revolution of the mind?"

"The what?"

Boris repeated his question.

Flynn smiled and replied that he doubted if he was a revolutionist of any kind. "Least of all with anything as complex as the mind."

Dick Drummond asked his views on psychoanalysis.

Clive said, "I'm a pretty old-fashioned sort, really. With so many phonies and charlatans about these days, old Daddy Freud is more than enough for me to handle on a day-to-day basis."

Last steadily examined Clive through half-lidded eyes. *Here it comes*, I thought. "Tell us, mon, if ye were a Partisan escapin' fr' th' Nazis . . ."

Clive mulled it over. "Well, Willie," he finally said, "The fact is, in the war I was a Special Forces bod. Commando. Narvik, Dieppe, the Long Range Desert Group, pretty much the whole show. Once, on a Benghazi oil refinery raid, I had to dispatch a dozen or so rather dim-witted Italian pipeline workers who got in our way. Civilians. I personally shot them—and went into analysis as soon as I could afterward."

Half angrily Clive turned to Boris Petkin. "My commitment is to the human race. To help myself by helping others, mad or not. I suppose I'm what you might call an emotional liberal. You chaps have an intriguing idea which has a fifty-fifty chance. I've an independent income and I might be able to lend you a hand. It really doesn't go much beyond that." For good measure, he added that madness was an ugly business, often violent and unhappy, and we'd be well advised to keep in with the local bobbies wherever we landed.

After a long uncomfortable silence, Dr. Last told Flynn we'd let him know, and he left.

The first reaction of most Councillors was to dutifully place on record their admiration for Clive's moral fiber, his frankness and honesty under fire. (Now he's had it, my UAW caucus instincts told me.) Then Boris waded in, verbal scalpel flashing. "Th' bugger hoodwinked us," he spat. "All that treacle about" (and here his gruff voice dripped sweet venom) "lovin' th' human race, the Errol Flynn stuff in the war, all the rest of his mealymouthed put-on. What crap!" Clive, he thundered, was a weak-kneed dilettante playing at being a worker who would rat on us in a crisis. The historical tendency of the liberal heretic—did Boris look at me?—was to worm his way into the ranks of the Elect only to sell them out when the going got tough. "Flynn's deaf to Prophecy and blind to Revelation, an existential washout, the very seed of corruption which if the Essenes had extirpated they'd be a living church today!"

(Why had Clive so upset Boris? Months later Davina confided: "The things Boris respects in me—my accent and private-school manners—he loathes in a man.")

Slowly, pushed by Boris, the scales tipped against Clive. Drummond decided, "Simple honesty—as a phenomenological study of fascism shows—isn't enough. Hitler wasn't stopped with Social Democratic scruple and our English Weimar won't be demystified by good intentions alone." Alf opted out, and Tony Straw wondered if we weren't being a little harsh on a brother ex-serviceman. "But, on mature consideration, we might ponder whether one more of us might not capsize this frail little craft, eh fellows?" Davina demurely passed.

Not wanting to be the odd man out again, I kept my mouth shut this time.

"An' wot've we here?" Last reached over for the notebook on my knee, but I grabbed it away before he could have a good look at it. It was, I explained quickly, my novel-journal, *Special File.* All during Clive's interrogation, I lied, I'd been scribbling an allegorical chapter about an American writer-monk named Lebdis (spell it backward) who saves his Teacher, Adam First, from a stab in the back by a traitor I called Judas C. Flynn. (A copout. Actually my notes described the growing rivalry between Lebdis and a mad shrink named Nick Tepp.) Blushing and sweating, I prayed no one would ask to see my notes.

Slowly, reflectively, Last rolled his head around his shoulders, a sure sign of deep cogitation. We waited for his judgment. Then: "Hmm. A li'l overdrawn that." Damn, I'd bet wrong again. "But"—saved!—"Brither Sid may've intuitively grasped th' main point. Clive's a better mon than any of us, that was painfully clear. Th' question is, is he *too* guid? Was Jesus betrayed by an *honest* neurotic?" We must not decide hastily. "In th' meantime, tae spare his feelin's, wha' d'ye say we nae invite him around—fer th' time bein' only, of course."

We never saw Clive Flynn again.

Last's glowing reference to *Special File* went to my head. I wrote a new chapter describing how Adam First's six disciples righteously sandbag Judas C. Flynn after Brother Nick Tepp shows them the error of their bourgeois-humanist ways, and distributed copies to the group. Boris muttered something under his breath and threw his away. Dick stared blankly at me, Alf winked in embarrassment, Major Straw sighed and belched. Davina quietly tucked the pages away in her purse without comment.

Last, my fellow artist, glared at them. "Wha's wrong wi' yew lot?" he remonstrated. "Brither Sid, th' puir mon, needs sumthin' fr' ye *right now.*" He stood up and began clapping his hands. One by one the others grudgingly rose till we all stood in a circle dutifully applauding one another, Russian style.

Thus confirmed (a favorite Last word), I turned back—with the group's full support, I felt—to my Heroic Task.

No matter how late I got in from Clare meetings, sunrise found me in the black wool, floor-length cowled monk's robe Coral had sewn for me my first English winter. So costumed, I greeted the London dawn with deep Om's and Yoga pretzel bends. "I always wondered how saints got that look," Lena said from the bed. "It's because they're ruptured."

I hadn't expected her to fully understand my work, but I was getting a bit annoyed with her little digs and wisecracks. However, she was shrewd enough to stop just short of outright insubordination—and anyway my little sergeant had her uses.

With Lena's slightly bemused help I boiled down my flat to strict essentials. After giving away most of the furniture to friends or the Salvation Army, I sealed up the master bedroom and study, then Lena and I covered front and back windows with double thick drapes to keep out light and sound. For a grand finale I junked the last reminder of Coral, her parting gift to me when I moved out of her ménage to a flat of my own: the secondhand king-size bed she and I'd slept in. "From now on you'll probably need this more than I will," she had predicted with a kind of sour triumph. Well, I'd show her that two could play at the game of sexual disillusionment. Henceforth, I'd use the floor as a pallet, just like a real monk. Watching the Borough dustmen hack up the ancient, broken-spring object, our crucible and battleground, and fling the pieces into the refuse lorry's saw-toothed grinder, I felt a great weight drop from my shoulders. Goodbye to the Nineteen Fifties.

"That's spring cleaning with a vengeance," said Lena.

In the following weeks I lost thirty pounds on a diet of honey and nuts. The acid I routinely took hit my thinning frame with the force of a locomotive; my eyes permanently sparkled behind Polaroids. An unbelievable mental clarity lit up the dark twisted corners of my life as mail and milk bottles collected outside the hall door, the phone went unanswered.

Lena fussed over me like a Jewish mother hen. "Eat, *liebchen*," she appealed. "How do you expect to get there—wherever it is—on an empty stomach?" She was really starting to get on my nerves. Eat this, eat more, take your umbrella: she even sulked like my own mother. Also, I noticed that whenever I fell off the Yoga wagon it was to gorge on Lena's masterpiece, her delectable fondue. What was she up to?

My copilot, Last, said he recognized the syndrome. "Yeh, Sybil pulls that stuff too, tryin' tae slow me down wi' love. I call it Dharma-envy." Women, incapable of "goin' up th' Mountain," instinctively kept men chained to base camp at ground level. But I must persist, he said. "Ye're like a plane flyin' over th' Atlantic tha's jes' passed th' point of nae return. Abortin' now c'd be more dangerous than if ye pushed ahaid tae yir objective." With rather less fervor he also advised me not to overdo it or draw undue attention to myself.

On returning home I told Lena I needed to fly solo for a while. "*Warum?*" her eyes opened wide in hurt surprise. "What have I done except try to make it a little easier for you?"

Exactly.

Raising LSD fuel intake to 500 mg a trip increased my air speed and brought a renewed burst of power. Euphoria flooded my control panel as, in my snug, Lena-less apartment, I loudly communed with the earth spirit Yetaita and Izanami the death goddess.

"Say fella, what's going on up there? Sounds like a madhouse." Pete Rich, the songwriter who lived on the floor below, stopped me in the hall one morning. (Had he heard Cheddi Bumba scream last night?) Sorry, I mumbled, a friend had an epileptic fit. Next day Pete again waylaid me. "Look chum," he began, "don't take this wrong. But me and the wife are worried about you. Are you okay?" He poked me in the ribs. "And how come we don't hear so much of that ol' choochoo train anymore?" (He meant my lovemaking bed crashing against his ceiling.) To change the subject I deftly lied and asked if he knew that our upstairs neighbor Susan VanOver was having an affair with the married dentist next door? "No! Really?"

I escaped this time. But for how long?

For the thousandth time, I checked my perimeter security inch by inch. Chubb lock and mortice (✓). Steel door prop (✓). Window bolts (✓). Optic peephole and anti-intruder grille for door (✓). Specially installed angled baffles to cushion my screams and grunts (✓). Yep, all in order.

Regents Gardens S.W.1 was nearly perfect cover for a soldier of the Light. A polyglot, mixed-class street practically within shouting distance of Buckingham Palace, it was a three-sided warren of bedsitters and converted flats rented to floaters, Italian waiters, Indians, students, Irish workmen, petty hustlers and a few middle-class lumpens like me. I had the entire third floor of a stately old Edwardian house, one of several in the area still maintained by absentee landlords who had bought the leaseholds cheaply before the war. My downstairs neighbors, Pete and Marcia Rich, were a song-writing team forever at their piano; upstairs Sue VanOver, a law student, rarely was home. All around were busy shops, cinemas, after-hours clubs, laundromats. Charabanc buses for Victoria Palace's long-running "Black and White Minstrel Show" and transient hotels catering to rail travelers kept the street loose and loud.

Half respectable, half occupied by ponces, racetrack touts, retired black marketeers, and even a GI-and-lesbian commune, Regents Gardens had almost daily visits from police and firemen. Amid all the hubbub, foreign gabble and clanging fire engines who would hear my 2:00 A.M. birth cries?

Bella Fior.

"Sidney, you naughty boy!" she exclaimed when I groggily answered the door one late March morning. Pushing a home-baked cheesecake into my unwilling arms, the playwright Danny Fior's wife strode inquisitively into the apartment and inspected my dark, now-barren place with hands on her ample hips. "They said you had the flu—not that you'd gone bankrupt as well!"

After I got rid of Bella, a faint anxiety set in. If the Fiors, who lived clear across town in Hackney, had heard I was "ill," I'd better activate May Day Plan #1. I taped the windows airtight and thickly greased the water pipe running up from Pete Rich's flat. Stepping past the soundproof drapes, I scattered pieces of broken bottles onto a wet cement base on my balcony. Pete, parking his Morris Minor below, looked up curiously. "See you've been reading all about these local break-ins lately," he called. "Better safe than sorry, eh?"

To conform with Dr. Last's policy of "purrchase in th' wurld," I did my best to pretend I was my old normal self. For example, before making my daily pilgrimage to Vauxhall Bridge, to pray to Ennuge the river spirit, I always shaved and changed into Infidel (Burberry's) garb. Friday nights I warmed my regular seat at editor Rick Sadler's poker game in Chalk Farm, and on Last's advice forced myself to keep the increasingly rare business lunch date. Ugh. I didn't know which was harder to digest, Prunier's cuisine—coquilles St. Jacques à la Provençale, Lobster Newburg, etc.—or Fleet Street gossip. Who th' hail were The Kinks? Jean

Shrimpton? Rohan O'Rahilly? All at once this kind of journalistic scuttlebutt made so little sense to me I figured it must conceal something more relevant, a secret code perhaps. Rick Sadler's constant moan "Oh Jesus, give me a hand I can *do* something with!" I read as a disguised call for hailp, and slipped him Dr. Last's office number under the card table. When *Vogue* by special messenger asked me to contribute to a symposium, "Mary Quant and the New Morality," I replied with my first article in months, "The Meaning of Meaninglessness in Fashion and Mental Illness" (never printed). I did a Herb Greaves while lunching at Simpson's on the Strand with the literary editor of the *New Statesman:*

"Lessing's
No blessing
Braine's
On the Wain."

Trouble was, my media chums never were surprised by anything I did or said. "Didn't quite catch that, old boy" or "You're in jolly good form today, Sid" was all I ever got out of them.

Bluidy fyools.

All that Beatles' winter I worked to silence my life. I stuffed rags under the door cracks, slept true according to energy quadrants I'd found in an old Druid's manual on a Charing Cross bookstall. Sometimes, like Percy-the-radio, I wore earmuffs in the flat. Sure, it may have looked odd—but it was worth it, because things were so *clear* now. Nothing, I saw, was as it seemed to be. (Relationships in Clare Council proved that.) The least significant event—the changing swirl of a passing cloud, the route a dust speck took settling to the floor, the page a book fell open to when I slammed it against the wall—were parts of a Universal Jigsaw Puzzle I was on the verge of solving. For the first time in England I felt my life to be in complete control. Before had been Coral years. Many of my English friends and contacts had sprung from knowing her. How would I have made out without her? Were these thoughts my own, or still controlled by her? Okay—I'd be my own man again and think strictly Bell thoughts. Never again would I be owned.

And Willie Last was the door I'd open to find myself.

My gratitude to this tough, stammering, gentle Scotsman was almost infinite. Whenever I had doubts about the "innair voyage" he always reassured me: I wasn't going mad, *I was going sane.* I felt I'd walk—no, crawl—through hell for him. The least I could do was to show him my stuff as Clare's P.R. man. But "tactical caution"—and the Medical Council's ban on doctors advertising—short-circuited my finest efforts. "Er, ah, Brither Sid"—Last placed a fatherly arm around me—"yir latest handoot describin' oor Center as 'the first genuinely Socialist lunatic asylum' is purty impressive as a personal statement. But don't ye think 'a revolutionary seizure of hospital power by a democratic dictatorship of exploited patients and militant staff' prematurely exposes oor battle strategy?" Reluctantly, on his orders, I watered down Last's field communiques into bland press releases about "after care" and "research into community therapy."

Even that wasn't mild enough. Last deliberately skipped me when giving out assignments for our next group patrol, a deputation to the House of Commons.

"Hey, what about me?" I said.

He coughed and explained that I'd been put in strategic reserve. The group had decided (when? where?) I had ascended to a Bardol so rarified that I should not be expected to lower myself to the level of the Parliamentary clods we had to deal with.

I was confused. What had I done wrong now?

Davina told me privately. Apparently I'd blabbed about pre-Minoan sacramental intercourse to a Bishop we were wooing. "And just imagine," she said, "going on about Bantu rebirth rituals to Enoch Powell the Minister of Health."

Like Jerry Jackson I felt like saying: did I really do that?

When I kept loudly protesting my right to contribute, to pull my oar, Last diplomatically suggested that we hold our first formal election of officers, and on his wink the Brothers unanimously voted me Chairman of Clare Council. I had been kicked upstairs.

Dick Drummond congratulated me. "Naturally, Sid, we assume you'll respect the parameters of our collective idiom and restrict communicating the modality of its totalized metanoia."

Boris crisply translated: "He means shut your bloody yap before you get us all struck off the Medical Register."

It was a Jewish hypochondriac's dream. To ride the medical whirlwind with revolutionary Cossacks against all those Establishment quacks who had misdiagnosed, misprescribed and mistreated me all these years.

GER-O-NI-MO-O-O-o-o-o!

Days and Nights in Conolly House: Spring

Before returning to O'Brien's Temple of Consciousness (as I'd begun to think of Con House), I set my "innair life" in order. It wasn't as richly complex as Willie Last's, of course, because I had to cut my coat to a coarser cloth.

Thus, my rebirth scenario was written less by Sartre or Eliade than by Monogram Pictures and Astounding *science-fiction magazine. A million buried fragments of a youth misspent in schlocky movie houses or glued to radio serials and drugstore comics was exploded up from my subconscious by LSD. The image I'd long had of myself—young Marx, a latter-day Clarence Darrow—gave way to a less political figure, a scientist-soldier in the best Saturday matinee tradition. He (I) was kindly but brave (Jean Hersholt as* Dr. Christian), *a 35 mm descendant of Colonel Gorgas, the U.S. army doctor (De Kruif's* Microbe Hunters) *who made possible the Panama Canal by eradicating yellow fever in the Isthmus (Robert Montgomery in* Yellow Jack). *I was sacrificing my own mind in the hazardous search for an antidote to schizophrenia (Muni in* Pasteur). *Before locating and destroying this deadly, infectious germ (Robert Donat blowing up the rotten sewage plant in* The Citadel), *I had to confront the monster in myself (Spencer Tracy,* Dr. Jekyll and Mr. Hyde), *and then transmit the secret of what I found to the spiritually helpless masses (wizened Sam Jaffe in* Lost Horizon—*or was I Ronald Colman?). My perfect, self-enclosed world at Regents Gardens S. W.1 had all the scientific precision of Flash Gordon serials, not to speak of the perpetual emergencies of "Buck Rogers of the 21st Century." ("Come quickly, Dr. Huer. Wilma's vanished off the time spanner!") The religious framework I patched together out of hazily recalled bits of Apache lore from countless Ken Maynard and* Three Mesquiteer *pictures, somehow mixed up with ancient Egyptian rites (Boris Karloff in* The Mummy). *This mystico-existential sundae I topped with the ideological whipped cream of F.R.E. ("family reciprocal exploitation") from Last and Petkin's case studies, sprinkled with Les O'Brien's "no goodness without badness." Plus Jew's journalism, dedicated to Isaac Babel; and 'jazz,' or how to jam in small groups; 'Becketing,' my updating of Hemingway's grace under pressure (the courage to face No-Theng) and New Marxism's 'quality of life.'*

All this I collected under the umbrella of my new job, Urban Shamanism.

"HEL-L-L-o-o-o there, Sid!"

This time Dr. Dick means *me.*

A. C. Corrigan, the Liverpool redhead, leans over to shake my hand. "Congratulations—and welcome to th' club, whack."

I'm in.

In monk's robe, dark glasses and stocking feet I'm at the 10:00 A.M. community meeting in TV lounge. The boys—those who remember me, that is—are mildly surprised to see me back. Nodding at my shaman's costume Jerry Jackson yawns, "Yeh, it *does* get kinda cold in 'ere." (The Administration still won't repair any broken windowpanes on the principle that it might encourage the boys to smash them again.) Florid Barney Beaton, also in pajamas, grinds his eyeglass Movietone camera at me, "Ho, it's the old upstager himself! When's the ice cream interval, Sir Laurence?" Long-haired Jeff H. hasn't taken his eyes off me since I brought back for him an autographed photo of his idol (and my old UCLA classmate) Jeffrey Hunter. He admires my outfit: "Terribly chic, m'dear. Didn't I see the original in *Harper's Bazaar?*" Looking wilder than ever, Herb Greaves angrily bunches the monk's cloth between his bony fingers and gives my elbow a hard pinch. Ow.

"Beau Bell's passion (he howls)
Any fashion
Mind's a vogue
To Grub Street rogue."

Lena dropped me too late last night for a proper recon, so I do one now. Statistically, not much change: a few boys gone, about an equal number admitted. Bit players I hardly recall from my previous visit have pushed reigning stars like Hurricane Hodge into the wings. All day I'm jostled 'accidentally' in the corridors by a big, blond, fiery-cheeked boy in white sweater, white duck trousers and white sneakers; even his neatly cut hair and pale eyes seem bleached. Derek Chatto, hitherto a shy, solitary chess player who blushes easily, is "coming out," as Les calls it. He treads on my heels while addressing his pocket chess set whose peg-in-the-hole pieces are beautifully carved Chinese ivory miniatures. "All right, Botvinnik, you got yourself into that corner—now think your way out!" Or he punches me violently in the back: "Don't rook me, Fischer!" Derek sticks to me like glue till I spin about and deliberately move one of his chess pieces. He looks suspiciously at me, "Clever, Lasker—but not clever enough!" Like Herb Greaves he hates it if you try to get under his guard or 'understand' him prematurely. Lord knows what happened while I was gone to nudge him over the line from being a brainy Milquetoast to an angry, sex-hungry Groucho Marx. When he isn't crowding me he chases any passing female he sees—but backpedals in panic and hollers "Checkmate!" if Bronwen or Sally actually lets him grab her. That bulge under his white fly is a seemingly permanent erection.

Toward evening Derek's rage overflows, and he corners me against the TV set. "You, Mr. Bell! Write books, go on the telly and lay famous women! What brings you here?" Jerry explains, " 'e's 'ere recrutin' for 'is new mental circus." Derek's face lights up, and suddenly he leaps into the air, almost hits the ceiling with his head and comes down in an attempted split, legs spraddled. Miraculously, be breaks nothing, slinks off cupping his crotch and muttering, "Chess is my game, dammit."

On this, my second trip, there's a flukier feel, more randomly impulsive hitting. The warmer weather, thawing out frozen impulses, causes a severe crisis in some boys. Last week Percy-the-radio slashed nurse Dave Foster with a broken milk bottle (the bandage is still on Dave's arm), and little Nigel Atkinson tried hanging himself while on home leave. The atmosphere has become so inflammable that Wally Walters has clamped a pair of Five & Dime toy handcuffs on his powerful hands, and Yorkshire Roy has buried his beloved knife in a garden halfway across the hospital.

What's going on?

At the dining room piano Herb Greaves bangs out part of the answer:

> "Woe me
> Mother Macree
> Annoyed
> Pretty Boy Floyd."

Translated : Clement Attlee Woodford is leaving Con House.

Like a mourner at his own wake Clem sadly confirms that he passed his university entrance exams, which he'd half-hoped to fail and thus stay longer in hospital. But Cambridge has accepted him, and now a gorgeous shiner decorates his right eye. "When I told Roy I'd gotten this grant to Kings College he slugged me and said it was just like a Socialist to want to keep living off taxpayers like him."

Around Clem's departure boys and staff weave a thick web of fantasy, hatred, envy and hope. A few optimistic souls say it's the start of a General Amnesty for schizophrenics, but most see it as a vague threat to themselves. Barney Beaton logically applies what he was taught in the family printing business. "We patients aren't earning a sufficient return on investment to satisfy the Hospital Management Committee. So they get their foreman, Dr. Dick, to hire an American efficiency expert, Mr. Bell who recommends shop-floor redundancies starting with Clem. My father says small independent enterprises don't survive at a time of mergers and take-overs." Curiously, staff pick up on this, somehow seeing Clem going as evidence of Admin's malice toward Con House. Even the normally pro-Establishment Sally Peel says, "They're picking us off one by one. The *Daily Telegraph* calls it baloney tactics."

But the most immediate casualty is Robin Ripley.

A Clean Well-Lighted Place

Robin hasn't been seen in Con House for over a week. "Dunno why," says her friend Jack Sweeney. "When I told her Clem was leavin' she jus' turned pale all over and belted me one."

As Jack and I cross King Eddie's silent, immaculate lawns, I ask why his knuckles are bleeding. He smiles shyly. "I git these fits, see? Jaisus Christ jumps outta th' bushes—or up th' toilet spout—for a little natter. Sometimes at night a big brown beast forces me tuh swaller him. Then he starts roarin' an' wantin' tuh git out. I git so scared I smash windows." Or, I think, Hurricane Hodge's prowlike, provocative chin. Jack, a shy sweet Tipperary ex-altar boy with a heart-stopping soprano, is part of the hospital's 'Irish Mafia,' mainly youths who cracked up while working as laborers on English construction sites. They meet Sundays after Mass for 'music mornings'—the basis of Hurricane's anti-IRA delusion. Jack's closest English contact is Robin, for whom he is a kind of substitute husband. Though they're always battling and making up like an old married couple, he insists they're only "best mates."

You can't just stroll unannounced into Pankhurst Ward, a tidy brick building with plastic boxes of flowers spaced precisely along sills of glistening, intact windows. First Jack has to press an outside buzzer, which summons a black starched nurse who peers at us through windowed double doors and lets us in only after we drop our names and home ward on a piece of paper through the mail slot. Then, once inside, she writes down our identities in a book hanging from a wall chain and turns us over to another Omo-laundered nurse who, clearly disapproving of us and the person we are visiting, wordlessly escorts us along a dead-quiet corridor smelling of wax finish. Our unnaturally loud heels leave visible scuff marks on the sparkling floor lino. What a nice contrast with Con House, is my first impression. (I forget just how offended by the boys' crappy habits I really am.)

Pankhurst is a doctor's dream. So silent, so clean. I've been in louder morgues. (And what a contrast, too, with Female Admissions which, when I saw it, was full of cursing, shouting women exploding with a lot more energy than I saw in Male Admissions.) We pass several doorless rooms whose beds would win gold medals at the hospital-corner Olympics. The mannequinlike patients, in frilly dresses or nightgowns, are glassy-eyed on drugs, and seem more a function of their tightly made beds than they're real human beings. "Jaisus preserve me," Jack crosses himself, "I t'ought sure they wuz wax dummies at first."

With a double set of keys the nurse opens a door and, after we're in, locks us inside a room with Robin. A gray blanket covers her up to her thin, marble-white face looking even paler under the orange-red pageboy bob with fringe she has cut and dyed her hair into. She turns sleepy, pain-filled eyes to us. "Oh, h'lo Jack, what's Mister Writer doin' in drag?" (I'm in my urban shaman's robe.) Jack and I take turns cheering her up. "Guess I had a fit," Robin says. "Kicked matron in the bum, broke the ward telly and bashed in some windows—a regular Con House do," she wanly smiles. "Don't remember much, really. Dr. Goldstein says Clem's th' reason. His exact words were that I'm reenacting my traumatic exclusion from the primal scene attributable to rejection by my surrogate brother." Painfully she withdraws her arms from under the blanket: they're heavily taped to the elbows from having been slashed with a razor blade. "Me, I'd say it was spring fever."

After Robin dozes off Jack and I wait to be let out, then creep from dust-free, spick-and-span Pankhurst Ward and almost run for our lives back to scruffy, dirty, smelly old Con House.

Praise God, She Will Protect You

The more I see of Con House the greater my admiration for Dick Drummond's special brand of horse sense. Wisely, he selected male patients with an eye to balancing off serious psychotics against less disturbed cases, and King Eddie's rigid segregation of sexes he has tried to outwit by recruiting three women who are as different as chalk from cheese.

Bronwen Meg-Owen Jones—the social worker—is forever lost in spiritual mists due to over-identification with Con House's most backward types. "She's got th' schizophrenic bends—a condition brought on by staying in too long beyond her depth," says O'Brien a little uncharitably. Sometimes, after coughing her lungs out in empathy with black Abe or rocking for hours along with Gareth, she is so smashed that they must help her into a chair. Ex-Cardiff CND, ex-Free Wales Army and Royal College of Nurses dropout, Bronwen is a born glory hunter, seeking her lost self in the murky waters of other people's problems. Every time her fiancé, Dr. Lewis Singh, tries to fish her out she takes it as a personal affront. "Oh Sid"—she takes my hands in hers while pressing her body against mine—"Lewis thinks Con House will kill our love. How can he be so paranoid?"

Sally Peel, the bouncy, full-breasted occupational therapist, admires her colleague's somber commitment. "Bron's *serious.* All I ever do is mess about and drink tea." Gallons of it, lubricating her shrieking, schoolgirlish laughter as she comfily sits, short plump legs tucked under her, knitting absentmindedly or gossiping with the boys who crowd around for a quick peep down her cleavage. (I saw one boy actually burst into tears at the sight of her Venus-like breasts.) Sally, a Cheltenham Ladies College graduate and the debby daughter of a Hampshire stockbroker, is the least likely candidate for schizophrenic work. Her life utterly changed course the day Dr. Dick spotted her ladling soup to a back ward of chronics. "There I was, all lah-de-dah and Voluntary Aide," she recalls. "Dick just grabbed my hand and practically dragged me over here by the hair and shouted, 'Invent yourself!' I felt like a starlet he'd just discovered." In time Con House transformed this primly gregarious fixture of Young Conservative dances into a lazy, sexy female presence who is content endlessly to gaze into the fire and do absolutely nothing. "I keep telling my husband it's an acquired skill." More than any doctor's therapy, Sally's easy somnolence hones the edge off many a boy's guilt and self-hatred about being in a mental hospital. Unlike Bronwen she instinctively respects the line between sane and insane, and the whole idea of a 'schizophrenic voyage' makes her giggle. "I'm rather afraid I keep thinking of it like a day trip to Calais, all underdone sausages and seasickness. I'll wait on the quayside, thank you all the same."

Around 5:30 P.M., when Sally and Bronwen clock off, *Robin*

Ripley punches in—literally. Wham, sock! Anyone who deviates from her romantic fantasy of what a proper gentleman is gets a taste of her knuckles. The worst crime in Robin's book is not the boys' feebly groping hands or their attempts to steal a kiss in the darkness of the TV room. Their real sin is introspection. "Thinkin' again, Jack? Disgustin'." Pow! All her life Robin has secretly battled against huge odds—a violently bullying father and a compliant but covertly hostile mother; a transvestite brother who killed himself; a minor form of epilepsy and an early forced abortion—to define her own stubborn idea of the feminine role. "I'm an inbetweener, I guess. Only wish I liked girls as much as I dislike boys." Though not by temperament a rebel, she is forced to rebel against stereotype-wielders who hold a knife to her throat, sexually speaking. Violently antiestablishment in Pankhurst Ward, she is passionately conformist in Drummond's. Schizophrenic—or the best of both worlds? From somewhere inside the eye of the bisexual hurricane she lays about with her fists like a modern Carry Nation working out her problems on the captive, willing boys who can never quite measure up to her Victorian standards of gallant chastity. Strangely, the boys didn't seem to mind. She is Con House's most consistent female support, and they love her for sticking with them into the midnight furies. After which—she'd bash anyone who even suggested she stay the night—a proud honor guard of Con Housers led by Jack Sweeney escorts her back to Pankhurst Ward. "Thanks fellas," she whispers as they shove her through a ground floor window. "Sleep tight. Don't let the psychiatrists bite."

Spring in Conolly House is sad, fine lightning. With everybody's young sap rising, our shoulders unhunching from the long gray cold, more fights (rarely serious), more broken windows. Days longer, nothing to do. Goaded beyond endurance by Dr. Dick's permissive regime, more or less undrugged, the Conolly boys try holding it in. Sometimes successfully, causing month-long depressions. Or letting it drip, seep, trickle out. Darting, paranoid, furious. At times I think Con House will lift off hospital grounds like a maverick rocket. And fly to where?

But (even in the spring) it's mostly 'contained.' "And that, my old mate," says O'Brien, "is what's commonly known as the double bind."

Bull Session

Sex, like a stray hand grenade, rolls around Con House; it fizzles and sputters, daring the boys to pick it up. No one does—directly. Instead, the itchiest spirits, magnetized by my shamanistic come-on and my ambiguous relationship with Dr. Dick, congregate in my room. Between midnight and dawn I professionalize their jitters.

S. BELL
Chinese Spoken Here

reads a joke card someone's tacked to my door.

Does Dr. Last get such problems? I can handle the more down-to-earth complaints—Social Security foul-ups, gripes about the food or Bob Featherstone's fear of losing his brewery job if they find out where he goes home after work. Other worries are trickier. Jerry wants to know how to curb his Jesus highs. (Wally Walters advises, "Try Bromo Seltzer.") Yorkshire Roy, tight with Clem Woodford till I came on the scene, wonders if alien Americans—"no names, no pack drill"—can be sued in British courts for stealing a person's best friend. ("Only if there were children born of the union," cracks A. C.) Jeff H. is furious because the hospital newsletter rejected his short story, *'Arf 'n 'Arf*, about homosexual dogs. Someone asks if kissing another man causes cancer. And Percy-the-radio, now back from the violent wing for attacking a nurse, needs advice on how to word a High Court petition demanding compensation from his mother for "attributing her delinquency to a minor."

The common denominator in this complex algebra of mangled Scripture, castration fantasies, tittle-tattle from outer space and repressed sadomasochism, is . . . sex. The same obsessions that I feared would drive me mad at their age have actually pushed them over the line. I was saved by masturbation and a street tradition of bravura confession ("Wow, lemme tell ya about this wet dream I had last night!"). But almost all the Con House boys I've spoken to grew up as private adolescents outside the sanity-saving circle of curbside confidences. Few of the boys have had any real sexual experience, apart from flirting back at their mothers and occasional encounters with a prostitute. But they cannot fool me. Behind their demonic sex fevers lurks an even deeper hunger, an unconscious longing to be adopted into the Cosmic Britherhuid, to become Men (not children) of Light. So I tell them stories from my bedroom past, an adaptation of the Igluic technique for initiating young warriors. For the first few years of adult screwing, I say, I always shouted "Mama!" during climax, and often mind-killed my father before he actually died. They look relieved.

But, I say, the problem starts *before* birth.

I was a sailor with Columbus, I say. A Stone Age pterodactyl, a Cathar monk. A. C. and I first met while laboring under huge back packs in Hannibal's Alps-crossing army. Until nearly dawn, my face set like Last's, I hold them raptly describing my LSD primal scenes. I've been a midget elephant, climbing up the slippery slopes of my ma's vagina, ejaculating through my baby trunk. Then a wee-wee bird, stuck into my ma's ass on her Great Bird Flight over prehistoric Earth. Then my pa laying into my ma who cursed him for not being a good enough provider.

"So ye see," I conclude, "*it's natcheral tae want tae fuck yir maw.*"

Shocked silence. Their embarrassed eyes avoid mine. Derek Chatto shouts angrily, "Knight into Queen won't go!" Nigel slips out blushing. Jeff H. (born Bernie Mendelson) rocks back and forth moaning "*oi, oi, oi.*" Jerry Jackson scratches his chin vehemently. "Oh no," he cries. "Oh no, no, no." He laughs against his will. "Ya creepin' soddin' bugger, ya." He too runs out.

Only A. C. remains. He fixes me with a skeptical eye. "You go easy on that stuff, Sid. Roman officers *never* carry their own baggage."

Brass

"Good Lord—HEL-L-L-o-o-o there!"

Never have I seen Dr. Dick or his staff move so fast. They're on their feet in nothing flat scrambling to find chairs conventional enough for two middle-aged ladies to use. The community meeting has been gate-crashed by a couple of the leading lights of the much-feared Hospital Management Committee.

The women slip into their seats with the ostentatious humility of visiting royalty. Which, in a sense, they are. Management committees, composed of doctors and lay members, rule the hospital roost, if only by their enormous powers to strip patients of their freedom for long periods. They're drawn from the same upper middle-class stratum—and as mysteriously appointed—as England's magistrates. (In fact, they're sometimes one and the same person.) O'Brien says that the civilian committee members, far from checking the power of hospital bureaucrats, dance to the psychiatrists' tune and do exactly what's told them. "Odd people. They're not in it for the money, just the itch to dominate other people's lives. Pardon me, to 'serve.' "

We know from the way the visitors don fixed nervous smiles that they've heard about us and expect trouble. Clearly they disapprove of Con House but are doing their utmost to conceal it. Mrs. Fiona fFlytch-Fraser is buxomly armored in a beige tweed suit of a style much favored by the Queen, a Tory-turban puce velvet hat, expensive leather handbag and rhinestone brooch fastened to her lapel like a regimental badge. (I've seen her before in the Assembly Hall distributing prizes to long-stay patients and hoping she'd see them again next year.) A local Justice of the Peace, and married to a real estate agent, she is much called upon to do voluntary work among the less fortunate. From her general bearing I expect her to bark, "Troops at ease!" Her co-committeewoman is Dr. Ethel Primrose, a consultant psychiatrist at King Eddie.

The boys sense the women's unfriendly vibrations and put on a gratuitous display of their worst traits. Abe, happening into the TV lounge for a rare visit, is the perfect patsy: black and withdrawn. "How come we let th' nigs come over 'ere for cheap nervous breakdowns on our National 'ealth?" rhetorically asks Jerry. "Blasted wogs," chimes in Barney, "rape our women, inflate our crises. We fought at Allah-mangle and Dumb-cork for the right of freeborn English yes-manry to take a pee in private. Now the golliwogs are trying to do it for us." A suggestion by Wally that all blacks be sent back to their native jungle is heartily seconded by others. Abe, apparently unhearing, drifts out again; moments later we hear him coughing louder than ever upstairs.

Mrs. fFlytch-Fraser and Dr. Primrose glance inquiringly at Dr. Dick but cannot find any overt sign of disapproval in his poker face. Offended to the quick of their liberal souls, they nod to each other, as if to say: what else can you expect from a doctor who runs a place like this? Dr. Primrose fingers a stethoscope hanging down her starched white uniform jacket as if it was Queeg balls. "Your little community seems rather disturbed today, isn't it, Dr. Drummond?"

"Oh, do you think so," Dr. Dick rolls about in his gold-monogrammed Diana Dors chair, in agony or jollity it's hard to say. "Or is their disturbance a consensual expectation of projected corporate violence?"

A great cheer goes up. One for our side.

Sensing that with a little effort they can unnerve our guests, some boys duly act out the committeewomen's expectations of them. Jerry pretend-masturbates in his pajamas while giving himself detailed landing instructions. "A little to th' right, no a bit higher, ya're undershootin'. . . ." Derek Chatto throws his pocket chess set at the women, "I'm fed up, you play with my things." Mrs. fFlytch-Fraser is so fascinated by Jerry's obscene performance that she forgets to duck and almost has her hat knocked off by Derek's missile; Dr. Primrose discreetly wiggles her chair against the nearest wall—a staff reflex, I've noticed.

This is Eric Raw's big chance. Since my last visit he's been wasting away for lack of nourishment and a fresh audience, and now he suddenly appears in tattered pajamas and flops his ninety-five-pound cadaver at the visitors' feet. "Shadow of his old self," he whines, "what's to become of poor Eric?" Dr. Primrose refuses to look at him; instead she tries to keep her annoyance at bay with a heavy joke aimed at another boy. "You there—water is free. When did you last wash?" But Eric isn't having it. He pushes himself up from the floor almost into the doctor's lap. "It's all my fault, isn't it?" he demands.

Dr. Primrose's leg jerks away from Eric's touch, and her eyes rove all over the room. Finally she bursts out: "And when did this patient have a meal last, Dr. Drummond?"

Calmly, Dr. Dick explains that Eric's prolonged hunger strike, like Nigel's famous thirty-day snooze, is an attempt to transport himself existentially beyond self-consuming guilts. Also, Eric is deluded that the hospital food is feces and therefore unfit to eat. "Ol' bag-o-bones ain't so crazy," interjects Jerry. " 'e's prob'ly savin' 'is life by not eatin' th' grub 'ere."

Dr. Primrose sharply reminds Drummond that his first duty is to his patients and not to a general theory of antitherapy, but when she continues to talk about Eric without ever looking at him, he grabs her hand. "Sailfish buoys always end up nailed on someone's wall, don't they? Not that I'm complaining, mind. I've had more than my share of ECT and blancmange." Failing to get a response, he ups the ante by thrusting an invisible object under Dr. P's thin suspicious nose. "Ha ha," he chuckles, "you didn't think I could make Bronwen pregnant, did you? Blamed it on poor impotent Clem." Even when he holds the empty air like a huge, unconscious cock aimed at Dr. Primrose's stomach, amazingly she won't look at him. He recoils. "What?" his voice harshly ventriloquizes to middle age. "Don't you know how hard your father and I worked to feed you. Going without, using our entire sugar ration in the war to keep our little Eric in sweets." Suddenly he screams at her: "DON'T PLAY WITH THE SAUSAGE—EAT THE BLOODY THING!"

That's more than enough for her. She points her stethoscope at Dr. Dick like a pistol and her voice has an edge of angry hysteria. "If that unfortunate boy"—looking at Dick, not Eric—"isn't given proper treatment he may die. And this hospital, not your so-called community, will be financially liable in a court of law." Barney says, "I knew in the end it would come down to dolors and sense."

Rather than lose control altogether—which presumably would drag her down to the patients' level—Dr. Primrose announces she has other wards to visit this morning, and she and Mrs. fFlytch-Fraser back out to cries of "Wot about th' grub, then?" and "Are ya 'ere only for th' beer?" But the English upper class hasn't ruled for a thousand years for nothing. From the safety of the doorway Mrs. fFlytch-Fraser flings us a regal smile. "Terribly ni-ahse of you to have us."

"Satisfaction, Jackson!" replies Jerry. "Come back with your problem any time."

After the visitors flee, Vince, the 'deaf' klepto who has been lolling near Dr. Primrose's handbag slung over a chair, delightedly opens his hand to inspect a five-pound note he's surprised to find there.

"Well, it might have been worse," says Sally at staff meeting.

"Sure," agrees Dave Foster. "Eric could've cut his throat all over Dr. Primrose's uniform."

Things are coming to a head, I'm told. The Management Committee's visit is just the latest incident in a campaign by Admin to subtly harass Drummond, to drive yet one more nail into Con House's coffin. Bronwen says they've weathered such storms before; "Con House is safe as long as the hospital still needs a scapegoat unit." O'Brien grunts, "Up to a point—Lord Copper."

Les Talks

"Sure, they used to think th' sun shone out of our arseholes. That was when we took in all their dirty human wash—the intractables the other wards couldn't handle. But now th' novelty's worn off. We cause too many headaches." He looks around. "And we ain't exactly a united front in here either."

How, I ask, do similar therapeutic communities make out? Les says that Maxwell Jones' psychotic unit at Henderson is allowed to function almost independently of its parent hospital, Belmont. "And I don't give you a plugged tanner for David Cooper's Villa 21 once he gets to our stage."

The crux, as always, is the knot that staff gets tied into. "On the one hand our patients imply, 'Go mad, be one of us, otherwise you're useless.' On the other, they tell us explicitly, 'Stay sane, go on playing at staff, otherwise you can't protect us.' Talk about double binds!"

Staff bind is only one of the mutually inhibiting relationships set in motion by Con House. "We may see ourselves as an oasis of sanity in a desert of medical ignorance. But we're still connected to King Eddie by a thousand ties of salary, promotion, law. Just plain proximity. We can't belch without instant repercussions elsewhere." Ripples of anxiety starting in Con House—a broken window, a dirty floor or fistfight—are like a tidal wave when they hit the doors of the Chief Nurse and Divisional Heads, Les says.

"And y'know, sometimes I actually feel sorry for th' brass. We ain't no tonic for their nerves. Staff *and* patients, they couldn't care less about Dick's schizophrenic voyage. As if just bein' in a loony bin wasn't hard enough. People here want a rest, not a revolution.

"In case you've not noticed, most patients are conditioned by us to think they've 'broken down,' like an industrial machine. Or else are suffering from a mysterious, unpredictable disease called mental illness. So naturally, it's a miracle, owed mainly to the tender loving care of doctors and nurses, when they're 'cured.' I've never seen anyone so grateful as patients who have let us bombard them back to normality with ECT and pills.

"The 'mad' are far more terrified of themselves than of us white-coated figures who soothe and comfort them. Having been trained to turn their mental guns on themselves they fire away dutifully until the pain gets too much—which is when we get them. Our job is to make them more efficient antiself gunners: relax them, clear their heads, set them up again to be their own clay pigeons. That's 'mental health.' "

Silent throughout Les' monologue Dick Drummond suddenly slams his fist on the desk. "WHAT IS THE BLOODY POINT?!" Con House, he aggressively shouts, must be returned to a saner, more structured day. As of this moment there will be compulsory cleaning, compulsory reveille and locks on all the doors. "And Eric *will* start eating—if I have to shove it down his throat myself."

Staff members nod knowingly at Dick's outburst—and ignore it. We've all felt this anguish at Con House's muddle so it's nothing new. Unconfirmed in his fury, our doctor squid subsides slowly into his usual inky, word-clouded depression. "Oh well, I suppose the extension of self into Not-Self implies a continuous plenitude of ambivalences. . . ."

"Dunno too much about that"—Jerry Jackson pops his head in—"but that lady shrink's back again."

A moth to the flame, Dr. Primrose flutters back to give the boys one more chance. Without warning she marches boldly into the TV lounge and, unconsciously positioning herself in the doorway so that no one can enter or leave, rasps with more aggression in her voice than she knows: "I believe you had questions about the menu." She then launches into an incredibly detailed briefing of why the meals aren't better. (Primarily a shortage of experienced chefs and the logistics of trucking in fresh produce daily, she says.) Amazed that anyone in authority is willing to discuss anything with them, several boys lay aside magazines and radios to allow Dr. Primrose to conclude her earnest, fact-filled harangue. "And if you have any complaints," she says, "I hope that you will give them to the Culinary Subcommittee of the Hospital Management Committee. And we'll deal with you—I mean them."

A patter of solemn applause.

Dr. P. glows. "I knew you'd want to be reasonable, lads—" Violated handbag drooping from her pencil-thin arm like a dead rabbit, she surveys the tea-sloshed, cigarette-strewn room and bursts out: "But how *can* you live in such pig squalor?"

"Oink oink!" "This ain't th' army, lady!" "Th' less we polish th' more we live!" Herb Greaves says,

"Don't mind mess
Fends off stress
Clears minds
Of double binds."

Dr. Primrose bravely smiles through the flak. "You know," she informs them in a real effort to be friendly, "I raised three grown sons, right in this very hospital. One has gone into advertising, one is a banker, my youngest is still at Oxford." What is she driving at? "But my children never would have got on if they had to endure filth like this. They simply would not have known how."

Filially, Jerry lays his head on her bony shoulder. "Not to worry, mum. You send 'em along an' we'll teach 'em."

In an access of goodwill Barney leads the group, "Three Cheers for Mrs. Management—"

"Hip hip HOORAY!"

Her eyes mist over. It *is* possible to break through. "Don't forget," she says as Jerry and Barney firmly guide her to the door, "submit all complaints to—"

"THE CULINARY SUBCOMMITTEE OF
THE HOSPITAL MANAGEMENT COMMITTEE!"

The boys make a poem of it.

They wave her off affectionately. "Good ol' cow," adjudges Jerry.

When the good old cow peeks into her purse and realizes she's been conned out of a fiver, she marches directly to the Medical Superintendent's office and delivers an ultimatum about Con House's distressing state.

It's a Barnum & Bailey World

On a slowly rising tide of obscure aggravation, a farewell party is organized for Clem, who leaves this weekend for a work-holiday in Devon before he starts college. A chance remark by Jerry got the ball rolling, "What about a last drink together—y'know, like wot th' condemned man gets before they top 'im?" A. C. Corrigan, the former seminarian from Liverpool, immediately saw the possibilities and roped Sally Peel into helping him create a theatrical send-off.

"I'm leaving too!" announces Bronwen, suddenly jealous of the fuss over Clem. Her excuse is that Dr. Singh has advanced the date of their wedding, the ceremonies to be held at a Sikh temple in Southall and later at King Eddie's multidenominational chapel to please both sets of parents. "Lewis insists on choosing the music, the flowers, the minister—even my bridesmaids," she says with a trace of bitterness. "It's nothing to do with me, really."

Her news causes hardly a ripple. Wally explains, "Bron ain't one of us like Clem. 'Er 'eart's in th' right place—but so's 'er 'ead."

"A. C.'s idea"—how most think about the party—splits Con House down the middle. For many it simply doesn't exist. Others endure it like Percy's radio anger: a slightly deafening irrelevance. Yet somehow it gets done, mainly because A. C., who has written the program and even chased up costumes from Occupational Therapy, hassles everyone to pitch in. Saturday 6:00 P.M. a circus ringmaster—A. C. with trousers tucked into Wellington boots, a ride-to-the-hounds red jacket, top hat and wax moustache pasted to his freckled sweat-shiny face—strides about banging two dustbin lids together. "Hurreh hurreh hurreh—take your places for The Greatest Show on Earth!"

Bug-eyed and eager we tumble into a TV lounge miraculously swept, Hoovered, even reglazed in Clem's honor. Sally personally cleaned out the usual muck and replaced it with Christmas tinsel, and someone has neatly lettered above the 'Shanghai Express' graffiti:

GOOD LUCK NORMALS

In a fancy tailcoat Jerry Jackson tends a makeshift bar built of empty Guinness crates supporting plastic cups and paper plates of cheese crisps. "Step right up, folks!" he shouts. "Tonight it's King Eddie Special—cider for th' ladies, cider for th' gents!" With top brass due later, Dr. Dick isn't taking any chances on the hard stuff.

Almost everyone is out of bed, including some people who have been under blankets so long I've never met them. Even black Abe and Mr. Wu mix timidly. By special dispensation the whole crew is in street clothes, so primped, combed and shaved that they're nearly unrecognizable. In a mod suit Gareth becomes a sharply handsome Kings Road toff, and Herb Greaves looks merely artistically intense in velvet jacket and pressed cord trousers. Clothes maketh the madman.

Not to be outdone I, in robe and stocking feet, have removed my Polaroids for the festivities.

Party's subdued. Not enough women, for one thing. Les got short shrift from Pankhurst Ward's matron when he asked for some. "No, Mr. O'Brien," he reports her as saying, "I'd sooner see my girls in white slavery." In anticipation of Con House's biggest riot yet, Mr. Tasker, the Nursing Officer, has ordered a temporary evacuation of patients from adjoining wards and canceled weekend leave of his huskier male nurses. Jeff H. gazes out at the suddenly depopulated landscape around Con House and says, "That's the trouble with this place. They expect too much of you."

Like a heavily tapped presliced melon the party falls away into its several segments.

In the center of the ring Clem is like a main event fighter almost buried in towel-waving seconds pouring advice into him. There is something almost sexual in the way boys slip up to pat or touch him, a last physical contact before he turns into a normal. Yorkshire Roy, still in shock over losing his best friend first to me and then the outside world, gives Clem a money belt as a going-away gift "so they can't steal thy hard stuff." "And if you lose your mind," Nigel says, "don't do what I did and ask for it at the nearest police station." For good luck Derek Chatto slips Clem his cherished chess set.

In another part of the lounge the staff sulk with their backs against one wall. Dave Foster, his arm still taped where Percy-the-radio cut him with a broken milk bottle, flinches and looks ceilingward every time the Muzak—supplied by his assailant—stops. His wife, a Female Division nurse, unsmilingly eyes the patients; Les left Mrs. O'Brien at home. "Never mix business with pleasure," he says. Which is which?

Dr. Dick, brooding over the loss of his two favorite protégés, drinks alone and morose in a corner.

But Sally Peel is in her element. Jolly and sexy in a low-cut cocktail dress, she introduces her tall young husband around as if she were at one of her Tory charity balls. "Jerry, this is Michael. He's a solicitor." "No kiddin', Sal. Must be awful embarrassin' fer ya."

Bronwen stands apart exuding a tragic air and watching Sally have a good time. Her brave martyr's smile turns slightly bitter when anyone looks her way. She is heavily shadowed by a darkly handsome man in a blue turban and a doctor's white coat, who suddenly strolls over to me. My neck prickles, I feel like John Wayne in Apache country. "Ah, the famous Mr. Bell," he says without introducing himself. He doesn't have to; I know he is Bronwen's husband-to-be, 'Screwy Lewie' Singh. Youngish, brown, hawk-nosed, he's built like a southern California tennis pro, all flashing teeth and forearm and grins like Jack Palance just before he guns down Elisha Cook in *Shane*. His small glittering eyes give my shaman's robe the King Eddie stare. "You *must* come and visit us after the wedding," the oily upper-class accent is as well-trimmed as the tiny moustache. "Bronwen will be much better then."

Oh, I ask loyally, is anything wrong with her?

Dr. Singh enigmatically looks for flies on the ceiling. "Dear Mr. Bell. You understand perfectly." He gives my shoulder a hard, patronizing squeeze and returns to guard Bronwen—followed by my Krazy Kat brick. Pok!

Soldiers' Talk

Willie Last says that the key to communicating with the forward battalions of the schizophrenic army is to break through their secret language. Like a spy I drift from group to group at the party and furiously scribble in my notebook. I'll decode it later.

"Help-o, Mus-turd Blip. Jimmy Pell Knee Jelly. I'm three. And how are you? Softly bees tunicht, sir. Caroline's lonely, can't reach us, Home-bird interference. I've written to the Government but never get a reply. Waswong? Maybe more school would help. One-hundred-foot hurdles are easier. If only I could sleep better. Kong bristles enumeration instability roger comecon. Oh well he's got his troubles too, I expect. Are you?"

Nigel Atkinson, fifteen. Cracked up while attending a top grammar school. A family-pressured overachiever, he has invented a stupid twin brother "Desmond" who is a petty pilferer, arsonist and would-be suicide, the author of all of Nigel's troubles.

Sudden like, I started 'avin' these dreams, see. Fair knocked me over they did. All about Bristol City, dunkin's Scotch eggs an' God's currant bun. Mixed up, like. At first I cows an' calfs. But when they din't go away, I bubbles to my china who says I'm goin' ginger beer. Me mum says, "You ain't no oily rag" an' takes me down to the English Channel. 'e gives me some soap which makes me all Mutt 'n' Jeff. Anyway they wuz apple fritter. I throws 'em in th' bread 'n' butter 'n' ducks into this battle cruiser. Me da' finds me Brahms 'n' Liszt from pimple 'n' blotch, which I'd never 'ad before. "Why ain't you out earnin' yer greengages?" 'e Diana Dors. So's I barry mokes 'im with my Chalk Farm, for g'd measure bangs 'im with th' Aristotle, then cock 'n' 'en bottles 'n' stoppers falls on top of me like a mouse. Brought me 'ere a year ago Whitsun. What a barney!"

Wally Walters, 275-pound lorry driver from Bermondsey, a once thriving dockland community disintegrating under the hammer blows of redevelopment. Wally's family rehoused from a friendly, ramshackle old street to a terrifying high rise twenty stories in the sky. An eleven-plus failure, too. The above story makes perfect sense in cockney rhyming slang—which no hospital psychiatrist understands.

MmmmmmmmmMnnnMssssssGfhhhhhhhhhM. . . . nnnnnnnnnnn. . . . .mmmmmm . . . nnn . . . . uhuhuhuhuh. Sssssssssssssssss. tu tu tu tu tu. Nahanananahanah. NO!

Gareth de Walden, Seventeen

"Howdy, Dicky-bird—where's th' action?"

All genial ferocity and a glaring mid-Atlantic accent, a balding attractive man in his fifties bounces in: Dr. Hugh Winstanley, the Medical Superintendent of King Edward VIII Hospital. Like a small-town mayor running for reelection he goes around shaking hands and making not-quite-right American wisecracks culled from his two years on the staff of a madhouse in San Antonio, Texas. He heartily slaps my back while sizing up my urban shaman rig. "If you can't lick 'em, join 'em, right Mr. Bell?" We met when he interviewed me during my first visit.

Dr. Winstanley cultivates his reputation for slightly radical eccentricity by dropping mysterious aphorisms like "R equals S minus P"—or (as one eventually learns), the (R)ecovery of a (S)chizophrenic varies in direct ratio of the distance between the patient and his (P)arents. "Wedlock is deadlock, the family is a graveyard of love," Dr. Winstanley cheerfully says. "Where I disagree with Laing, Last and that lot is that they aren't mad enough to run a State hospital. Ha ha!" Before I can reach into my head for the lever marked 'Talk-Professional,' A. C.-the-ringmaster bangs his dustbin lids again. "All ashore who's goin' ashore—up anchor for

THE CHINA FOLLIES!"

Led by the Medical Super with his arms impartially around Drs. Drummond and Singh—who constantly battle for his ear with stories pro and anti Con House—we file into a miniature theater-in-the-round (ex-dining room), where the stage is a cleared space circled by chairs and tables. A. C. has found it easier to make a theater than get the boys to act in it. The few who give a damn are bashful; the others indifferently wander off as soon as A. C.'s attention is elsewhere. The result is unusually entertaining though not always in the way he intended.

It's amateur hour—with a point.

At first it doesn't go off too badly. A barbershop quartet of Con Housers led by A. C. serenades Dr. Dick with Cole Porter's "You're the Tops," followed by Jack Sweeney reciting Kipling's "Danny Deever" (he mischievously inserts the names of Divisional doctors in each stanza, "Oh they're hangin' Screwy Lewie in th' mornin' . . ."). Barney Beaton enthusiastically cartwheels around the room while passing out small square cards inscribed in a tiny but beautiful copperplate:

BLARNEY BEATEN
Family Circus Artiste
(mummer's wag
father's fool)
Available Immediately for Engagements
and Other Forms of Intercourse

R.S.V.P.
Randy Stripling
Very Paranoid

Agent: D. Drummond
Conolly House
King Edward VIII Hospital
Low Wick
Berkshire
England
United Kingdom
Europe
Western Hemisphere
Free World
Earth
Solar System
Universe
(not before 11 A.M.)

Barney refuses to give up the stage until A. C. hisses, "Get off—it's Sid's turn!"

A. C., sweating with the effort of knocking heads together to keep his program going, has prevailed on me to "Go on out there,

Sid, and knock 'em dead." All I can think of is to mumble 'Om' without drawing a breath for three minutes by Yorkshire Roy's watch. For a finale, Jerry Jackson reveals a fabulous football skill by keeping a soccer ball in the air with his skull, knee and instep à la Pelé, then aims a powerful header at Dr. Primrose which almost knocks her glasses off. (Her alarmed glance at Dr. Winstanley he cheerfully ignores.) Incited by Jerry's bravado, a few boys blow razzberries at the doctors or trip each other up in small scuffles, which A. C. controls by sheer muscle power.

The big surprise, though, is Robin Ripley, bright red pageboy bob and all. Escorted by her ward shrink Dr. Goldstein and wearing a longsleeved jersey to hide her bandages, she makes a grand entrance and is immediately engulfed by Con Housers happy to see her. "Hey fellas, lemme breathe." By reflex she swings a friendly punch. "Ouch—I forgot." Her appearance disrupts the program, which she rescues with a show-stopping number. Holding her slashed arms away from her wiry body, a gay professional smile on her small intent face, she soft-shoes "Bye, Bye, Blackbird"—sung at Dr. Singh—to much racist applause.

Intermission, for cider and smuggled beer. The booze is an excuse for some boys to shove others into the laps of Drs. Singh and Primrose who are getting pretty fed up with A. C.'s show and make moves to go but sink back to their seats under the disapproving stare of Dr. Winstanley. He is hugely enjoying the show—even if some of it is at his colleague's expense. Conolly House, you can see him thinking, isn't as bad as it's cracked up to be. Or is it?

If the first act was unpredictable, the second—which A. C. wrote as a traditional English music hall pantomime—is an Abbott and Costello movie run backward. The plot seems fairly simple, or so A. C. has been telling us for the past week. Actors portraying the rival doctors, Drummond and Singh, are instructed to fight over Bronwen. Singh must win by foul means, and is supposed to kidnap Bronwen, who is then rescued by a posse of heroic Con Housers. (Nobody is quite sure what A. C.'s message is, and he won't enlighten us beyond, "It's paragorical, old whack.")

It is a shambles from the word go.

Yorkshire Roy, turbaned and blacked up to resemble Dr. Singh (they both sport small moustaches), comes jabbing in, with blood in his eye for Barney Beaton designated by a placard around his neck as TRICKY DICKY. Noticeably cheered up by having an outlet for his aggression, Roy/Singh pummels Barney/Drummond with everything he's got. It was supposed to be a play-fight but when Barney socks back they slug away with gusto until A. C. has to separate them. Following his whispered orders, Barney kayos Roy to the patients' applause (the real Singh is not amused) and Tarzan-style drags 'Bronwen' under a table with paper roses tacked all around it, an idyllic cottage labeled CHINATOWN. Jeff H., who plays Bronwen, is fetching in white split-to-the-thigh skirt, a green scarf tied like a bra and red spike-heel shoes, an only slight parody of the Welsh nationalist colors the real Bronwen wears almost every day.

Offstage, to signal the next morning, an alarm clock rings. Tricky Dicky emerges from a night of love under the table, yawning and happily patting his privates. He carries a stethoscope and butterfly net, and has on a white coat, Drummond-type winkle-pickers and a jockstrap with sequins sewn into it. After passionately kissing Bronwen (Jeff H. likes this part), he entrechats around the room to catch his day's quota of loonies. Right here is where Roy/Singh is supposed to creep in and kidnap Bronwen, but Barney/Drummond refuses to stop his dance. "Stick tuh th' effin' script, ya bastid!" A. C. screams from his prompter's box in the corridor. Roy, stomping around now in stormtroop boots and a Wehrmacht helmet over his turban to emphasize the point A. C. wants to make, has to push Barney off. Then, twisting his crayon-enlarged moustache, Roy dives under the table to sexually attack 'Bronwen' who, instead of fainting as per script, begins to cuddle him. Roy kicks Jeff H. in disgust. "That's not how I wrote it!" yells A. C. Too late. Completely oblivious, Jeff and Roy tightly lock in a half-wrestling half-amorous embrace until Eric Raw, wearing red Indian feathers, jumps on top of them shouting, "It's all my fault, isn't it?"

Around now is when A. C.'s rescue party was supposed to charge in for the climax. In odds and ends of costume which A. C. 'borrowed' from Occupational Therapy—a policeman's helmet, cavalry sword and jodhpurs, KKK hood, caveman's skin, etc.—they shuffle onstage, led by Clem more than a little embarrassed but bravely carrying on. They're in total disarray, stumbling over one another like a Dad's army of a war yet to be fought, and despite A. C.'s frantic attempts to organize them, they begin to wander out the door—even an open window. With his beautiful script falling apart, A. C. does the only thing he can and rings down the curtain by herding his players back on stage in a well-rehearsed chorus of

> "I'd like to get you on a slow boat to China
> All to myself alone
> Get you and keep you in my arms ever more
> Leave all you lovelies weeping on the faraway shore. . . ."

A. C. then steps forward to deliver a Greavesian envoi:

> "And so we bid you fond goodbye
> We hope you liked our modest try
> Clem's away to have a ball
> Bronwen? Well, can't win 'em all."

After the applause, including his own, dies away Dr. Winstanley makes a special point of going over to congratulate the troupe. A. C. is depressed but philosophic. "Maybe I shouldn't've tried puttin' Method actors into music hall." Clem tries not to show his embarrassment.

Once the brass go the party loses momentum, and a sense of real loss breaks through: for the moment there we'd forgotten that Clem, our most successful part, is leaving. Boys high on smuggled wine race through the unit playing slightly drunken tag. Featherstone-the-Flasher ferociously play-masturbates to Percy's resumed blast furnace, while "What Do You Want if You Don't Want Money" rips the old walls apart. Derek Chatto weeps uncontrollably, "I've lost my king," and Greaves chases Mr. Wu up and down the stairs shrieking

> "Mingle
> Mongol."

Clem—the object of so much of this despair—staggers over to me, his eyes full of grief and anger. "Congratulate me, Sid. I've turned out to be a voyeur just like you. I didn't have the guts to go all the way to China, did I?" All his life he'll regret not having had a true schizophrenic breakdown. He knocks the notebook from my hand, but instead of scrapping about it we hug and kiss each other. Then, suddenly aware of what we're doing, we pull apart and turn on the most convenient target, Con House's Oblomov, Jeff H. For no really good reason we rail at his detached dreaminess and trancelike passivity, his lazy acquiescence to a condition others define for him. Still in his Bronwen dress, Jeff languidly defends himself while unbraiding his hair in the wall mirror. "Oh, I've taken some hard knocks since I was thirteen, I can tell you." (Jeff's orthodox Jewish family in Golders Green treated him as mad because he let his hair grow to shoulder length and refused to go to his father's funeral. On his eighteenth birthday he announced that he was really Ann-Margaret O'Hara from spaceship Moonglow and was going to dock with a bisexual cosmonaut named Evelyn. He claims that all his mother wanted to know was, "Is this Evelyn Jewish maybe?") When Jeff and Clem suddenly buddy up to compare suicide attempts, I leave in disgust. I hate it when schizos talk so easily of checking out. "To hell with both of you!" I shout, full of wine. "Don't go with a whimper, go with a bang!"

Like their patients, the Con House staff feel disconsolate and ill at ease, and they, too, snipe at each other, reopening old wounds and digging up long-forgotten slights. Dr. Dick, who is least adjusted to losing Clem and Bronwen, drunkenly wraps his arms around the latter. "This is your real, your first home—never forget that." Les glares tipsily at his boss. "Let her go, you bastard. You're trying to make this hellhole too attractive to her." With exaggerated dignity Dick straightens up and offers Bronwen a fulsome toast to a happy marriage, an existentially fruitful life, a— From the back of the crowd someone says: "He means he'd like to fuck you."

Followed by Dr. Singh's scowling eyes, Bronwen tearfully grabs my hand and leads me out to the wire-enclosed porch. "Oh Sid"—she clings to me under a full April moon—"I feel like a soldier going to a war I may never return from. Lewis can't go beyond the line, but he knows in his heart that The Beyond exists. I'm lost in the cold. I need your strength, to help me toward the Sacred Mountain, away from the Evil Prince." She lifts her face for me to kiss, then gothically fades away into the darkness.

A muffled explosion shakes the building.

I rush back inside to help drag Jeff H., coughing and spluttering, from the smoke-filled kitchen. Covered in soot black he collapses in a shaken but unhurt heap on the floor. "How's that for a bang not a whimper?"

Slowly, Con House's *geist*—lying in wait since morning—takes over. Things collapse after the women depart. Les and Dave, once again custodial, help several boys to their beds. Others are left where they drop, under tables and chairs. A few sad bodies float anticlimactically through the corridors, sober. Maleness, dry, charged, settles in again. Only Hurricane Hodge, who predicted an IRA outrage, strides smugly about.

The party is over.

Les O'Brien and I, left alone in the TV lounge, look at the empty cider and wine bottles, torn Yule decorations, broken furniture. Everyone is gone. He looks immensely tired. "Nobody's ever on to the other bloke. You travel all your life to find that. Haven't found it yet. We, none of us, would be here if we thought it existed."

Finishing his drink he fixes me with an unblinking stare. "And that," he murmurs, nodding at the party's debris, "is the best . . . the very best we can do."

3

Spring also crept into Clare Community Council.

By Easter Bank Holiday (I missed another Aldermaston march) we had shaken down to "oor fightin' weight," as Dr. Last put it. The dross—Clive Flynn and his ilk—we'd got rid of simply by letting them come to meetings. No stranger ever survived a Lastian interrogation. "Wha's th' point in suckin' up tae ootsiders," he declared. "Suiner or later they'll only find oot th' truith aboot us." And he'd giggle unhappily.

I thought that this blackballing of outlanders contradicted Last's stated policy of courting all possible allies, and said so. (After all, it had provoked my first quarrel with the group.) He looked right through me as if I wasn't there. Though I'd been elected chairman—admittedly, to keep me quiet—Last still ran Clare meetings in his own way. Head in hands, he punctuated the agenda with doleful comments on our shortcomings. "Dav, stop mumblin'. If ye've nuthin' tae say, shut up." "Git tae th' point, Boris. Yir Stalinist prattlin's drivin' me up th' wall." "Sid, I swear if ye was a mite more wi'drawn ye'd disappear up yir own arsehole."

Strangely, we lapped it up. Davina said, "Willie gives one such a feeling of being nobody, of not even existing. That's the first step to satori, isn't it?"

The plain truth is, we jumped whenever Last cracked his whip. His decisions, usually handed down in the form of soft-spoken suggestions or off-the-cuff guesswork, had the force of Law. A strange collective chemistry transformed even his slips of the tongue into group canon. Will-lessness emanated from us like plants stretching out to their light source, Willie Last.

Hell, I'd been through all this charismatic b.s. before, in American politics. And the other Clare members had been around, too. Why did we stick it?

If Last had been nothing but what he seemed—a vain, truculent stage Scotsman with a talent for "puttin' th' buit" into our emotional soft spots—we would never have followed (and loved) him so. He could also be sweet, tender and wise, caring, fatherly, without side or swank, retaining—even in fits of arrogant temper—that sly, warming grin, which seemed to say: "Och mon, what're we takin' oorselves so seriously fer?" He had a trick, of enticing you into dark, twisting mental labyrinths and then suddenly abandoning you to find your own way out, which we proudly thought of as his liberating us from "th' chains o' love." Though he made much of his dislike of the role of Master, which he said we foisted on him, he seemed to accept such eminence as we gave him with a humility that bordered on arrogance. At the same time as he poked fun at my habit of always calling him "Doctor Last," a respectful hangover from our previous analytical relationship, he made it equally clear that in practice Clare's democracy of souls meant he had every right to lash us for (among other things) our dependence on him. Perversely feeling more inferior with him than my previous mentors, I whipped myself on to get to "th' hahrt of th' matter," to become a master of No-Theng in my own right, and thus put an end to his discomfort at my fathomless stuipidity.

At bottom, of course, couch power dictated Clare relationships. Part of Last's abnormal authority over us came from our fear of blackmail. Not pure and simple blackmail but the possibility, however remote, that he would somehow exploit to our disadvantage the inmost crimes and disorders which, at one time or another, we had confessed to him in analysis, over drinks or on LSD. Our deepest emotions were locked into his. Yet perhaps our gravest disservice, to ourselves and to Last, was that we Clare members hardly ever discussed personal problems collectively, among ourselves—only with him. This put an intolerable psychological burden on him, which he vented with public lambastings of us that we never could be quite sure weren't rooted in what he'd learned about us privately. Whether he intended it or not, it was enough for us merely to know that he knew to produce an instant obedience among us.

There was also a feeling, which he discreetly encouraged, that he had picked each of us out of the Sludge of Error and firmly put us on the Road to Enlightenment. It got so that a word from him could make or break our day. He was our sun, moon and guiding star—understanding ("standin' under") us when we did not understand ourselves, redeeming past sins and absolving future mistakes, filling up the cracks in our broken souls. We needed him.

But why, I once asked him, did he need us?

Last chewed thoughtfully on his cigar and said, "Innair solitude is essential tae my personal voyage. An' I cannae imagine a settin' more congenial tae feelin' so utterly alone as oor li'l gruip."

> *In weaker men I would have called Last's aggressive despondency nothing but self-pity; in him it seemed to stem from the tragic detachment of a great seer who dares to look into the Abyss avoided by us lesser mortals. It wasn't only affectation that made him refer to us Clare Councillors as "terminal cases" and "lifeless shadows pretendin' tae be hyoomin." He genuinely perceived life as pure terror, a concentration camp to which we had been condemned by a hahrtless, random fate. Everything he measured by standards of Auschwitz. Mothers and fathers were kapoes of the bourgeois state, family love a crematorium. Not only Last but all three doctors were so spooked by, almost in love with, their patients' self-disgust and self-hatred that paltry human emotions like laughter and affection were considered "unseemly" (a favorite Last word), even a betrayal of the Task.*
>
> *"Serialization"—the modern individual's moral numbness—was our greatest ainemy, Last taught. Yet when Dick's father died in Canada of a stroke, not one Councillor offered him a word of sorrow or comfort, nor did he appear to expect any. When I asked why, Last said–as if explaining to an idiot that two and two make four–"How else d'ye think we presume tae call oorselves healers? We are th' disease we're tryin' tae cure."*

As an ex-committeeman myself I had to applaud Last's committee skills, which often dissolved my doubts and misgivings before they could become fully conscious. How he got us through all that dismal, boring business agenda I'll never know. His sardonic smile seemed forever challenging us to get bogged down in a morass of detail, and when (predictably enough) we did he'd suddenly shift gear. His face hardened, his back stiffened. One! two! three! he clipped off the items we had been floundering in. He had a genius for unraveling the knots we'd tied ourselves into (some of his making). Explaining, urging, directing—he sliced through our woofle to lift our tired, frazzled hearts. "Th' Task is tremenjus an' oor Covenant puir," he'd bark. "I c'n see in yir faces ye'd like tae pull oot. Right then! I'm willin'. This minute if you say." Silence. "Aw-right, le's strap up oor boots an'—*muive off!*"

("Cor," whispered Alf, tapping his chest, only half joking. "Gets you right here, doesn't it?")

A kind of martial chauvinism gripped Last then. "It's really funny when ye think on it," he said. "Millions of men destroyed like sheep in th' First War wi'oot sayin' baa. Even th' froggy French mutinied—th' servile sassenachs niver. An' ever since then th' milksop Ainglish'v'b'n like whipped puppies or chronic patients that niver got over their ECT." Once, goaded beyond her usual meekness, Davina muttered, "And what about your wonderful Scots, eh Willie?" He glared happily at her. "Oh *them.* Wi' their Wee Free consciences an' Red Clyde heritage *they'll* niver bow permanently tae th' Ainglish colonial whip." He warmed to his subject. "Y'know tha' flick *The Longest Day*—where th' Scots pipers lead th' whole Allied army ashore on D day? *Tha's* th' forgotten so'jery I'm daiscended fr'. *Tha's Scawtlan'!*"

He was the first native Scot I'd known well since my days with the United Auto Workers union in Detroit. Scottish-born UAWers had been the best guys on a picket line and the worst Stalinists in committees. What kind was Last? A romantic, left-wing nationalist, he regarded Scots like himself as "Jews," with the historic mission of filling the shoes of Europe's traditional intellectual-cosmopolitan elite, the Jews Hitler had murdered. He took more or less literally this self-elected Jewishness. England south of Carlisle was a "Diaspora," and Scotland, like pre-Israel Palestine, a marginal land of broken dreams. But one day soon the spark of a primitive, kirk-based egalitarianism—the democracy of souls snuffed out by the Culloden massacre and the Act of Union (1707)—would burst into vengeful flame, and Scotland (like

Dixie?) would rise again. Then he, William Angus Bruce Last would hurry back to his native lowlands to raise the consciousness of his awakening countrymen from mere bourgeois nationalism to the heights of the psychic revolution.

"But first I'm gointa plunder th' fucken Ainglish like they did us fer 250 years!"

If Last hated England so, why didn't he follow the examples of men he admired like Aldous Huxley and Alan Watts and emigrate, to America or elsewhere? I asked. He shook his head and said, "Nae doot that's what they'd *like. I won't give 'em th' satisfaction." He refused to desert his post on the lawng Ainglish wall because, he claimed, here was where it was all happening. London was the Vienna of the 1960s, the Havana of the schizophrenic revolution.*

Did Last see himself as a latter-day Freud or a psychiatric Castro?

Smiling modestly, he allowed the question to be its answer.

Freud and Castro probably never had the trouble with their followers that Last said he had with his. He ceaselessly nagged at our "puir covenant," our lack of commitment to one another, and demanded that we speed up the process of britherhuid. If we simply sat back to wait for fraternal bonds to grow naturally, the gravitational pull of existential apathy—"oor innate drive tae mediocrity, which we use as armor against cosmic risk"—would destroy us. In some crucial way the fate of millions depended on the quality of personal relationships we achieved within the group. "If sech hahrtless shits as us c'n fill each uther's Emptiness, there's still hope fer a broken-hahrted wurld." Last drove us into mutual affection as if we were conscript soldiers storming an impregnable fort. He insisted that we dine together whenever possible and also make positive efforts to learn about each other's problems (though he did not see the death of Dick's father as one such problem). All the while he kept repeating; "Close ranks, Brithers—or die!"

We tried to love each uther, but it was a hard, often embarrassing slog. In an England notorious for its reticence, and where friendships less than fifty years old are considered brief encounters, our attempts to warm each other up were stiff and clumsy. "I suppose Willie's right to force the pace this way," said Major

Straw ruefully, "but, dash it, I wish he'd given us a bit more basic training before we set off." Even I, used to an American style of easy intimacy, found it hard to achieve Last's sort of sponsored love. But gradually, annealed by acid and countless drives into the countryside to inspect estates, his policy *did* begin to pay off. Those terrible English barriers relaxed. "Gee fellas, that's super," moaned Alf when we took turns massaging his slipped disk. I gladly sheltered Major Straw from his wife's private detectives (she was suing for divorce), Alf baby-sat for the Drummonds. Viv Petkin taught Davina how to cook Boris' favorite dishes. "Vegetarian he may now be," Viv said complacently, "but my Boris likes it *tasty.*" Friday nights, *shabboth,* we ate communally at a meatless restaurant in Leicester Square.

Around Last buds of britherhuid burst into bloom, a little garden of fellowship where we could begin to discover tiny areas of common interest. What surprises! Boris and Major Straw found that they'd soldiered at the same camp in India. (Boris, an army medic, smuggled pistols to the nationalist agitators; then Lt. Tony Straw shot them down in pre-Partition riots.) Alf and I had identical birthdays, Davina and Last were Sagittarians. Dick and Alf both were hooked on Woody Guthrie, and Davina had been at school with an old girl friend of mine. Last was satisfied that these were more than trivial coincidences; somehow they sanctified our union. In an ever-growing atmosphere of the need for such mystical confirmation, the group temporarily submitted to my jotting down more of their biographies.

Little by little my Clare Council identikits took on light and shade. Davina talked to me in between making us sandwiches and coffee, writing up the minutes, nursing us through LSD trips and even mending our socks. I learned that after a High Anglican games mistress had platonically seduced her at school Davina had tried to enter a convent. "Mummy and Daddy couldn't have been more horrified. Drawing attention to myself that way. I suppose they thought my wanting to be a nun was pushy and vulgar. Anyway," she smiled sadly, "it wasn't my dish of tea. I'm afraid 'Woman's Hour' at the BBC was the nearest to it I could find."

I was lucky enough to tackle Dick Drummond at the right moment—during a three-day whiskey and acid binge. (All that booze was adding pounds to his already corpulent frame, which was starting to look like the asexual Buddha Last said was the physical aspect of gaw'd-haid.) Dick had rebelled against his wealthy Montreal parents by going to Black Mountain, a radical North Carolina college, and marrying a black student there. In the 1950s the Border Patrol had caught him helping to smuggle into Canada a couple of New York Communists dodging the Smith Act, but only Dick got probation. All his other comrades got prison terms. Convinced that his parents had pulled strings in order to castrate him, he fled to Europe and psychotherapy (on their money). "Dialectically speaking, it was the perfect start for an existential outlaw. I became a revolutionary Bolshevik of consciousness against all my upbringing and conditioning. I raped my bourgeois mind to bring it back to life."

Boris was his old charming self, and I beat a hasty retreat before he could start yelling at me again.

To bind us even closer together, Last hired a projection room in Wardour Street, Soho, and for an entire afternoon had Major Straw lecture us on small-squad tactics while we watched war documentaries. Then Last split us up into two-man 'buddy' teams—"tae cover yir partner's blind side in everyday matters," and thus leave our minds freer to concentrate on the assault approach to Infinity, he said.

Dr. Last	chose	Dick Drummond
Boris	"	Davina
Major Straw	"	Alf

Nobody picked me.

Being buddyless was an honor, Last persuaded me. "There's nae point tae slowin' ye doon tae oor snail's pace. From now on, ye're a collective responsibility. We'll protect ye Crossin' th' Great Water."

Oh.

Still, I couldn't help feeling that he was getting revenge on me for somehow letting him down. Well, I'd *tried* to recruit the cultural big shots he'd badgered me about. But Danny Fior, my playwright friend, had just shrugged, "Honestly Sid, I don't see much for myself in your group. Plays about Rasputin always bomb in the West End." Coral was equally indifferent though I'd heard that she was quietly playing the same hunch as me. "Christ, darling. Do I have to? My next novel is all about how the world nearly ends and is saved by the mentally ill. From what I'm told, if I met your dotty Scots boyfriend I might have to change the last chapter and it's already written."

To be fair to Last, he probably didn't do anything to me he didn't do to the others. But I mediated my emotions so exclusively through him that it was impossible to check this out. Hence, I felt sure that I must be the only weed in his rose garden, and to keep my anxiety at bay I moved around taking notes compulsively. If a Councillor objected, Last shushed him by diagnosing my scribbles as an 'illness,' which ought to be respected "like any uther form of schizophrenia." Once he convinced them that their talking to me was part of my therapy, I had no further trouble collecting further fragments of my Brithers' histories.

Alf's life turned out to be a rural horror tale. After he had almost brained his mother in a homicidal rage and then botched his own suicide-by-drowning, a Dorset magistrate committed him to the mental hospital that Dr. Last worked in. "The first doctor I saw was Willie. He looked down at me and said, 'Och mon, she probably deserved it.' It was just like getting a Royal pardon." Alf felt that he owed his very life to Last, and wisely safeguarded his adjutant's post by steering clear of LSD and ideas he couldn't handle. Of the Sartre and Eliade paperbacks I carried around with me he said: "Yeah, Willie started me off on that stuff, too. The side effects almost killed me."

Major Straw was still the hardest for me to figure. Which made two of us, since—like Con House's Robin Ripley—he abominated introspection. As far as he'd thought it out, his presence in the group was a logical culmination of his early religious training (his father had been active in church affairs) and later military career. "It's a gut feeling, I suppose. Willie's version of brotherly self-sacrifice and a Higher Design—it's just the Golden Rule with a little spit and polish added, isn't it? And, who knows, maybe all this pounds, shillings and pence stuff (LSD) will solve my old drink problem." Loosened up by acid and Last's frequent references to the bisexuality of the Life Force, the Major went around slapping our bottoms and physically embracing us on all possible occasions—everyone, that is, except Davina on whom he'd conceived a romantic schoolboy crush. "Th' gel's absolutely topping—one of the chaps, really."

Even Boris Petkin slightly thawed now that chatting with me could be viewed as 'treatment.' I found out that we actually shared an experience: Coral, whom he had briefly psychoanalyzed on her rebound from Jung to Subud. "Daft woman passed through me like a dose of salts. Pretty promiscuous, analytically speaking."

So it went. Every day revealed new links drawing Clare Council together in the now smaller village of London. What a fantastically close-knit community 'the smoke' was, once you got to know people.

Weeks, then months passed without our finding a Place. Alf, who had practically abandoned his travel agency to work full time on Clare business, reported that several times he had almost clinched a deal for an empty house, but the Borough Council or private angel had reneged at the last minute. "That word schizophrenic puts them off," Alf said. "Why don't we switch to something more acceptable like ax murderers or child rapists?"

Superficially, things were going badly. The Ministry of Health, to whom we appealed for support, told us to get lost, and influential sponsors wouldn't touch us with a barge pole. The group 'kitty" was almost broke. Despite such setbacks, group morale was surprisingly high. Last's constant exhortations to love one another or die were bearing fruit, in closer relationships and a generally tighter feeling among us. Yet the strange thing was, Last couldn't stand it. Several times I noticed that no sooner did the group groove in a fairly affectionate way than he was moved—driven, almost—to torpedo its precarious stability. It was eerie, to summon up tentatively friendly feelings toward a Brither and then to have Last say that you'd fallen into "slawbby sentimentality" or some other form of spiritual flabbiness.

The latest form of his ambivalence was speak-bitterness sessions. "Self-criticism on the Chinese model," as Dick Drummond described it, became a Clare Council art form. Led by Last, we Councillors kept in existential shape by socking it to one another. Originally, to show us how, he'd teed off on Boris—blam, right between the eyes. In front of us all he flayed Boris for incompetence, greed, emotional exploitation of and fatal insensitivity to his patients: all the sins in the medical book. "An' mon, ye're even stahrtin' tae *lewk* like all those pre-Raphaelite virgins ye tout fer." (Petkin's specialty was middle-aged spinsters.) Boris, who was used to Last's needling, sometimes played dumb or sometimes fought back according to the tactical advantage he gained. "Willie," he'd sneer, "you may smarm th' top people better than me. But when it comes to the sheer athletics of the job—sitting in that chair without moving a muscle for fifty minutes—I've got you beat hands down." If it suited him, Boris pretended to be deaf, or else deflected Last's fusillades onto Dick Drummond, who was coming up fast on the inside to challenge Boris' position as Last's No. 1 medical collaborator. "I'da fuckin' sight rather cream a few lonely old biddies," Boris snapped, "than get my rocks off on a gang of underripe pubescent psychotics. Watcha tryin' to do, Dick, jolt 'em back to sanity with that outfit?" (Drummond's latest ensemble included an off-mauve patch pocket suit and black Borsalino hat.) Here as in Conolly House Dick's counterpunches were disguised as self-libel. "What's the point, Boris? Why waste your breath on a deracinated First World turd like me?"

Last's other gambit was to play the doctors off against each other by 'protecting' the underdog with hurtful slurs (a technique of his I knew painfully well). "Don' jes' sit there, Dick—it's th' puir mon's way of beggin' fer frien'ship." Or, "Stop insultin' Dick, Boris. Cain't ye see he likes it." Provoked to lam away at each other, Boris and Dick writhed like puppets in the grip of Last's remote-control aggression—until, with a gracious smile, he chose to release them. "I ken how 'tis," he patted Boris' shoulder affectionately, "I'd suin lose my finesse too, if I had tae knock off Viv every night." And he and Boris, two working-class boys sharing a dirty joke, would laugh quietly, conspiratorially. Or Last would wink at Drummond. "What's wrong, Dick? Nancy bellyachin' agin?" Dick's face sagged. "Oh Willie, if only you knew," thus reestablishing intimacy with the man who was selling him and his wife down the river. I suspected that down deep Last hungered for us to stand up to him; at some level, he hated the toadiness he inspired. But we denied him this pleasure. Indeed, Boris and Dick knuckled under so slavishly—which egged Last on to such extremes of vituperation—that I sometimes wondered if they weren't 'setting up' our leader, but dismissed these thoughts as unworthy of a true comrade.

As time went on a pattern of brotherly recrimination developed, often reflecting the current state of play for Last's love. Combat rules were arbitrary. While Last considered all six Councillors as fair game, only the doctor-samurai had the right (however unexercised) to nail him. Attempts by Alf, Tony, me or Davina to grab a piece of the action were snubbed with a curt nod or glassy stare: sailf-criticism was an officer's prerogative. We noncoms, divided among ourselves by Last's system of capriciously shifting his affections from one Brither to another, compensated by hassling each other. When I tried rallying the other nonmedics against the doctors' elitism I ran into the old CP-style taboo on 'inner-party factions,' and Alf promptly reported my behavior to Last.

Lapdogs aren't always loved, and Last spared no one—not even informers. "Cannae ye lift yir snout outta th' trough of slawbby pragmatism just once, Alf?" he would demand. Or he'd skewer Straw for just those virtues the Major most prided himself on. "Ye've swallered other people's orders so long, Brither Tony, ye've gone all soft an' cringy." Of me Last said: "Every time Sid sticks his cock intae th' twat of success he wi'draws it afore he c'n come. A flyaway bird fueled by curiosity an' a mortal terror of commitment."

But it was poor Davina who got the worst of his tongue. Something about her cool upper-class manner got Last's goat. Once, as we were driving back exhausted from yet another wild-goose chase into rural Hertfordshire, he suddenly roused himself at her expense, working himself up to such a pitch of proletarian fury that I thought he'd slug her or blow a gasket. He accused her of class exploitation, of freeloading to salvation on the backs of her social inferiors—the Clare men. "Wha' th' hail d'yew rich bitches know aboot th' stagnant shit at th' bottom of society's cesspool—my people! Or are ye jes slummin, Dav?"

Blushing in the backseat of the Bentley, Davina gestured weakly. "Oh I know you all think I'm a mouse. But you try getting a word in edgeways with six shouting bullies." At once, Last braked the big car on a country lane. "Okeh," he said, "fair enough. Now ever'body but Dav shut up. Fer five minutes there'll be complete silence while she says anythin' on hir mind." He glanced down at his vest-pocket watch. "Stahrtin' . . . now." He raised and dropped his arm like a race starter. Finally, Boris came to Davina's rescue by yawning loudly. "Drop it, Willie. You can be a real prick at times." Davina sneaked Boris a grateful smile, and they sat closer on the trip back.

> *Meetings were like indoor rodeos where riderless animals and horseless cowboys tumbled each other into the dust. Or an intolerably sandbagging poker game sans limit. How much could—would—the Other take? In the doctors' vision of Hell, hope existed only in the microscopically small spaces between institutionalized madness and existential therapy, and we danced a high-wire act of muted violence stretching from one meeting to the next.*
>
> *A terrible fear—of rejection? uselessness?—seemed at times to make us emotionally drunk. As if—call and response—we had to match the true schizophrenic's sense of loss. "It's perfectly unnerstan'able," affirmed Last. "Characters who cannae say a significan' hal-lo tae one another are doomed tae a perpetual state of farewell."*
>
> *Having evolved techniques of emotionally lassoing a Brither Councillor without drawing him to us (which would be a violation of our nonimprisonment code), we stood off at a psychic distance, giving playful little tugs on our invisible ropes. The resulting pain, Last assured us, was designed "tae toughen th' Other against oor most formidable ainemy, th' fear of th' fear of loss, so tha' wi' each karate kick we render oorselves slightly less sensitive tae Draid."*

The goal was freedom, from bourgeois hypocrisy, from neurotic hangups. Above all, from the need to be needed, starting with psychoanalysis, the basis of our association. "Nuthin'," averred Last, "gies me more satisfaction tha' seein' some puir dailuded bastid tell his shrink tae fuck off." Boris promised, "One day they'll give an analysis and nobody will come." "The therapist who gives up his patient commits a revolutionary act," said Dick Drummond. Dapper little Major Straw looked dubious. "It's fine for you fellers, you've been commissioned in the field. But what about us Other Ranks who've just enlisted?"

For, despite everything, we were still prisoners of the psychoanalysis we rejected. Alf hopped up occasionally on Last's couch, and Davina saw Boris professionally as well as personally. Tony Straw went to Dick Drummond on the side, and offstage, Last saw *his* training analyst, Dr. Phineas Maud, as did Boris and Dick theirs. And, of course, the doctors' incomes were still based on good old-fashioned capitalist transference.

The pecking order went something like this:

Completely analyzed	Last
Almost c.a.	Drummond
Partly a.	Boris, Alf
Novice a.	Davina
Un-a.	Tony

When I showed my journal, with this notation, to Last he frowned, "An' where do ye stand? Outside-a.?"

Perhaps the most painful irony of speak-bitterness was that its instigator, Willie Last, was himself the chief victim. Chinese-style sessions left him depressed and drained. ("Postcriticism blues," Alf called it.) At such moments he openly doubted that we'd make it as a group, because the very qualities that had brought us together—"spiritual funk, ontological despair an' a simple feelin' of goin' rotten at th' core"—would sink us. "Then ye'll stahrt luikin' fer yir Chosen Victim," leaving the rest just hanging in the air. Always these days, under cover of his stringent search for fellowship, Last's gentle gray eyes furtively sought out his Betrayer. He was calmly, almost serenely certain that one or other of the Councillors would do him in, and he absolved us in advance. "Oh, ye'll nae do it on purpose. Judas probably had th' best of motives, too. . . ." His likening himself to Jesus, which had begun as a joke, sounded more serious nowadays.

His evident disappointment in us went hand in hand with a revival of fondness for outsiders. The more he found Clare Council wanting the more he foraged (again) for strangers to put us right . . . find the house . . . tone up our souls . . . or straighten out our finances. Someone to fill the vacuum our lack of commitment (he said) created. Every month or so, right on schedule, such a fairy godperson appeared. The portents were always the same: under new business, Last would clear his throat and say, "Er oh yeh, I wuz lunchin' t'other day wi' Larry Olivier at L'Escargot"—he took a child's pleasure in dropping show-biz names and the restaurants he ate in—"an' Ringo (or Vanessa or Sean) came over tae oor table an' tol' me aboot this fan*tas*tick frien' of theirs willin' tae help us. . . ."

And so shoals of new fish swam into view. Always with talents we allegedly couldn't do without: a clairvoyant Romanian businesswoman, a Swedish ethnographer just back from a study of Haitian voodoo, an emotionally cracked-up BOAC pilot fleeing a Detention Order, a lonely Somerset bachelor with a derelict farm and a passion for UFOs, etc.

Two newcomers, Frisbie Blue and Sy Appleby, almost took.

Place: Armistice Hall, a Quaker-pacifist country house outside Dorking, Surrey

Time: A Friday evening in early June

Event: A weekend conference between NON-RUT (spell it backward), a "multimedia intercommunications network" of fashionable working-class poets, action artists and ex-Committee of 100 militants still looking for a way to blast the public conscience; and Clare Council representing existential psychiatry-cum-Eastern metaphysics. In effect, a Mafia summit of Britain's madness radicals.

Things aren't going too well.

Even before the conference officially opens, a thick wall of suspicion separates the two supposedly fraternal groups. Boris Petkin makes no secret of his contempt for the "lumpens" personified by Frisbie's henchman, the American junkie novelist Sy Appleby. Most NON-RUTters couldn't care less for Clare Council's heavy eschatological view of the world. But it's too late to back out now because Last has shelled out thirty quid of our money to rent Armistice Hall for two days.

It doesn't start well. Friday evening Sy overdoses and collapses during Boris' talk on "The Hasid Way to Tao"; Tony Straw takes a swing at a NON-RUTter baiting the Army's imperialist role in

Malaya (where Straw served). A second punchup is narrowly averted when a NON-RUT satyr runs off into the woods with Davina, and it takes several of us to restrain a fiercely jealous Boris. NON-RUT is all over the place, doping, free-form painting and fucking in the bedrooms (not yet on the parlor carpet, that will happen tomorrow), while Clare Council huddles together like a tourist party of nuns strayed into a Paris brothel. Nobody really wants to talk to anybody else. In disgust, Clare Council votes to pack its bags and go in the morning.

Saturday A.M. Phineas Maud, Last's father-figure, arrives with a contingent of elderly ladies. When Alf reports that several of them look like wealthy widows, we decide to stay.

All Saturday, operating in relays, Clare Council relentlessly hammers away at the politics of madness. Before this, we and NON-RUT had insulted each other lustily; now we try persuasion. The two organizations, Last argues, are capable of providing the natural "generals" in the war against bourgeois society's (in)sanity. "We both attack th' same problem fr' a different angle, is all. But p'raps Clare Council's angle is th' more . . . er, ah . . . acute." Last dogmatically concludes that our perception of the dialectics of schizophrenia—the assault on capitalism through its soft underbelly of the normal family—is more revolutionary than NON-RUT's concept of struggle through art and "th' mindless banality of marchin' tae hear th' sound of yir own feet." The conference almost breaks up as Sy explodes, "Shit man, your old Marxist cunt juice is dissolvin' this happening. We're splitting." At a hurriedly convened caucus in an upstairs bathroom Last dryly orders a change in tactics. "We're nae exactly overwhelmin' them wi' oor icy logic. So whyn't we drap oor defenses an' interact wi' their experiential mode?" Translated: Alf had just said that he was making too many useful contacts among Dr. Maud's flock of well-heeled geriatrics to go now. We plunge into NON-RUT's thing.

Not in Conolly House's maddest moments have I seen anything quite like this. A NON-RUT painter aerosols a wall, another hangs polystyrene stalactites from the chandeliers. "In the holy name of antiugly" a girl strips off to do a nude dance in the greenhouse next door, and Frisbie Blue contemplates slicing the music room's 150-year-old tapestries to shreds as his statement on bourgeois art, but gives a poetry reading instead. We Councillors dig the scene, too. While Last revives Sy who has OD'd again, Davina strums her guitar and warbles off-key flamenco to Phineas Maud's elders beaming uneasily at Major Straw and me dancing cheek to cheek to some old Joe Turner records I've brought. Boris stalks drunken Davina who exults, "I say, one has had more passes made at one here in twenty-four hours than in all the time one has been a Clare Brother . . . Sister . . . Brister." Last and Sy boozily drag race their cars across the fields.

Late Saturday afternoon, Dr. Maud insists on reading his paper, "Time Is the Healer But Who Is the Patient?" He doesn't get very far. Frisbie and his girl friend begin a silent dance of the flowers around him, which Sy films with a 16 mm camera. Bewildered but tolerant, Phineas keeps lecturing through a shower of marigolds flung at him by the girl, but falters when she peels off to bump and grind. Abruptly, Phineas stops when she wants to unzip his fly. Dr. Last shouts alcoholically, "Show 'em yir life force, Finny. Or di' ye hock it along wi' yir soul t'all those superannuated biddies ye're gigeloin' fer?" The aged doctor, now white-faced with anger, tells his entourage to collect their luggage and then leads them out the French windows. (A lovemaking couple have barricaded the front door with their bodies.) The last we see of them is a procession of Daimlers and Rolls-Royces disappearing down the driveway. "There goes our potential bankroll," moans Alf. "Why couldn't Willie have worked out his Oedipal conflicts somewhere else?"

For the next twelve hours we all sing, dance, read theoretical papers, break the family piano, nurse Sy out of a cocaine trauma, turn on the gardener and film-tape record ourselves for posterity. We and NON-RUT separate before the police—called by Armistice Hall's pacifist owners who have sat up all night with shotguns on their knees—arrive. Speeding wildly away in Last's Bentley we Clare Councillors feel great. "Tha'," says Last, "is how tae *meet!*"

Soon afterward we hear that Sy and Frisbie have abandoned art for commerce to open up a striptease club in Manchester.

Armistice Hall left behind a sour taste (not to speak of hangovers). If NON-RUT was a sample of what to expect from "th' ootside wurld," to hell with it, and we relapsed into an embattled, defensive xenophobia where all strangers were presumed guilty until proved otherwise. Willie Last, temporarily confounded, turned his attention inward, from persons to ideas.

Last's decision—to seclude himself at home "tae wurk oot one or two things fer myself"—gave us a temporary respite from his hectoring, and group tension eased a little. The Councillors had a rare chance to unwind. Including Mr. Stiffneck, Boris Petkin, who junked his sweaty old workman's rig and smartened up with flowered shirts and sandals to make himself more attractive to Davina. The effect was more like a beatnik Godzilla than anything else.

Normally uncongenial (as only ex-Party members can be), Petkin and I grew closer after Armistice Hall. "You were the only serious person there—aside from me," he said. We had been the only Clare members not to pass out. Before long we developed an almost therapeutic relationship, in which I (usually stoned) sat listening to Boris' problems: his dying marriage to Vivienne . . . his guilt at being infatuated with a "class enemy" (Davina) . . . his pride at achieving, if by a detour, Grandfather Petkin's dream that one day little Boris would grow up to be a famous *tsaddik* . . . his past deprivations and heartsores. Boris' harrowing tales of his Whitechapel boyhood outdid in pure horror even those Last and I spun. "Compared to me, you and Willie were practically born with silver spoons in your mouths," bragged Boris, the eldest of six raggedy children of a demented mother who died in an asylum and a father who tried burning up the family along with his tailor shop. "My soul was murdered on the cobblestones of Commercial Road—I'm dead, an emotional corpse," he wept. Clinging to me for support he confessed: "Mine is a psychosis of indifference. I cannot give freely. All my life I've been looking for a community to set this undead ego of mine at rest." Just when I half-dissolved in pity, Boris jerked up his head. "My one hope is the group. Helping me back to my lost karma. But we cannot relent."

Relent? "Yes. In ultimate circumstances we must execute heretics. Or exile them. If the disciples of Jesus and Baal Shem Tov hadn't lost their nerve, none of us would be so tightly strapped to the Wheel of Existence. The best thing we ever did was to banish Clive Flynn. D'you reckon it would've been kinder to kill him?"

Boris started coming to my flat, to escape from Vivienne's migraine protests and, surprisingly, to take acid. Politically he still didn't approve of LSD, but rationalized it as his contribution toward forestalling a take-over of the psychic revolution by "social democrat opportunists"—Tim Leary, Ken Kesey and R. D. Laing.

We prayed together—Boris in Hebrew, I in shaman-jabber (pig latin mixed with Oms) to match his swaying wail. His immense, hairy body naked except for *yarmulke* and black tapes pressed to his forehead and wound round his ham-size arm, he moaned 'our' Diasporic loss. "You and I, Schlomo, must awaken Brother Alf. An unawakened Jew is a dead Jew." (I thought: but Alf is C of E.) Ever interested in self-improvement, Alf came over but recoiled when we asked him to strip and take LSD. "I don't mind taking off my clothes—but can't you put on a little heat first?" Boris and I were climbing the Tree of Life when Alf said, "You know, this stuff makes me nauseous," and vomited. Poor Alfie: we cried for hours over his spiritual failure. But two acid-dropping Jews like Boris and me were a *minyan* anywhere else.

After ritually exchanging my Siberian rattle and Papuan sacred beads for Boris' skullcap and phylacteries, we chanted "Hatikvah," the Israeli national anthem—ending "Masada—NEVER AGAIN!"—and Boris asked Davina to join us. I, reluctant to pollute our monastic purity, argued against it, but he was keen to penetrate her upper crust. I gave Dav the lowest possible dose, 50 mg. Boris and I, on 500 mg, were grunting our way back to ancient Palestine ("Hold on, you sodding buggers, we're coming to the rescue") when Davina stirred.

"Fuck me," she said. Boris and I, busy holding back the *bubelah*-eating Roman hordes, didn't hear.

"Fuck me!"

Stripped, solemn, Davina sat cross-legged, Buddha, in each hand a breast pointed at each of us.

"In the name of Abraham, woman, where is your sense of decency?" cried Boris. She leaned back on her elbows, smiling but still gunning her tits at us. I got up to move out of range.

"No, you don't," she said. "Gotcha covered."

"HARLOT! JEZEBEL! HAVE YOU NO SHAME, YOU WHORE OF BABYLON!" roared Boris. Davina reached over, lazily tweaking his completely erect prick. She turned to me. "I think I'll have you."

After packing off Davina, I comforted Boris, who sobbed, "Can't you see, Schlomo, she's trying to drive a wedge between us."

Alas, as soon as Boris sobered up he put me back on his Enemies List, and added the seduction of Davina to my other doctrinal crimes. To replace him I asked the Major over for LSD cocktails. One Sunday he swayed unsteadily on my doorstep. He'd already taken some acid. "Greetings, Sid-the-Superman. Shall we go up, UP and AWAY-Y-Y!" He swallowed 500 mg, then another 250. Eight hours later, when I came down, he was sobbing in my arms. "I've never done anything like that before. Promise you won't tell."

Tell what? I'd been away in Medina talking to Mohammed and hadn't a clue what the Major was on about.

A few nights later Dr. Last materialized at my place. He had lost weight and his eyes glinted with an unnatural brightness which I recognized as the result of a long, private LSD trip. He had been back in circulation a day or two, and wanted to warn me about something he'd heard in the group.

What was that?

"It's Boris. Ye've made an ainemy there fer life. He goes aroun' tellin' th' Brithers ye're th' rotten apple in oor barrel. What did ye do tae him anyway?" After filling me up with anxiety about Boris' intentions toward me, Last assured me that he was on my side.

After Last left, I dumped my worries into the lap of Davina, whose basic steadiness (except on LSD) I found increasingly comforting. "Oh, didn't you know?" she said. "Willie and Boris have hardly been on speaking terms since Armistice Hall. Each accuses the other of wrecking our golden opportunity to 'milk the bourgeoisie.' Willie's probably canvassing for your support."

Thank Gaw'd he still needed me.

To my intense pleasure, Last began courting me all over again. And it wasn't only to line me up against Boris. He wanted company in a new venture.

Mother Amelia entered our lives.

A bangled, Margaret Rutherford–looking woman in a Gypsy skirt and bandanna, she read fortunes in a small dark room above an Old Brompton Road tea shop. "Hyoomunly speakin', of course," said Last, taking me up for the first time, "she's a silly ould bitch. But her command over th' Dark Powers is sum'thin' else."

Amelia never charged us Councillors for readings. "We're all in the same fight, dearies," she trilled over her green baize table.

Singly and in pairs we trooped upstairs to confer with her. Almost always she recommended holidays abroad. (She sometimes sounded more like a Pan Am ad than a spiritualist.) "Brother Bell rides furthest and wears the lightest armor," she told Last. "He is in the greatest danger from Old Nick. I would advise a fortnight in Kitzbühel and plenty of Bio-Strath in honey to clear the mucous membranes."

Mother Amelia was only the tip of the thaumaturgical iceberg.

I should have seen it coming but it loomed out of our fog unobtrusively at first, in bits and pieces. Among the early warning signs had been Last's literal interpretations of his patients' (and his own) psychotic visions. ("I *was* at Troy.") And I suppose the timing came from his feelings of political despair and isolation after our failure to cement the link with NON-RUT at Armistice Hall. Whatever the ins and outs, Last broke his seclusion to announce: "Brithers, *magic* is th' rock tae take oor stand on. It is th' class struggle carried on in uther-wurldly terms."

Somehow he had synthesized science fiction and existentialism with Lenin, Harry Stack Sullivan and Aleister Crowley, 'the Beast 666.' After first distributing copies of Asimov and *The Dawn of Magic*, he said we could no longer wait to reveal our ultimate objective: namely to reenter the occult mainstream forced underground by two millennia of Establishment suppression. We must reopen our minds, darkened by long centuries of scientific rationalism, to the whole spectrum of original insights which went under the name of wizardry, or magic. Throughout the ages, Last preached, a titanic duel—between the Galactic Guides, or white witches, versus "th' Overlords of Night," or "th' Dark Kings of Belial"—had been waged for control of the Pearl of Knowledge.

Politics was simply the modern name we gave to this struggle, backwards and forwards in time, to gain access to long-hidden founts of supernatural wisdom. In this interpretation, psychiatry was but the latest mask worn by the Devil in his ancient conspiracy to destroy Light. Thus seen, the Nazis were in reality an anti-Rosicrucian plot, Mussolini a corrupted warlock possibly from hyper-space. Trotsky had been murdered not for crimes against the Stalinist bureaucracy but for possessing secret galactic powers. Even the 1926 General Strike had been a late-flowering Gnostic heresy.

"Don't lewk so put oot, Brither Sid." Last, noticing my startled expression, brushed aside my stuttered objection that perhaps politics concerned the struggle for economic power. Couldn't I see—he asked with the superbly confident air of student nurse Bert Karp telling me about the pH factor—that my youthful Marxism was only a pitifully clumsy attempt to retrieve a memory of something lost hundreds of years before I was born? In some dim way I must have sensed this, he said, for by outgrowing the rigid rationality of the Old Left I had unwittingly made my own "leap intae th' Light." "Subjectively, ye may've thought ye were breakin' oota stereotyped Stalinism—but willy-nilly ye've landed up where th' real action is, in th' Principality of Unreason." My lingering doubts he wiped away with a grandly liberal flourish. "There are many ways tae skin' th' spiritual cat—an' every road leads tae . . . Lhasa."

Well, perhaps it did make sense. Certainly we Old Lefties had struck out for reasons that never *quite* added up.

"Tha's right," Last said. "Ye thought of everything—except th' superstructure's superstructure."

Soon I didn't turn a hair when Councillors criticized someone not for their stupidity but for their "low astrological sign." Or at Last's "When a patient tells me she's jes' come fr' another planet, and is so sure, th' integrity of her statement slices my rationality off at th' knees." He leaned forward a little, seriously, "*Of course she's bin thar!*"

I'm not sure which changed first, Last's ideology or his lifestyle. Both seemed to come together, a new passionate commitment to sci-fi mysticism and a sartorial transformation. Suddenly he was out of his funeral-black suits and those incredible lace-up ankle boots and into Indian cotton shirts flowing over white linen trousers and gaily embroidered slippers. (So *that's* where Boris got the idea.) Alf, a constant visitor at Number 4 Crimea Street, reported that Last's escape into nonattachment and Eastern clothes was causing a lot of domestic havoc. "Sybil says Willie's sworn off eating meat and fucking her. And she says she'll strangle him if he doesn't take a bath soon." To us Last merely referred to his troubled marriage as a "demonic pseudoreality, an illusion I've stopped believin' in." *Real* reality was the self-liberating search for Paradise Lost, "tae discover who among us are Captains of Armies, Lords of Battle and exiled Princes of th' time continuum."

Like a housewife anxious to keep up with the galactic Joneses, I kept fretful track of how my Brothers hunted down their lost pre- and posttwentieth-century selves: who had been who when. To discover his primordial essence, Last spent his lunch breaks studying Asimov and Arthur C. Clarke or at the British Museum reading room browsing acid high through musty volumes of Tibetan and Sikkimese theology. Boris, who had taken up Yiddish folk dance, hora'd his way back to Essenian Galilee, while Alf dickered with the possibility that he was a Glastonbury Druid from outer space. Trying to reunite with the ur-logos, Dick Drummond woke up from a mescaline trance to assert: "I am ka-ka, the universal shit"; he also began hanging around the primate cages at Regent's Park zoo. "Bloody big buggers know something we've forgotten." And Major Straw, after weeks of delving through archives down at Somerset House on the Strand, proudly announced: "I am the seventh son unto the seventh son unto the direct line of descent from the great Saxon warrior kings. Henceforth please call me Brother Hengist." Poor Davina felt out of it. "I'm hopeless. Tunbridge Wells through and through. (Pause) Come to think of it, just before the war some Gypsies did come through. . . ."

With Mother Amelia's help I located myself as Father Sebastien, a thirteenth-century Provençal monk sent to England to propagate the secret faith. "A bit *moderne* tha'," suggested Last. "Wi' a li'l more research ye oughttae hit th' Byzantine Empire at least."

Research? Immediately I taxied down to my favorite mystic bookshop in Charing Cross. "What, you again?" exclaimed the owner. "Don't tell me you've forgotten something. You practially cleared us out of stock last time." Afraid I might have overlooked something, I took home yet another armload of books on ESP, astrology, alchemy and flying saucers. In a moment of sobriety Dick cautioned me: "Don't take our statements too literally, Brother Sid. They are meta-remarks structured to commemorate the tragic incomprehensibility of our individual extraverbal continuums." Despite Alfy's rider—"he means blarney"—I soon hoisted more canvas on a sea of eschatology.

Trying to follow Last's philosophic twists and turns was driving me nuts. He was a guiding star who constantly changed position and never appeared in the same place twice. As I loyally stumbled after him, from Freud to Sartre to Goffman to Crowley, I began to falter and lose my bearings. His habit of picking me up and dropping me whenever it suited him didn't help much either. Up down up down, a yoyo on his string, I relapsed into my childhood stammer. At Council meetings I waved my arms and opened my mouth but nothing came out except strangled little grunts and futile gestures. Last rejoiced: "Brither Sid is finally breakin' through!"

Into what?

The more uncertain I stood with Last, the sharper Boris' attacks on me, the more I withdrew into identification with the Eternal. (. . . below primeval water, above molten land, the songs of Cuchulainn and bullroarers of Zagreus . . .) Birth and rebirth, paradise's nostalgia, *ab initio*—the sacred, irrational and ahistorical. Although I knew Zen had greased Japanese atrocity swords and that some of my favorite writers on occult or primitive religions were pro-Fascist, I adjusted such facts in my vast polyhedron of Knowledge-Needed-for-the-Voyage. When a universe of communion was opening up for me, why niggle? Distinctions between 'right' and 'wrong' melted away in the blazing furnace of No-Theng. Who was to say whether a Beatles lyric or Lyndon Johnson's invasion of the Dominican Republic was more 'it'? What the world needed was not the divisiveness of social change but unity—the self before it was a self, when it was One with the Cosmos.

Bolstered by the knowledge—so often implied by Last in our talks—that I was above normal moral and political categories, I smugly patronized my old pals on the left. Bypassing demos and picket lines with a superior smirk, I wrote letters to *The Times* defending the monarchist principle, and gave $25 to the League of Empire Loyalists. As a Yankee Consciousness Pilot, I redrew the political map to exclude Voiderica (USA) and magnify SWINE—anagram of (S)cotland, (W)ales, (I)reland, (N)orth, (E)ngland—the world's first psycho-Socialist nation, the geographic-historic base of Clare Community Council, rescue mission to the cracked minds of the dying West.

Nobody was happier at my swing to the right than Brother Hengist (ex-Major Straw). "With a few more chaps like you in the Conservative party, Sid, we might weather the storm."

Tony Straw was not often so contemporary these days. After stoutly resisting Clare Council's more radical tendencies, he now capitulated entirely to Last's magic Marxism. As reinterpreted by Brother Hengist-Straw, this meant a kind of romantic paganism in which the group was a reincarnated Round Table and Willie Last its once and future king. The Major must have seen himself as an Arthurian Winston Churchill, for he went around warning us in pidgin-Saxon that he could offer us nothing but blood, toil, sweat and tears. It didn't make sense—but who was I to judge?

For me, losing left politics meant losing not only my inner balance wheel but language as well. Tongue-tied in the horizonless fields of extraverbal communication, I felt hopelessly outclassed by the verbal tumbling acts Last and Drummond engaged in like gum-chewing kids competing to see who could blow the biggest bubble or pee the farthest. Their new enthusiasm for the occult rendered their language even more opaque than usual. (Boris still talked fairly straight.) I wrote down a couple of samples.

Drummond: "If the person being mirrored by the other person sees nobody but the mirroring person he fails to reflect his Oneness into the Other's Otherness which mirrors to the unmirrored person only the mirror-Person's self-mirror. And so it goes, spiraling down the staircase of untold generations."

But as one artist to another I had to take my hat off to Last who looked immensely pleased with himself after juggling something like this: "Th' identification of th' eternal Self wi' th' historically deconditioned fantasy of th' archetype by whom one is seen splits th' primary self intae Observe-th'-Observer-Self an' Observed-Self dividin' th' Observer-Person into Self-th'-Observer of th' Observed-Self an' Other-Observed until th' Self tha' is Observed disintegrates intae a million flying fragments of selves projectin', fantasizin', explodin' roun' th' Self-Invisible-tae-th'-Self starin' unutterably at It-Self in th' incommunicable vastness of Nae-Self nullifyin' itself." And he'd weave his body in time to the cadences like a headless horseman on a word-pebbled road, I jogging falteringly behind, ever behind.

> *In my more depressed moments I wondered, was I becoming the unofficial idiot—the Gareth de Walden—of Clare Council? To Brother Hengist I confessed that on acid I hallucinated the group was using me to dissociate from their own unacknowledged schizophrenia; that I might be a mere pawn in the doctors' personal rivalries. In short, that I might be the double-bound child of Clare Council's normal family.*
>
> *"Hey, that's very interesting," said Tony, cocking his head at me. "Mmmmm." Then rearing back, he slapped my knee and shouted with laughter. "I wouldn't carry that much further if I were you. That way . . . madness lies."*

Like a weathercock, in times of stress I kept turning back to Lena. But, maybe in revenge for my throwing her out once too often, her responses to my troubles grew smart-alecky, even irreverent. Worst of all, she sometimes insisted on talking about herself. Quel drag. Where was the cheerful, elfin fraulein I'd once known? "In the bloody soup like the rest of you crazies. Except that nobody seems to think *I'm* such an interesting case." She had, unbeknown to me, been hustled closer to Clare Council by her fiancé Irv. Unable himself to break into the closed circle of the Sacred 7, he had asked Last to see her as a patient (which presumably would have given him the personal link to Last he was looking for). But Last had not wanted to get involved professionally with anyone as problematical as Lena and had palmed her off onto Boris Petkin. (The two doctors often scratched each other's backs this way.) Lena's sessions with Boris had been dreadful, she reported. "He kept yawning and belching in my face and when I turned away to avoid all that boiled cabbage on his breath he said I had a bad transference problem." In the end, a little the worse for wear and tear, Lena had gone back to her Harley Street man. She was perfectly aware that Irv—and to a growing extent, I—were mucking her about, but she couldn't let either of us go. Irv was her passport to married respectability—and paid the bills; in a vague way I represented her 'better' self. So she resigned herself to making slightly bitchy remarks, such as pointing out that both Irv and I now spoke with faint Scottish accents. "Some women are accident-prone. I must be Willie Last–prone."

Poor li'l Lena. Surrounded by Men o' th' Light yet incapable of partaking of our splendor. Not out of any sense of grievance or disapproval—I told myself—but to help ease her burden, I broke off Second Holy Most Ultimate Contact (Schmuc). Stopped fucking her. Most of the Brithers were now experimenting with Last's model of TSA, total sexual abstinence.

Lena panicked and accused me of treating her as Last sometimes treated me. "You're throwing me over—and not even for another girl!"

What damn cheek. "Until you learn better manners—and how to take orders—you'd better sleep in your own bed for a while," I said coldly. And out she went again.

Next day I learned just how close to the edge Lena actually was. A middle-aged German woman loudly knocked at my door at Regents Gardens. "I am Hebbie. Lena zed you vould not anzer ze televone. She haz overdozed again." Lena's apartment was in Notting Hill, a garden flat partly converted (at Irv's expense) into a workshop for making costume jewelry, which she hoped might one day set her free economically. When I arrived a squat, gray-haired man, Hebbie's husband, was pouring hot coffee into the semiconscious girl with expert brusqueness. He glared at me. "You are all crazy," he muttered angrily while propping Lena up against a long table laden with welding equipment and polishing wheels. "Why do you and Irfing leave Lena so much alone. Iz like her monthlies, she chews zleeping pills like Polo mints."

After Hebbie and her husband left—they were her landlords who lived in the top flat—I slapped Lena out of her stupor. Dumb bitch, disobey me would she? I put extra sting into it, and she put up her arms to protect herself. "Why don't you let me die? One less Jew-killer left," she groaned. How corny could you get, blaming yourself for Hitler's massacre when you'd been hardly born at the time?

Crisply, I diagnosed Lena's suicide attempts—this was her fifth or sixth, she boasted—as internalized aggression. She must learn to express her anger toward others more openly, I said. Lena laughed weakly. "If I did, you and Irv would be dead by now."

Skilled help, that's what Lena needed. Plus care, affection and human warmth—all the things I'd dropped as so much excess baggage. (Anyway, shamans never doctored their own girl friends, I'd read somewhere.) So, after she shook off the sleeping pills, I jollied her into coming along with me to see the great man himself, Willie Last. He still didn't want to take her on for analysis, but reluctantly agreed as a special favor to me when I pointed out how much she disliked Boris. Lena unhappily listened to us discuss her as if she wasn't present in the room but later let me convince her that Last was the best thing for her. "Best—or dearest?" she asked helplessly. For Last had insisted that she now stand on her own two feet and pay his fee herself. Which meant risking her (relatively) secure relationship with her landlords, Hebbie and her husband, by borrowing heavily from them. (On principle she never asked me for money.) "Your Scotch headhunter better be worth all this *tsooris*, Sid," Lena warned. "I don't think I have the energy to divorce any more shrinks."

As spring days lengthened, thus giving us more light to look for country houses, it became clear that I wasn't the only Brother having trouble controlling his woman. The doctors' wives were absolutely fed up slaving over intricate vegetarian diets for absent men whose asexual detachment they perceived as a put-down, and they began openly to rebel. Never exactly quiescent (especially since I showed her my memo favoring a womanless colony), Sybil Last now let off her big guns.

"So-o-o, it's this month's Pin-Up Patient. When's Alf suing you for alienation of affections, Bri-ther Sid?" she'd answer the front door at Number 4 Crimea Street. Or tackle me in the kitchen. "And how's Paul? No *real* man would've taken that crap from

Hannah." ('Paul' was the heroine Hannah's American lover in Coral's novel, *Loose Leaves from a Random Life.*) Once, after Sybil trod hard on my foot with her spike heels, Last took me aside. "Go easy on th' lass, Sid. It's harder fer her, bein' ootside th' Circle of Light." Overhearing, Sybil went after me hammer and tongs. "Gaw eas-eh, Bru-thair Sid," she flounced around the parlor sniggering. "Sucking up to shrinks could produce sex changes." Behind her back Alf, who had been Sybil's previous target, theatrically wiped his brow and whispered, "Thank God it's your turn now."

Nancy, the black New York wife Dick kept at King Eddie's married quarters, first blew up at the wedding reception the Drummonds threw for Screwy Lewie and Bronwen Singh. We goggled as Nancy interrupted Dick's usual soliloquoy on "bourgeois marriage, love's murder" to stalk into the nursery and bring out the smallest of her tan, sleeping kids, then defiantly breast-fed the baby with one hand while knocking back Vat 69 with the other. "Wake up, you li'l bastud, yo daddy's talkin' 'bout you!" She turned to a male guest. "Baby, I sure got those nuclear family blues. Y'know, locked up inside a nut house all day like I am is just like bein' in th' movies. You ever see *The Snake Pit*?"

Even that longest suffering of migraine martyrs, Viv Petkin, threw in her cards. Tired of Boris' radical-sounding rationalizations of his tomcatting around with Davina, she decamped with the children to her mother's in Bethnal Green. Boris lamented, "Poor Viv. It's all my fault for not equipping her better to grasp the nettle of sexual emancipation."

Later, as the doctors' marital situations went "into a state of flux and reflux, crystallizing at higher stages of understanding, if necessary of spiritual separation and purification," as Dick described it, we got used to their new girl friends.

Clare Council's attitude to women embraced both extremes without a middle ground. Females either were exalted Light Bringers or slightly subnormal Earth Mothers. In practice, a woman stood or fell according to how well she bounced 'light' (knowledge) off her man.

Davina seemed ill-disposed to challenge this view. She cooked, sewed and typed for us without complaint, a kind of masochistic dues she exacted from herself as the price of experimenting with her other possibilities. Such subordination to men somehow helped buy off guilts triggered by that original act of liberation, taking a job against her family's wishes. "In a way," she said, "Clare Council isn't so different from the Beeb. You tolerate women as long as they're gentlemen." She wryly admitted that Boris, with his traditional Jewish attitude to women as kitchen comrades, was the perfect lover for her.

I, too, usually treated Dav as one of the chaps. What a relief it was to have a modest, silent woman around who never made vulgar personal demands or drunkenly tried to kill herself. It took months before she dared raise her hand to speak at meetings. Yes indeedy, she was the perfect . . . er, Brister.

But sometimes it was a close call. One LSD afternoon in my flat I suddenly stripped naked and used my penis as a joystick to maneuver around inner space. My trusted sitter Davina, knitting and reading *Lady Chatterly's Lover*, calmly lay aside her book to stare at my enlarging prick till I fell onto the bed and groaned, "Pilot to base, pilot to base. I'm lost up here. . . ."

"Do you want some radar?" Davina said helpfully. She came and sat at my bedside and put a cool competent hand on my cock. It glowed like a red-hot iron, then shriveled. I hid in mortification behind the velvet double drapes and hallucinated badly. Then, sobering up in the street outside, I told her that under acid I'd recorded her true selves—a Mother Superior with a BBC microphone for a belly button and too sacred to screw, Lizzie Borden chopping off my *shlong* with a bloody ax while singing the suffragette anthem "Shoulder to Shoulder," a butch-looking Tinker Bell burying me at the foot of the weed garden, Saint Mae West burned at the stake in Rouen. When she stuck too menacingly on androgynous Maori with a war club in her fist, I decided her black body-painted war dance was too much, and brought myself down.

Davina smiled stoically. "I know. Willie and Boris tell me much the same thing. Sometimes after listening to all your fantasies about me I say a litany to myself, 'Davina Mannix-Simpson, daughter of a Tunbridge Wells bank director. . . . Davina

Mannix-Simpson, daughter of a Tunbridge Wells bank director . . . Davina—"

But one woman could give the exploiters a lesson in exploitation.

One late June night I answered a weak knock at the door of Last's home (Sybil was away sulking at *her* mother's in Edinburgh). When I opened it Bronwen Jones Singh, bruised and muddy, slumped melodramatically across the threshold. "He tried to kill me," she whispered before passing out in my arms.

After brandy and cold compresses brought her round, wild horses couldn't stop Bronwen pouring out her tale. It all started with her wedding at King Eddie chapel, she said, where Screwy Lewie had ejected some gate-crashing Con Housers. ("Herb and Jerry had as much right to be there as anybody," she sobbed. "So what if they were naked?") After the honeymoon Bronwen had changed her mind about her promise to quit Con House, and also demanded her right to sleep in a separate bed. When Singh complained to Nancy Drummond that Dick was breaking up his marriage, Bronwen stormed out with her bags to a refuge room Dick kept for her in Con House, whereupon Singh wrote a long, libelous letter about her and Dr. Dick to the Management Committee. ("That's all we needed—to get caught in the crossfire of an escalating sex battle," O'Brien told me later.)

Earlier this morning Singh, informed by Bronwen that she wanted an annulment, had blown a fuse and run amok, dragging her out of Con House by the hair, kicking and punching her all the way to the Chief Nurse's office, where he demanded that Mr. Tasker fire her on the spot. Tasker, bowing to Singh's superior medical status, begged Bronwen to leave quietly "for the good of the hospital service." "He didn't even say anything about my bloody nose. Just fired me and sneaked out for a cup of tea," cried Bronwen, whose humiliation was complete when Singh abducted her in his car and dumped her in a ditch miles from nowhere. None of the three motorists who helped her get to London commented on her disheveled state. "No wonder the English go mad—nobody notices you here!"

Bronwen looked up at us with frightened eyes. "Lewis says he'll kill me if I see any of you again."

After she was put to bed upstairs, a war council. We were fairly pissed. Last narrowed his eyes, set his jaw and massaged first one fist then the other. "Well?" he demanded.

Silence.

"Are we gointa take this lyin' doon?"

More silence.

"What do you suggest, Willie?" asked Alf mildly. "We knock him sidewise into yestidday?"

Last harshly, eloquently cracked his knuckles.

"Why not?" Davina squealed in delight.

A few more brandies, a bit more knuckle cracking, and I could feel the lynch fever rise in all of us. At last—something to *do.*

We piled out of the house with a primitive roar and in Last's Bentley sped through sparse presunrise traffic toward Low Wick. On the way Boris suddenly remembered an urgent appointment elsewhere, but shamefacedly stayed when Davina, not especially sober, chastised, "Oh ye man of small faith!" Major Straw-Hengist kept shouting happily, "Reminds me of Calcutta, communal riots, '46. Sergeant, ready, load and aim at that trouble-maker at the edge of the crowd." At the hospital's rear gate Last solemnly shook hands with Dick and me—the "assault force"—and stayed behind with the rear guard. (Davina had to be restrained from coming along for the scrap.) The Bentley, motor running, waited in a nearby lane as Dick and I crept along the dawn-lit path to Dr. Singh's cottage. I couldn't rightly recall how I had 'volunteered' but this was no time to argue. Kneeling at Singh's doorway I asked: "What'll we do if he's home?" Dick replied boozily: "Confront his epistemological disturbance with our heuristic intentionality." And then? "Kick the shit out of him."

But the cottage was unlocked, empty. "Oh is that you, Dr. Drummond?" called a passing grounds keeper. "If you're looking for Dr. Singh I think he's staying over at the Medical Super's."

Disappointed, we returned to London, boasting of what we'd have done to Singh . . . if. That night, at Number 4 Crimea Street, smiling appealingly under her black eye and cut lip, Bronwen sat in our midst and kissed all the men for rallying to her defense. We all held hands, cried a little and sang old war songs until one by one we dropped asleep, Bronwen in Boris' arms (much to Davina's displeasure). Dr. Last, mumbling his favorite tune, fell upon Alf, Boris' squawking attempts to sing woke us up, Tony Straw joined in heartily and the night ended for the Sacred 7, plus Bronwen, arms intertwined, softly in unison:

"Oh the roses are shining in Picardy
In the hush of a silver dew
Roses are flow'ring in Picardy
But there's never a rose like you. . . ."

Going back to King Eddie had given me a powerful urge to stay behind there. Con House's yellow brick chimney, glimpsed over the tidy hedgerows, had looked so beautiful in the early morning sun. Somehow life in a schizophrenic unit seemed simpler, saner.

After months of pretending otherwise, I had to admit to myself that a void was opening between the group and me. Small doubts and hesitations, which I'd once felt as the tiniest pinpricks, now spurred me to *kvetch* endlessly and ineffectively at this or that minor aspect of Last's line. He almost never seriously discussed my objections with me, just let me ramble on pointlessly until I sputtered out in the face of his pained, tolerant grin. When he did talk to me it was usually to attribute my uncertainty to "yir ol' kawn-flict fer kawn-flict's sake syndrome, a neurotic projection of yir ambivalen' longin' fer th' perfect political family."

With all my heart I inwardly fought against this deepening alienation, and tried to bridge the gulf with feverish activity on behalf of Clare Council. After a long absence I hit the left's Chautauqua trail again, beating the drums for the politics of madness in front of Ramsgate CND, Dulwich Anti-Apartheid, Kilburn Young Anarchists and Fulham Fabians. My old comrades, who had once cheered my Wobbly songs and Bevanite views, now sat in polite silence as I harangued them on "The Politics of Antipolitics" and "Schizophrenia: or Back to the Socialist Grass Roots."

"How'm I doing, *schatzi*?" I asked Lena. Now that she was safely tucked under Willie Last's wing, I felt easier about letting her chauffeur me around again. She grinned wanly. (That she was more subdued these days I put down to Last's good influence.) "They may not always know what you're talking about, Sid. But that old Socialist sex appeal sure hits the old ladies where they live."

Out of a sense of political obligation to Clare Council, I even forced myself to do BBC stints. But I soon discovered that LSD and the cyclops eye didn't mix. The night I appeared with C.P. Snow on *Monitor*, a TV book show, I got the shock of my life when an apparition in my mind—Con House's Herb Greaves, armed with a kitchen knife—came crashing past the studio lights screaming:

> "I'd like to take a Ronson
> To Pamela Hansford Johnson. . . ."

Depression, gray and familiar, surfaced.

So did Jerry Jackson.

"H'lo Devil! FORGET IT—IT'S PAST!"

Blackened by the anti-intruder grease I'd smeared on the outside drainpipe, Jerry pounded on the rear window of my flat, which I untaped to let him in. He brushed his shabby suit and looked around at the bare, dark apartment. "Gee I knew writers was poor. But ain't this carryin' it too far? FORGET IT—IT'S PAST!"

For the next twenty-four hours, cross-legged and sitting eye to eye, Jerry and I picked at the verbal knot he had tied himself into: he could not stop hiccuping "FORGET IT—IT'S PAST!" By morning he was tired, down, and for advice I phoned Les O'Brien who told me to bring him back to King Eddie—"Pronto, before he scares himself half to death like he usually does." At Victoria Station Jerry broke away to tootle "It's Just One of Those Things" on his invisible clarinet and to jitterbug with a corgi-holding lady. "Shake it or break it, fat stuff. FORGET IT—IT'S PAST!" He bore down menacingly on a bearded, turbaned man with a monocle: "Mornin', Gunga Din. FORGET IT—IT'S PAST!" And tossed a frozen-faced City gent's bowler down an open manhole. "Easy come, easy go, Moneybags. FORGET IT—IT'S PAST!"

We ran for it back to my place.

I was getting slightly scared by this time and again rang Les, who said in a tired voice, "Get th' rozzers—but don't leave Jerry alone with them." In response to my 999 call three big, surprisingly gentle policemen came, and almost tenderly took Jerry down to the station, where he sat on a bench joking and flirting with a policewoman—until O'Brien and Dave Foster showed up. Suddenly alarmed, Jerry jumped up and backed against the station wall, doubling his fists. Half a dozen cops tensed for a fight.

"Hey Jerry," I yelled.

He looked at me.

"Forget it—it's past!" I cried.

He collapsed on the floor, laughing.

But he wouldn't go back to Low Wick without me.

"Sure, why not?" said Les. "Th' old place don't seem the same without you."

Days and Nights in Conolly House: Summer

It was like coming home. By now my only anchor was Con House and its amused tolerance (if not total acceptance) of me. Yet my fear and underlying shame at mingling with madmen, some of them half my age, made me yearn for a definition of sanity that would keep a safe distance between the boys and me. Were they mad, ill, existential travelers or what? Granted that the majority had been railroaded into hospital on one pretext or another—the voluntary admission gimmick could be the nastiest Catch-22 of all—I still couldn't swear hand-on-heart that they were not *genuinely batty. Where, in all of Jerry Jackson's American jazz fantasies, Derek Chatto communing with the chess grand masters and Featherstone's phallic self-exposure, had Last's light broken through?*

*"You're as blooming crackers as they are," Les O'Brien, the charge nurse, asserted. "You keep looking for madness which is mad itself. What's wrong with them is that they worried someone. But it has nothing to do with justice, the nub of the case. Take a look at their parents next Sunday and tell me who's got a screw loose and who hasn't. You know what gives the game away? I'll tell you. Not one papa or mama has himself been a mental patient. Not one! Statistically, it's an impossibility." O'Brien slapped his head. "For Christ's sake—*it's a hype."

Safe harbor.

As Lena's red MGB slowly rolls up to Conolly House a bathrobed boy wearing a police bobby's helmet crashes out the front door and takes the porch steps in one leap, closely pursued by someone in a KKK hood waving a chair leg and a pajama'd Indian chief in full war bonnet. With wild yells they disappear round a corner chased by purple-faced Bert Karp, his nurse's white smock flapping about his knees. "Mornin', Mr. Bell," he shouts. "Wondered where you were past few days!" I've been gone two months.

I examine Con House through Lena's windshield. Dick Drummond's struggle with the hospital bureaucrats to keep the lawn dirty and 'natural' has apparently not yet been lost. It's an even worse garbage heap than usual, if that's possible. Empty beer bottles, bread crusts and bits of newspaper litter the uncut grass on which a French musketeer wrestles with a boy wearing angel wings and another who is one of Dr. Who's mechanical Daleks; someone partly dressed in pirate gear reclines on a mattress up on the roof. It looks as if A. C.'s "China Follies," like the Windmill theater, never closed.

A barefoot butler jumps on the MGB's hood, causing Lena to brake sharply and almost throw him off. Jerry, back in tails and striped trousers from Clem's party, comes around to the driver's side and pokes his head through the window. "Is copper's little nark 'ere turnin' you in too, miss?" Lena replies, a little too seriously, "I hope not." She waits for me to get out then roars off in reverse toward the front gate. The hospital terrifies her.

I apologize to Jerry for calling the cops last week. He winks. "Ah forget it—it's past." We collapse, laughing.

Flopped alongside me on the warm dry grass under a July sun, Jerry complains that he hasn't had any visions lately. When I suggest that maybe he's not so crazy anymore, he asks worriedly, "Anything I c'n take for it?"

In answer to my questions Jerry says the odds and ends of costume are leftovers from the party, which the boys 'forgot' to give back to Occupational Therapy. It's also their way of needling Dr. Singh, who ever since Bronwen left him has been snooping around Con House looking for her. (Bronwen, almost deliberately provoking her husband, has retaken her room in the unit.) "Screwy Lewie is really screwin' us up," Jerry says. Singh and Dr. Primrose, the Management Committeewoman who feels rejected by the boys, have teamed up in a campaign of harassment, which has made everyone even more nervous than usual. There have been two more suicide attempts and several escapes. (Light-fingered Vince loves taking off to faraway places—Scotland and Cornwall are his favorites—in order to enjoy the Government-paid train ride back. Nurse Foster, who often acts as escort on these return trips, but can't afford to visit his own hometown, says: "I wish th' deaf little bugger'd hole up in Manchester once in a while.")

"On th' positive side," Jerry winds up his report, "Nurse Karp 'as a summer flu, Sally's pregnant an' Robin's pa died."

A shadow falls over us. "ON YOUR FEET, SCUM, WHEN AN OFFICER APPROACHES!" A large angry boy in dirty pajamas kicks the ground next to our heads. Shading my eyes I don't recognize the filthy character with dirt-matted hair and bloodshot eyes.

"Oh yeah," says Jerry lazily, "almost forgot. Derek Chatto 'as gone tuh sea as Lord Nelson."

I've never seen a 10:00 A.M. community meeting so divided into two hostile camps. In their weird, wonderful scraps of costume the boys sit smoking or cleaning their fingernails while Dr. Dick, flanked sternly by Drs. Singh and Primrose, stares at a blubbering mass of bedclothes in the center of TV room. Derek Chatto, his face gluey with filth and tears, rolls fetuslike from person to person, a weeping tumbleweed grabbing at legs, the floor, himself, moaning, "What's wrong? There is nothing wrong. Get it out of you. Get what?" From the weary way O'Brien and the boys yawn like bored theater critics when Derek crashes past, I gather he's not exactly hot news around here. Only Drs. Singh and Primrose seem unhealthily fascinated with his behavior; everyone else is fed up with it.

Not me. Swiftly I kneel over his sweating, struggling form on the floor and mentally roll up my sleeves. Ah yes, reckon his Astral Calibration at ninety degrees, Flight Path Trajectory Zero Zero approaching Critical Moment One [1]. Thank Gaw'd the Sacred 7 trained me to guide the lost and marooned down from the High Pass country of the mind. As I make magic signs over his body, Derek jumps and twitches as if hit by gunfire; he grapples with me and reaches up to kiss my lips, arches his back to draw me down. Sumbitch is strong as an ox. Bert Karp moves in to grab Derek but I wave him away: this one is mine. (I can feel the astonished eyes of Singh and Primrose boring into my back.)

Bubbling and cursing, Derek stiffens to attention on the floor and bellows: "Mustn't bash the lower ranks. Conduct unbecoming a Prussian officer and English gentleman. Don't want to hit anybody. DON'T!"

Barney Beaton, wearing a MISS BOGNOR REGIS swimsuit, walks over to Derek and pours a jug of water on him. "Cool off, Admiral Nelson. You're dragging your chancre."

Meeting's over.

Why Derek, of all boys, should cross over from a mild obsession with chess into full-scale psychosis remains a mystery. True, on my last visit he'd already begun to "come out" by chasing girls but reportedly had been shocked back into his old, shy repressed personality when Bronwen fell into his arms and let him fondle her. The flash point came soon afterward, on a Sunday visit from his father, a naval officer based in Portsmouth. A quiet afternoon huddled together over a borrowed chess set climaxed when Derek smashed the board over his father's head and shouted, "Stop trying to break down my defenses!" After which he refused to eat or wash, then proclaimed himself the ghost of Baden-Powell, the Boy Scout founder, and when that proved too namby-pamby to contain his aggression he switched to Martin Bormann back from the Paraguayan jungle to complete Hitler's mission of wiping out all Jewish chess players. O'Brien says that the Bormann personality actually helped Derek for a time. "But he's basically too nice a kid to sustain a Fascist fantasy system. Bad luck for him, that." I can see that O'Brien is worried. Derek's explosions, he fears, are far more active and formidable than the essentially passive, ritualized punchups of, say, Hurricane Hodge. "We've tried everything, from leaving him alone to practically breast-feeding him. Nothing helps." I ask why Drummond's methods, which assuage at least some boys 'problem of anger,' don't work with Derek anymore.

"How th' hell should I know?" O'Brien cries despairingly. "Maybe he don't put enough sugar in his Weetabix!"

When the coast is clear I slip into Observation Dorm on the ground floor where my patient Derek nods dopily from O'Brien's hypo of 5 cc paraldehyde. "H'lo, Master Petrosian. Putting all the Jews in concentration camps almost purified the game, didn't it? Only one more to go—Bobbie Fischer!" He grabs me again and starts to wrestle me into bed with him.

"Tyger," I murmur, extracting myself with some difficulty. "Tyger Bluefish." Something in my manner quiets Derek, and he lets me place my fingertips at his temples, bend and whisper a phrase from the *Iranian Manuscript*. Glassy-eyed, he grasps the Gnostic Pearl; gently bites my finger. Dear Tyger.

And like Claude Rains in *Phantom of the Opera*, I fade away.

Of course, I'm seen doing this, but no one takes exception to my fluttering around Derek with strange, incomprehensible passes and chants. The general attitude is: you want to shamanise, who's stopping you?

All day Derek's vibrations control Conolly House. Later he shows up on the lawn, shaved, combed and contrite, his Hitlerian power fantasy having shaded into something more familiar and nautical again. "It's out of me now. I had a dream. The Lord High Admiral told me not to hurt the patients but to lead them against the Zionist armada. That's why I'm here, isn't it?"

It happens at tea time. In the dining room a great brain-destroying roar, scraping of chairs. Sally screams. I dive out of the way just as Derek Chatto, arisen like a blond King Kong, upends his table and sends people, utensils and china flying. Before the table hits the floor Les O'Brien is on him, sliding with incredible skill between Derek and the scattered cutlery, and wrestling him along the floor to the nearest wall. O'Brien pins him there without hurting him and lets Derek flail away until he ineffectually punches himself out. When, weakly and unconvincingly, Derek grabs for a bread knife, Bert Karp, straining at the leash of his own violence, takes a running leap and lands his 200 pounds of frustrated police cadet failure squarely on his head. Thump! thump! Bert slams Derek's skull on the floor again and again, dispassionately, like a picador pushing his lance into a bull, his broad red face slightly abstracted with pleasure. Les O'Brien reaches over to pry Bert's hands from Derek's throat and says, in a mollifying tone usually reserved for violent patients, "Okay Bert, let up on him now." To Derek: "Relax, boy. Nobody's going to hurt you." Derek crumples, crying.

O'Brien orders the two nearest gawkers, A. C. and me, to collar Derek while he tries to find Drummond. When I shove up against Derek the way I saw Les do I can feel his 'body electricity' running through me like a physical current. "Boy," says A. C. still in his ringmaster's coat and pressing on Derek's powerful, shuddering shoulders, "I don't mind a schizophrenic breakdown every now and then. But this is ridiculous."

Emergency meeting in Obs Dorm. O'Brien scans the crowd. "Hmmm. Full house. Ominous."

Derek, propped up in bed, smiles dreamily and returns a salute no one has given him. "Mustered the crew then, Master-at-Arms?"

The simple reason why so many Con Housers have turned out so spontaneously is that we have learned that Dr. Singh is pushing hard to have Derek imprisoned in the violent ward, Churchill Wing. It is generally suspected that this would set a precedent for anyone else in the unit who ever goes 'florid'—at one time or another 99 percent of Con House (including me).

Instinctively, the boys look to Dr. Dick Drummond for advice and comfort, but he's so into one of his paralytic trances disguised as noninterference he might as well be on another planet. Perched uneasily on a cot as far away from Derek's as he can get, he swings his chubby legs back and forth like a moonstruck child. His whole manner suggests a trauma of indecision which only his patients can alleviate. He is in a genuine dilemma. On the one hand, getting rid of Derek has its attractions because he is such a painful reminder that community therapy has its limits. But Dick is committed to keeping the boys out of a hellhole like Churchill Wing. In his heart he knows that submitting to Dr. Singh's pressure must put everyone else at risk.

Finally the penduluming legs stop, the Drummond voice speaks: "Prima facie, Derek bears the unbearable burden of our reductively totalized psychopathy—"

Groans. Wally loudly whispers, "Blimey, th' guvnor's off again."

Just this once the boys can't really enjoy Dick's longwinded prevarications. They need firm guidance in navigating through their own ambivalences. A lot of them wouldn't mind seeing Derek shipped out because he's become such a threat to their stability—but they also know that Singh would not stop at Derek once he smelled their blood. Who will put the options clearly? As usual when Dr. Dick goes into shock, the boys turn to Les O'Brien, who, with a tired glance at his chief, says: "One, we give up Derek so we can all take a breather. Two, we keep him in Con House but doped up to the eyes, which is agin our antidrug principles but since when has that stopped us? Three, he stays here . . . undoped. And every one of you takes the consequences."

A. C. cocks a trigger. "That's right, why not look after him ourselves?"

A tremor passes through the dormitory. While nobody comes right out and calls A. C. nuts that's the gist of it. The boys' protests and catcalls only make A. C. dig in his heels. He may have meant it as a joke at first; but sure, why *not* let everyone take over Derek's nursing until he's better?

Half-incredulous questions fly thick and fast, mainly at O'Brien. A. C.'s kidding, right? I mean, Derek is much too sick for Con House . . . isn't he? Also isn't he, uh, kinda dangerous? Wouldn't it be better to help him get, er, specialized treatment? ("Like th' twisted towel therapy," mutters someone who's obviously been to Churchill Wing.) Terrified of patient power—of effectively erasing the reassuring line between themselves and nursing staff—the boys almost beg O'Brien to label Derek an incurable chronic withdrawn. "He's too much for mentals like us tuh handle," beseeches Jack Sweeney who pipes down when Robin, now sporting a platinum-blond urchin cut, shakes her bandaged fist at him.

O'Brien refuses to back down. "He's got what you've all got—no more, no less. Call it what you want."

Some boys are nothing if not inventive. "It's against union rules, i'nt it?" asks Wally Walters who suddenly recalls he's got a card in the Transport & General Workers. And hearts begin to bleed for staff who might lose their jobs in a patient take-over and then who'll feed their wives and kiddies? After much palaver the boys offer a generous compromise: they will *help* the staff to nurse Derek but nothing more.

O'Brien flatly dispels this illusion by pointing out that there simply aren't enough nurses around to contain Derek in his present excitable state. So, either he gets shipped up to Winnie Wing—or, in one way or another, the Con House patients must take virtually total responsibility for him. O'Brien bluntly adds: "If you guys are fantasizing that Dave and I will pull your chestnuts out of this particular fire, think again. We vote to toss Derek out, right Dave?" Nurse Foster nods agreement.

O'Brien's candor so angers some boys that they turn their spite full on Derek and cuss him out. In effect, the names they call him—lazy, self-dramatizing, indulgent, perverse, just downright vicious—regurgitate many of their parents' voiced and unvoiced resentments at their own breakdowns. "We did everything we could for him—where's his gratitude?" snaps Yorkshire Roy. Herb Greaves decides,

"Eeny meeny miney mo
Derek foe
If he hollers make him go
Eeny meeny miney mo."

Big Barney leans over Derek with an improvised stethoscope (the nozzle section of a garden hose) and pontificates, "Acute mania of the tabula rasa. Send for his sister and shag her."

My biggest disappointment is Jerry Jackson, who panics at the sudden prospect of exchanging his present unhappy security for the risks of self-nursing. "Ya fuckin' clap-poxed fairy twit—why'nt ya take yer medicine like a man!" he screams at Derek, then looks around in fury at us and slams out of the dorm.

A. C. tosses his hot potato at me. "What's your opinion, Sid?"

I'm so keen to keep my urban shaman's hands on Derek I vote to retain him, free and unsedated, in Con House, and my enthusiasm swings over one or two waverers, who fear I may be expressing an Administration view they must obey. For an hour or so the arguments roll back and forth across Derek's blithely grinning torso. Normally Con House splits between the gut liberals and hard-line conservatives, but this issue produces a large crop of switch voters. The mad are spiritual Californians.

In the end, tired out by wrangling, the boys want Drummond to settle it. "You must collectively decide," is all he says before ducking out.

"What's wrong with Dr. Dick?" someone asks. Robin dryly says, "Incurable ditheritis."

The upshot is, we—the patients—are taking over.

The Florence Nightingale Caper

First shift, Derek rota.

From 6:00 P.M. we're operational. People in false beards, KKK hoods, a MISS BOGNOR REGIS swimsuit, a clown's red nose and a shaman's cloak (me) surround Derek like a Praetorian Guard, watching his every move in bed. There's no shortage of helpers; the boys queue up to volunteer. Which is just as well, because Dr. Dick and O'Brien refused to live in with us. "My staying would invalidate your authenticity," said Dick loftily. O'Brien was blunter. "You don't catch me goin' over the top without some officer showing me th' way first." As a gesture of solidarity to us, O'Brien arranged for Mad Monahan, the dreaded night nurse, to be assigned elsewhere. We're on our own.

Night. Obs Dorm lit by the dying rays of a summer sun setting behind Low Wick. Derek lightly moans, a few nearby shapes change position, sleep on. Whenever Derek moves uneasily one of us holds his hand or talks comfortingly to him. Snores.

Three A.M. Shifts come on and off every two hours. (Yorkshire Roy is the timekeeper, of course.) The self-appointed captains of the guard—A. C. and me and A. C.'s lover, the dud shell Keith Whitworth—dig in for the night and take turns catnapping in Jerry's empty bed. Jerry has quit the dorm in protest against "yer dumb Florence Nightingale caper." An unusual peace descends. Percy's radio is silent courtesy of an anonymous pair of wire cutters, and hullabaloo artists like Greaves and Hurricane Hodge have caught the spirit of the thing and are in temporary retirement. Shadowy shapes scurry in to peer down at our sleeping monster or bring us mugs of tea; out in the corridor some boys, unable to cope with the anxiety produced by our challenge to the hospital's authority, cower together and wait for retributive lightning to strike them down. Eric Raw wobbles in plaintively. "It's all about me, isn't it?"

Four A.M. The only sounds are Gareth squishing into his rubber sheet, Jack Sweeney sleepily crooning "Maria," Barney laughing at jokes in his dreams. Like Henry V's yeomanry before the battle of Agincourt, lacking only campfires, A. C. and I keep each other awake with whispered gossip and our life stories.

Lantern Slide: *A. C. Corrigan*

Albert Cavanagh Corrigan is one of Con House's naturally commanding voices, an influence which owes much to his Liverpool-bred skills, almost equal to O'Brien's, at subduing the unit's wild men. Also his frank, good-humored admission of private torments which drive the other boys crazy in the effort to cover up. "Not that I didn't try, old whack."

A. C. is a homosexual, a fact he discovered at seminary. ("I wanted to be a priest out of guilt. Good God, what a priest *that* would've made.") When his Merseyside Irish family threw him out—"Offshore micks like us are a funny race, more tolerant of loonies than queers"—A. C. decided to go mad or, failing that, to kill himself. On a last spree in London he tucked himself under Charing Cross railway bridge and got sick on cheap wine and sleeping pills. And he had his first vision, of Nelson's Column as a gigantic phallus pumping sperm into Pope Paul's mouth. "Took six of the boys in blue to wrestle me into King Eddie. I was ravin', had every hallucination in th' book." Dr. Dick, scouting a good patient mix for his new unit, rescued him from a Churchill Wing straitjacket and padded cell. "I suppose he needed a few classy I.Q.'s to impress visitors." Since then, A. C. has become one of Drummond's ablest helpers, a veritable Pancho Gonzales of group therapy, lobbing back with perfect accuracy the boys' furious salvos of self-deception. "Me, an expert? Maybe so—if that means bein' in th' same bloody boat as them. Anyways I enjoy it. Soothes th' sadist in me."

Though A. C. deeply mistrusts the theoretical side of

Drummond's work—"I wuz born an'll die a Catholic near miss. Dr. Dick's a blasphemer,"—at the same time he has a marvelous talent for sussing out the practical implications of antipsychiatry. (Drummond himself could take lessons from him on this.) However, A. C. is still his respectable lace-curtain parents' son, and hedges his bets with a running patter of self-protective, self-denigrating jokes about "us schizo animals in th' zoo" and the airier absurdities of "funny money logic" (phenomenology).

Is he sorry he came to Con House, then?

A. C. exchanges a glance with Keith Whitworth and replies quietly, "This grotty bughouse? It fuckin' saved my life."

Near dawn A. C. and Whitworth doze with their arms around each other, and I have a chance to check on our patient. Derek's eyes flutter open when I kneel at his bedside. I guide his heartbeat till it's locked into the Universal Clock, then satisfied it's all I can do now, I kiss the blessed Brither's hand and go off to my room—followed by A. C.'s sleepy, puzzled gaze.

In a corner of my room Jerry crouches, tense and miserable in his cutaway coat and wretchedly fingering "Don't Blame Me" on his invisible clarinet. He leaves plenty of musical gaps for me to fill in, which I don't because I'm less forgiving of him than he was of me for turning him over to the cops.

"Fuck off, Jackson," I fall tiredly into bed and turn to the wall. Splat! The plaster flies away only an inch from my face—Jerry has kicked the wall so savagely I almost hear the bones crunch in his bare foot. "Ya cuntish, patronizin' intellectual bastid! Everything was okay till ya came!" Jerry towers over me, eyes glowing with pure hatred, and shouts that I will wreck Conolly House with my far-out stunts like the Derek rota. There is a rational, terrified quality to his nonstop cussing. Then, suddenly afraid, he 'wipes' his anger. "Boy, am I glad ya're 'ere," he mops his brow in exaggerated relief. "Us schizos need proper doctors like you an' Dr. Dick."

Bullshit, I reply. And all through the morning and into a warm afternoon we argue the rights and wrongs of Derek's case—of patients supervising themselves. Once he loses his temper and punches me; a second time I hit back, without squeamishness, and we slug it out until I remember his weak point and tickle him into helpless, laughing surrender. Then it's back to jaw-jaw, and it goes on like that most of the early night, each of us dozing off while the other drones on, until finally Jerry shakes me awake.

"I think I got it now. It's like Jesus whippin' th' Gadarene charge nurses outta th' Temple, ain't it?"

Having worked it through for himself, he is now ready to help, but something still puzzles him. "Wot's so important about Derek anyways? 'e related to someone big?"

I suggest that Drummond semicreated the crisis. "He may be trying to get us to commit ourselves to Con House as his last line of defense," I say.

"Us?" says Jerry. " 'e's got a hope."

But the hope persists. At first, with shifts relieving one another at surprisingly punctual intervals, there are almost too many volunteers. Curiously, it's the Con House conservatives more than the progressives who pitch in to help. For their own reasons, of course. Roy says we are saving the Chancellor of the Exchequer money on staff salaries. On the other hand, the CND anarchist Jeff H. has opted out—oh, how familiar this sounds!—on the superradical pretext that A. C. and I are making a bad system work.

Hyperactive morning. Con House's level up, up: last night Percy rewired his amplifiers, causing the building to float on a sound cushion of Beethoven's "Eroica." Someone has even scrubbed out the TV room, and for once the dinner dishes get washed promptly. I've never seen Con House so orderly, calm (if noisy). It's like a well-run consultative assembly about to legislate a vital bill. A constant stream of boys on vague errands passes in and out of Observation Dorm, looking for an excuse to nurse Derek. As we gravely dodge past one another, exchanging businesslike smiles, purposefulness spreads like morning sunshine.

The takeover galvanizes Con House. Madness does not disappear; but something changes, moves. With a slow smile of comphrension Eric Raw ends his long hunger strike and, between bites of a huge jam sandwich, says, "Maybe it's Derek's fault this time." Black Abe becomes so curious about what's happening that he forgets to cough, and as if it's the most natural thing in the world a number of boys get out of pajamas—the patient's Yellow Star—into street clothes or China Follies gear. On the debit side, few of the anonymous withdrawns have really come awake, and one or two boys unable to adjust to the new situation look like joining them in the mental boondocks.

The effect on staff is almost as disturbing. Released from their chronic need to look after and be in charge (as some patients need to be looked after and obey), they euphorically bounce around looking for something—or someone—to do. When their attempts to 'help' us are politely rejected they slowly regress to huddle in corners for private, worried talks and even begin to develop symptoms. Dave Foster falls into deep, unpremeditated sleeps; and Bert Karp goes around passing out not pills but apples from a brown paper bag. Pregnant Sally complains of the cold (in July) and sits all day in a rocking chair in front of an unlit gas fire, knitting. And Dick Drummond, whose office we have occupied, sits part of the day in his yellow Morgan parked in the driveway and stares ambivalently at Con House. His equivocation only heightens the tension. As it is, too many of us already incubate dark guilts over some nameless, terrible thing we are doing to Derek. Bert Karp echoes what six or seven people have told me: "Where did I go wrong with Derek, Mr. Bell?"

No sign yet of the Demented Duo. Are Drs. Singh and Primrose giving us enough rope?

Another moment alone with Derek. I tenderly place my hands on his stomach. Dear Tyger Bluefish nods and sits up, beautifully in tune. Mustn't hurry. My shaman arms accept the tremors flowing from his Vital Center, I feel his disconnected sickness in me. I almost faint. Tyger, I whisper, will you come with me? "Yes." Now? "Yes." Thus legitimized, I point my clasped hands at his heart to make the incision, then we're both tossed into the Universal Plasma, streaking for the wild light. Along the way I teach him how to spear the bush kangaroo, heave rocks at low flying birds, trap the marmion. At first stiffly scared, his responses awkward, he warms, oils, flows, at last slowly flies apart. His True Voice is born. We jive.

Far, far below on earth Eric and Wally, in their newfound

friendship looking like Laurel and Hardy, return from supper to their guard duties. Quickly I reassemble Tyger Bluefish back into Derek Chatto. "Oi," says Wally, "whatcha bin doin' to 'im, Sid? Look at 'at smile. Like a baby wot's jus' bin burped."

Rotten luck tonight. Somehow Mad Monahan, the bully boy nurse O'Brien was supposed to sidetrack for us, is back on duty. The very idea of a unit run by its patients gets up his nose. "Stuff this carry on!" he bellows, and breaks up the rota by poking and kicking us into bed. Derek's moans he stifles with a double syringe of paraldehyde, and anyone who even looks at him wrong is threatened with incarceration in Churchill Wing, "where you bleeding fruitcakes belong." Me he freezes with a look of withering contempt. "And that goes for you too, Yank!"

My honeymoon with the staff is over.

This morning, hung over on dope, Derek shambles into group therapy—one of the Con House institutions we decided to keep—and pushes Dick Drummond out of his customary Diana Dors chair. (Dick, hassled by hospital busybodies who wanted to know what he was doing all day in his parked car, decided it was safer in here with us.) "Well you see," Derek begins reasonably, "my father can't admit his sexual aggressiveness. Transfers it to me where I can't discipline it. It doesn't belong to me but to him. I love my father. He loves me. How can you lead the Home Fleet into battle on only four O-levels?" He breaks down. "I'm scum, sirs."

Barney Beaton, rushing up to place his nozzle-stethoscope against Derek's head, diagnoses: "Inflammation of the eat-a-pussy complex," and just as Derek lashes out to kick him Drs. Singh and Primrose, with Chief Nurse Tasker riding shotgun, stalk in like Mafia hoods. The sight of patients in tuxedos and false beards running Con House does not please them.

"Who is in charge here?" demands Dr. Primrose, struggling unsuccessfully as usual to keep the anger out of her voice. Dr. Dick lies silent as a statue on one of the mattresses now.

"I guess all of us are in charge," cheerfully responds A. C., who explains how we work the rota system: two guards on Derek at all times, replaced every couple of hours, a flying squad always alert for emergencies. We're also trying to wean Derek off the paraldehyde Monahan keeps squirting into him.

The Indian doctor, Singh, only half hears A. C. because his small, suspicious eyes are busy roving around for Bronwen (who is upstairs therapeutically cuddling Mr. Wu). When he finally registers what A. C. is saying, he smiles frostily. "Ah, Mr. Corrigan, my naive friend. So you and your Falangists think that the way to cure Derek is by projecting onto him your own unresolved totalitarian tendencies?" Dr. Primrose butts in to ask if Derek has been violent during the night. "Yeah," interjects Jerry. " 'e killed a woggy shrink. Chopped off 'is crockers 'n hung 'em up to dry."

Screwy Lewie laughs mirthlessly. "Ha ha. Good joke, sir."

"Don't mention it, Gunga Din."

An outburst of weeping by Derek brings Dr. Primrose instantly to his bedside, where she makes sympathetic noises and smooths back his evil-smelling, unkempt hair. Before anyone can warn her Derek grabs her long pointed nose between his strong fingers and gives a powerful tug.

O'Brien and I watch Screwy Lewie help his colleague to the infirmary, leaving behind a delicate trail of nose blood droplets. How much longer, I ask, does he think we can keep Derek in Con House? He replies, "The question is, how long can we keep Con House itself?"

Les Talks

Can't O'Brien do anything about it?

"Who, me? Naw. I'm boxed in. Totally exposed. I'm a family man with a wife and kid who need my seventeen quid a week take-home pay. And there's a house tied to the job."

Then why not taking his nursing expertise somewhere else?

"Where to? Private bins are as bad—or worse. Anyway I don't want to make money out of lunacy. Just live off it." He gives his gleeful spine-chilling laugh.

"Listen, chump. For nearly two decades I've been one of the businessmen of breakdown. I make my living off severe psychosis, the people who have it, the people who label it. It's an open question if I could survive, economically or psychologically, without it. I'm hooked."

O'Brien reminisces. "You shoulda been here when Con House started. Especially when we got the first patients—half from other wards, half new admittances. All Grade-A specials. Hallucinating, lively, drugged, a couple in straitjackets, a few near catatonics, the usual religious maniacs and obsessional robots: all young and half killing themselves to keep that ol' sex and creative drive properly repressed. I thought the place would fall apart when Dick announced they could get up and go to sleep when they felt like. Nothing compulsory—no 'treatment,' no drugs, no therapy. My God how that frightened them!" He cackles. "And if th' kids were scared I was paralytic. Talk about fright."

At first, Les says, he and Dick had gotten along poorly. "He didn't like my institutionalized ways. And I resented that Bond Street getup and his glib, bolshie style. Uh oh, I thought, another whiz kid bucking for a rep. So I did what any other self-respecting old nursing lag would do—my duty eight hours a day and kept my nose clean. After he got shot down I still wanted my job." But Dick avoided all the obvious traps. He moved his family into the hospital, faithfully attended staff meetings and parties and never made an important move without first clearing it with Chief Nurse Tasker and the Medical Superintendent. "Within six months we had ourselves a unit. Once I saw Dick wasn't a flash-in-the pan, I relaxed. Then the real problems began."

Les says he was an "institutional wreck" by the time Drummond showed up. "I knew what was wrong, knew the system inside out. Even had a few ideas how to put it right. But there was nobody to talk to. My wife Peggy listened, but what was the point in that? *I* was the one had to go through those swinging doors every morning. All I could see in front of me was another twenty years. Of slugging or tying up people, giving them smaller doses of more sophisticated tranquilizers, pretending they were crazy and the rest of us sane. When Dick came along he could have been a five-horned purple-dyed demon for all I cared. He meant *change* and I jumped at it."

That, says Les, was a little over two years ago. "It probably saved my life. But what th' effin' hell for? I keep asking myself. Before, in the good old days, I only suspected what was wrong and kept my mouth shut. There's a kind of contentment you get from observing the evil and tellin' yourself there's nothing to be done about it. Ah but wait! Once someone raises your hopes you start getting *unhappy*. You commit yourself to all these petty schemes for improvements. For shifting the weight just a tiny fraction off patient types. And the backlash begins. You, Sid, have arrived at a time of backlash."

Les says the irony is that in its death throes Con House has become fashionable. At precisely the moment when Admin's stooges are hovering for the kill, the unit is deluged with requests from social workers, journalists and "itinerant idealists" to come and work in it. "We get everything we need except understanding. Without that, sooner or later, we're for the high jump. More and more I hope it's sooner—before we make too many promises we can't honor."

Someone shouts, "Hey, Derek just raped Bronwen!"

Wally, an eyewitness, says Bronwen sashayed into Obs Dorm to do her compassionate bit and leaned over Derek in her Vampira outfit, a low-cut jumble sale dress. " 'er tit was 'arf 'angin' out so 'e did th' logical thing an' 'ad a nibble."

Obs Dorm resembles a Victorian painting titled *After the Storm*. Her dress mussed and ripped, Bronwen sobs against the protective breast of Chief Nurse Tasker, who let Screwy Lewie beat her up only a few weeks ago but has become her champion now that she has been 'victimized' by one of the boys. Sally, looking a trifle skeptical, holds her hand. Screwy Lewie is speechlessly angry at his bride.

Another full house. Plus the Mafia don himself, Dr. Winstanley.

Derek gaily calls out to me, "H'lo, Master-at-Arms. Did it again, didn't I? Messed up. Still, it proves I'm no homo, doesn't it?" He points an accusing finger at the Medical Super: "I ordered that man put in irons."

Dr. Winstanley blinks amiably at Derek and, ever unflappable, tries to rouse a still-catatonic Drummond with a joke. "Court's in session, Dick, monkey's on the bench—next case, please." Some joke.

With carefully controlled rancor Screwy Lewie Singh puts the case for the prosecution, which is that Derek's behavior, contrary to Drummond's view, is not a potentially healing descent into chaos but a destructive attention-getting device. "By indulging your patient you collude with his most infantile fantasies. You prevent him from adapting to the reality principle—and you also threaten the existence of the community you say you want to protect." Already, says Singh, Derek's stunts have so upset some Con Housers that they've quietly asked him to arrange a transfer to another ward. (We quickly look around: who are the traitors?) Summing up, Singh lays an iron hand on Derek's shoulder. "Would Mr. Derek's prognosis not improve in surroundings more stable?"

Derek whinnies like a horse and makes Screwy Lewie jump when he tries to sink his teeth in the doctor's hand.

Con House's defense team may not be up to Queen's Counsel standard, but it is impassioned and fairly rational. Jerry Jackson argues, "Derek din't exactly kill Bron, did 'e? An' 'e din't do nuffin' she wasn't askin' for. If 'e needs a good 'idin' we c'n do it jus' as good as those Churchill Wing basta—nurses. I thank you." He bows as a barrister would to an Old Bailey judge and retires with a great swishing of nonexistent robes. A. C. follows by saying that sending Derek to Winnie Wing would probably only feed his violent masochism. "If we don't take care of our own we're just goin' along with all those creeps who keep sayin' th' mad need to be treated. Who can tell—if this works maybe we can abolish loony bins." Dr. Winstanley looks a little daunted at that prospect.

Swim-suited Barney Beaton sidles up to Dr. Winstanley. "Hugh, old chap," he harumphs, trying a hearty class approach. "Missed you at Boodles t'other evening. Cough cough. Now about this cheeky snipper whopper Chatto. Known the family donkey's years. Father's Cudgels Chatto, rugby blue and bloody good oar, too. Sound English stock there. Trouble's this pox the boy picked up on French leave. Trying to think for himself. How venereal! 'Pon my soul, Hugh, not a bit of it anywhere else in the family. All he needs is a trifle more jelly in his sore bun, hur hur hur." Barney then strides jauntily over to Dr. Singh. "Tell *that* to your damned fuzzy wuzzies next time they try to break the thin red line!"

Staff keep mum, except for guilt-stricken Bert Karp, who volunteers to give up all of his free time in order to help Derek tame his runaway pH factor. (Robin whispers, "That's all Derek needs.') The boys' enthusiasm has put Dr. Winstanley in a box. Conolly House, once the apple of his eye but now the hospital's leper unit, has become a dangerous liability, even a threat to his position. For months, pressure—from dissatisfied Consultants, angry nurses, frightened parents and even patients—has mounted to "do something" about Drummond's unit. Yet in his own devious way Winstanley believes in Con House and doesn't want to get rid of it. As usual he straddles the fence in a classic King Eddie way.

Clamping down firmly on his pipe in a schoolmasterly fashion, he launches into a radical analysis of schizophrenia, its origin as a weapon of invalidation in the normal family, its use as a tool of social mystification. (Knowing his audience, he doesn't even hint at the possibility of a physical cause to schizophrenia, even though that is the basic medical principle of his regime.) All this he speaks not at us directly but to Dick Drummond, doctor to doctor, as if nobody else was in the dorm. It's a technique he has perfected over the years to mediate among various hospital factions. By making progressive statements he seems to tell patients (and radical staff) that he's on their side—but he does so in a typically bureaucratic, disconfirming style that immediately signals to the more conservative doctors that really he's on *their* side. After all, who but a totally institutionalized psychiatrist would talk about patients as if they weren't there? It is a fiendishly beautiful method of subverting the patients he's ostensibly defending.

Little by little, Dr. Winstanley feels his way into a comfortably unconventional position, and piles on the rhetoric. "By their bold and adventurous experiment in autonomous nursing, Dick, your patients have lighted a candle in the dark abyss of human ignorance." Pause. "However, it is a very *tiny* candle—don't you agree?—and the wind is rising." American accent, with a wink at me the Yank. "Gents, the nitty gritty is, is now *quite* the time to fight City Hall?"

He makes a major production of knocking ash from his pipe against his chair leg. Here it comes, I think.

"Mr. Tasker, care to toss your two bits in?"

With Bronwen's pale head still adorning his chest, the Chief Nurse insists that staff is stretched too thinly for him to spare even a single extra nurse to look after Derek.

A. C. is exasperated enough to tear his mass of tangled red hair. We want to release, not bring in more, staff, he protests. Mr. Tasker's eyes glaze over and he repeats: "It isn't that I don't *want* to assign more nurses here. . . ." Somehow he has hysterically converted the boys' case into its opposite. Dr. Winstanley torpedoes his subordinate with a 'isn't he hopeless' grimace to us.

Just as (it seems) the Medical Super is about to rule on Con House's fate, Bronwen meekly raises her hand. Ever since Clem left, she's craved the spotlight, and this is her big chance. A madonnalike smile spreads over her tear-stained face as she makes the grand gesture. "Derek didn't take a very big bite," she says.

Dr. Winstanley exhales audibly. Thank God, Bronwen has made his decision for him. He rubs his hands like a poker player raking in all the chips and says, "Right then, that's it—for the moment." And heads for the door with the usual glad hand for all. Abruptly he stops and turns to us: "Lads, don't you believe all that about romance and orange blossoms. Marriage is a compact of murder to see who gets who first. R equals S minus P." And before we can figure it out he adds:

"There is nothing so powerful as an idea whose time has come. *But is Conolly House a premature ejaculation?*"

And is gone.

We look at one another uncomprehendingly.

"Oh no," groans O'Brien. "A reprieve. Th' suspense'll kill us."

It does.

For several days the unit quivers on a knife edge. The way Dr. Winstanley saved Con House insures its downfall, for not many boys want to be associated with a premature ejaculation. After the rota disintegrates due to lack of personnel, Derek is left without adequate supervision, causing the inevitable to happen.

At 3:30 P.M. Friday afternoon an enormous cracking sound fills Con House: out of bed, Derek Chatto has weaved upstairs to the Anything Goes room and ripped out the metal base of the punching bag, and he uses it to smash windows and splinter doors, screaming: "BATTLE STATIONS TO REPEL JEWISH BOARDERS!" Then he flings the heavy metal object through a window, almost braining a nurse passing below. Those of us who subdue Derek find a scrap of paper in his pajama pocket:

ORDER OF THE DAY

TO WALK THE PLANK

MAO TSE TUNG

MALCOLM X

F. CASTRO

They are the real names of three mutinous seamen—Mr. Wu, Abe and Gareth—he confides.

Possibly to the secret relief of some Con Housers, Derek's flip-out forces Dr. Winstanley's hand. In a typical compromise the Medical Super reassigns Derek to Churchill Wing, but allows him out for evening meals with us. Nobody is fooled. Derek is *kaput.* Staff reoccupy their office, and the crisis is over. Con House reverts. Percy's electronic garden bursts into bloom again with Louis Armstrong's "Bucket's Got a Hole in It," and rather sadly the boys climb back into their pajamas. Clowns, pirates and beauty queens become patients again.

Herb Greaves keens a valedictory:

"Tried
Died
Brave
Knave."

WILD TRACK:

Sally (staring at a winged insect on the lawn): "Oh look at that butterfly. It's doing a Con House. Fluttering its last wings."

Ian Fleming died today, which some boys feel must be connected to Con House's present trouble. Most of them are fans of

James Bond, who, together with "The Man from UNCLE" and Steed of "The Avengers," they fuse into a single all-powerful superhero. I ask why such a strong identification with Bond?

Jeff H. says, "Well, he's a retarded adolescent doing dangerous work under the orders of M for mother."

Just before the nurse goons from the violent unit come to collect Derek, I slip into his dorm. He salutes and pipes me aboard. "Master-at-Arms—give this message to the crew," and hands me another piece of paper.

PISS OFF

Without Derek the unit seems absurdly empty. Depressed like many others I relapse into an institutional King Eddie shuffle and trudge from room to room vainly seeking consolation. Through an open office door I eavesdrop on Dick Drummond talking earnestly to some fresh-faced Oxford students down for the day. He is suddenly his old buoyant self.

"The concept of 'cure' for mental illness belongs to a reactionary, outmoded ideology," he lectures. "Conolly House has transcended the bourgeois fallacy of health and sickness. We stand on the threshold of a new era—schizophrenic sanity."

That night Clare Council's Alf Waddilove rings me at the hospital. "Guess what?" he shouts exultantly over the line. "We've got our Place!"

ALFIE'S PLACE WAS a huge decaying ex-Congregational church on a quiet side street in Brixton. It backed onto a railway viaduct and bombed-out wasteland. A neat little row of terrace houses faced the five granite Ionic columns that supported the building's portico. A bell tower, knocked off in a wartime raid, had never been replaced. The church, over 150 years old, had peeling paint, a roof long ago stripped of its lead and a wild undergrowth of bushy vines around its moldy foundations. The front door was just charred planks of wood nailed together, and corrugated tin blocked up all the windows. Moss and dead leaves blanketed the gravestones under two ancient plane trees. It was a far cry from our dream of a gracious country estate.

It was known locally as Meditation Manor.

Alf, who had winkled it out of its Quaker trustees at a peppercorn rent of 21 shillings a year, proudly showed us around on a cold wet Sunday afternoon. The sodden old church looked like a cross between Baron Frankenstein's castle and Wormwood Scrubs jail. "It may not be the Ritz," admitted Alf, "but isn't it gorgeous in its way?"

Basically a disrepaired shell, the church had two slightly sagging floors and a dank basement. Within its mildewed walls a three-sided balcony overlooked a main hall half the size of a football field. Both floors were gutted of their pews. "Slightly Moorish effect, don't you think?" said Brother Hengist (ex-Major Straw) who had let his trim little moustache grow long and drooping to resemble an illustration of a Saxon warrior chief he'd seen in the Imperial War Museum (once the site of Bedlam Asylum, I suddenly remembered). Dominating the hall at ground level was a magnificently phallic pulpit flanked by tattered Union Jack and Church Army flags. Several musty private chapels were recessed into the side walls, there was a makeshift kitchen out back. The toilets were broken, pipes long burst. Debris lay everywhere. "It's practically a masterpiece of filth," marveled Davina.

Wrinkling our noses against a stench of graveyard urine—not even Con House smelled this bad—we gingerly stepped over sleeping bundles of aging, wrecked men and women who Alf said were tramps and meths addicts allowed to use the church to sleep in. How had Alf hustled Meditation Manor? I asked. "Dead easy," he replied. "I promised we'd raise the tone of the place."

All around the grimy cheerless walls ("Great for finger painting," said Dick Drummond, whose whiskey belly and overflowing beard now made him look more like Father Christmas than Buddha) hung reminders of previous tenants and benefactors. You could read the church's long social history—Theosophist Hall, Salvation Army mission, Labour party office, etc.—from its accumulated litter. A banner proclaiming KICK OUT THE TORIES lay brokenly among scattered yellowing leaflets. Oleos of William Morris, Joanna Southcote, General Booth and Keir Hardie stared down from the walls in geological strata of good intentions, and down in the basement, behind a disused boiler, we stumbled on a dirt-encrusted bust of Robert Owen, the utopian capitalist and Marx's friend. A thinner, more ascetic-looking Willie Last, in sandals and a knee-length Indian shirt over white linen trousers, knelt reverently and cleaned the inscription at its base:

> "I therefore now proclaim to the world
> the commencement on this day, of the
> promised millennium, founded on rational
> principles and consistent practice."

"Owen was a Lanarkshire mon—it's an omen," breathed Last. Boris Petkin, his six-foot-plus frame encased in a long Hasidic coat and who had grown curly black ringlets that swung gaily whenever he turned his head, had to help Last carry the marble head upstairs. They stood it on a chair just inside the plank door so visitors would encounter it first thing. Later, a twenty-four hour 'eternal' spotlight was fixed to shine on it.

Alf led us over the Manor and ticked off its virtues like a used car salesman trying to persuade us we weren't buying a lemon. The foundations were solid, the brickwork still good, and the location unbeatable—a long bus ride away from the distractions of the West End, but firmly rooted in a real working-class community. We couldn't have wanted better neighbors, Alf promised. True south Londoners, they were used to minding their own business and to seeing all sorts of odd types hanging around the Manor so they were hardly likely to be shocked by us. The trustees, despairing of finding anyone to take the building off their hands, had been overjoyed to give it to us as a 'community health center' for the rehabilitation and after-care of mental patients.

"Well," Alf finished, "and what do you think?"

Last looked around at the foul smelling rubbish, broken plumbing and sleeping drunks. His gray eyes clouded with emotion. "It's shit awful. When do we move in?"

Overnight we were in business. Hardly had I, as Clare Council's chairman, signed the guinea-a-year lease than the Manor began filling up with people in urgent need. Without blankets or sheets, without heating or adequate light, improvising from meal to meal, we Councillors stood welcome as they showed up, round the clock.

The first one to find us was an impeccably groomed lady barrister in her late forties who appeared with her harassed-looking brother the morning after we moved in. "Howja do!" boomed Anna Shepherd in a commanding courtroom voice. "I'm too exhausted to go on swimming against the tide—may I rest in your snug harbor?" Anna's brother had his own large family to look after and could no longer cope with her aggressive behavior and strange hallucinations. "It's been sheer hell, I promise you," he pleaded wretchedly. "It's not that I don't love my sister, just that I'm not competent to deal with someone who thinks she's an octopus one day and a porpoise the next. Why, only last week she tried jumping from Albert Bridge because she couldn't live on dry land—and then tried to strangle me with one of her tentacles when I pulled her back." Padded cells in mental hospitals had only worsened Anna's condition, and he had been on the point of agreeing to a lobotomy when he chanced upon a *Times* profile of Dr. Last. "You're our last hope," said Mr. Shepherd, leaving Anna on our doorstep and driving away before we could think twice about it.

After Anna they came in droves.

Sir Marlo Snell, ex-Battle of Britain pilot, was angrily depressed over business partners who had allegedly cheated him; he dive-bombed everyone in sight shouting "Bandits at nine o'clock!" Ramsey and Roxie, a rich New York divorcée's fourteen-year-old twins, had been expelled from Summerhill school for behavior offensive even to A. S. Neill. Jenny Potts, a pretty miner's daughter from Wigan, was possessed (she believed) by the spirit of Jennifer Jones, star of *Song of Bernadette*, which she'd seen sixty-two times; Jenny walked about in a self-designed nun's habit swinging a large wooden crucifix she wielded like a shillelagh. Chuck Biberman, a California Rand Corporation dropout, had accidentally killed his wife and child in a car smashup. A black Milwaukee novelist, Bobby May, and his Swarthmore girl friend Trish Wakefield, were on bail awaiting trial on dope-smuggling charges. Dr. Andrew Horn-Green, retired Adlerian analyst, had just absconded from a forty-year marriage to pursue his more authentic sexual interests (boys). Alluring Taya, the dark-eyed teenage daughter of a Pakistani businessman, had not spoken a word in any language for several years. NON-RUT's junkie poet Sy Appleby and his buddy Frisbie Blue were on the run from creditors after their Manchester strip club had gone bust. Plus half a dozen more freelance schizophrenics fleeing fed-up families and/or Detention Orders.

Sleeping alongside the tramps on the floors, benches and up on the balcony, they were ready before we were. May Day calls drew heartening response from friends and sympathizers, who, now that we had a physical place to show them, pitched in with emergency carpentry, electrical installation, etc. (Clive Flynn's offer of help we quietly ignored.) Some who came to hammer nails stayed to live in.

With an enthusiasm I had not seen since that first New Year's Eve, Clare Council rolled up its sleeves to make the Manor into a palace of healing and whole-y-ness. Every night for weeks, often to the accompaniment of my Leadbelly work hollers, we scrubbed the old church down, flues, kitchen, floors, everything. The bangs of hammers and slaps of whitewash brushes eased, temporarily at least, the wounds of waiting. In a frenzy of comradeship (and because we lacked official support), we poured our own money and time into the Manor; kitty contributions were doubled and each Brother pledged several duty nights a week. For the first time our energies were hooked into something useful and outside ourselves, and it was the making of some of us. Alf, for so long a cipher living in Last's shadow, came into his own, emerging as a dynamo of business efficiency. Swiftly he steered us past the scrutiny of the Charity Commissioners for tax-exemption purposes; got us insurance cover, ordered letterheads for a fund drive, hired and supervised heating engineers; made round after round of diplomatic calls on nearby police stations and churches; and—arguing that it was cheaper for the taxpayer to maintain a person in Meditation Manor than in a mental hospital—somehow persuaded the area National Assistance Board (dole) manager to cough up a small sum toward the upkeep of the Manor's poorer residents (not many, it's true). Later, it became convenient to charge stiff fees all around.

We were all systems go. Except for the tramps.

Nothing was possible, Last decreed, until we got rid of those moaning, smelly, stupefied old wrecks who took up so much of our energy and the Manor's space. Davina's suggestion that we share the church with the down-and-outs was contemptuously rejected. "Aw, save tha' sentimental sheep-dip fer 'Woman's Hour,' Dav," he snorted. He was not about to jeopardize salvageable "walkin' wounded" like Anna Shepherd and Sir Marlo for basket cases like the dossers. The problem was, how to dump them within the letter if not spirit of Alf's promise to give the tramps plenty of time to find alternative winter quarters?

Last said slyly, "Let's put it tae th' entire community."

Clare's new residents jumped at the chance to help their benefactor. Sy woke up the sleeping lumps by shouting Khalil Gibran verses into their dirty, uncomprehending ears; Frisbie kept them awake by beating on a toy drum while Ramsey and Roxie jumped over them in a wild hopscotch contest. By midday most of the boozers had fled. The last drunk stayed on—till Anna Shepherd, naked and dripping wet, rose like a lank-haired, androgynous Neptune from the basement where Davina had been hosing her down. "Cor," the old man croaked, "it's the DTs." And he blearily tottered out, never to return.

Last watched him go without regret. "How's that for nonviolent direct action?"

Having cleaned out the Manor's rubbish, human and otherwise, our little community began to groove. A rota was set up so that at least one Councillor was always on hand to deal with crises. Boris, who distrusted amateur psychiatrists—primarily Tony, Alf and me—argued for a qualified doctor to be present as well, but because Clare's three 'officers' had to tend their practices and (what remained of) their families we noncoms ran Meditation Manor. We held the residents' hands, played incessant Ping-Pong with them and listened to their troubles, shouted and screamed with (and at) them; cooked their food and cleaned up their shit. I'm not sure what it did for the Manor's schizophrenics—but it certainly put lead in our pencils. Alf, who seemed to grow in confidence and stature with each passing day, was truly reborn. We could not have survived without him. He knew exactly which type of plywood at what price to buy for cubicle partitions, how to set up a clear and simple bookkeeping system and how to get the local glaziers and plumbers bidding against one another. He threw himself heart and soul into the Manor but refused to move in, and when I asked him why he gave his broad countryman's wink: "Just because I like to work in a brewery doesn't mean I have to become a drunkard."

On Major Straw the Manor's effect was equally bracing if a little more bizarre, for it released him entirely into the personality of Brother Hengist, a pre-Conquest Saxon chief. He was like a liberated transvestite. The moment he was safely inside the church he joyfully dropped his City gent's uniform—brolly, bowler hat and pinstripe suit—and got into a self-invented battle dress, which consisted of a short fur cape he flaunted over one arm like a war shield, a kiltlike skirt and a ceremonial dagger stuck into knee-length stockings. (He reminded me of Ralph Richardson as the barbarian chieftain in *Things to Come.*) The

Major's eyes burned with the fever of self-realization. "To think that all these years my real identity was hanging in the rented costume department of Moss Brothers."

And, in her exacting role as the Manor's resident housekeeper (and Boris' girl friend), even some of Davina's timidity sloughed off. Coping with day and night emergencies brought out her wry, realistic, headmistress side. "I joined the group to go creatively mad like Sylvia Plath or Artaud. Instead I've ended up as the ward matron in *Carry On, Schizophrenia.*"

I was least enthusiastic about the Manor. In my eyes its intake compared unfavorably with Conolly House's. Though we didn't deliberately plan it this way, Clare Council's liberal, middle-class version of the old-boy network effectively screened out tough working-class nuts like Jerry Jackson and Wally Walters in favor of ones like Anna and Sir Marlo—people whose private hells were socially insulated by professional status, expensive educations or artistic ability. Broadly speaking, money and class position became the determining factors for admission. Nobody got into Meditation Manor who didn't know somebody who knew somebody. Or who could not seduce us. It almost made me feel anti-middle class, until I remembered that Herb Greaves, Barney, Gareth, Hurricane Hodge and Derek—in fact, about half of Con House—were anything but working class.

As a member of the selection committee for Manor candidates I grew disturbed at the criteria we used. Only attractive cases who corresponded to the doctors' idea of what a good schizophrenic was got accepted. Didn't this make Clare Council a kind of accomplice of privilege? I wondered.

At first Boris appeared to agree—or so I thought. But it turned out that what he really resented was the American influx. The flood of Americans that threatened to overpower the Manor caused him to spout darkly about "thinning our blood with Yankee spiritual imperialism." (Why did he look sidewise at me when he said these things?)

Last swept aside both Boris' and my arguments as "provincial." Clare Council's prime mission was to establish a bridgehead on public opinion, and for that we needed *articulate* madmen, he said. "One reintegrated patient talkin' tae th' newspapers'll do more guid than a hundred satisfied but silent customers. As fer th'

Amahricans, they're ridin' tae oor rescue like th' fookin' Seventh Cavalry. An' we'll make 'em pay through their noses fer th' privilege."

Recruited from Last's transatlantic lecture tours and Stateside publicity about him, the Americans insatiably organized Meditation Manor. In their hunger for a grass roots counterculture, they turned the place upside down, saddling us with a 'free university,' a season of antipoetry, political teach-ins and a neighborhood outpatient clinic, which the locals stayed away from in droves. The harder we and the Americans tried to get across to our Brixton neighbors the more strained relations grew, and perhaps to compensate for this failure of communication the Manor threw its doors open to every aspect of the alternative culture. But it only made matters worse. "Those nut cases up th' road are invitin' their crazy relatives now," I overheard a street trader complain.

As Berkeley and West 72nd Street accents mingled with, sometimes drowned out, those of Stepney and Lancashire, Boris hit out at the American invasion. "Bloody Yanks own our factories and dominate our arts. Do they want to colonize British schizophrenia, too?" (Hear! hear! echoed Brother Straw-Hengist patriotically.) Last defended 'his' Americans from a curiously nihilistic, left position. Sure, their influence was likely to be as pernicious as Boris said, he admitted. But so what? Had not American-made products, and a whole style of Americanized mass culture, done more to undermine the traditional British establishment than anything else in the past twenty years? "An' who knows?" he laughed. "Mebbe one or two more Yankee shrinks'll be enough tae finish th' job."

On a more realistic note he added, "Anyway, what choice d'we really have?"

Too true. Even Boris had to concede that nearly two years of taking our begging bowls around the doors of official British medicine had netted us exactly one seventy-year-old retired analyst and a failed med student from the Orkneys. By contrast, a single interview with Last in the *Village Voice* or *New York Review of Books* got us dozens of inquiries from young psychiatric interns armed with revolutionary sentiments and foundation cash. "Aren't they luvly?" he purred. "Know fuck-all—but wha' eggistainshul hustlers."

The radical Scotsman—and the filmgoer—in Last dug Yanks, their irreverent *chutspah* and their capacity for hard, zealous work. They were, he fondly said, "New Frontiersmen of psychic border country." (Sometimes I thought he expected us Americans to wear coonskin hats, spit 'baccy juice and roar 'Tarnation!' like Walter Brennan or Arthur Hunnicutt.) Like blacks we had existential rhythm, an almost inborn drive "tae explore th' impawssible pawssibilities of yir pawssible impawssibilities" arising out of the insanity of American life. Nothing amused him more than the ironic spectacle of Americans recrossing the Atlantic to enthusiastically 'improve'—i.e., destroy—the mother country's quality of life.

Me, I had mixed feelings about my compatriots. Who could deny their incredible energy? What touchers, wrestlers, feelers, slappers—very un-English. Alas (like me) they'd brought their imperialist egos over with them. Davina said, "Have you noticed how it always ends up with you listening to *their* problems?" Sometimes, out of pique or envy, I inserted anti-American caricatures in my novel-journal, *Special File*, which I read aloud to groups in the Manor. "Man, that's really vital, groovy stuff," exclaimed Dr. Marve Munshin. "Can you make a copy for me to send home to Mom?"

Munshin, in particular, gave me the whim-whams. A crew-cut, tanklike ex-linebacker from Syracuse University, he had large staring eyes that never blinked and oversize pawlike hands that constantly hugged and patted you when he talked. I didn't like him touching me. Whenever he noticed me flinching or backing off he'd trap me with a heavy arm on my shoulder and turn his piercing Peter Lorre stare on me. "Are you all right? Feel like talking about it?"

Not all the Yanks were like that. A jewel was Larry Goodman, a Bellevue hospital staff dropout who arrived one morning with no money, a string-tied suitcase and a pet parrot named Lyndon he'd somehow smuggled past quarantine. "I read about you guys in Krassner's *Realist*. Got room for one more?" Gentle and dazed, Larry lacked the ham-handed push of guys like Munshin and vainly wandered around the Manor looking for a place for himself. A couple of weeks later he gave up. "It's kind of funny," he morosely told me as he packed to go. "I escaped from a straight medical system that encouraged patients to collude with their doctors by pretending to be sane—to this system where they've got to go crazy to please their doctors. I'm honestly not sure now which I prefer." He shook my hand. "I tried losing my mind here. Honest I did. Just couldn't hack it, I guess. I hate going home feeling such a failure."

The American problem was a pushover compared to a continuing one much closer to home.

Initially the Brixton locals had been rather pleasant. The vicar and his wife had us in to tea, the neighborhood bobby said to call him Tom and ask his help any time, and some of the wild street kids even helped us move in. Our stock had risen especially high after we got rid of the tramps. "My dears," gushed Mrs. Conway, the minister's wife, "you succeeded where even the Borough Medical Officer and police failed." As a goodwill gesture we kept the church's traditional policy of giving the main hall to community groups free of charge.

The honeymoon was brief. Soon I noticed people along Walworth Road giving me the fisheye. "Och, stop yir frettin', mon," scoffed Last. "They've put up wi' a lot worse'n us." Alf agreed. "If Brixton survived the Blitz, it can take Clare Council."

In fact, Brixton had a long history of tolerance and live-and-let-live. Solidly Labour, working class and increasingly black, the people who lived around the Manor greeted us with good-natured indifference when we moved in. After all, this part of the Borough had over 100 years' experience of absorbing without fuss all kinds of evangelical do-gooders from across the river. But in counting on a warm welcome we reckoned without current feelings. Massive redevelopment had shifted large hunks of old Brixton to the outer suburbs, shattering long-established neighborhoods and relationships, and isolating in high-rise flats the families who stayed behind. The Notting Hill race riots exposed a racial infection that had spread southward with deadly, unpublicized swiftness. Their street life eroded and communities breaking up, psyches blasted by accelerated change and identities threatened by blacks and foreigners, the "guid, wurkin' class" Brixtonians were less able to cope with a bunch of trendy loonies in their midst.

Clare Council, insulated by the Manor's teething problems and a New Leftish view of Brixton as full of happy ramified family units, caught on much too late. By the time the penny dropped Frisbie's caterwauling electric organ, Taya's inchoate screams, Sir Marlo's abuse of the next door neighbors ("Jerry on your tail, you blind bastard!"), the twins Ramsey and Roxie pilfering local shops and black novelist Bobby May's midnight strolls through the streets shouting "AH'M A-COMIN' FOR YOU, JIMMY BALDWIN!" had drastically depleted the fund of goodwill we'd started out with. The street kids began speaking for the Brixton community in no uncertain terms by making faces from the pavement, then inviting themselves in for a quick giggle, then smashing the windows we had so meticulously repaired and setting small fires outside the improvised door. Not that they had anything against us personally, Last kept saying, "They jus' refract their parents' irrational fear of what they dinna unnerstan'." Boris, less sentimental because he came from an area like this in East London, wanted to import some tough friends of his as security guards. "If we don't, th' lumpen sods out there will tear the place apart."

Last was confident that Boris had it all wrong—"as usual." Properly analyzed, our neighbors' behavior could be the start of a meaningful dialogue. "Cain't ye see? It's a call fer help, a strangled but intelligible protest aboot their whole alienated eggistence—their exile fr' wha' is True an' Real."

That weekend on the streets of Brixton we passed out leaflets inviting one and all to an Open Tea at the Manor.

A marvelously peaceful silence hung over the church, mainly because Davina and Boris had corraled the freakiest residents deep into the basement with orders to keep them down there till the coast was clear. The main hall, usually cluttered with semiconscious bodies and dirty blankets, Alf and I had faultlessly cleaned and also Air Wicked away the normal clouds of incense and marijuana. A long oilclothed table held a tea urn and mountains of cakes and mugs. Murmuring "Om" to himself and pacing up and down in his Harley Street mai-dical disguise, Willie Last serenely awaited the expected throngs.

Three thousand leaflets had gone out.

Ten locals showed up, including two whiskey-smelling Irish workmen from a nearby building site, several pensioners and Kenneth, a teenage ted who stoked the boiler in exchange for our letting him rehearse his rock 'n roll group in the church. Scattered among the rows of rented folding chairs, they seemed even fewer in number than they were.

Last was obviously disappointed by the derisory turnout but stayed on his best behavior, turning on the charm and shaking everyone by the hand personally. While our guests munched cakes and slurped tea he described Meditation Manor as a "community center meant tae bring new life, a new hahrt, tae a stricken part of Brixton neglected fer too long." (This didn't go down too well with the pensioners, who didn't look as if they saw themselves as neglected.) Warming to his subject, he stressed his and Boris Petkin's working-class roots but also lovingly lingered over the names of the titled peers and bishops on our growing list of sponsors. Then he introduced us present Councillors—like him, in our Sunday best suits and ties—as a "prominent West End businessman" (Alf), a "well-known author and TV personality" (me) and a "BBC executive." (Davina, looking rather the worse for wear, rushed up from the basement to take her bow, then rushed back to help Boris with their restless herd.) But it was Major Straw who knocked them out. Wearing a miniaturized set of campaign ribbons on his sober stockbroker's suit, he captivated Kenneth and the old ladies by describing in rousing detail how he'd earned his medals, from Palestine '39 to Suez '56. (Did I hear one of the Irishmen mutter, "Imperialist bastid"?)

After the Major softened up the visitors, Last went in for the kill. He explained Meditation Manor—which the locals insisted on calling 'Medication Manor'—as the first of a linked chain of mental health clinics designed to get back on their feet and into the community those people who might otherwise languish in mental hospitals. Our friends (never patients or clients) were not forced to work, or get up in the morning or go to sleep if they didn't feel like it. Staff and patients—terms we abhorred—mixed on equal terms, "Wi' a view, p'raps, tae th' day when us doctors can go mad an' be treated by th' so-called patients."

"That'll bloody confuse the issue," I heard some irreverent soul whisper.

Blandly, Last asked for questions.

A wizened, bundled-up old dear, Mrs. Rascoe, slowly wiped crumbs from her puckered, tiny mouth. " 'ere naow," she said in a surprisingly forthright tone, " 'oo controls yer nutters?" Mrs. Rascoe had lived all her seventy-three years in the same street, just opposite us.

Last gave her his strobe eye flutter and shy smile. He sweetly explained that the nub of existential therapy was allowing the person in distress to heal himself. Our job, as helpers, was to conduct him through an experience of death, journeying in the Other World and rebirth in the here and now. Mental health, as we understood it, involved a safe voyage back from aboriginal Chaos. ("Can you get a cheap day-return?" someone sniggered.)

Mrs. Rascoe protested that Last had not answered her question. " 'oo controls th' nutters?" she persisted.

He stonewalled again. Madness was not a disease, but a spiritual quest, and by letting it happen here we restored to the old church its lost religious identity.

Kenneth mildly inquired what kind of people the Manor took in.

Shifting uneasily in his chair, Last said: "Er ah some deluded psychiatrists call 'em . . . er, um, . . . schizophrenics. But—"

That did it.

Tea mugs suspended, some visitors sat bolt upright.

Mrs. Rascoe sharply piped up: "D'ja mean Jekyll an' Hyde, like?"

That *was* the popular fantasy, Last allowed.

"Fantasy moi bleedin' eye," retorted the larger Irishman. "Moi sis's bin locked up these five years wid schizzo-waddayecallit."

Last heavily corrected him: didn't he meant what misguided or quack doctors labeled schizophrenia?

"All oi know is she wen' aroun' liftin' her knickers tuh ivry pimple-faced kid in th' road," said the Irishman.

Last forced jocularity. "Surely *tha's* nuthin' fer a big bruiser like ye tae be afeared o'."

The Irishman's mate roared with laughter. "Ye've niver met his sis!"

An old man timorously raised his hand. "Are . . . any of *them* 'ere naow?"

This was the moment we had been waiting for. "Oh Jenny, w'd

ye come in please?" called Last. On cue, Jenny Potts toddled in, and my heart sank. We had rehearsed her over and over again in how to dress and what to say. She was out of her nutty nun's habit, all right—but into another costume of her own design: black knee-length leather boots over flesh-colored tights and a rough wooden crucifix reposing on the cleavage of her extremely revealing sweater. To me she looked like an ad in a soft porn magazine. (Later, she apologized and said she hadn't wanted to shame us by appearing shabby in public.) Straight as an arrow she went and sat next to Mrs. Rascoe and said brightly: "You see, I had been to *Song of Bernadette* sixty-two times and had this terribly unhealthy identification with Jennifer Jones. My friends here have helped me gain insight into why I needed to dissolve my ego in a fantasy object, which phenomenologically was my invalidated self engulfed by an ontologically inauthentic family disjunction. Of course I'm not Jennifer Jones anymore. Who'd want to be *that* old has-been? Please call me Brigitte from now on." She looked over at Dr. Last, who seemed pleased by her performance, then she flounced off waggling her hips like a shimmy dancer.

Mrs. Rascoe looked puzzled. "If yer arsks me I'd say th' gel's still crackers."

Last's smile took on a fixed aspect. With just a hint of impatience he said that Clare's first rule of therapy was never to impose your own idea of sanity on anyone else. "One way o' luikin' at it is, Bardot's a significant clinical advance over Jennifer Jones."

We had one final card to play, and I wish we hadn't. Partly to demonstrate our interracialism, Bobby May was called on. But the instant the black novelist appeared Mrs. Rascoe leaped from her chair and pointed a wrinkled, accusing finger at him. "That's th' bloke wot give our Jim sech a nasty fright. Yer oughter be ashamed, yer oughter!" She declared that her favorite nephew, a pipe fitter named James Baldwin, had hurriedly packed off from the area when told a strange black man was out to get him. ("Ah'm a-comin' for you, Jimmy Baldwin!")

Bobby (high on hash) roared "Racist bitch!" at Mrs. Rascoe and ran up to the tall pulpit to denounce us all for complicity in Britain's old slave trade. Alf whispered to me, "We're not doing too well. Maybe Willie should close the show."

Anna did that for us. An ear-splitting screech, followed by a long low moan and muffled shouts, seeped up from the basement. A disheveled, water-soaked Davina burst in: "Willie! Come quickly. Anna says she's spawning!" Then Anna Shepherd herself emerged, or rather floated in. Naked except for some rubber sheeting tied around her knees—a makeshift mermaid's tail we'd fitted out at her request—her long, black hair matted over her flushed vibrant face, she bumpety-bumped along to us as in a potato sack race. "Oh hello there," she beamed proudly at us, wriggling from Davina's grasp. "I've just laid a very large egg." ("So've we," muttered Alf, eyeing the stunned locals.)

Her large breasts swaying to her naked waist, Anna flipped onto the trestle table, scattering cakes and crockery. Last kept his cool. In for a dime in for a dollar, his expression said.

"How're ye, Anna? Enjoyin' yirself, are ye?"

She rolled off the table and crawled to him. "Oh yeth," she relapsed into a childish lisp. "Ith tho thweet thwimming around with no other fith to bother me. God ith a thord fith, you know. He put hith thord into me and now I'm jutht an itty-bitty thalmon hopping ith way upthream to lay my eggth and become a momma fith. God fith would love me then, wouldn't he Willie?" She dug inside her mermaid's tail and came out with two large handfuls of her excrement. "Thee my eggth?"

Last smiled compassionately down at our sacred, stinking fith. "Er ah Anna, w'd ye care tae tell oor guests wha' ye did afore ye came here?" Abruptly she switched to her normal, stentorian voice. "Of course, Doctor. I had chambers in the Middle Temple and specialized in estate probate and litigious trusteeships. . . . But that wath before I met Willie-fith and Borith-fith and. . . ."

While Anna squatted on the floor to audibly do her "thits" inside the mermaid's tail, Mrs. Rascoe firmly put down her tea mug and scuttled from the hall. With embarrassed nods the others also crept out.

"Ta ta," said the Irishman with the mad sister. "Oi'll sure tell me Maeve about yez. Might be just th' place for her."

Only Kenneth, the rock 'n' roller, stayed behind to admire Anna drawing a floor mural with a watery-brown substance in her hands. "I've never seen anybody do that before. Is she *made* of shit?"

That night local kids smashed all our street-facing windows and relit fires outside the door. More rocks were thrown. In the morning, obscene graffiti and 'KBW' were smeared all over the Manor's stone columns.

"Hey man," asked hung-over Bobby May, "is that old Mosley's 'Keep Britain White' gang?"

Alf sighed wearily. "More likely 'Keep Brixton Well.' "

The abortive tea party seemed to confirm the truth of what Last had been implying ever since Armistice Hall: all outward roads were blocked, only the Inner Road counted now. We had failed to connect with NON-RUT, and we had failed to connect with the Brixton community. The signs were unmistakeably clear that the world was not yet ready for us. Why shilly shally any longer? "Let's move oota this desert of compromise an' plant oor standard on th' heights off eggistainshul risk," he urged. The Manor was the spiritual orgasm we had worked so long and hard for, and we didn't want to cheat ourselves of it by trying to win some sort of cheap popularity contest among our neighbors. It was their lookout if they refused to be Enlightened. In a word, to hell with everyone else, let's concentrate on saving our own kind.

Boris strenuously objected that Last's "left-infantile adventurism" was a counsel of bourgeois despair, a product of imperfect political analysis which put us at risk for no tangible return. Though he held no brief for the Brixton yahoos, he urged a policy of continuing to plug away undramatically at friendship with the locals, no matter what. After all (Boris said) if Stalin could sign a nonaggression pact with Hitler to buy Russia time to build its defenses, we could show similar "revolutionary patience." Post-Leninist Russia had many such lessons to teach us if we cleared the liberal rubbish from our minds.

In the weeks that followed Last and Petkin clashed repeatedly over how best to manage the Manor, but always masked their personal differences in grandiose jargon. Last argued that Boris' need for medical accountability, for a chain of command with a man at the top where the buck stopped, was simply another form of his neurotic craving for the original family situation. The kind of rules Boris demanded were the enemy of spontaneity and simply encouraged dependence on a system we were out to destroy. Anyway, true authority should never be imposed from without, it was a personal quality that people instinctively responded to. Only those who did not possess this inner authority had to force their will on others—"like Beria and Joe Stah-leen," said Last, looking squarely at Boris.

The issue was joined over Anna Shepherd.

It was some time before any of us realized just how completely Anna needed to regress. She'd taken to Meditation Manor like a duck to water—literally. We were used to residents going back to infancy; Anna was our first case of someone retreating to the primal slime. Fortunately, one or two of us Councillors had experienced ourselves on LSD as animals and birds and had little trouble adjusting to a female fish. We regularly hosed Anna down and built her a corrugated tin tank in the basement, where she became the special project of Dr. Marve Munshin, the ex-jock from Syracuse U. They became incredibly fond and possessive of each other. Anna wouldn't let Marve out of her sight, and Marve hated anyone else touching her. Many a harrowing night he slapped and roughhoused her out of hysterics; they were the battling Maggie and Jiggs of the Manor. Anna loved it. "Oh Marve, you big ape."

With Marve's encouragement Anna began to ascend the ichthyological scale, from an amoeba state up through the fishy depths to human age three or four, old enough to launch a campaign of sustained aggro against the community. She laid her 'eggth' (shit) all over the Manor, including in our beds, and enjoyed waking us at all hours to imperiously demand a bottle or get one of us to burp her. Even in the throes of 'therapeutic reintegration' she remained a bossy old battleax, haughtily ordering us around like junior counsel in her courtroom. But telling her to fuck off also meant tangling with big Marve Munshin, and no one felt strong enough for that. Anyway, she was mad and vulnerable and too much rode on her as Clare's first success.

Anna split the community into hostile camps. Some residents, whose clothes or peace of mind she had ruined, wanted her thrown out, and others, mainly Americans, agreed with Last that letting Anna run riot was a supreme test of what the Manor was about. A confused minority wanted something done about her, but weren't sure what. The Anna Question grew like Donovan's brain till it threatened to wreck the whole community. (I reckoned she'd have lasted about five minutes in Con House.) Deepening personal animosity between Last and Petkin ensured that Manor opinion hardened into a bitter factional struggle. You had to line up behind one or the other—there was less and less room for compromise—and because each doctor, typically, tried to outflank the other from the left, it also meant buying into their particular version of twentieth-century history. Boris never tired of pointing out similarities between the Manor and Lenin's Russia after 1919; we could survive, he said, only by suppressing our antisocial elements and enforcing (sinisterly unspelled out) "administrative measures," preferably imposed by a supreme Medical Director (guess who?). Last, while cheerfully admitting that Anna was a big pain, contended she was also our revolutionary moment of truth, our Kronstadt. He loved needling Boris with historical examples of "Stah-leenist treachery," from the massacre of the kulaks to Trotsky's assassination. In their loud wrangle over the precise nature of the Soviet—was it a deformed workers' dictatorship, or bureaucratic state capitalism?—Anna got forgotten. Most residents were too hyped on dope or their own miseries to follow the Talmudic ins and outs of the doctors' slanging matches replete with opaque quotes from Marx and Sartre, so in the end what counted was which man you were emotionally hooked on. I, of course, was a Lastian because, among other things, he had the LSD. But I never completely suppressed a slightly guilty leaning toward the things Boris represented.

Though Boris smiled less than any man I'd ever known, and had the soul of a Lord High Executioner, his commitment to stability and his unanarchist sense of direction undeniably satisfied a deep hunger in the community. Some people needed a respite from the whipsawing effects of Last's romantic narcissism. Even Anna, when ordered by Boris to clean up her mess, obeyed meekly. Without a qualm, he confiscated Sy's cocaine and locked yammering Ramsey and Roxie in their cubicle until they came to heel. While the rest of us endlessly debated how to negotiate peace terms with the local teenage vandals, Boris did not hesitate to dump pails of cold water on them from the roof. Lacking Last's charisma, he staked his authority on blunt charmlessness and never truckling to the residents' whims, traits that endeared him to the Manor's more anxious types. For the first time since the Communist party (Stepney branch), he had something organizational to bite on, and—Stalin to Last's Lenin—he quietly set about building a power base.

After so many Lastian storms, Boris' unhip obduracy felt solid and reassuring under my feet. For all his sneering bluster he was something familiar to me, basically a reformer in the great Jewish authoritarian tradition who saw the Manor in a Communist perspective of mass struggle for a better life rather than as a psychedelic adventure playground (Last's view). As a party type he hewed to his original belief in man's ability to control the movement of history, to plan a rational social order. He still believed in the mind Last had lost faith in.

Before I could piece together all my tangled emotions, the Martins showed up.

They came like the Holy Family, with stars in their eyes and carrying nappies for their small baby. Without having consulted anyone Last had talked Sam Martin, a former patient of his, and his wife Rose into locking up their TV repair shop in Chichester and signing on as the Manor's full-time housekeepers. "Aw, jes' move in an' do yir thing," he said and promptly forgot about them. Nervous and insecure, the Martins slung a hammock-cradle in the pantry for "wee Willie" (named for Last) and tried to fit in, but Boris wasn't having it. What the hell was the idea of hiring an unqualified, former hospitalized patient as staff? Last replied that Sam's breakdown *was* his qualification, and as usual the doctors ended up on a lofty theoretical plane, slamming away at each other with Lenin's *What Is to Be Done* and Stalin's *The National Question*. Caught in the crossfire, the Martins grew alarmed and confused, which only confirmed Boris' poor opinion of them. When Rose, still in postbirth blues, had bouts of weeping, Sam appealed to his sponsor, Last, who washed his hands of them. "It's a community decision, nae up tae me alone." Clearly, the Martins were not worth a full-scale showdown with Boris—just yet. When Sam approached some of us Councillors we didn't want to know either. Why sacrifice our newly forged unity for the sake of a couple we hardly knew? Rose resolved the problem by breaking down completely, and Last peremptorily and without notice sacked the Martins.

"It's fer their own guid," Last told me. "Rose's turned oot pure psychotic—mebbe tha's why Sam teamed up wi' her. Hell, they oughttae be grateful that we showed 'm how incompatible wi' this wurk they really are. Probably saved 'em years of wasted effort."

Charitably, we didn't ask the Martins to pay us back their wages.

Shortly after the Martins left, Willie Last approached me in his old charming, tentative way. Would I move into the Manor and help him protect its integrity against er, well, "unkawnshus saboteurs?" (I.e., Boris.)

Would I? Oh boy. Back together at the OK Corral!

Lena was aghast when I rang her with the news, and begged me not to move bag and baggage into the Manor. "Have you gone absolutely bonkers, Sid?" she exclaimed. "Last and his crew of professional crazies will eat an amateur like you alive. Please, please don't go." Ah yes, I thought, that was to be expected of someone having transference difficulties with her new shrink; at least she was getting the hostility out of her system. Seeing that she couldn't change my mind, Lena helped me shut up Regents Gardens and then drove me across the river to the Manor. "I'll be waiting when you get out, *liebchen.*" Sad and tight-lipped, with the sorrowing eyes of a convict's wife, she watched me disappear into my new home. The church's burned-plank door crashing shut behind me brought back all the prison films of my youth, from *Each Dawn I Die* to *Mutiny in the Big House.* What had Ida Lupino sobbed when her lover Mad Dog Earl (Humphrey Bogart) had been shot after being released from San Quentin in *High Sierra?* "Free at last." Except that I'd find my freedom *inside* the walls.

Closing my eyes to the Manor's stench of disused jailhouse, the ghostly odors of Labour's pacifist piety, the sheer ugliness of the joint, I grimly pitched in to help my war buddy, Wille Last.

Heady, euphoric days. Sleepless nights. Hand holding, embracing, breast cuddling, wild screams. Terrible insults, even more unendurable silences. Most times I felt like a tiny psychiatric submarine floating through the boiling bloodstreams of Anna, Sir Marlo, Frisbie and the others—all, in Last's words, "goin' through that special agony reserved fer those fyoo obstinate souls who refuse, at th' cost of their lives, tae relinquish their whole-y humanity." Trouble was, where Last saw Holy Suffering my Con House-sharpened instincts experienced Manorites as temperamental prodigies. God knows we had our share of prima donnas at Con House. But because Dick Drummond frowned on individual therapy, nobody got special treatment. The unit's rough and ready democracy, which inhibited personality cults, made madness as common (and often as unnoticed as) dirt. In Con House *everybody* was crazy, so—in a sense—nobody was.

But at Meditation Manor the mad were exalted. At times it reminded me of my days in Hollywood—the same struggle for Harry Cohn or Jack Warner's favor, the studio infighting, petty malice and publicity consciousness. Even the same star system. Indisputably, Anna Shepherd was the Manor's queen bee, its Joan Crawford-Bette Davis figure. She was a star in every way, including (I suspected) how she conformed to her bosses' image of her. So different, I thought, from the anonymous, drably defeated, cases in Last's book *The Unhealed Heart*.

But I liked Anna in some ways. You couldn't help but sympathize with her long heroic struggle to save her sanity through one awful padded cell after another. Before Willie Last came on the scene, no doctor had even remotely grasped her impelling need to gamble everything on total, uninhibited regression. That's why I didn't mind sharing the sacred if filthy job of cleaning, feeding, hosing down and nursing her. If we could help Anna, then all the crap we'd heaped on one another all these months would take on a certain dignity, even splendor. My doubts didn't begin till the night I took rota alone.

Making my usual rounds I went downstairs to check the water level in Anna's tank. She panicked if it got too low. Gently I knocked on the broken door of the womblike coal cellar and entered the pitch black, foul-smelling place. A scratchy, whimpering sound greeted me. In the darkness I squatted down, waiting. The odor of sour milk, feces and stale water was overpowering; it was more fetid than a coal mine.

"H'lo Anna," I said. No reply. Then I heard a soft breathing, a sniffing close to my face. A bony forehead touched mine, then rolled back and forth across it. I sat while she moved her scalp against mine, grunting and pawing me. Suddenly she stopped. Her long matted hair dropped on my neck and shoulders, as she wordlessly straddled me, hooking her legs around my waist. Secure, she began rocking swiftly. Harder and harder she jerked, I held on till she said "Ahhhh! . . ." Three or four times later she climbed off. I heard her lie down in the corner. In the faint slit of light from the basement light bulb her eyes glittered with pleasure, then shut. A baby's gurgle, then more cooing. She chewed savagely at one of her large, drooping breast's nipples, then lay back and clawed the air in frustration. I gave her her usual bottle of sugared water, which she sucked, then I turned her on her side and smacked her bottom; she burped gratefully. "Fank you, Marvie-fith."

I said I was Sid, not Dr. Munshin. The coal cellar light snapped on. Covered with a shit-smeared blanket and shaking with rage, Anna stood up in the tank. In her most sonorous Queen's Counsel voice she cried: "How dare you molest me, you damned impostor!" And chased me out with wild, judicial curses and pieces of excrement.

Clearly I had little s.a.—schizophrenia appeal—for Anna. Nor, I discovered, for the other residents.

On a routine check a couple of nights later I found the twins unhappy. "Where's Willie?" snarled Roxie, backing against her cubicle wall. I said Last was at a Paris human rights conference with Sartre and Genet. "What about Boris or Dick?" sullenly asked Ramsey. All the doctors were temporarily away, I said. The fourteen-year-olds glared at me. "Listen punk," said Ramsey, "our dad shells out alimony for the best in the house. We don't want no flunkies like you."

As I increasingly did, I went and confided in Davina, who agreed that the residents had all too quickly picked up on how to manipulate Clare's internal pecking order. "Strange, isn't it? They're all supposed to be in ecstasy, withdrawn, possessed and all the rest of it. Yet they fly like homing pigeons straight into the arms only of men who have medical school diplomas."

Jurisdictional disputes were rife. Everybody had 'their' schizophrenic. Once, when Marve Munshin and I heard curvy Jenny Potts cry out, he practically ran over me to grab her first. Another time Chuck Biberman took luscious, speechless Taya out of my arms: "I saw her first." Competition was keen for the younger, more excitable women. As Davina watched Boris wrestle with hysterical, chair-smashing Trish Wakefield (36″-22″-36″), she remarked: "Oh well, I suppose she's got something I haven't. Schizophrenia, I mean."

Stimulated by American homage and growing, if grudging, recognition at home, Last began actively courting the mass media. No longer were television and newspapers th' ainemy I'd once prematurely exposed oor battle strategy tae with my ultraradical press communiqués. Now they were instruments of capitalist mystification, which we would turn against the mystifiers themselves. The media was not slow to warmly reciprocate Last's embrace, and competition soon hotted up in the Manor to see who could snag the most lineage and prime TV time. Anna Shepherd and Jenny Potts became all the rage, and well-publicized visits by the Beatles and Princess Margaret ensured that, media- and trendwise, we were in like flynn.

Boris hated it. "Have we lost our senses, comrades?" he stormed. "Why did we suffer in the wilderness if it was only to whore after the gutter press at the first crack of a clapper-board. They're just using us to paint a shiny gloss on their incurable syphilitic sores." Even Dick, who had learned the hard way that Conolly House gained no long term benefits from publicity, wondered if it didn't put us in an "inauthentic position."

Last bridled, "Ye don't think I *like* wastin' time on those Fleet Street hacks, d'ye. I feel like pukin' after every interview." He must have been sick a lot, for those hypnotically fluttering eyelashes and that soft elliptical brogue were now familiar to millions of readers and viewers. He was much in demand as a polished, photogenic TV performer (which Boris was not). 'Lastian' became a vogue word—*Vogue* magazine profiled him in its "People to Watch" section—and for a time you couldn't open a newspaper or magazine without finding an interview with him. BBC-2 sent a "Man Alive" crew to shoot him narrating a documentary on Anna's shit murals, and a couple of journalists were so dazzled that they became his private patients.

Through it all Last insisted that his basic attitude to the press had not changed, only "tactically adjusted" to take account of our acquisition of a stable base in the Manor. To Boris' skepticism Last had a pat answer. Had not Lenin taken capitalist money and a sealed German train in order to reach his rendezvous with world revolution at the Finland Station? "Th' only dif'frence is, th' Bolsheviks used pistols an' bombs—we've got th' *Sunday Times* color supplement."

Almost overnight, it seemed, Clare Council had acquired a wurld ootluik and a political perspective. The Last/Petkin hypothesis, rooted in flashes of insight and modest research among a fairly narrow spectrum of unhappy Scottish and Home Counties families, was made to apply to any struggle anywhere—not only to the double-bound 'Harrisons' of Pinner, Middlesex, but also to South African miners and Brazilian peasants. "Oppression" was the same whether it occurred in small family units and mental hospitals or exercised by whole governments. Mississippi white racism was "macro-social terror imposin' pseudomutuality on pathogenically perceived aspects of th' false-self system" (Last). Britain's Great Train Robbery was "an existential dysfunction of capitalist serialization" (Petkin). Even the current Tokyo Olympics was "a replication of Western imperialism's subject-object colonizer-colonized torturer-tortured duality" (Drummond).

Davina and I attended one of Last and Drummond's 'Liberation Psych-Ins' at the Manor. Standing at the rear of the s.r.o. crowd of students, Americans and ex-New Lefties, she confessed: "I feel a bit thick. Why *is* Fidel Castro an ontological externalization of Lyndon Johnson's castration fantasy?"

Clare's swing to the left threw me into a fine tizzy. Had I read the signals wrong again? How in hell had the Tao which depoliticized me made Bolsheviks of my Brothers? I listened intently to Last's public speeches for a clue, but his 'two track' approach only confused me further. To medical audiences he spieled diagnostic concepts and family classification systems; students and beatniks got the mystical inner trip. Rarely did the twain ever meet. Yet he denied that there was any inconsistency—except in the minds of his audiences, who were "hongry sheep" that had to be spoonfed, gently and gradually, only what they found easiest to ingest. (In the war, he reminded me, Allied troops had unwittingly killed many of the concentration camp walking skeletons they were liberating by thoughtlessly gorging them on too much food too soon.) "I'd hoped Conolly Hoose'd taught ye tae communicate wi' deluded cases in their own language." By deluded cases Last meant his own followers.

An assumption of total spiritual superiority now underwrote almost everything we did. Manor residents—indeed much of the outside world—were hongry sheep and Clare Council the Wise Shepherds. A cult of Last permeated the Manor. Let him coast to a stop even for an instant and flocks of breathless adorers surrounded him like baby chicks. Once I saw a sari-clad girl reverently lotus sit outside a toilet he was perched on. It would have taken a tougher man than Last to resist. Sometimes, as a gesture to our old agnosticism, if he saw me watching he'd surreptitiously roll his eyes up to heaven as if to say: *wha' fyools these mortals be.* But, so long as he could also convey a token embarrassment with all this adulation, Last dug having his own ashram. How often I came upon him, in the dead of night, comforting a raving blond in his arms or dropping a mixture of hashish and Scotch whiskey (Dundee Dynamite he called it), his face a mask of unendurable agony. Shadows now seemed to darken his gray eyes, his stoop became more pronounced. He looked worn out. Once I caught him coming exhausted out of Jenny Potts' cubicle at 5:00 A.M. carrying his kimono. Grinning strangely, he slumped against the wall. "Brither," he groaned, "they're crucifyin' me." Martyrdom agreed with Last. He might try to look like hell, strolling about dressed only in a haggard expression and an elegant silk robe sexily open to the waist—but I had never seen him so carefree. Though he wasn't at the Manor all that much, the time he did spend with us was all up front and conspicuous. He liked to greet visitors at the door with a gentle smile and hand bow while Buddha sitting beside the Robert Owen bust so that the twenty-four-hour spotlight shone on him too, and his private meditations were conducted so publicly that they were virtual happenings. When I asked him why he didn't use one of the Manor's secluded cubicles, he replied with an absolutely straight face that generals not only had to risk their lives along with "th' troops" but had to be *seen* to be doing so.

Of course we did not dare interrupt him with mundane chores.

He might symbolically wash an occasional dish or change a soiled sheet but, by and large, we accepted his view of himself, that his real job was ceremonial, to be a Presence. Above all, he enjoyed presiding over communal dinners, the high point of everybody's night—and day. At the head of the long table heaped with plates of spaghetti, French bread and bottles of red wine, Last jovially engaged the American interns in cutting contests to see who could tell the goriest operating room story or bantered philosophically with our show-biz visitors. Illuminated by candlelight, dramatically outlined against the main hall's high, lead-braced stained-glass window, he did indeed seem a Highland Jesus Christ.

These dinners often lasted well into the next morning. Our neighbors had already gone to work before most of us were in bed. Last's stamina was amazing. A fifteen-minute snooze left him fresh as a daisy; the rest of us spent the entire day recuperating. Meditation Manor's 'night' was over only when everyone had dropped off to sleep around Last, still enthroned in his chair and ready to take on all comers.

His self-promotion to a Christ figure coincided with a shift in Clare's attitude to insanity. Originally, Last had taught me that madness was a comprehensible, but definitely psychotic, response to invalidation. By subtle stages it had become something else, a kind of supersanity implicitly superior to the alienation which normals called normality. Indeed, anyone at the Manor who wasn't totally off his chump was treated as a second-class citizen. So the competition was to go as crazy as possible the way some kids will try to appear brighter than others for a teacher who gives gold stars for the right kind of answers. Last not only encouraged this worshipful attitude to insanity but also personified it. He had nothing but contempt for social workers and doctors who kept their psychic distance from the mentally ill; such detachment he likened to the voyeurism of the bullfight critic who is afraid to enter the arena. Insisting on the oracular powers of schizophrenics, who were "foreign correspondents back fr' uther wurlds wi' battlefield reports we haven't th' wit tae unscramble," he said that the only way to decode such reports was to climb into the schizophrenic's soul—be one.

At least that's how I understood it. It did not occur immediately to me that while I (and others) risked everything on Last's magical mystery tour, the way he freaked out rarely took him too far from his couch or desk. At his nuttiest he never stopped lecturing or writing.

Perhaps to compensate for his inability or unwillingness to break down, Last went to extreme lengths to identify with schizophrenics, to proclaim them the teachers and he their pupil. (Was this why he lavished praise on me the madder I got?) In a sense, he'd become one of his own patients. Marxists used to call this kind of flattery of the masses 'tailism.' At the Manor we called it creative madness.

Creativity was the big thing. You were nobody at Meditation Manor, even considered odd, if you didn't 'do' something artistic. That was almost as important a qualification for residence as madness. Cued by the attention Anna received—she had progressed to carving clever little soap ducks in her tank—many Manorites tossed off poetry and paintings as if schizophrenia hadn't been invented. Even our worst withdrawn, Taya, felt able to hold an open-air exhibition of her handwoven rugs in Brockwell Park. All this was nothing compared to the suddenly released energies of the doctors. Away from their nagging wives and kids, and turned on by the Manor's abundance of libidinal outlets, they churned out an impressive number of monographs and book chapters. It was as if a creative dam inside each of them had broken. Dick Drummond wrote an entire book within a fortnight and had time to start collaborating with Last on a Penguin Special, *Schizophrenia: Imperialism of the Mind.* He had more or less dropped Con House for an 'anti family' of young sexual communards near Regent's Park—and to be close to his beloved gorillas (guerrillas?). Not to be outdone, Boris grew his own Old Testament beard and buckled down to a monumental study of sex and Hasidism called *Baal Shem Tov in Love;* the free time for this he'd bought by installing Davina as his 'anti wife' (unpaid housekeeper) in the Martins' old flat next to the kitchen. She cooked, washed and ironed for him, and divided her (much reduced) leisure between flamenco guitar lessons and fighting off a takeover bid for Boris from Bronwen, who had flown into our coop from Conolly House after Screwy Lewie made life too hot for her there. (Boris, who missed his own children, adopted Bronwen as his karma-daughter.) Meanwhile, horned and helmeted Major Straw-Hengist kept busy drafting his memoirs, *A Thousand Years of Blighty*, subtitled *A Reborn Officer Remembers*, and Alf took up morris dancing.

How could I compete against this burst of activity? The atmosphere that stimulated everyone else's creative juices drained mine. In its nineteenth volume, I shut down my novel-journal, *Special File*. Stopped writing. *Finito*. Last, welcoming my "cessation of egoic activity" as a sign of Grace, kissed me with tears in his acid-blurred eyes and said: "Brither Sid, *yir time has come.*" Had it?

Were almost two years of LSD, acorn tea and Yoga hernia going to pay off? Glory be.

With a clear heart and empty head I made plans to lift off.

Up on the farthest tier of the Manor balcony, in one of the plywood cubicles built for residents who had cracked up, I prepared my launching pad: a London version of a Siberian shaman's hutch. In the middle of the floor I screwed a Tree of Life (ex-broom handle) and four pegs, covering them with the sacred blanket Lena had stitched for me, and at the top of this blanket-*yourt* I cut a hole for spirit-escapes, then notched the pole with symbols copied from Eliade's *Shamanism: Archaic Techniques of Ecstasy*. Inside the hutch I laid out the tools of my trade: dark glasses, Siberian drum and rattle, surgical rubber gloves, a box of comb honey, an 8″ x10″ glossy photograph of Charlie (The Bird) Parker, and medical forceps to assist rebirth—but minus the Corona portable typewriter I no longer required to write my *Special File* communiqués on. At each of the tent's corners, to signify the Zodiac elements, I deposited a jar of Thames River water, a box of Swan matches, a plastic bag of earth from St. James Park and a toy balloon I had to keep inflating. After a brief purifying ceremony, I invited in Willie Last, who took one look and said quietly, "That's pretty mad, Sid." With this blessing, I knew I was in business.

now
summon tutelary spirits
softly drum on earth-covered floor
drop 750 mg LSD
chant mixture hard-driving chicago blues & shamanjabber
sing song to dead alive at center of earth

hey oo oo oo oo ah ah   hey oo oo oo ah ah

weightless

go clare sessions one better   *am* animals
growling jarga panther   chuffing doonto bear
let altaic ghosts dance me into nonhuman hearts

ANIMALS TAKE OVER

grrrrrrmmmmmmmmmmmmmmmmmmnnnnnnnnnnnnmmmmm
chmmmmmmmmmmmmmmmmmmmmmmmmmmmmmmmmmmmnh
owwrrrrrrrrrrgghh

!

zero gravity

hey oo oo oo oo ah ah   hey oo oo oo ah ah
i want a little girl   just to
call my own

cherry red!

scared   hope someone come in & stop me   nobody does

A new spirit, along with the usual flying snakes and scowling griffins, oozed out of my ruptured brain. Its cunning, watery eyes gloated over spectral bifocals. "We'll knock 'em dead, kiddo," it said in a fruity pitchman's voice. I called it Bilko.

Security-wise, Meditation Manor was a vast improvement over my apartment and even Conolly House. You could flip out without scaring the neighbors or bringing down a herd of hypodermic-bearing nurses on your head. The madder you were the better everyone liked it. Anyone stood ace high who dropped their "socially cripplin' role tae stand naked an' exposed tae th' Light." I didn't stop to think that every morning Willie Last went back to *his* socially crippling role.

Word quickly spread that one of the Sacred 7 (no less!) was going up the spout, and I took over from Anna as the Manor's No. 1 box-office draw. People began to stop by my door to leave flowers, or meditate or just simply hang around in the hope that my baraka would rub off on them. Clare Council seemed to be solidly on my side, too. Last fondly smiled at me as I imagined L. B. Mayer had done at Lassie and Mickey Rooney, stars he'd personally promoted. Alf helped me rewrite my will; Tony Straw read me to sleep with chapters of his book. Twice daily Davina came around with a bedpan to see if I was "regular," and every morning Boris shone a pencil light into my eyes and took my blood pressure. "Can't afford to have you croaking on us here," he grunted. With such support how could I fail?

An idea fixed itself in my bursting head. It was that Clare Council was the London equivalent of the civil rights movement in America and that I was a freedom fighter like the SNCC field workers I had met in the South last year. I began to croon to myself songs I adapted to the present struggle.

"Oh freedom, Oh freedom
Oh, freedom over me
And before they label me mad
I'll fly to China and be bad
And go home tae my Gaw'd an' be free."

and

"We shall stand under, we shall stand under
We shall unner'stand some day
Oh, deep in my haid I do believe
We shall unner'stand some day."

Free a' Last. Free a' Last. Great Gaw'd-amighty—free a' Last!

Except of Lena the Leech, whose constant carping about Last was becoming pretty intolerable. He found her so uninteresting, she complained, that he hadn't even bothered to show up for the past few appointments "What do I have to do to win his approval—go as nuts as you and Irving?" She was sore as hell but as usual kept it tightly bottled up; not for Lena the open defiance of Sybil Last or Nancy Drummond's drunken fury. Instead she produced her version of Viv Petkin's migraine aggression: stomachaches, which she parlayed into false appendicitis and then a tumor no X-ray could detect. When I refused to take all this nonsense seriously, she began leaving me neatly typed translations of Rilke (he and Sylvia Plath were her favorite poets) under the church door every evening.

"Alas, as I was hoping for human help; angels
suddenly stepped silently over
my prostrate heart."

and

"Shine, oh shine and let the constellations
look upon me. For I fade away."

and

"Oh, to be dead at last and endlessly know them
all the stars!"

Silly, foolish girl. Didn't she know that I handled a dozen such grandstanding false alarms every day at the Manor?

I ignored Lena's bullying notes—after all, she was Willie's pigeon now—until Hebbie's inevitable phone call. The scene back at Lena's place was a rerun of her previous suicide try. After Hebbie's husband washed out the sleeping pills with hot black coffee and he and Hebbie left, I walked Lena back and forth while she babbled on and on about a nightmare she'd had. "You and Irv had fallen into Willie Last's web and I was next. Save me from the human spider!" I pushed her away and told her to get a better grip on herself. "How can I?" she cried. "He'll kill me—and you'll be next." Then, protected by her stupor, she took a deep breath and turned really nasty. "You think Last and the others are your brothers—but they're not. I know how the human spider talks about you with Irv. Laughs at you, says you're like a *schicker*, a drunken clown on roller skates. Don't you see, *liebchen—Willie Last hates you!*"

Something snapped. I grabbed Lena's throat and pressed her back into bed, exploding with curses. My grip tightened until I felt sperm coming down inside my trousers, then I crawled into bed with her. Next morning before I left I scrawled a bit of Shakespeare on a pad beside Lena's heavily sleeping form:

"So shalt thou feed on death that feeds on man
And, death once dead, there's no more dying then."

But did that bitch know something I didn't know?

Back in the bosom of my Clare Council family I felt strange vibrations. The novelty of my shift in status from 'oxygen pumper' to 'pearl diver'—Manor terms for staff and patient—had begun to pall, and Boris dropped broad hints that I was putting on a crazy act for Last's benefit. Even my confidante Davina groused that I was letting the side down. "One less viable Councillor means more work for the rest of us, Sid. Someone's got to stay behind and clean up the mess." The message I got was that the Holeh Fire was okay for mere plebs but we Brithers had to have enough strength of character to abstain from the disintegration we urged on others. Here I'd sweated so hard to produce my madness to Clare's specifications, and now they treated me as if I was . . . well, mad. It wasn't fair.

Last refused to deny or confirm that the old freezola was on, or that I was being given the Clive Flynn treatment. All he said was that I was so far out there ahead of everyone else that I mustn't lean on him anymore. "If anything I should come tae *yew*—Master."

Shit, I'd been kicked upstairs again.

> *The parallel between my situation and that of the double-bind children in* The Unhealed Heart *was getting too close for comfort. I had painstakingly learned to fight shy of sanity to gain Last's approval. But now my madness displeased the other Councillors whom he needed to keep the 'family' going. Would I become expendable like Rose and Sam Martin?*
>
> *As a Lastian diagram it might read like this:*

I say	Last says
Something has changed.	*Nothing has changed.*
The Brothers dislike me for going mad.	*You're projecting your own self-hatred.*
I'm not invited to Clare meetings anymore.	*We don't want to disturb you. Anyway they're only informal get-togethers.*
You're trying to kill me.	*'Killing' is a metaphor for rebirth.*
Nobody loves me anymore.	*You're imagining things.*

The more I felt disconfirmed by my Brothers the greater my need to show my urban shaman's flag in Meditation Manor as freely as I did in Conolly House. Not so easy, this. Most residents were already spoken for. Poaching went on all the time but you had to be quick off the mark. One night I blocked my soul sister Brudwif (nee Bronwen, now Boris' 'daughter'), wafting through the drafty old church in a transparent cotton shift tied at the waist with a Welsh St. David's flag. "No . . . don't," she shrank from my embrace. "I am the Whore of Babylon moving along the Time Bend toward Mary Magdalen. Reb Boris says I will be lost forever in inner space if I let you touch me."

Boris, the clever sod.

Such noncooperation forced me to look outside for non-Manor patients. (It was also a good way of ignoring Lena, who was bombarding me with farewell letters in the form of Rilke poems.) My first nonschizophrenic patient was Mrs. Alexis Shane, a *Life* magazine writer. She had come to talk to Last and was thrilled at finding me ("Well, I declare, it's Sidney Bell, my fa-vorite cult author.") as a bonus. A fragile, pretty Charlestonian, Mrs. Shane dug the Manor scene. After shucking off her clothes in my shaman's cubicle, she let me tune into her vibrations by touching her all over, and she shivered as I probed her sex parts for 'the trouble.' (This was standard procedure at the Manor.) Ah yes, a father fixation plus slipped disc. Nothing to worry about, I told Mrs. Shane. Her head flew up, eyes shining. "How did you *know?*" Then buried her head in my lap, sobbing loudly. On terminating the usual treatment I crawled exhausted into my tent. "An' don' fergit," I yawned, "th' writer ye're tryin' tae interview is th' yew tha's tryin' tae interview him."

Swifty wasn't such a pushover.

A tall, beautiful, spectacular-legged air hostess from Arkansas, she regularly flew into town. Her salutation at my apartment door usually was, "H'lo, Sittin' Bull, le's fuck." She'd sail into my arms, loaded with duty-free Cognac and kisses, and before I could stop her she was halfway out of her dress, singing in her Grand Ole Opry accent, "Ain' choo nevuh gonna cum tuh bed John Dillinger-boy?" And gobble me up before I could protest.

When sweet reason and broad hints about my sacred state failed to dampen Swifty, I made my point more forcibly. The first time she called at Meditation Manor I waited for her in my stone amulet, sandals, dark glasses, shaman's cloak and nothing on underneath. "Oh boy," she grinned, "Mandrake the Magician. Where's Lothar?" She peered inside my little tent. "Phew!"—she held her nose—"you raisin' chickens in there, honey?" Her attitude to the Manor was no less disrespectful. She called Anna Shepherd in her water tank "Esther Williams" and said the kimono'd, stoned doctors were the funniest thing she'd seen since *A Night at the Opera.* She shook her head disbelievingly at the Manor's passing parade. "If th' gals was purtier Ah'd say you was runnin' a real high-class bordello. You sure this environment is good for a growin' boy?"

Eventually—under the influence of plenty of brandy and my Siberian chants—Swifty submitted to sitting nude lotus position, touching only my hands. "Ah'm sorry, darlin', Ah nevah c'd do that hootchie-kootchie stuff. Cramps mah legs. Say, with you it's much easieh. Golly." For several hours I told her forgotten past, reading it out of her head like stock market tape.

"An *African* princess? You sure now? My momma in Li'l Rock ain't gonna like that one danged bit."

As Swifty grew sleepier our tunes began meshing. "Christ-amighty baby, this is tremendous. Ah been sittin' like this for *hours!*" I removed my cloak, rolled it up and hung it over her bare shoulders, horseshoe-style. I forced her against the wall. She fell down on one knee, I atop her, arms akimbo. I tightened the cloak as hard as it would go. When her breathing stopped I slid to the floor, dog-tired.

The next thing it was morning. Swifty gone. A note on the tent floor.

Gumdrop:
What DID you put
in the likker last
night. Kisses.
S.

My hunger for self-confirmation demanded a constant supply of cases, so when not enough outsiders showed up at the Manor for me to practice on I plunged back intae th' wurld of dinner parties and pubs, shamanizing anyone and everyone I met, in coffee bars, on park benches, even in public conveniences. (And almost got arrested for importuning near Oxford Circus.) Long-buried talents surfaced, intuitive powers raised to frightening heights. My LSD-dilated eyes X-rayed bodies to locate badly knit bone fractures and lesions, which no doctor had ever found, including old emotional scars. I laid hands on friends' wives to ouija their cosmically lost femininity, and knew what people had been in previous lives. The dead and absent spoke through me. Sir Marlo was thunderstruck when I mimicked his RAF wing man. "Good lord. Fortescue went down over Arras in '43." As a party trick I handed out racing tips which turned out remarkably well (I refused a large gratuity from one delighted Manorite).

It wasn't all peaches and cream. For example, some bigoted parents resented my telling their kids to run away from home to follow the psychedelic Children's Crusade, and one jealous husband almost knocked my block off. "I don't mind you making a pass at Juliet," Tom stormed, "but you've half convinced the idiot woman she's the Queen of Sheba and now she expects me to kiss her feet when I get home from work."

Since no Marxist, however lapsed, can work entirely free of a theoretical justification, I wove one around my activities. I was (I deduced) a catcher in the rye of lost souls, a guide-guardian of the Children of Light; my task was to go around confirming the forgotten divinity of a few Absent Friends, that miniscule force of closet schizophrenics who might yet redeem oor Gaw'd-fersaken epoch. Mine was undercover, secret work. If the Evil One twigged, then I—Philip Marlowe, Shane, Lamont Cranston the Shadow—was finished, and I'd be forced to begin my Wheel of Existence all over again. The risk was absolute and unconditional, as Last said. But as he also said, "Th' darkness is closin' in, th' lights are goin' oot, only a fyoo of us stand between th' Beast of th' Night and . . . and . . ." and here he often broke down before specifying further.

I told no one about my theory, not even Last. After all, does Macy's tell Gimbel's?

A gorgeous transparency (and 1000 mg LSD) flowed through my veins, which enabled people to 'see through' me to Last & Co. 'I' didn't exist anymore, only my skill at funneling people to my guide-guardian Brothers. When Ida, my Long Island cousin, rang me from her hotel to complain of tourist tummy, I sent her to Boris for deep psychotherapy. And I told Ellie Newblatt, my novelist friend, that Dr. Last handled all my hysteria cases the night she called and screamed that her London publisher wanted to be beaten with his collection of whips. The Clare doctors accepted my referrals without comment. In our work who expects thanks?

Yes sir baby, my luck had changed, I was now in full possession of my True Faculties. I must have been *crazy* all these years, wanting to write. Write? Egoic activity, Mayan veils of typewritten puke. Shamanizing was infinitely more creative and satisfying. One day, perhaps thousands of years in the future, the unlocked secret history of our times would reveal the incredible nature of my work and destroy at a stroke the fly-by-night reputations of those airthly hacks, Mailer and Hemingway.

So why did I feel so lousy?

Hollow-eyed, jaw-tight, my face began to lewk like Willie's, my Scottish accent thickened. Waves of murderous rage (against what? whom?) tore me apart, exposing me to echoes of Last's accusation that I was just a flyaway bird fueled only by curiosity. Damn him, I'd show him—I'd show them *all*—just how committed I could be, even if I still wasn't sure what I was committing myself to. Disregarding the most elementary rules of personal safety. I crowbarred greater and greater doses of LSD into me and behaved accordingly, but in the Manor's circuslike atmosphere no one took a blind bit of notice. Like Avis, if I wanted (as I half consciously did) to get caught, I'd have to try harder.

It wasn't easy. Every night I slouched back into the Manor worn out by street encounters the bizarreness of which shook even me. Old ladies in Lambeth to whom I whispered kabbalisms while helping them across the road merely complimented me on how well I spoke English for a foreigner. Limehouse dossers snored through my readings from *The Unhealed Heart*. The schoolgirls I astral-goosed on the Old Kent Road gathered in clusters to giggle at me, and even my doing midnight capework in front of speeding autos up and down Denmark Hill failed to stop traffic. Bloody limey phlegm. Nothing worked. I could not break down altogether or get arrested. Conduct that would have rammed Jerry, Herb or Featherstone-the-Flasher into a mental hoosegow in five minutes was infinitely tolerated, especially by my permissive middle-class friends. Americans thought I was superhip, the English hardly noticed. Despite myself, I knew the rules too well.

Could nobody stop me?

"H'lo, Devil!"

A bony, bespectacled head under a Jungle Jim pith helmet poked through a hole in my tent. Knapsack on back, binoculars hanging from his neck, Jerry Jackson crawled in. He looked at my surroundings. "Th' housin' shortage really hit ya hard, din't it, ya ol' Diabolo." Jerry said that he had run away from a dying Con House to find Dr. Dick "an' bring 'im back alive."

Searching for Drummond took us around the church on a normal Manor day. In the incense-choked hall Ramsey and Roxie held a Black Mass over a dead cat; Marve Munshin crying "This hurts me worse than it does you!" was slapping a delighted Anna Shepherd all over the place, and a TV camera crew lay out cold under blankets. Bronwen Jones floated about trailed by a photojournalist from *Elle.* I tried introducing Jerry around. Some Manorites, registering his shabby ordinariness, looked right through him; others, like Sir Marlo and elderly Dr. Horn-Green, condescended when they heard his lower-class accent and called him "old man" and "dear chap." Boris took one look and snapped: "Right—get him out by sundown. We don't want his institutionalization to infect the rest of the community." When Last, on the floor of the main hall playing word games with some visiting Californians, invited him in, Jerry—who loved games of any sort—hunkered down with pleasure. "Le's see," Last said, "where were we? Oh yeh. Jill is angry tha' Jack is nae angry tha' Jill is angry Jack is angry at Jill nae bein' angry—" Jerry's smile quickly faded. This wasn't his thing at all. Suddenly he began hiccuping helplessly "Forget it it's past, forget it it's past, forget it—" and let me pull him away. Last and his friends looked embarrassed.

On a dirty mattress behind some packing boxes upstairs Jerry and I found Dick Drummond cradling a mewling infant in one arm and with the other stroking the hair of a sitar-strumming girl beside him. Food crumbs and droplets of Chivas Regal (a nearly finished bottle lay to hand) hung from his mangy beard, and he cried softly to himself. Jerry's eyes bugged but he managed a friendly wave at Dick; Dick was too stoned to notice. Pale and anxious, Jerry asked me to ring Les O'Brien at the hospital. "I dunno, Sid," he said unhappily when I helped him back to my cubicle, "guess I ain't got th' stomach for normal life no more." By dusk, when O'Brien and Foster came by in a King Eddie van, Jerry had the shakes. "B-boy, a-m I-i g-glad t-tuh see y-ya," he pumped Les' hand. "T-thought I'd g-go m-m-mad 'ere." O'Brien asked Foster to drive Jerry back, then said: "Think I'll stick around a bit, Dave. Never seen schizophrenia in wide screen Technicolor before."

As my guest that night Les mingled with the Manorites and took it all in silently. In the morning he urged me to return to the hospital with him, but I stubbornly refused to desert my post. "Okay," he shrugged, "it's your funeral."

Stuipid Les, puir Jerry. So institutionalized they couldn't see that the Manor was therapeutically a million miles ahead of King Eddie hospital. Any doubts I had on this score were settled by the news media, which overwhelmingly preferred Meditation Manor to Conolly House.

Good Sojer, I manned my post all summer. Emptying out slop buckets, sterilizing Sy's needles, keeping Ramsey and Roxie from murdering each other—serving as a kind of ward orderly to a dozen or so crying, screaming, finger-painting, poetry-writing schizophrenic prodigies. (By now several residents, who considered the Manor too phony or upsetting, had quietly departed.) But no amount of my shit-shoveling could buy back the Brithers' love. They really didn't like me fizzling on the pad as I did; like conventional nurses, they wanted mainly peace and quiet from me. Their unspoken disapproval stuck to me like flypaper, and like a lost child I wandered from cubicle to cubicle seeking what I no longer knew, but getting only those dreadful gargoyle smiles that seemed to fix me forever into the patient's position. It dimly occurred to me that the Manorites were doing to me what I often had done to Willie Last, making me an object of their aggressive love, a mere icon of their quasireligious whimsy. But I was too freaked out to appreciate the irony. Between the residents' implicit incitement of me to blast off, and my Clare brothers' silent disapprobation, I felt myself being yanked off the ledge of reason without a karmic parachute. By habit more than choice I approached Last again for help, but when I did he withdrew behind an impenetrable wall of homage and called me "Father Sid." Oh boy, what a bind. There I was, technically still chairman of the Council, while daily meetings were called to which no one even thought of inviting me. Weeks ago, I learned, Marve Munshin had taken over my Council seat if not yet my empty title.

Maybe they were right. Maybe I had overstayed my leave on airth and it *was* time to go. If so, better under my own steam than to be pushed.

Willie agreed to have a Last (acid) drink with me and afterward we dined at a fashionable Kings Road bistro and dropped in for my farewell visit to Mother Amelia in the Old Brompton Road. The fortune-teller solemnly warned him, "Help Sidney. He is astride the Horse of the Night that has broken loose. I left him as a holy friar in Circenster but have lost all trace of him now." As usual she refused any money. Outside I laughed. Amelia, I said, was losing her marbles. "It was Toulouse, not Circenster."

I was so tired, thinking
a) for myself
b) for others
c) for myself-as-others
d) for others-as-myself-being-others
But I supposed that's what existential psychiatry was about.

From here on I cut myself off totally. From Lena, from the world. Disregarding Amelia's warning to take a holiday, and on a rising tide of hysteria, I crawled inside my shaman's yourt for a Final Effort. I stripped for action by devouring books about galactic warfare and jungle combat (Ogburn's *Merill's Marauders*, Syke's *Orde Wingate*). Most days I woke around dawn and lay staring through the blanket hole while steadily swigging acid and distilled water. My chest had Band-Aids all over it where I'd tried to scratch away the cosmic Itch of Perfection (the same one that Con House's Derek Chatto used to complain about?). I was utterly fatigued, more tired than I'd ever been in my life. Like a sick pregnant cow I lay in my dark tent day after day, waiting. Speaking to no one, eating nothing. Topping up with almost hourly doses of acid.

Nothing happened. Not No-Theng. Nuthin'.

I got bored. Was this gut-aching ennui 'it'? Surely not. Didn't something . . . er, happen?

Old-fashioned anxiety flew back into my nest.

The animal needed to get out.

In the small dark hours of the night, when the others were too stoned or sleepy to notice, I crept out of the Manor to lope the quiet empty streets of south London. From Crystal Palace to New Cross, from Catford to Woolwich, I heel-and-toed it to escape the thing that was chewing me up. All night and into the next morning, up to twenty miles a day, I tramped, a 1960s *Werewolf of London* dreading only the bright sunlight. Sometimes in the dawn mist I met Bilko-spirit who rubbed his hands and grinned, "Don't worry, kid, we got It made."

Just like the old bums we'd kicked out of the church I slept under bridges and in doorways, and slowly slipped back to my movie-watching roots. No longer Shane or Bogart's Rick, I was now Paul Muni in *I Was a Prisoner on a Chain Gang* forever fading into the Brixton fog to elude pursuing cops, Frankie Darro in *Wild Boys of the Road* running from the switchyard bulls.

Songs, forgotten till now, bubbled to my lips. This time not black civil rights songs but labor hymns from an earlier period of my life.

"Get thee behind me Satan
Travel on down the line
I am a union man
Gonna leave you behind. . . ."

A vision. Of Chicago, my hometown. I am striding alone down Roosevelt Road, confetti blizzarding down on me, the returned war hero. A one-man V-E Day parade. In both my hands, held aloft in a boxer's triumphant gesture, a Corona portable typewriter into which is stuck my Report from Nowhere, the holy grail of the writer's quest. Old school chums send out thunderous cheers, lovely girls in Marshall High sweaters line the curb and clap hands for me. UCLA Homecoming queens strew my path with long-stem red roses. (Rita Hayworth and Ty Power in *Blood and Sand.*)

> "Hold the fort, for I am coming
> Union men be strong
> Side by side we battle onward
> Victory is ours."

Sonofabitch. 'It' still would not come.

I had to force the issue somehow. Conolly House might be on its last legs, but so was I.

Days and Nights in Conolly House: Fall

"MR. K. TOPPLES"
"HAROLD DOES IT"

Nursing a bruised arm, I'm lying half-asleep in the back of Lena's MGB splashing past rain-soaked news placards. Nothing surprises me anymore, not even Harold Wilson organizing a putsch in the Kremlin. Lena breaks in to say that Labour just won the British General Election and, coincidentally, Khrushchev is out in Russia. Oh.

What a hangover. For weeks Bilko-spirit and I have been prowling the streets by night and by day helping Last turn on relays of American acid novices (he still trusts me to do this). Yesterday an elderly Vermont poet almost cranked my arm off thinking I was his first Model T Ford. Favoring my twisted shoulder, I'm still a sea gull leading the Yankee geese home on one good wing.

Lena interrupts my reverie with one of her own. "Last night I dreamed you were a bird lost high over the ocean. Flapping around and making such crazy noises the other birds thought you knew where you were going." Cold beads of terror pop out under the shaman's cloak I'm wearing under my raincoat. The Kraut vampire is at it again, bugging me by trying to read my mind. Heading west on the A-40 I ward off Lena's evil spell with shaman jabber under my breath until she drops me outside the hospital gate. "Can I come get you soon?" her lower lip trembles. A passerby stares as I burst out, "No, you goddamn witch bitch. Tell your control, Irving, I've blown his cover. And say, next time don't send a girl to do a man's job!" I slam the door and stalk off.

Where is Conolly House? My tired LSD-soaked eyes can't spot it anywhere. And no wonder. With its yellow bricks sandblasted clean and its broken windows repaired it now looks exactly like all the other wards. The wire mesh around the front porch has been replaced by glass, and even the tell-tale lawn is neatly mown and free of debris. Something must be wrong. This time no one jumps at me with an invisible clarinet-rifle—because the front door (for the first time in my memory) is locked. My knock is answered by a strange white-coated nurse who takes a long time checking with higher-ups inside before he admits me to a scrubbed, gleaming, Gareth-less corridor. Inside, the place is unrecognizable. Disinfectant and wax polish have erased the familiar stench, the walls are bare of China graffiti. It's dead quiet, too. Has someone finally strangled Percy-the-radio? One or two new boys sit around wearing bathrobes and doped, vegetable faces and utterly ignore a couple of men in business suits who skulk near them scribbling furiously in notebooks. What in hell is going on? Part of the mystery clears up when my nurse-escort unlocks the door to staff room to reveal not Dr. Dick or Les O'Brien but Mad Monahan with his feet arrogantly propped up on O'Brien's old desk and over in the corner Drs. Singh and Primrose burrowing through Drummond's confidential files. All three throw me the King Eddie stare. "Ah yes Mr. Bell," medically smiles Screwy Lewie. "So sorry I could not keep your old room reserved for you. It was necessary to assign to another patient." He accentuates 'another.' Confused, I back out in a hurry and start hunting for friendlier faces. Upstairs, as I go past the loo, a strong anonymous arm snakes out and jerks me in.

"Welcome back, ya ol' devil," says Jerry Jackson. "I knew ya'd be in time for th' wake."

The old bunch is all up here, in the large upstairs latrine which they have turned into a carbon copy of their funky old nest in the TV lounge, complete with mattresses and the television set with wires trailing into Percy's room. Only up here can they get any peace and quiet, they say. "Mad Monahan harasses us everywhere else—then calls us mentals for living in a toilet," says Jeff H. Almost everyone is out of China Follies gear and back to their standard drab pajamas and gowns.

All the news they give me boils down to one basic fact: Drs. Singh and Primrose are exploiting Drummond's prolonged absence to impose a vastly stricter regime on the boys. With the Medical Super Dr. Winstanley's tacit approval, the Demented Duo have already banned 'unauthorized' activities, such as the disorderly, almost continuous meetings which were the unit's heart and soul. Dr. Winstanley has also agreed to the reintroduction of compulsory reveille, regular bed check and locked doors. But so that he can sleep nights with a good conscience the Super has quietly advised Singh to continue a show of Drummond's old policy of minimum drugs. (Except that Mad Monahan's idea of minimum is enough to choke a horse.)

What happened to Derek Chatto whose breakdown triggered this debacle?

Jerry says, " 'e comes outta Winnie Wing real quiet like an' callin' everyone 'sir.' 'e stops chasin' girls an' says 'e wants to enlist in th' Royal Navy like 'is dad. So they discharged 'im as cured."

> *The boys carefully refrain from blaming the new regime on anyone but themselves. It is obvious to them that they must have done something odious to cause Dr. Dick to abandon them. Snide insinuations by staff that Drummond has deserted his ship in its darkest hour the boys refuse to countenance. All they will concede is that maybe, just maybe, a few of his outside interests like Meditation Manor drew off his energy at a crucial time. Even then they are prepared to give him the benefit of their doubts. Free-enterprising Barney says, "Dr. Dick saw the National Health was going too Socialist. So he wisely balanced off the pubic sector with his private parts."*

Dr. Winstanley's new broom, wielded with unholy joy by the Demented Duo, sweeps Con House clean of his precious mess. What used to be the only King Eddie ward run as much for the patients as for the staff now reverts to its original function: to keep staff anxieties under control. Ironically, the very first victims are Drummond's old crew of nurses who drift rudderless and demoralized amid squalls of 'I told you sos' rained down on them by staff colleagues who always believed that Dr. Dick would dump them once he got bored with Con House. Bert Karp, whose basic zaniness Con House supported and disguised for so long, chomps apples all day and like a back-ward senile stars glassily into the gas fire of TV lounge; to anyone who'll listen he blames the unit's collapse on the elusive pH factor. Very pregnant, Sally Peel idly knits and consumes gallons of ice cream while brooding over the possibility that she has become a 'carrier' of schizophrenia to her unborn infant. Dave Foster endlessly plays Ping-Pong in Staff Canteen, and O'Brien has vanished. "Probably getting pissed out of his mind," Dave says.

The boys adapt more quickly—and more realistically. Several have already abandoned ship or are making plans to do so. Yorkshire Roy has hustled himself into a halfway hostel in Ruislip next week; if he stays, he says, Mad Monahan will rob him blind. "Ah don't know if it'll be mah money or mah manhood. Either way I'll be th' loser." Jeff H. also sees no point in hanging around, not since A. C. Corrigan, who Jeff fancies, fell in love with the dud shell Whitworth. "Before coming here I went mad because I didn't know who or what I was sexually," says Jeff. "Now I know—and the pain may drive me crazy again." And little Nigel says that his ectoplasmic alter-ego 'Desmond' has told him to go home. "Des is there already with no one to protect him against my family. I'd best go and look after him."

With the unit's top layer creamed off, the rest of Con House is left more defenseless than ever. Guilt saps the spirits of those who had committed themselves to helping Derek Chatto; they blame themselves for not doing their job better or, increasingly, for getting involved at all. As Nigel says, "We tried to sucker a lie-in and now they're throwing us to the Christians." When I confess my own share in provoking Derek's flipout—all those bedside séances—I'm told to relax, he apparently seduced most of his visitors into believing they had supernaturally curative powers.

Very few patients seem bitter toward the absent Drummond. Or to me, as his surrogate. "Even th' blokes wot figure you for an Interpol nark think you're jes' **th'** spy wot got left out in th' cold—like th' rest of us," says Jerry. Anyway, there is no time for recrimination. The urgent thing is to get right with the incoming staff, to do violence to ourselves before it's done to us. An example is set by Herb Greaves making a funeral pyre of his copies of Laing and Goffman on the manicured front lawn while incanting:

"Sikh socks sick
Kick kooks' kocks
Punish penis
Intra Venus."

And others aren't slow to catch on. Barney Beaton turns his eyeglass-camera—usually pointed at doctors or his parents—on himself, "Hold still, dammit man, how can I shoot a moving target?" Wally Walters goes back to his old habit of shutting out the world with his small red radios clamped to either ear, and Hurricane Hodge lays off Jack Sweeney to punch himself silly with renewed fervor. Jack, deprived of Robin Ripley's support (she has been banned from Con House) and the emotional comfort of Hodge's assaults, sinks into his ancient Tiperrary mist. Eric, who had begun eating under the stimulus of Derek's crisis, resumes his fast. And Abe, a terrified witness of Mad Monahan strapping an overactive Mr. Wu into bed, stuffs a dirty rag into his mouth to stifle his coughing. "Ain't never seen a purple blackie before," says Wally.

With truly frightening authenticity a number of boys have started to impersonate the affectless tics of chronic seniles: this must be what they were like before Drummond came on the scene. Conolly House is a doctor's heaven now: clean, quiet—and nuts. The old solidarity has evaporated, and it's every man for himself. The important thing is to underwrite staff's sanity by writing off your own.

Except for Jerry Jackson.

Off Largactil, out of his hospital-issue gown, Jerry has found the confidence to get his first paid job in years. Nothing very hard, he says with self-deprecating pride, just capping hair oil bottles part time in a Slough factory. Every night, dog tired, he drags himself back to the hospital utterly drained by paranoia and bus sickness. After years of crippling depressions he was encouraged "tuh mek something of meself" by the part he played in the July revolution (Derek's rota). The very ferocity of his inner battle with the seemingly impossible thought of taking personal responsibility for another person, did it. He has not stopped being mad: he still has visions and hears voices. And—is this crazy?—conjures up a picture of himself as the lone survivor of "The Four Just Men," his favorite TV adventure series. (The others being Clem, A.C. and me.) With the last of his political juices he circulates a SAVE CON HOUSE petition I helped him write. Among his demands are better food, the right to change doctors and union wages for mental patients. (I got him to drop the clause about an immigration ban on Indian doctors.)

"Dr. Dick's allus goin' on about how us schizos are vital tuh th' nation's health," he says with irresistible logic. "Why not get paid th' rate for th' job?"

Lantern Slide: *Gerald Jackson*

An elder statesman of schizophrenia, Jerry has been in and out of mental hospitals since adolescence. He is twenty-four now. His career as a schizophrenic began unassumingly when a childhood bout of measles temporarily left him deaf, which got him misdiagnosed as a 'high grade subnormal.' By easy stages social workers and then doctors labeled his extreme boredom with classroom studies as 'backward,' 'disturbed' and finally 'paranoid schizoid' when he began yelling bad names at the people who were calling him classification-type names. He wears such stigma like war medals, as if to boast, well at least someone has paid attention to me. A sense of defeat is a Jackson family tradition.

Jerry's dad, a Rhondda valley collier, was starved out in the '26 General Strike, then had to quit with black lung in '38 (without a pension from coal pits still privately owned). War conscripted to a Coventry munitions plant after wandering the roads looking for work, Mr. Jackson was struck on the head by a falling factory girder in the famous Luftwaffe raid of November 14, 1940. A six-month coma left him incapable of focusing his eyes, and he steadily slipped down the job ladder till he was grateful for a position as lavatory cleaner for Wandsworth Council, London. Helped bury blitzed bodies '41–'45, then hit the road again and never came back. "'is mind wanders, so does 'e."

"Ya c'd say me folks helped mek ol' bloody England," Jerry says. "Me mum died in service, y'know, cleanin' th' nobs' 'ouses. Da' was a funny ol' bird. Every mornin'—jes' before goin' off to clean loos—'e got up whistlin' an' singin' 'is 'ead off. Wot'd 'e got to whistle about?" Jerry's only sister succumbed to pneumonia in the terrible austerity winter of '47.

Basically shy and acquiescent, Jerry never dreamed of arguing against the life verdicts passed on him by his middle-class judges. Anyway, his inner life lay elsewhere. As with so many English working-class boys, his artistic-intellectual drive had gone to his feet, and what couldn't be expressed in words in a classroom was said on a soccer pitch by heading, kicking, dribbling, flicking and curling goals from thirty yards out. At fourteen a miracle! A million south London boys' fantasy came true when a scout for Chelsea Football Club told him to report for a tryout with the junior side. But Jerry so hooked on failure "I wakes up that mornin' an' me leg aches so bad I turns over an' goes back to sleep. Never did mek it to th' grounds that day." When I suggest his leg was psychosomatic Jerry takes off his glasses, seems to claw up the wall in merriment. "I can't stop laughin', don't know why, that's so funny." His face empty, blank, tired.

These past few years a new fantasy has driven him: to marry his vicar's daughter, Caroline. To qualify as prospective bridegroom, he began attending church regularly and then so loudly and passionately that the vicar had to call the police. Somehow fucking and religion got confused, Jerry's been trying to untangle them ever since. His main obsession is to become respectable enough to tie the knot with Caroline in a fabulous all-white ceremony attended by every single member of the Chelsea soccer team. Figures the best way is to out-Jesus her father by cleansing the world of impurities like himself. His hospital days alternate between dreams of ravishing Caroline and bouts of guilty blankness when he forgets that he's . . . he's . . . 'effin' 'ell, forgot again! When he can't remember who/what he is, Jerry fingers his 'clarinet' (held between his legs and moved up and down Cotton Club style) and shouts the GI-imported blues until God's tune—and his identity—spurts out.

A daylight patrol in my combat gear, urban shaman's cloak and dark glasses. The boys generally accept that my ostentatiously cradled arm is an injured sea gull's wing, but are divided on whether it happened in a previous life. My insistence on this point—considered normal by Last and Clare Council—causes some Con Housers (a few for the first time) to amiably doubt my sanity.

I can't walk in any direction without colliding with a sociologist or research psychologist writing in a notebook like mine. They are strays from the Sixth International Congress of Psychotherapy now being held in London, I learn. Before tea I bump into several such visiting foreigners who want to interview me as an unusually interesting case. Ha. With nineteen volumes of *Special File* already written I've got the jump on them.

Whenever Mad Monahan sees me on his rounds, I slump into a deferential slouch and, following the boys' example, call him 'Mister' Monahan.

"Oi—Dr. Dick's on the telly!"

He sure is. Upstairs in the latrine a crowd avidly hunches over the TV set, watching Dick Drummond being interviewed on "Nationwide" about a speech he made earlier today at the Psychotherapy Congress. Tie askew, beard uncombed, he's pissed. When the lady reporter asks him a particularly irrelevant question Dick growls into the camera, "What's the point? Why should I help the BBC colonize the fractured minds of those atomized ciphers out there—the great British public?" he hiccups. "THE REVOLUTION STARTS WHEN WE WANT IT TO!" With that he flings his typed speech into the studio air and is blotted out by a snowfall of unbound pages.

The boys stare at the screen. Wally Walters says, "What would happen if any of us did that?"

The boys are genuinely puzzled at the double standard used to define insanity, examples of which they see in their daily lives all the time. Take radio. While keen TV watching is assumed to be a symptom of depression—commercials especially offend their sense of logic ("You can't *be* whiter than white!")—a lot of boys like listening to BBC radio's popular morning Light Programme. Wally Walters unplugs for a moment to explain one reason why. "Well, y'know 'ow Dr. Dick wuz allus natterin' on how we schizophrenics are th' wave of th' future. Cop a load of this—we done arrived, I reckon." He gets me to listen to Jimmy Young, the housewives' favorite disc jockey on BBC:

"The J.Y. prog with Jim at the Beeb. If you-lee-o would like-ee-o to participate in same send-ee-o a postcardio. Want me to call you? Must have your numero for phonio. It's Jim at the Beeb. . . .

"Mrs. Hart—pumpin' away, ay?—of High Wycombe-an'-go writes to say if you could give a little link-up for us super super super. That's what we're here for. It's seashore biscuit time. That's th' name of our rah-dee-o ray-see-pee. You have three mins to get yourself equipped . . .

"Two oz wholemeal flour speedily followed by two oz . . . Am I going too fast? . . . crab paste, which brings me to the penult item. I shall audit the books. Do you have six? Wun. Tew. Three. For. Five. Six. Six. Five. For. Three. Tew. Wun. Do you have six? A quick sock through the 'ceep for you, a quick recap . . . then you have seashore biscuits delicioso."

Cooler weather keeps us in like caged animals. Behind locked doors, spied on by the omnipresent Demented Duo, the boys pace up and down; a few even begin to stake out little corners of Con House that belong to them and no others—a chronic pattern I've not seen here before. One of the boys sobs theatrically, "Boo hoo, if I'd known I'd never have started it." Where the hell is O'Brien?

Les Talks

I track him down in the little-used Anything Goes room where he sits disconsolately against the wreckage of the upright punching bag Derek tore apart. A carpet of cigarette ends and empty brown ale bottles around him, Les is buried in Faulkner's *The Mansion*.

"H'lo Sid," he wearily raises his eyes and taps the paperback novel. "Y'know, these Snopeses, they'd make good mental hospital staff." He looks awful. Shriveled, almost.

"Knackered is the word. Like Conolly House." He tells me that the unit is finished for all practical purposes. And him?

"A relief in a way. Maybe I can take my accumulated leave and visit with the wife and kids. Man, they haven't *seen* me in years."

And look for a different job?

"Nah. I'm an addict. Hooked. Working with the mad is the only sane thing I've found in this mad, mad world. . . ."

And Con House?

"Soon we'll be nothing but a distant memory. A historical landmark. Like Stonehenge. A legend'll spring up. You, Dick, others'll write about it maybe. The fight, for a better deal, may spread to more mental hospitals.

"The impulse will go on. But we—Con House—will get left behind. A myth, no longer reality. Trendies like your Brixton mob will interpret even our failures as successes for 'family oriented phenomenology.' Doctors and nurses closer to the shitwork will remember mainly our disasters. Of which there were one or two, may I remind you. Any Con House kid who goes chronic or kills himself will be our fault. We went too far, they'll say. Too noisy, too dirty, too this or that. Some of these lads never will leave a mental hospital. Too far gone when we got them. Still, we'll get the blame. Staff'll fall into a schizophrenic habit: they'll keep that part of our praxis which makes their job more bearable and reject the other side of what we tried to do here. They'll say Gareth or Herb or Abe might've survived better without Conolly House.

"God help me—they could be right."

For the next few days and nights Con House revolves around Jerry's one-man petition and occasional, unannounced drop-ins by delegates from the Psychotherapy Congress in London. It is typical of British medical incuriosity that visiting foreigners eager to know about us outnumber English by ten to one (the one, an Ipswich-based psychiatrist, said he was thinking of starting a Con House-type community—in Australia.) From the methodical way the foreigners tromp through we must be somewhere on their tourist checklist between the Tower of London and Madame Tussaud's. Gregarious Dr. Winstanley, our executioner, likes playing host.

"This-a-way, comrades."

Protected by platoons of King Eddie nurses, half a dozen square-faced men in wide-cuffed business suits invade our upstairs latrine sanctum. The Russians have come.

Their escort, Dr. Winstanley, is at his ebullient best, describing Conolly House as a major breakthrough in community therapy. "The pragmatic English tradition is to bend without breaking. So we gave a little power to the patients before they could overthrow us," he jokes. The Russians take him seriously enough to confer with their hefty, unsmiling woman interpreter about possible questions to ask. While they're deciding the Soviet psychiatrists and the boys settle down to a mutually uncomprehending stare session. Jerry, trying to be friendly, politely fractures the silence. "Oi then, wot 'appened to Moscow Dynamo's goalkeeper after 'e lost ya th' game to Barcelona last year? Did'ja shoot 'im?" After translation, six square Russian heads slowly swivel toward Jerry. Is he sick—or a provocateur? The interpreter woodenly replies, "We have been nice to visit in your British Islands. The weather is pleasant." The Russians are deeply upset by our laughter. It's raining out.

Undeterred, Dr. Winstanley—out to make an impression—asks if any of the patients will explain "in your own words" how Conolly House works. Nigel, fifteen, complies.

"Once upon a time
the world was blown up by a big bomb   a huge radioactive tidal wave almost drowned everybody   to make sure they survived the remaining adults decided to build a dike of the brains of their best children   they hoped this would keep the flood from drowning them all   for many generations a way of life arose based on the production of children for the great dike   then one day a man named mad dick actually a child in disguise who'd never grown up like peter pan built a large wooden boat and announced he was sailing to china and could take a limited number of children with him   parents furiously denounced mad dick for threatening their supply of dike children and therefore all of civilization   but mad dick no flies on him cleverly convinced the parents that the only

> kids he'd take to china were defective ones their porous brains were no use against the flood just as the ark full of unwanted children set sail for china the parents changed their minds it was all a trick they said their submarines sank the ark all hands including mad dick drowned the torpedo explosions caused a crack in the great dike which collapsed and then everybody else drowned too i thank you the end

The interpreter goes to work, then says: "Dr. Vukovich inquires, what is the moral of this fable?"

Nigel says brightly: "It's an east wind that blows nobody any good."

Suddenly, Jerry bounds forward waving a piece of paper, which sends the Russians scampering behind a wall of nurses. But all Jerry wants is their signatures on his SAVE CON HOUSE petition. The lady translator grabs the paper and hastily scans it, then barks, "We unanimously condemn this unprovoked interference into the internal affairs of the Soviet Union!—"

"Oh no, lady," Jerry protests, "ya don' get it!"

She plows on. "The rights of all minorities, including psychiatric inmates, are guaranteed by our Soviet Constitution." She turns venomous. "And what about the Irish question?"

The Russian doctors all look ill. Everybody has been so polite till now, not even mentioning KGB hospitals. One says in perfect English to Dr. Winstanley, "My sympathies, Comrade Medical Superintendent. Your capitalist schizophrenics are remarkably like our own." They edge toward the door. Herb Greaves stops them with a new version of "The Internationale":

> "Arise ye disconfirmed of Britain
> Arise ye red shit of mind's splittin'
> Iron bars do not a prison make
> When you've had a diagnosis fake. . . ."

He shoots out a clenched fist salute, which accidentally catches Dr. Vukovich under the chin, and is buried under an avalanche of nurses. Whatever chances Con House ever had waft out on the dying echoes of Herb's

"Tis th' final *Con* flict
Let each man take his stand
Before the Doctors' Internationale
Has us stacked, labeled and canned."

Tonight's Nine O'Clock BBC-TV news carries a film clip of part of a speech by Dr. Ronald D. Laing to the Psychotherapy Congress. (Willie Last snubbed the meeting partly because he knew Laing would be there.)

> "Perhaps [says Laing] we will learn to accord to so-called schizophrenics who have come back to us, perhaps after years, no less respect than the often no less confused explorers of the Renaissance. . . ."

Black Abe delivers himself at the TV set feet first, kicking and stomping on it till it explodes with a squawk and curl of smoke. O'Brien, playing solitaire in a corner of the latrine, helps the overexcited boy up. "Haven't seen Abe so active all year. This bloke Laing must have powerful magic."

Lantern Slide: *Abraham Clewes*

I'm ashamed to say that sometimes I think of Abe Clewes as the black bogeyman in *I Walked with a Zombie:* the same stark staring eyes, the same ju-ju ability to appear out of nowhere like a Halloween ghost. Like Mr. Wu, that other butt of Con House's racial jokes, seventeen-year-old Abe never speaks except through his marathon coughing sprees. What makes him tear his larynx to shreds—is he trying to spew up his blackness?

Abe's family is hard-working, honest and docile, a paragon of immigrant virtues. London Transport recruited them from Jamaica in the 1950s to clean subway trains and serve tea in a bus depot. Ma and Pa Clewes came expecting to work themselves up from poverty and to be touched by a little of the powerful aura of middle-class respectability exuded by their totemic goddess, young Queen Elizabeth, but found themselves enshrouded in a racial fog of knowing nudges and nasty little jokes. The peculiarly subtle forms of English racism eventually sent them into a kind of shocked withdrawal ("They likes to keep to themselves th' blackies do."). They numbed themselves with gargantuan amounts of overtime to earn the mortgage down payment on a semidetached in Lewisham. When Abe, their eldest son, came over from Kingston, they promptly indoctrinated him into the ground rules of English Uncle Tom. For example, if Abe came home from school with stories of racial bullying, his parents insisted (1) it wasn't happening and (2) it was his fault. Thus, his blank impassive expression—to most doctors a symptom of affectless schizophrenia—is actually the result of careful family guidance. Abe couldn't be pious or clean enough for the elder Clewes, self-appointed surrogates of English Jim Crow. Work, pray, turn the other cheek.

Abe tried. But the hostile reception he found in Britain—so different from the liberal, tolerant image he'd been taught back in Jamaica—and the fierce competitiveness of other West Indians, knocked him into himself. One day he came home bloody from a minor race riot (reported in the papers, as always then, as a "teenage scuffle") and Pa Clewes stropped him for unwittingly walking into the incident. Without a Black Power vocabulary of anger, Abe began seeing angels, devils and cherubim, all in white.

If Abe's folks are a black parody of the normal white double-binding family, Con House is the concentrated essence of English attitudes to color. Its saving grace is that it's open racism openly arrived at. On the outside, Abe never really knew what he was fighting against; but in Con House he can be in no doubt whatsoever.

The tragedy is that he was already so messed about by the time he arrived that it's impossible to know how deeply the boys' frankly shouted antiblack gibes get into him, or if catharsis is available. Our only clue is that Abe's only real enjoyment seems to be popping out of closets to scare the bejeepers out of people, a terrifying spook who corresponds to the most primitive racial fantasies of the white English boys. That's when Abe absolutely cracks up. "Ho ho ho ho ho ho hich hich hich hich," he cackles, slapping his sides in utter satisfying delight.

Every afternoon a couple of the village kids come through Con House hawking the *Evening Standard.* They are brothers, about fourteen and twelve, and pretty hardened to being around a mental hospital. In other wards, I've seen them zip in and out with hardly a backward glance. But in Con House they gawk and snigger as if at a zoo outing, and in a perverse display of shame some patients play up to them. Jerry Jackson in particular has always pretended for their benefit to be a stupid gorilla, scratching under his armpits and loping after them in a thoroughly moronic way. The newsboys laugh and jeer at him before running off.

Why do you do it? I angrily ask Jerry.

"Aw, fer a giggle—an' 'cuz they sorta expect it," he says.

I suggest that since he's been able to break a lot of other bad habits recently, then maybe it's time to change this one, too. So for the next few days Jerry either ignores the newspaper boys or buys a *Standard* from them without his usual simian capering. At first the brothers look at him strangely, then with growing apprehension, then begin to avoid him. Soon they stop delivering papers to Conolly House altogether. From now on we have to trek into Low Wick village to get them.

Jerry asks me, "Got any more labor-savin' ideas, Dr. Freud?"

Limbo bound, the Shanghai Express starts grinding to a halt, despite Jerry's best efforts to keep the unit and himself going. Some boys already refer to Con House in the past tense. "Wasn't all there but I liked it 'ere." "You din't 'ave to be nobody—made you feel somebody." It really scares me, the way so many now look and act like deteriorated chronics, right down to the sloped shoulders and King Eddie shuffle. A "they know what's best for us" attitude replaces the previous anarchy.

Only Jerry continues to say 'is.' Pale with anxiety, he camps outside the office and holds aloft a large bit of cardboard

WE WANT OUR RITES

and heckles passing staff, "Jesus saith th' meek shall inherit th' booby hatches, what's that lot of Gadarene swine doin' 'ere . . . ?"

Improbably, the Con House idea has lodged in Jerry's head.

Singh and Monahan at first try to laugh it off, then angrily chase him away. No one gives Jerry a hand with his campaign, not even A. C. Corrigan who is leaving soon and doesn't want to jeopardize his imminent release. When I point out to Jerry how vulnerable he is, he reminds me: "But it was you wot tol' me if a thing's worth 'avin' it's worth fightin' for, Sid. Wot made you change your mind?"

How do you dialectically reason with a schizophrenic? Like a tree that's standing in the water, he will not be moved.

Well, if Jerry is not scared of the hospital authorities, I am. Why risk my privileged position as an urban shaman for the sake of . . . what? As discreetly as I can manage it, I cut out on Jerry and retire upstairs to reopen my clinic at the rear of the latrine-lounge. My only professional competition is the latest patient, Joshua.

His full name is Joshua Redcliffe-Nightingale, and he is a hardy perennial who crops up in mental hospitals all over southern England when the urge hits him. A balding, thirtyish man in tramp's clothes but wearing a monocle, he also happens to be a molecular chemist, a Fellow of All Souls, Oxford, and of the Royal Society. "And a paraldehyde addict," says O'Brien. "Joshua's got it scientifically worked out. Gets himself admitted to a different hospital every few months, kicks up just enough fuss to get his dope, but not so much they ECT or Section 29 him. Brainy type." O'Brien says Joshua constantly needs to fill up on his peculiar fuel and recharge his batteries by contact with young boys.

Friendly and loquacious, Joshua tours the unit, waving hello to old pals, then climbs into an Obs Dorm bed and bawls like a baby until Kelly, the No. 2 night nurse, hurries in to pacify him with evil-smelling paraldehyde in water. Over the next few days Josh holds a kind of teach-in on schizophrenia to the kids who never tire of his theories. Apparently, he has a different one for each visit.

"Chaps, I think this time I've finally got it," he says excitedly. "After following up a number of experimental false trails—pink spot, hormone deficiencies, endocrine imbalance and the like—I now can demonstrate conclusively, mind you *conclusively*, that the primum mobile of schizophrenia, wait for it chaps—is the asychronous discharge of neurons in the cerebrospinal fluid caused by the presence of an extra 'Y' chromosome. In laymen's language—bad blood." The captivated boys nod knowingly; they always suspected this.

At night, Josh totally regresses and, in a sad echo of Derek

Chatto's rota, we take turns bottle- and breast-feeding him. (Happily nibbling and sucking our uncovered chests, Josh refuses only mine. "LSD get into your milk?" asks Barney.) Mad Monahan, usually so eager to massively dope his patients, sadistically withholds paraldehyde from Joshua, who bawls even crawls for it. "G'wan back to bed, ya pervert!" Monahan bellows. Tonight, unable to bear the craving, Josh feebly claws and sucks the air, then gets out of bed to groggily stumble into the staff office. From behind my Forward Observation Post under the rear stairwell I hear Josh fiddling ineffectually with the lock on the medicine cabinet, much to the scornful laughter of Monahan and his assistant, Kelly. When Monahan loses patience and pushes him back into bed, Josh slips from the nurse's grasp and lurches into the office again; Monahan grabs his hair, drags him across the corridor into Obs Dorm and roughly backhands him twice in the face. Then he slugs Josh hard in the stomach. The sound is sickeningly loud.

Enraged, I run into the office to tell Kelly who looks up from his *Racing Mirror* and says, "Seeing things again, Mr. Bell? We got pills for that."

From Observation Dorm another sound of fist on flesh, but this time it's Monahan on the receiving end. Kelly rushes past me across the corridor to help his colleague up from the floor. Jerry Jackson, who saw the assault from his bed, stands over Monahan, fists cocked. "Leave 'im alone, ya fuckin' Fascist creep!" he yells as the two burly nurses drown him in punches and kicks, then haul him off into the staff room. Monahan wipes blood from his lip and reaches for the desk phone. "All right, you cunt," he tells Jerry. "Your new home's Churchill Wing."

Despite Jerry's screams and protests behind the closed office door, nobody—including me—stirs in Con House. I stand under the stairwell with fingers in my ears until I can't take it anymore. Okay, I'll be brave. My timid knock brings Monahan, daubing at his split lip. He bunches my shaman's robe at the throat and shoves me against a wall, and in his angry grip I really feel the loss of the forty pounds I've given as a hostage to vegetarianism; my injured 'wing' hangs helplessly at my side. All these past weeks of my obsequiously mistering Monahan mean nothing to him. He snarls, "Keep your nose out of this, Bell—before I show you th' biggest needle in th' business." Dry, frightened, I run upstairs to the dorm where I now live and pull the covers over my head.

In the morning when Les O'Brien gets my indignant report his eyes harden, his tone goes deadly flat. "Why tell me? It's not my affair." I can't believe it. Won't he do something? "You must be joking," he says. "Do you really expect me to grass on a colleague? Who I may have to depend on to save my skin next time one of you schizos goes for me with a broken bottle? Do me a favor!"

I am stunned. O'Brien is a 'cop' again—actually siding with the Con House-hating nurses who give him such a rough ride. "So what? Remember chum, I have to work with these blokes after you're long gone."

Not very convincingly I threaten to kick up a row to rescue Jerry from the violent wing.

"Go ahead—if you dare," says O'Brien. "But before you do, *Mis*-ter Bell, take a china at yourself in a mirror. That Count Dracula getup, the loss of voice and weight—th' ecstasy bit. A license, even yours, extends just so far in a place like this—then it expires." My position is difficult, he says. If I were a genuine patient I could lay a formal complaint against Monahan, if staff I could go through channels to report him to Chief Nurse Tasker. "As it is, you're nobody around here—a role you chose for yourself. Remember?"

But what about Jerry?

"Not to worry. Jackson's an old Churchill hand and knows the rules. I reckon we'll have him back good as new in a week or two."

I tell O'Brien that Jerry has changed and is less institutionalized, more sure of himself now. O'Brien stares at me. "For his sake I hope you're wrong."

With Jerry incommunicado in Churchill Wing, his campaign to Save Con House falls apart. Even that poor cousin of rebellion, sullen resentment, becomes too dangerous to show—look what happened to Jerry—and hence to feel. With a weary practiced air a number of boys slip even deeper into the institutional groove, the chumminess gone, each now more than ever separated from the others. Percy-the-radio goes ominously silent. A. C. Corrigan, hand in hand with his lover Whitworth, accosts passersby with mordant sarcasm: "Clap hands if *you* believe in fairies." Herb Greaves makes a final effort:

"False
Dawn
Balls
Gone."

It's official. Conolly House shuts down next week. The coup de grâce was the Soviet Embassy's complaint of a vicious attack on six of their nationals by two agents provocateurs (Herb and Jerry). That's all, folks.

Impassively, the boys read the announcement pinned to the office door. Only little Nigel is visibly upset. "Why?" he exclaims. "We tried to please them. Where did we go wrong?"

Joshua, our aging baby, puts his unsteady, paraldehyded arms around Nigel. "Silly boy. You frightened the horses in the street."

Les O'Brien and Dave Foster, the two northern-born nurses, meet for a smoke in the empty TV lounge. Seemingly asleep, I sprawl in the Diana Dors chair nearby.

LES (*drawing deep breath*): Sliced off at the nuts, eh Dave?

DAVE (*glumly borrows cigarette from Les*): Aye.

LES: Y'know, somehow I thought we'd evade it. Beat th' system. Or Admin'd lost interest in us, like before.

DAVE: Steadfast men, bureaucrats. Long memories. Must be their training. (*Lengthy silence.*)

LES: Well, it's back to the salt mines. Wonder where we'll get assigned next. Winstanley told me this morning he didn't want to lose my expertise. Said something vague about a new self-governing unit. With quote more supervision than Conolly House of course unquote. Wonder if he was serious?

DAVE: He told *me* he was thinking of a new mixed sex ward. Wanted to know if I was interested.

LES: Are you?

DAVE: Think I'll quit. Been thinking on it a year or so.

LES: Do what?

DAVE: Anything. My brother-in-law owns a couple of automatic laundries. Maybe ask him to put me on.

LES: My brother-in-law's in Australia. Maybe I'll emigrate.

DAVE: There's mentals there. You'd find 'em. (*They laugh.*)

LES: Well, Australia's closer to China.

DAVE: China. Only a figure of speech. Symbolic and all.

LES: D'you think we almost made it?

DAVE: To China?

LES: Yeah.

DAVE: With a few, maybe.

LES: No, I mean—for you.

DAVE: I learned . . . something. It's a possibility. A definite possibility. The easier thing, for them, even for us. It's bound to happen. Like progress. Even tha' fooker Winstanley says we're pioneers.

LES: You believe all that?

DAVE: Aye.

LES (*dubious*): Th' word's out, I suppose. Maybe it will . . . get around. I wonder what form it'll take.

DAVE: A new self-governing unit. Mixed sex ward. Broadmoor goin' up in flames. This bloke Laing. Dr. Who blowing all the ECT machines to hell. (*Pause.*) Who knows—maybe some day we won't worry so much about the nutters. People will be kinder.

LES: They'll be set free. We'll still be here.

DAVE: Not me. I've a brother-in-law who likes me.

LES: I wonder who likes me.

Reluctantly, watched by a few boys, I pack. This is my last trip. Les advises that in my present state is would be suicidal for me to follow the boys into a normal ward. He gets Kelly to unlock the front door for us.

Robin Ripley joins us outside and kisses me. "Don't take it so hard, Mr. Writer. One day maybe we'll outnumber them." She looks more relaxed and together. Her hair, which in the past I've seen in varying lengths and the colors of a rainbow, is cropped boyishly and almost completely gray. She admits it's her natural color. "I've looked like this since I was a kid. But I hate th' shrinks to know. They think I'm crazy for dyein' it all th' time." She says this with a 'that'll fix 'em' smile.

We exchange addresses, and several boys ask me to send them copies of the book I intend writing about Con House. How they'll ever get through the nineteen boxed volumes of *Special File* I don't know.

We move in a group up the hill to Churchill Wing's massive iron door and ask to see Jerry Jackson, but a voice behind the slide-away panel informs us that Jerry is "resting" and slams the panel in our faces. "Damn cheek of the help nowadays," says Joshua, little the worse from Monahan's hammering.

A small party accompanies me down to the front gate. My damaged 'wing' is an excuse for some of them to take turns carrying my bag. On the way Josh recites Baudelaire to us:

De même qu'autrefois nous partions pour la Chine
Les Yeux fixés au large et les cheveux au vent
Nous nous embarquerons sur la mer des Ténèbres
Avec le coeur joyeux d'un jeune passager. . . .

which he translates:

Just as we once did, we set out for China
Our eyes fixed on the horizon and our hair blowing
in the wind.
We will embark on the sea of Shadows
With the young Traveler's joyful heart. . . .

It's a beautiful Indian summer day. We're the only noisemakers in a silence that engulfs the fifteen hundred other patients. On a nearby lawn Herb Greaves and several more Con Housers play a game, using a bat and ball, with a group of girl patients. There are more nurse-chaperones than players. A. C. says it's Dr. Winstanley's latest innovation. "Calls it baseball therapy. Th' revolution goes on, he says."

I turn around for a last look. From here we can see the huge, calm establishment, its passionately orderly paths, hushed wards, Churchill Wing with Jerry locked somewhere inside. Suddenly Con House explodes the immense quiet. A choir of hi-fi amplifiers splits the soft English sky with Elvis Presley's "Jailhouse Rock."

Robin smiles a little. "Percy must be over his depression."

What had I learned from these visits to Conolly House? A fairly simple thing. That patients and staff conspire to build a certain type of social order within a mental hospital, a community of sorts. In most wards this mini-society is based on the patients' fear of staff who treat them as 'ill' which eases both their minds about why they're there. Con House itself is not exempt from such a power system. The difference is, an effort is made not to violate the patient's fundamental right to heal himself. True, this greater freedom raises anxieties which doctors and nurses (and patients) have about themselves. But the resulting chaos, it seemed to me, is preferable to the buried, warped terrors of straight wards. And, for the majority of people who break down without benefit of antipsychiatry or money, a saner alternative than Meditation Manor. It was the best thing I had seen.

Also it's free on the National Health.

That may not be China. But it's something.

5

On my way back to Meditation Manor I stopped off at Lena's. She was an absolute mess. More frightened and upset than I'd ever seen her, she lurched around her workshop bumping into furniture and scattering semiprecious stones. Though she was slightly drunk and cursing in German, eventually I got it out of her. Within the past twenty-four hours two of her main life supports had been kicked out from under her: Irv had broken their engagement and, after weeks of showing up late or not at all for appointments, Dr. Last had sacked her as a patient. Why? Yesterday she had really blown her top for the first time. "I barged into this session between Last and Irv and gave them both hell. But it didn't change anything—except for the worse." Last had demanded on the spot that Irv choose between his bad-tempered girl friend and his doctor. "No prizes for who got the chop." And, on Last's suggestion, Irv was going to move into the Manor. "Last calls him th' Trusted Twelfth or some such codshwallop." I thought: hell, nobody had told me Clare had added five new Councillors.

Lena bitterly regretted blowing her top. "Why did I ever lishen to you, you Judas goat?" She laughed almost hysterically when I offered to give her refuge with me at Meditation Manor. "*You must be joking!* I haven't lost *all* my marbles yet—you queer." She pushed me away. "Don't touch me. You're all queers!" Her lovely, palely freckled face collapsed in tears and she clumsily put her arms around me. "I'm shorry. I apologize. Now you'll never want to see me again. I don't blame you. Only a Nazi could hate two Jews th' way I hate you and Irv. Shomeone should lock me up or shoot me."

I put Lena to bed with a couple of the hundreds of little red Seconals she kept by her night table. She held my hand tightly. "I didn't mean it. You're not a Judash goat. Just a blind little bird looking always for a cage to fly into. . . ."

In my absence, relationships at Meditation Manor had "recrystallized" again. All three doctors had left their wives. Last had settled in with Jasmine, a lushly beautiful ex-patient from Buenos Aires. Dick popped in from time to time, but was otherwise occupied with a menage à trois in Kentish Town involving two ex-patients, one a man the other a woman (Dick slept in the same bed with both, but wouldn't tell us which one he made love to). And Boris had his hands full refereeing between his housekeeper-mistress, Davina, and his surrogate daughter-mistress, Bronwen. Of the doctors' ex-wives—Sybil, Nancy and Vivienne—I heard no more.

As for the nonmedics, Alf was happy as Larry mapping out a string of mini-Manors all over England—"You Yanks don't have a monopoly on franchise operations." And the Major was on Cloud Nine, chewing peyote like Life Savers under the basement boiler where Anna's water tank used to be. (She was somewhere upstairs sculpting Marve Munshin, lifesize, in lard.) Straw's wife had just served divorce papers on him. "Don't mind, really," said the ex-war hero, "just wish th' old gel hadn't charged me with desertion." Then he smiled blissfully and said that despite his legal problems everything was ticky boo, because Willie had agreed to adopt him legally. "Changed my name by deed poll. I'm now officially Anthony Last Straw."

Weirdsville.

The Manor was jumping like a Kansas City juke joint. Residents, many of whom I didn't know, sang, danced, shouted poems and walked about in costumes copied from the dhoti- and sarong-wearing doctors, like extras in a De Mille epic. An exhibition of Anna Shepherd's soap figures took up a part of the main hall, and the loss of Chuck Biberman and a few others from the original intake—Davina said they'd skedaddled because the Manor was getting too much even for them—had been more than made up by curious Americans and show-biz types who easily outnumbered genuine schizophrenics.

The change in Last was stunning.

He'd grown a wispy beard and looked like a zonked-out Ho Chi Minh and spoke v ... e ... r ... y s ... l ... o ... w ... l ... y, almost inaudibly. Gone was the foul-mouthed Dundee street brawler I'd come to like; in his place lotus-sat a frail disciple of Gandhi, loincloth and all. Quarrels he'd once escalated for the sheer joy of it he now avoided by insisting that he was lesser than the least, "a mis'rable speck o' dirt on Gaw'd's face." I recognized it as a variation of the Dick Drummond Ploy, or aggression disguised as submission. Last now conceded everything, including his rival Boris' right to manage the Manor as he saw fit. "All ... social ... questions ... end ... in ... *maya*," he gently wheezed. This tactic drove Boris wild. "Th' wily bastard's found a way to have all the fun while I do all the work," he grumped.

I, too, felt Last's limply transcendental mode as covert hostility. When I asked him yet again to help me untangle the knots in my head he meekly smiled at me: "As ... if ... *yew* ... din't ... know, Master," and insisted on treating me as his spiritual superior. He no longer even wanted me to help him turn on visiting Americans, a function that, along with my Council seat, Marve Munshin had taken over. (Had I been formally impeached as Chairman? No one told me.)

Last's wholesale conversion to Eastern pacifism ("loss of ego boundaries") set up one more barrier between us, and when nothing I said or did made the slightest impression on him, I decided to pack up and go. But when I tried to leave the Manor Last's emissaries stopped me. Big Marve Munshin easily lifted the bag from my hand and gave it to the Major. "Only we know how to protect a Holy Fool like you, Brother Sid." Marve pronounced it Holeh Fyool nowadays. Their strong-arm tactics intimidated, but also flattered me. Someone Up There, in the balcony where Last and his ashram mooned about on mescaline, still liked me.

Almost routinely then, I reerected my shaman's hutch in my old cubicle upstairs. A bit of th' ol' bacon 'n eggs (LSD) and I was back in the Divine Slot. Time passed effortlessly. Far, far below on Earth things happened. Work, wars, revolution—how funny it all was. So irrelevant to *atman.* For hours I lay in my tent laughing and weeping at the pointlessness of all human activity. Except here, at Meditation Manor. For the first time I understood love. Love was my brother Clare Councillors suffering me to fly solo as high as possible on my crooked wing. Sacrificing their still-valued egos for the sake of my egoless flight. And Willie Last, lighting my Upward Path with his incredible self-abnegation, was giving me this chance to break the Cosmic Tape before he did. Only a true Christ figure could be so generous and self-sacrificial.

Yes. If (a) Willie was Jesus—a comparison he'd never altogether objected to, and (b) he was confessedly my spiritual inferior, then (c) was it possible that I was—No no. Not that. Not that.

"Sid, this is Robin. Robin Ripley. Is that you? Your voice sounds so funny. Yes, I s'pose it's this line. (Pause.) I can't stop cryin'. Can you hear me? You sound so weak and far away. Jerry. He's dead. They killed him. Jack Sweeney's been drunk all day over it. I wish I could drink, it goes to my head. Are you there, Sid? Sid? Are you there?"

Les O'Brien confirmed it when I rang the hospital. "Yeah. Allegedly in his sleep. At Churchill Wing. A few of th' usual rumors floatin' about. Bed straps, a straitjacket, a bit of a punchup followed by too much calm-juice. Just rumors. No, no postmortem. Inquest ruled it 'death by misadventure.' You can say that again. Buried him in the King Eddie cemetery, beside the chapel. No family, couldn't locate them. Only me and Sally and one or two of th' blokes were there. Am I going to do what? Ask for an investigation? Investigate what?!" O'Brien slammed the phone down on me.

I found Dick Drummond wearing an ape's papier-mâché head and precariously perched on a ladder helping Sir Marlo with his huge autobiographical wall mural *From Spitfires to Meditation Manor: A Life Up in the Air.* Had Dick known about Jerry? I shouted up. Oh yes, he'd heard about it a few days ago. Then why hadn't he told me? "What's the bloody point?" came through the ape mask.

I needed to talk to someone about Jerry, someone who even vaguely remembered him which nobody at the Manor did. All

Last said was, "If ye'd brought him tae me on time, I'd'a done him fer nuthin'." So I phoned Lena, who agreed to pick me up at the Manor. She seemed more in control, subdued if deadly pale. As she drove me slowly around Brixton, I pounded my fist in fury against the MGB's dashboard. They killed him, I said bitterly. I'll write letters to the Home Office and demand a public inquiry. Get revenge on those murdering bastards at King Eddie.

Lena glanced over at me. "Forget it, Sid. He's dead. If you want to appease your conscience buy him a nice stone. Why don't you worry about the living for a change?"

I was struck by her angry but unhysterical tone. Her very calmness seemed a rebuke to my own confused wrath. "You're sick," I screamed. "Really sick!"

Lena braked the car and held onto the steering wheel for support. Her voice held a note of cold, steady finality. "*Ja.* I'm sick. Sick of you and Irving and that ridiculous Scotchman of yours. I must be sick to want to please all three of you." She struggled with herself. "Maybe *I'm* not the Nazi. Maybe it's you and Irving. You're both more German than me. Following Führer Last like Nuremberg sheep. *Heil* Last!"

A stream of obscenities poured from me. I'd kill the bitch in another minute. She clung to me as I made a grab for the door handle to get out. "Don't go away, Sid," she cried. "You're my only chance. I'm sor—"

I hacked her hand away and jumped out shouting "Take your problems to Willie Last!"

This time I didn't need Hebbie to tell me. The next day one of the Manorites came up to my cubicle and said, "Hey, Brother Sid. Some foreign-sounding chick rang up yesterday and left a message. Said to tell you goodbye."

She wouldn't dare. Anyway, people who were forever trying it never actually did it. Slowly—but in my heart knowing what I'd find at the other end—I walked from Meditation Manor to Notting Hill. Even as I used my key to open Lena's door I told myself it was just one more of her bullying tricks. Anything to mess me up.

In Lena's apartment were Hebbie and a young Brooks Brothers-type American with a fixed,, agreeable smile. The place was neat as a pin again. My books and pajamas were in a cardboard box at the foot of the bed. Hebbie said, "Zeventh time lucky, eh?" She fluttered around, idly sorting out Lena's jewelry-making equipment and crooning, "Zuch a ztubborn girl, zo ztubborn. Ziz girl could have been happy. Bad luck, *hein?*" She looked at Brooks Brothers and me. "Why do you look zo bad you both? What right do you haff to zympathy. Go away."

She walked out of the apartment.

The American introduced himself. "I'm Irving Goldman. You mustn't blame yourself too much, Sid." He'd made all the arrangements before I got there. Sent a telegram to Lena's mother who was flying in from Munich for the funeral; and talked to the police who seemed satisfied that it was suicide. Though Lena had left no note behind, Goldman said he was confident an inquest would confirm her intentions. So I needn't worry. He sounded businesslike and quite affable.

I'd lost so much strength along with my weight that he had to help me lug out the carton of books to his white Mercedes convertible. I let him drive me back to the Manor. "Did you know I was moving in next week?" he said pleasantly. "We'll have a hell of a lot to talk about." He gave me a friendly smile as I got out.

First Jerry. Now Lena. Yes, of course. *Now.*

With immense care I washed and dressed myself in my shaman's tent. Bare feet. A white cloth around my middle, a newly cleaned cloak, dark glasses, Boris' old *yarmulke.* There.

I was ready for my Last Supper.

Full house. Around the food-laden communal table in the main hall sat the usual contingent of spaced-out residents and American doctors and kibbitzers. A news magazine photographer hung with cameras discreetly crept around snapping pictures. At the head of the table, sipping from a Vat 69 bottle and softly joshing with Jasmine, who was in a patterned sarong to match his red silk kimono, Last presided. The flickering candlelight caused his shadow to jump and dance on the windowed back wall. All the other lights were out except the usual spot on the Robert Owen bust.

With extravagant humility I slipped into a chair at the table, and Last gravely acknowledged my Presence by steepling his hands and bowing Indian-style. I returned his blessing with the sign of the cross then gestured to the others to go on eating. Like Pope John I hated unnecessary pomp. Fragments of talk floated around me. ". . . So Willie said the I I'm trying to grab is the me that's . . ." ". . . Willie says the nearest tae Gaw'd we ever get is watchin' a snake swaller its tail. . . ." "Willie thinks. . . ." "Willie says. . . ."

The buzz of talk died away as the others noticed how Last's moist gray eyes had fastened on me. Open-mouthed, a few stopped eating, then more. On his signal everyone fell silent, waiting.

Obviously, they expected something of me.

I pushed back my chair and got up. "Comrades. Brithers and Bristers. La-deez an' gennulmen. . . ." Words rolled off my tongue like little balls of mercury. The stumblebum, strokelike paralysis, the stammer that had tied me up for so long in agonizing incoherence, had vanished. It was a miracle. I'd found my voice again. With surprising fluency I made one brilliant point after another—on buying new lino for the Manor kitchen, on Bobby May's literary problems, on a plan for commercially marketing Anna's soap ducks, on the need to build a grass-roots coalition with Brixton Labour party—

Boris rudely cut in. "For Christ's sake"—he knew!—"how much of this rubbish are we going to sit and listen to? He's been spouting almost an hour."

Ah, Judas.

Disciple W. Last came around the table toward me, talking to Boris all the while. "Have ye nae eyes in yir haid, mon. Cain't ye see—*it's . . . happenin' . . . tae . . . him.*" (Even now a tiny voice within me asked, is Willie using you against Boris? I stifled it.)

Last stood before me. "Er, ah . . . ye must fergive Brither Boris, Master Sid. He forgets. Ye remember fer us all. W'd it embarrass ye tae lead us in th' Laird's Prayer?" When I hesitated he swiftly knelt at my feet, and automatically everybody bowed their heads except a glowering Boris and Davina who merely looked disbelieving. Last intoned,

"Oor Father, who art only in oor split minds
Hallowed be thy Nae-Name

Oor kingdom's come
Oor will's bein' done
Here
As niver in heaven.

Gi' us each day th' strength tae *be* in thy Absence
An' fergive us oor fergitfulness
Nor lead us intae sailf hatred
An' d'liver us fr' alienation
Fer thine is th' Chaos, th' Alpha an' Omega an' th' Nuthin'-ness
Forever, amen.

I gazed over a forest of bent heads. Only Boris kept eating.

Rising, Last embraced me emotionally. He turned and faced the assemblage. "It's his time."

They all, including Boris this time, had no choice but to follow Last out of the hall.

I was alone.

An incredible pain gripped me. It squeezed and ripped my heart section, causing me almost to pass out. The dark great empty hall filled with a low powerful growl rising to a scream and fading away to grunts and snorts. My animal was loose again.

A light snapped on inside me. An LSD flashback, I thought. Cool.

After the usual leap backward and forward in time, from primeval grume to the Inter-Galactic Convention of 4965, passing through by-now familiar epochs (Thermopylae, Calvary, St. Bartholomew's Night) as bird, fish and human, I arrived where I'd never time-trekked before. I was a year-old baby in the arms of my mother picketing the gold-domed Massachusetts State House in Boston, and I could read the placard in her hands:

FREE SACCO AND VANZETTI

followed by scenes and incidents from a montage of America's industrial agony, which my parents had in some way been connected with: the Triangle Shirtwaist fire, the Lawrence textile strike, the Fisher body sit-down, Republic Steel massacre. . . .

Then I shot back to the dawn of Time and began to recapitulate not so much the biological ascent of man as the slow, painful history of my personal species, writer. With an infantile gurgle I fell to my knees. Awkwardly, without my willing it, my right arm moved, reenacting the drama of man first learning to write. Eons passed. From crude Cro-Magnon slashes I gradually progressed to pictographs, hieroglyphics, the Hebrew alphabet.

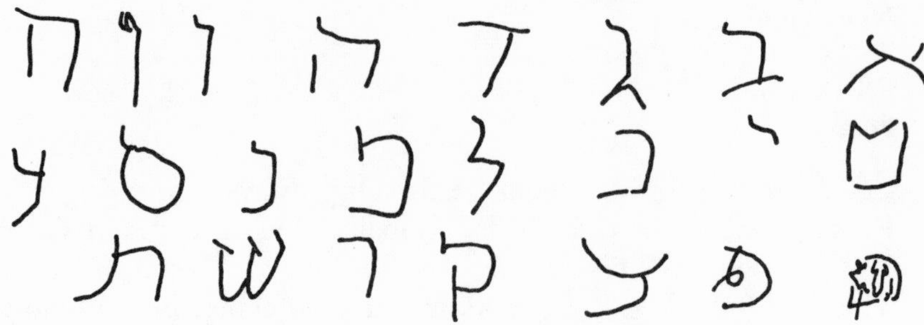

I'd never consciously known how to speak or write Yiddish let alone Hebrew, yet somehow I managed all the letters.

My arm felt so tired. But I must master the language the Hidden God had entrusted to me. At last, sweating and sobbing with the effort, I scrawled out in the dust of the floor of the main hall the highest, most sophisticated literary form known to Aldermaston Man:

SUPPORT OUR STRIKE

WORKERS OF THE WORLD, UNITE

NO PASARAN

BAN THE BOMB

I was a writer again.

Before I knew it the others came in, led by Last.

Ah, an audience. I bounced up from the floor and shuffled forward to bless one and all. It seemed perfectly natural to wrap an imaginary fringed shawl, a *tallus*, around my shoulders and chant and bow up and down as I imagined a cantor did (having never actually been inside a synagogue, I didn't know). It was late September, the High Holidays, and I was a Jew again—or for the first time? Not your ordinary, drab, garden variety Jew but a cocky, scene-stealing Yid, a stand-up *schpritzer* like Lenny Bruce. I tilted the *yarmulke* so it looked more like a UAW cap and in a soaring, Moishe Oisher voice sang them old Almanac and Woody Guthrie ballads,

"Oh which side are you on
Which side are you on?

Don't scab for the bosses
Don't listen to their lies. . . ."

One onlooker was so affected he fainted dead away. Major Last Straw embraced me so hard I thought my bones would break. Bronwen knelt to kiss my bare feet. Even Boris weakened and began winding a black phylactery tape around my arm. In the background Last sobbed quietly.

A great hush fell over the hall. Crazy, baby.

For I don't know how long I gave a one-man concert in a strange medley of tongues, oriental in flavor. I prayed, sang, sprinkled imaginary holy water and sanctified couples in love-marriage. Last's expression of awed anguish, which I caught out of the corner of my eye, was a model for the others.

Seeing nothing in the faces of my Brothers except the approval for which I'd hungered, I began my Questing Dance. Around the communal table. Eyes shut, playing to the gallery. Seeking my Rightful Place. Shuffle-dancing, I tried everyone's chair, even Last's. None felt right.

I grew confused and tired, but with everyone's eyes on me I had to keep it up. I hopped, skipped, jumped, jitterbugged, Suzy-Q'd, told jokes, recited bawdy limericks—anything to keep my audience. For extras I did Jimmy Cagney's "Camptown Races" number from *Yankee Doodle Dandy*.

Splat. Exhausted, I did a pratfall. Residents rushed to help me up. No no. Keep away. No touchee Chinee. I had to see this through on my own, just like the books on shamanism and Willie Last had always told me to. Gradually my frenzy diminished, and the silliness of it all began to dawn on me. I was pooped. What a shindig. Like the host of a party that had gone on too long I wanted my guests to go home.

Wham. Suddenly I leaped on the table and stood absolutely rigid. It, finally and at last, came. The Message.

My skull detached from my trunk and shot out into space. It grew large as the moon, circling the planets, seeking. Out of nebulae, condensing from stormy gases, angelic voices spoke to me. In a swirling mist I made out Jerry Jackson in Chelsea Football Club's blue and white uniform he'd been too depressed to get out of bed for. Gracefully dribbling a soccer ball toward an immense, heavenly net he arched his leg back and kicked a magnificent clean goal. He threw up his hands in a victory salute and shouted: "Forget it, Sid—it's past." Then Lena, enshrouded in the celestial perfume of her favorite fondue. "*Schmuck!*" she called sweetly. "Fly, fly away now, schmuckie bird!" My dusty face wept upon the sizzling sun below. Her softly scornful laughter echoed down the Ladder of Meaning I was climbing. On the way up I held a dialogue, increasingly political, with the strangest seraphs I'd ever seen. They were not Rubens cherubs but were wingless men and women, all ages and colors, who briefed me on 'the immediate perspective,' as we used to call it. It was ridiculous, even disappointing. The Great Breakthrough was no more ethereal than a copy of *I. F. Stone's Weekly* or an Isaac Deutscher biography of Trotsky. Indeed, Stone and Deutscher were among the polemical angels I thought I saw. They also included Clarence Darrow, Leo Huberman, Emma Goldman, George Seldes, Lincoln Steffens, Sam Grafton, Harry Bridges and Edmund Wilson—my early teachers. Though each one had something different to say (and how!), they all agreed on a few essential points:

I must stop romanticizing the heroic in life and politics.

The threats to socialism now came from unexpected quarters.

No true Socialist held himself above other people.

The Socialist position was far more complicated than it had ever been, and common sense and decency were more important than theory.

This simple, corny stuff sounded curiously fresh and new-minted to me.

With each step I could hear a voice, like a great soloist amid the choir, urging me on with a slight trace of impatience. "Hey, kid. Shake a leg, will you?" Slowly His voice dominated the others, which faded sweetly away.

"You will eat, by and by
In that glorious land above the sky;
Work and pray, live on hay
You'll eat pie in the sky when you die."

Soaring through Lena and Jerry's nimbus, past the serried ranks of didactic angels (now arguing with each other), I landed in the lap of God Himself. He was a fantastic old man at least ten stories high. Instead of a long white gown and flowing beard he wore a railway brakeman's denim cap, sweat-stained red bandanna at his seamed throat and patched but clean overalls. His bony, shaven face was that of Eugene Victor Debs, the American Socialist labor leader, and the voice belonged to Swede Hammeros, an old Wobbly I'd known in Chicago. The only religious emblem he wore was a small IWW—International Workers of the World ("One Big Union")—button stuck on his frayed, much laundered work shirt.

Swede—that is, God—smiled sternly down at me. "Listen bo," he said with a slight old-country accent I remembered from dozens of late-night rap sessions in his tiny Halstead Street room. "How'd you ever tie in with that *Nuthouse News* bunch of tinhorn sky pilots anyway? No, don't tell me—guess you've just got a natural talent for mixing with screwballs."

He lifted me up to his knee and gave me a severe look and a gentle, fatherly shake. It had none of Last's clubby, ambivalent quality. I listened.

"Here's the real McCoy. The left-wing movement is made up of thousands upon thousands of men and women who've woke up to the exploitation of one geezer by another. As long as we have the present system, which seems a while yet, there'll never be a shortage of red hots. Y'know, th' jungle buzzards who shout th' loudest and then shove you into a cop's billy and highball it when th' heat's on.

"Th' point is to change the system in a way that makes people better, not worse. And you don't do that by handin' over what little gray matter I gave you to some piecard who says he's got the answer to *all* your problems. Even my Son, Jerusalem Slim, never promised that. 'An injury to one is an injury to all,' is what he preached.

"Where you went wrong is in thinkin' there's only one kind of scab—the professional fink who breaks your strike 'cause he's paid to do it. There's another kind we call the 'union scab.' He—or she—isn't an ordinary scab. Won't sell you out to the boss. But he'll push the union to act against its own interests so he can chase after his own private fantasies of getting even against society or management or what-the-hell. He's the scissorbill with a permanently bitter thing going, drawin' up hatred into his vitals like a kid sippin' a sarsaparilla soda through a straw on a hot day: there's no stopping him. Injustice—the sheer shock of it day after day after day—is enough to fuel him (or her) until he's ready to call it a day and move on to another Holy Roller crusade. He may be a pretty fair short-term fighter but basically he don't understand what th' struggle's all about. Somewhere, very early on, his heart or wherever I put the soul, got trapped or branded, in the system's gears and he came out without knowin' who or what he was: except he's got a debt to repay. And he'll repay it in *your* blood. Someone has done him a bad thing and, damnation, he'll never rest till he gets his revenge. These are the grotesques—in circuses they call them geeks—of the Movement. How come you're a geek, Sonny? How'd you become your own worst enemy?"

I woke up.

What in hell was I doing half naked on a big table in the middle of a semidark room? What were all these people down there staring at?

Whoosh, it all came back. How silly I felt. Some revelation! I had to go through all that—and for what? A Wobbly lecture. Things Swede could have told me any time. What a terrific anticlimax.

Mortified, I shakily climbed down and headed for the Manor front door. Many hands 'helped' me over to Last. "Hey Willie," I cried, "tell your goons to leggo."

Last looked awful. He gasped, "Master Sid—*ye've made it.*"

Oh shit. "Schmuck," I said, reverting to basic Chicagoese. "I haven't made anything except one big fuckup."

Last turned his bloodshot, glazed eyes from me to the crowd. "Th' shock has confused th' puir lad. Let's pray fer oor Brither's safe return." His pious mumbling dropped their heads.

"*Schmendrick,*" I said. "Pray if you like—to get our asses out of this creep joint." To emphasize my point I gave Last a West Side knuckle burn, rubbing my fist into his skull. For just an instant, I thought, our eyes met in the mutually frank hostility of two street-wise kids. Last collapsed into a chair and appealed to the multitude. "He's bin thar an'—an' . . . forgot awraidy."

"I haven't been anywhere," I retorted, "except up the creek without a paddle. We're both so full of crap it's comin' out of our ears. Two of my best friends are dead, I can't write anymore and I've got this terrible hangover. That's where *I've* been." I looked down at the wet-eyed psychiatrist in the fashionable silk kimono and laughed. It was great to hear the sound of my own laughter again. "Willie—it's a hype. Come out in the fresh air with me."

When Last didn't move I looked at the other Clare Councillors. With the discreetly grinning exception of Davina they were all furious with me. What had I expected: roses and champagne?

With a disloyal 'up you' gesture to one and all, I raced upstairs to change into my old street clothes, which fitted my scrawny frame like a potato sack. On my way back down Marve Munshin and the Major, looking like Mutt 'n' Jeff but weighing about quarter of a ton in the aggregate, barred my way. Aiming to kick at Marve's balls in case of a fight (for some reason my Chicago instincts were waking up), I eased past Tony Straw whose outstretched arm felt like an iron bar across my egress. "Major Jerk-o," I said, "step aside before I kick in your lousy teeth." I got to the front door. Again I was blocked, this time by most of Clare Council. (As ever, Dick Drummond brooded indecisively in the background.)

"You'll have to kill me to stop me," I said quietly.

"Okeh. Le' him go," Last curtly ordered. I went past them into the cool, quiet London night.

What a fantastic city London was. I'd never before realized how serene yet incredibly alive the town looked, even at night, with shops and pubs shut.

At first unsteadily then more confidently I walked up Brixton Road past the Oval cricket ground toward the Elephant and Castle. People, even policemen, passed by with hardly a glance. Beautiful, anonymous, indifferent London. I felt like kissing each and every person.

At Waterloo Bridge I paused to take in the Thames, dully glittering under a cloudy crescent moon. Incredible to see the dirty old river for what it was and not as a sacred lair of demons and serpents. St. Paul's looked close enough to touch. A Borough cleaning lorry went by, its brushes rotating spray on my baggy trousers. London was real, not the holy sepulcher I'd imagined it to be these past two years. The ordinariness of it overwhelmed me.

I knew I was high. Had torn through that thin membranelike tissue separating sanity from psychosis. But I was alive. That's what counted. High octane elation pumped through my veins. I'd bloody well made it. And with life came pain—actual, felt pain. For the first time, like a blow to the heart, grief for Jerry and Lena hit me.

Gazing out at the great, dark river I made plans. My mind worked too fast for any but the simplest. First a good hot bath to soak out the spooks. Then a nonvegetarian meal. I ached for an American-style charcoal-broiled two-inch-thick T-bone steak, medium rare, side of Idaho baked potato oozing with sour cream and chives, crisp romaine lettuce salad and Roquefort dressing, real (not acorn) coffee and cream, and a huge slab of strawberry shortcake topped with globs of whipped cream. Yum!

Then a solid week of sleep, to rest my mind and let it start functioning normally again. It wouldn't be easy, this. I'd given myself a nasty knock, and I knew from other schizophrenics that coming back would be a lot harder than the outward trip. The poison would have to work itself out of my system gradually. But it never would unless I began to face facts squarely. I had been, to a degree I didn't understand yet, responsible for the deaths of Lena and Jerry. I'd made too little fuss about Jerry being exiled to Winnie Wing and none about his 'accident' there. And I'd treated Lena as the other Clare men had treated their women—except that Lena, not Sybil or Nancy or Viv, had done the dying. Even with death the doctors had somehow managed to protect themselves and their families.

A safe return from madness now depended on my figuring everything out. Why had I let Last do my thinking for me? Maybe old friends could help me piece it together. I'd have to plug into normals again—if, after the way I'd patronized and snubbed them, they'd see me. Where were Arnie Greenberg and Flo the clippie? Had Larry found his sunken treasure in Australia? Did they still drink at The George?

And I'd get my hands on a typewriter and reams of paper. What a story!

Impatient to get going, I hopped a night bus on Victoria Embankment. Upper deck, naturally. Shift workers and night cleaning women swayed tiredly with the jouncing red elephant of a vehicle. Brimming with cameraderie, I chatted up the Jamaican lady in front of me. (About the age of Abe Clewes' mother, I guessed.) When she got off I went downstairs to the clippie, a small Irish boy who reminded me of Jack Sweeney, and we *schmoozed* about soccer. (I was two years behind in the League placings.) Simply to talk, without astral-analyzing him or trying to outmaneuver him phenomenologically à la Clare Council, was terrific. What a relief.

I swung off at Westminster. Big Ben, looking as always like part of a movie set, struck 4:00 A.M., and I walked along Millbank past the Tate Gallery toward Regents Gardens.

Ich, the flat. First thing, I'd unlock my workroom and rip down those gruesome black curtains. Untape the window frames and get rid of the security grille and sweep up the broken glass I'd cemented into the balcony floor. Wash the anti-intruder grease off the outside drain pipe and reconnect the phone. See how much of my furniture I could get back. And somehow smooth it over with the Riches and Sue VanOver, my neighbors.

I jauntily took the hall stairs two at a time. On the third floor, as my key slid into the apartment door, I heard noises inside. I froze. Hearing things again? Shadows moved across the frosted glass upper part of the door. Ah fongoo. Burglars on this of all nights. Anxious and unsure, I retreated down to the street. Was I going crazy again? Should I call a cop? (Not in my state.) I leaned against a lamppost figuring the odds.

Across the street my hall door opened. Five dark figures moved down the front steps toward me. Whew. Only Willie Last, flanked by Boris, the Major, Marve and Bronwen Jones. Boris and Marve, each over six feet tall, looked like giants in the empty road.

Light-headed with relief I greeted them.

"Hi fellas," I said. "Look, I'm okay, really. Just tired. I need a bath and a helluva long sleep. Call you soon, promise."

A flicker of cold, comradely smiles. Major Straw, a greatcoat thrown over his Saxon chief's costume, broke down and cried. Last, dressed straight, hovered worriedly a few paces away.

Boris put an unusually friendly arm around me. "We're worried about you, Brother Sid," he wheedled. "Why don't you come back to the Manor with us?" I smiled, shook off his arm and said no thanks. (It occurred to me: had Last and Petkin made it up and if so over whose dead body?) Big Marve Munshin loomed up on my other side. "Come along now," he said, sounding just like a New York cop. He wrapped his ham hand around my shoulder.

I laughed and slipped from his grasp. "Knock it off, guys. Enough's too much, as Jimmy Durante used to say."

I crossed the street and went inside my hallway. On the dark stairwell a thousand pounds of flesh thunked me.

My Roosevelt Road reflexes had grown rusty. Not until I was almost pinned did I lash out. I rammed my elbow in Tony Straw's moustached face, kneed Marve Munshin and socked Boris in the mush. *Goddamn, they're trying to kill me,* I thought.

When I started to yell, Munshin clapped his hand over my mouth. I bit it, fighting back and struggling with every last ounce of strength. Then something sharp stabbed me. I looked down. Willie Last was withdrawing a hypodermic needle from my leg. Oh no. He gave the hypo back to Bronwen holding his medical bag.

"For a junkie he's pretty strong," grunted Munshin, hammerlocking me so Boris could pull down my trousers. "Better sock it to him again." Last quickly refilled the syringe from his bag and slipped the needle into my behind. "Please," I said. "Please don't. Don't. Don't. You can't know what you're doing."

I forced myself to relax when I saw their eyes—full of pure concentrated compassion and hatred.

"Don't panic," I said. "Don't hurt me. I'll go with you." I had to calm them before they did anything more to me.

We lay like that for a few moments, Major Straw, Marve and Boris catching their breath on top of me. The drug took hold. I thought, Clare's lynch party for Screwy Lewie Singh had been a rehearsal for this, and I'd helped.

I was shoved in the backseat of a black Bentley between Boris and the Major. As Last drove toward Brixton and the brightening sky, Bronwen in the front seat turned to me and said: "You're beautiful, Sid. We love you."

I heard someone roar: "WHAT'S WRONG WITH YOU PEOPLE!" And passed out.

A tickle in my bare toes woke me up, and I looked down. In one of the Manor's cubicles (up on the balcony, near my own former hutch, I sensed) Bronwen Jones penitentially washed my feet while Boris Petkin leaned over me like a Sergei Eisenstein boyar, his lantern jaw chomping up and down as he *davened.* In a corner Tony Straw still sobbed uncontrollably. I lay naked under a white sheet, like Jesus on a Good Friday—or John Dillinger on the coroner's slab.

Last, his eyes wild with awe, shouldered Boris aside and bent over me. I tried saying something but the drug had shattered me. All I felt was despair and anger. I muttered, "You knew not what you did, asshole."

Overcome, Last knelt and kissed my feet. "When in doot read this," he whispered, and put a piece of paper in my hand. I blacked out again.

For two days and two nights (I reckoned later) I drifted in a doped, timeless sea. Slimy phantasmagoria, horrible shapes and sounds, the worst depression I'd ever known clobbered me. Sometimes I hallucinated Lena and Jerry alive and telling me how to escape. O'Brien, Jeff H., Gareth and other Con Housers paraded through my mind, shaking their heads at my naïveté. Though presumably brought to Meditation Manor to be looked after, I was left alone and untended for hours at a stretch in a balcony cubicle with easy access to an open fire exit leading out to a hundred-foot drop. Clare Councillors, who I'd always believed were there to protect me during a psychotic episode—what else were we about?—ignored me except for their occasional weeping, self-indulgent pilgrimages to beseech a blessing or absolution. It was too much trouble for me not to give it. My friend Davina tried to bring me a little tea and toast but Boris drew her away. The Americans were a little less hysterical; at first curious, they soon got used to me as just another trip-out. Bobby May lifted five quid from my wallet. "Pahdon, old chap," the black novelist burlesqued an English lord, "you won't be needing this immejutly, will you?" Thank God *somebody* around here acted normal.

I waited for my head to clear, but when it did all I wanted was to kill myself. Suicide, born of guilt for what I'd done to Lena and Jerry, seemed easier than escape. Bleakly I crawled out of the utterly unguarded room up to the Manor roof. It was cold. Hauling myself over the parapet, I dangled my naked legs over the street, three stories below. I gazed out across London's lights and gathered strength to let go.

Last's piece of paper was still crumpled in my fist—the message he said would inspire me in my darkest hour. I looked at it. It said

OM

Laughing so hard I thought I'd *plotz,* I backflipped inside the roof and staggered back down to bed. I laughed myself into a long, refreshing sleep and when I awoke I planned how to split.

I wasn't strong enough to fight my way out, so I'd have to play their game. Slowly, while rehearsing my Colditz escape script, I dressed. Everything now depended on how well I'd learned from Con House and even Last himself.

Downstairs, in the late afternoon, people were starting to stir. A few yawned at me. I waved with a papal gesture and they turned over, reassured.

None of the Councillors was awake. Except Last, under a blanket with Jasmine. He was between me and the front door, and watched me approach.

I prodded him with my shoe and nodded back toward the kitchen. He followed me in his red silk kimono.

Over Nescafé we held our last talk together.

He peered uncertainly at me, his impishly handsome face searching mine for signs that I knew he knew it was all a complicated Zen joke and nobody's fault, really. "Er, ah, mm . . . How ye doin', Brither Sid?"

I gripped his shoulder in a formal gesture of comradeship neither of us believed. "Oh Willie," I moaned. "The Light is so strong."

For a moment I thought he'd drop the pose and laugh out loud. Instead he smiled, his fear and anxiety allayed.

I slowly finished my coffee and, feeling a twinge of guilty regret, stepped past Willie Last through the quiet church to the sunny, strident street outside.